Caszandra

Touchstone:
Part Three

July to November

by Andrea K Höst

All characters in this publication
are fictitious and any resemblance
to real persons, living or dead,
is purely coincidental.

Author's Note

Touchstone is a diary in three parts, commencing in *Stray*, continued in *Lab Rat One*, and concluded in *Caszandra*.

A glossary of terms and phrases, and a character list, have been included at the end of each volume.

In the previous volumes

During her month alone on the abandoned planet of Muina, Cassandra Devlin found food, shelter, and mystery: glowing ruins, moonlight condensing to intoxicating mist, and hills which moaned of sorrow and loss. When the psychic soldiers known as Setari stumble across her on a lightning visit to their dangerous home world, she is more than ready to be rescued.

Taken to storm-wracked Tare, Cass is processed as a stray, a refugee of a disaster which tore gates between multiple worlds. Despite the wonders of Taren nanotech computers, Cass struggles with a new language, aching homesickness, and the question of what kind of place she can make for herself on a planet where no-one has even heard of Earth.

When the Tarens discover that Cass has the ability to enhance psychic talents, she is sent to work with the Setari, and learns more about their never-ending battle to keep Tare clear of monstrous creatures known as Ionoth. The strict military life led by the Setari is more than a little different for an Australian schoolgirl, but among them she still finds kindness and some measure of worth, offset by an increasing loss of privacy.

A near-disaster leads to an investigation into Cass' time on Muina, and an expedition is formed to search for answers to the phenomena she observed. The secrets of the planet's past are critical to the battle to hold back the Ionoth, and the Tarens have long been prevented from hunting among their home world's ruins by inexplicable deaths.

The sentry-creatures known as Ddura prove to be key to both death and safety, and when Cass identifies the Tarens to the planet's defences, it is a watershed moment. Cass believes that unlocking Muina will free her to concentrate on finding a way back to Earth, but an offer from a different faction of ex-Muinans to return her home leads her to reject the idea of abandoning the Tarens who first rescued her.

Exploration of Muina leads to the discovery of a strange underground installation, well-protected, and the site of many deaths. The malachite marble 'power stone' which shields the installation is a new mystery, but it is not until Cass inadvertently triggers a teleportation system to the teaching city of Kalasa that the Tarens discover a link between the Ionoth known as Cruzatch and the power stones.

As the Tarens search for answers among the ruins, Cass grows closer to the squads assigned to care for and guard her. Every bond she forms is complicated by the wild card role she plays, and her potential value as a key to unlock the mysteries of the past.

JULY

Sunday, July 13

Hero 101

It's one thing to decide to save the universe, another altogether to find a way to go about it. Today I catalogued my various abilities to try and work out how they could be used to fix fracturing spaces. Enhancement, hearing Ddura, sleep-walking to Earth, making soap bubble copies of real and fictional places, and seeing blurry. Somehow, surely, it must all fit together in a way where I can do something tangible to help.

Mostly, though, I thought about sex.

I doubt I'm going to make much progress toward saving the universe by constantly replaying images of naked Kaoren Ruuel, but, damn. Naked Kaoren Ruuel.

The subject of all my steamed-up imagining opened a channel to me when First and Fourth returned from rotation to say he'd be busy for a while, and knew that I'd very likely fall asleep after my Sights training, but that he'd bring me dinner when I woke. I managed an 'okay' which sounded completely shy and though he just said: "I'll see you then," before breaking contact, I could hear the smile in his voice. Or think I could.

This is going to be a continual mental adjustment. Not just for us, either, as I found out when Zee came to see me before we were supposed to start off for my Sights training.

"Maze says he's not quite equal to having this conversation with you," she said, wry and amused. "I expect you know what about."

"Everyone in First Squad know?" I asked, thoroughly daunted. I'm not really at the stage where I want to talk about this with anyone but Kaoren.

"Not as yet. Although this does have some impact on our roster for waking you if you can't escape one of your dreams. Is it something you wanted to keep secret?"

I was kind of yes and no about that, and she laughed at my confused mumble, then gave me a warm smile.

"I don't really need to know more than that you're comfortable, and remind you that we're here if there's anything you want to discuss."

There was something she was the right person to ask. "Is Kaoren somewhere right now get huge lecture because of me?"

"Not quite," Zee said, after a moment's pause. "Though it's good that you're conscious of the potential complications. He must, let us say, justify his actions, but he won't be collecting more demerits on your account, at least not simply for this."

"More?" Any demerits were news to me, but I hit on an obvious reason right away. "That Sights training session?"

"Indeed. You don't often see below the surface decisions to the cross-factional aspects of KOTIS Command, but that session, which Tsee Ruuel initially refused to carry out, led to a minor drama. The previous occasion was when he retrieved you from your home world's near-space."

"Demerits for rescue me?" I asked, startled.

"For far exceeding the number of spaces he was permitted to trail you. Sight Sight talents are tremendously rare – too valuable really to be risked even within the limits he was allowed on that foray – but very difficult to argue out of decisions made based on that Sight."

She was giving me fair warning, and I could hardly deny her point. "He sort of apologised for being sort of wrong, once. Plus couldn't keep to his own decision to stay away from me." And had, at least, shown no more sign of being angry because he was unable to stick to that choice. "Don't think he'll manage to convince me he's right all the time, anyway," I added, and figured it was well past time to change the subject. "How did two squad rotation go?"

"Very well. One stilt, but not the crowds of deep-space roamers we'd feared. It works especially well with an exploration squad, of course, since they must remain in a newly-cleared space much longer than a combat-oriented squad. We only fought together on the stilt and on one particularly populated space – one which Fourth would have been very unlikely to have been able to clear on their own. We'll also be trialing eight-member squads, and the next few weeks will involve a great deal of data collection to gauge which approach results in fewer injuries. Possibly it will be a question of using both options, depending on the spaces involved."

We went down to Keszen Point a little early, and put in a really solid session of testing – again repeating earlier tests, but with manifestation as well as Sights. I guess seeing things is where I might most logically contribute, and we're making progress on finding out my limits. Zee didn't question me any more about Kaoren, which I thought nice of her, but the test session left me so exhausted I fell asleep on the train back and woke on my couch.

Kaoren's in another meeting, but it shouldn't be much longer. He told me to eat without him. Squad captains are kept very busy, even when they're not getting hauled over the coals for smexing strays, and I bet I'm going to have fun dealing with how little time Kaoren has for anything but being captain.

Though right now I'm still pretty much champagne bubbles and incredulous gloatation.

Monday, July 14

More than a rumour

When Kaoren came to my rooms after his meeting, there was a red line, a cut, following the line of his jaw. The everyday danger the Setari face wasn't something I enjoyed being reminded of, and I reached up and touched the thin mark.

"Is that my fault?" I asked. "Because you not concentrating?"

He ran his thumb along the cut, as if he'd forgotten it was there. "Flying Leaves space. You went through it with First. The population increase there has made it exceptionally difficult. And the effort of not thinking of you has been far more distracting than–"

I kissed him, effectively putting off any chat till this morning, and then we were nearly late for our respective training sessions. I think neither of us wanted to talk about how much harder the spaces are getting, or how much easier Flying Leaves space would have been if Lohn had been able to create a Light wall with me. Or maybe we just didn't want to talk at all, to try and frame words around the transition we've gone through. We've skipped stages I know how to label – first dates and movies and working up to going steady – straight into an undefined state of together.

I guess 'together' will do as a word.

During our bout of stretching/yoga torture, Mara pretended Zee hadn't told her anything, having great fun at my expense asking if I had had any nightmares, and whether I was moving stiffly because I wasn't getting enough training. But eventually she stopped, and gave me a hug.

"It's too fun making you blush. You should have seen Lohn's reaction. He kept saying: 'With Ruuel? Are you sure?' Then he asked Maze if he felt like a father whose little girl had grown up."

I smiled at that – it was just what I'd expect Lohn to say. But I had something more serious it had occurred to me to worry about. "Unsure

Fourth Squad reaction," I said. "Fourth Squad with Kaoren bit like First Squad with Maze – respect him and protective of him – but don't tease him the same way. And they've been good to me. I think might be uncomfortable about this."

"Probably at first," Mara agreed, with the blunt honesty which lets me ask her questions like that. "Every squad, even First, places their captain into a special category. The authority captains have over their squad, and the need to trust their orders in situations of extreme danger, makes it very difficult to treat them as a peer. In many ways it's better not to. Captain training is difficult to pass, and balancing a squad around a captain is usually the main reason for delay in forming new squads. Ninth showed you where even a competent captain can fail to cope with a squad member wrong for her type.

"Ruuel is an excellent captain, a very strong personality, but distant. It works well with Fourth. They are proud of him, strive to live up to him. I know that if he was my captain, I would find it difficult if a friend of mine became his lover. If you are close to them, and he is not distant with you, it changes their relationship with their captain. Don't be too surprised if their initial reaction is a little more than surprise. They'll adapt."

"If they don't?"

Mara gave me a wry smile. "Then they won't be living up to their captain. If nothing else, this should remove some of the pressure they've been under because of *The Hidden War*. If you are happily bedding Ruuel, there can't be much basis to this villainous Lastier." But she went on more seriously. "Don't underestimate the situation generally, however. Maze was very concerned – he hadn't suspected at all – and since Ruuel *is* such a strong personality, he was worried about how much of this is really what you want." She snorted. "Zee pointed out that you're the girl who gave him a lecture on how annoying our transparently manipulative psychological tactics were. You're not an aggressive person, but whenever we've come up against things you care about strongly, you've grown unexpectedly firm."

I felt my face burn, and looked away, but said: "Liked Kaoren since he brought back from Earth near-space. He has tried very hard discourage me."

She tousled my hair. "Can't say I'd want to get into bed with a piece of living history either. Now with this next set of stretches, stop bending your knee."

I had medical for the afternoon, so Mara gave me an early break for lunch and of course I ran straight into Mori, who grabbed my hand and dragged me into a corner of the canteen. "I'm feeling very uninformed, Caszandra. Tell me if the rumours are true."

"Which rumour?" I asked, wishing I'd been sensible and eaten in my room.

"The Els Haral and Caszandra Devlin spending lots of time together rumour. We saw you the day we came back from Muina, but no-one bothered till now to let me know there was more to it."

I tried not to look too relieved. "Els chatted to me couple of times at lunch, and gave me very good idea for making projections from memories rather than visualisations."

"There's more to it than that, I bet. I hear he's not hiding his interest."

"Not going to happen," I said, firmly.

She looked tempted to press me more, but Glade, Par and Halla had found us, so Mori settled for murmuring wickedly: "After all, we have it on record that the Third Squad captain is the best looking."

Fortunately Glade was more interested in talking about the various squad pairings, letting me play coward and put off changing the way they treat me. They seemed pretty pleased with how yesterday's rotation went, and no longer quite so worried about being 'junior squad'. First, of course, are easy to work with and Glade was super happy that Mara had complimented him on the way he'd taken down one of the Ionoth. From that conversation I finally learned that Maze and Mara are considered the best hand-to-hand fighters among the Taren Setari, with Kaoren's Sight Sight believed to give him a mild advantage over pure technique.

How Mara puts up with training me I don't know, but I am exceptionally pleased that she and Zee think I'm not a complete pushover, despite my combat failures. I don't think I've ever had a nicer compliment.

I'm in medical now, having the usual scans and another round of cosmetic work on my legs. Fleshy blue bandages for the next few days. And Kaoren wants me to come to his room after the medics are done. He says the door will open to me.

Tuesday, July 15

Cheer Squad

Kaoren was still training when I was let loose from medical, so I footled about for a while, changing clothes and brushing my hair a lot and looking doubtfully at the small amount of makeup I'd been given by Nenna. When I've been out in the city with Zee and Mara and Ketzaren and Alay they've sometimes worn a little makeup, but it's not practical for their day-to-day work. I've been following their lead, but felt like, I don't know, marking the transition I've made, I guess.

Although briefly tempted to see how Kaoren would react to Cass the Goth, I settled for a touch of lip gloss and felt tremendously conspicuous walking down the corridor on Third and Fourth's floor, for all I knew perfectly well both squads were elsewhere. And even though he said he'd added me to his apartment's permissions, I still felt weirdly convinced Kaoren's door wouldn't open to me, until it did.

Kaoren didn't have any active images in the public space of his apartment. Instead he had pictures on the walls, real pictures in deep frames like glassed-in boxes. Inside were little landscapes, cities, forests, all cut out of what looked like stiff white paper, some parts outlined in black or delicate colours but most just white on white. Incredibly complex and beautiful and amazing, with so much detail that you'd need hours to look at a single picture properly. He had four of them and in one, which reminded me a lot of High Forest space, I saw some miniature figures which I realised were Setari.

Deeply impressed, I spent a long time finding other tiny details, then moved on to the rest of the main room. Very tidy, which didn't surprise me at all, with white and blue colours for the furniture, including long, dark blue shelves on the wall without pictures, full of evenly spaced objects. A specked-green stone statue which looked vaguely Mayan. A small, palm-sized curved bowl. A set of thick shiny metal links all joined together like an oversized puzzle ring. A really smooth pebble which looked like it had come from Pandora. An origami crane, the one I'd handed to him in my dream. It was a disjointed collection.

The bedroom and bathroom were very bare and clear by comparison, and I wandered around briefly, then curled up in one of the surprisingly comfortable chairs (they looked very firm, but were wide and deep) and immediately dozed off, and then Kaoren was there looking down at me with his eyes half-closed, as if trying to decide whether to wake me. I held out a hand and he slid into the chair beside me, which just snugly held us both.

I enjoyed the way his expression lightened, as if just sitting down with me lifted his mood, though he went on to say, "You have a slight temperature. A side-effect of the reconstructive work."

"Don't feel that bad," I said. "Bit groggy." I curled my hand around the back of his head and kissed him slowly because I could, because I was allowed to, then said: "I like this room. First time I've seen real pictures on walls since came to Tare. Get lost looking at them."

"My brother creates them for me."

"Good illustration of how little I know about you," I said, sleepily accepting the idea of Kaoren having a brother, though I've had a chance since then to get a bit nervous about meeting any of the Ruuels. "Will you tell me about your family?"

He didn't reply immediately, and I wondered if he didn't want to, but then he started off, voice detached:

"My mother is Teor Ruuel. A sculptor. My father, Paran, a mathematician. I was five and Arden – my brother – six when the Setari program shifted to phase two, and both of us tested as strong talents. Sight is very much a part of the Ruuel bloodline. Our parents did not try to prevent our removal by KOTIS – they would have had little chance of succeeding any legal challenge – but they are very opposed to the concept of Setari. Of 'squandering gifted on futile violence, best left to the untalented'. When we were permitted home visits, we were forbidden to speak of our training."

I was staring up at him, but his eyes were focused on someone not there so I didn't say anything.

"Arden has my Sights, not Speed, and is vastly my superior in Light element. He loathed the program, rebelled in every way. Many Kalrani do, and KOTIS is generally successful in directing that energy more usefully, but Arden's resolution was beyond them and he was allowed to withdraw at eleven. He is becoming increasingly known for his creations."

"He couldn't accept learning to kill?"

Kaoren turned his head to look at the pictures on the walls. "That didn't matter to Arden. He simply considers his time better spent."

"Do you enjoy visit home?" It seemed to me that Kaoren's family was a bad fit for someone who is so very serious about being a Setari.

"No. I only return now to escort my sister, Siame. She is in her forties, a Kalrani. I want you to meet her, on the free day we have scheduled. She will be painfully jealous of what you are to me, but will try not to show it."

First a brother, and then a sister, one who was going to be jealous. "I'll try not to be–" I paused, thinking about it – and reminding myself that the forties are the mid-teens. "Try not to be threatening."

He let out his breath, a short 'tuh' of amusement, but then kissed me and had an interesting time stopping kissing me, particularly since I don't take a slight temperature nearly as seriously as he did. He'd ordered in food (a selection of spicy goop, hot and cold, with something which could have been naan bread) and after we ate he told me the origins of the seemingly random items on the shelves in the room. Some of them were very unremarkable to look at, but were all about his Sights and the way they felt to him in Place. The way he spoke made me wonder if he'd ever talked about them before.

My blue bandages meant no indulgently long showers, but even a short one was sufficient to convince Kaoren that my temperature was probably not really a concern. I experimented with how he reacted when I tried to take the lead, and found that he'd let me do anything I cared to, but that not being in charge drove him completely insane. It was very fun for me to let him stop passively taking it.

I wonder if Kaoren's parents still think the Setari are a futile waste, now that they've recovered a world.

Wednesday, July 16

Home sweet

First and Fourth were away for a really long time on today's rotation. It's so frustrating to be too valuable to go with them. Instead of finding a way to save the universe, I feel like I'm being packed in cotton wool, just spinning my wheels instead of making any progress. But I guess there's not much I can do about that except work hard during my exercise sessions so they think I'm recovered enough to contribute. No more medical dramas or fainting fits or conjuring things up to hurt me.

As it is, I'm going to have to make sure to start doing something which takes all my attention – like playing my historical mystery games – around the time First and Fourth are due back because I was climbing the walls by the time they finally returned. Zee cancelled my Sights training because she was so tired and had missed when it was supposed to start.

She told me it had been a great success, though, since they'd finally tracked down the home space of those hairy roamers which have been causing all the squads grief since the spaces realigned. One thing I hadn't realised about roamers which originate in spaces, rather than in deep-space, is that if the roamers leave their home space long enough, the space 'remembers' them again. So the numbers can really build up.

Kaoren came and found me almost straight away, which surprised me since he likes to get his report writing out of the way before coming near me and my tendency to kiss him. We found something to eat, and then he began to talk about the roamers' home space, voice his usual detached tone, but his hands moving restlessly, which is very unusual for him.

"They're one of the most unpleasant Ionoth we've encountered. They kill for trophies, and torment and torture the occupants of the spaces they invade. Trap paths. And engage in ritualistic ceremonies which make uncomfortable imprints in Place. Their home space was large and beautiful – orchards, a village apparently woven from thin branches – but so ugly in

Place that it was almost impossible to view that way. And it is also like the Castle space – the space is a memory of the occupants of the village being invaded, overwhelmed, driven into the surrounding orchards by a different type of Ionoth. We arrived in the portion of the cycle where the roamers are being pushed out, and instead of engaging with them, we removed the conquerors. There is a strong chance that if we continue to do this during the critical period, they will not roam. It is a rotation which will take at least two squads to achieve, if only to discourage them by force of numbers from attacking us."

"There still roamers from previous cycles out there, yes?"

"More than likely. Even if there are not, the traps they've laid will remain until the spaces revert."

"Be strange for roamers if go back to home space and have fight with themselves," I said. "Can see why Zee so pleased with today's result, though."

"Dual squads are working well for exploration," he said. "Not so well for some of the clearance rotations because two heavy-strength squads are overkill for many spaces, and unless they continually leave one squad a space behind they're encountering the greater numbers of deep-space Ionoth predicted. We've been drawing them, too, but only when we pause too long in the same space."

He tucked me against his side and settled down to work on his reports, which I thought an excellent way to deal with so much of his time having to be devoted to being a squad captain. I don't think it was only for my benefit, either. The roamers' home space was obviously really difficult for him to deal with – he and Halla both study new spaces closely for evaluation purposes – and I think that being with me put some of the nastier aspects at a distance for him.

I spent my time educationally, watching a documentary on seaweed (the source of much of Tare's oxygen, which I had been wondering about given the lack of trees). An entire ocean of seaweed, great heaving masses of it so thick that it heaps up above the water and then gets ripped apart by storms. It's a bit like earth worms – being cut up is a way for it to reproduce.

Taren documentaries are so entertainingly weird, but I really should stop watching them. I still can't sit anywhere near an air duct without picturing that cleaning snot glooping about on the other side. Waiting. And the other day there was one about how the toilets work. They're lined with a nanite similar to the cleaning snot, which engulfs anything in there when the lid closes and moves it away beyond the membrane of goop through pipes all the way to waste recycling. Not only did I *not* want to hear about what they did with it after that, but they kept comparing the process to what happens to a mouthful of food when you swallow it. Now whenever I put the toilet lid down, I *swear* I can faintly hear:

Om nom nom nom

Anyway, the seaweed documentary was nearly over when a channel request came from Els, who asked me if I had anything planned for my free day.

I blushed; a silly thing, but Kaoren was right there and it felt so strange to have someone else trying to arrange a date 'right in front of him'. "Els very nice person–" I began, carefully.

He laughed. "I can hear the 'but' already. I improve on further acquaintance, I promise."

"Believe you." I paused and looked up at Kaoren's face, mouth a straight unsmiling line, eyes half-closed, blackly unreadable. "Sorry, but am very in love with someone else."

Els really is a cool guy, and he gracefully said: "Then I can only be envious of that person. We can still chat at lunch, I hope, if that won't make you uncomfortable."

That was fine with me, since I doubted anyone would take seriously rumours about us much longer. I said goodbye to Els, and have spent the next while catching up on this diary entry. I think I'll try projecting some music once Kaoren's reports are done. I've been thinking about recording some classical music for Zan (presuming I can remember what little classical music I've heard – Mum only likes classical in small amounts and I never really paid much attention). Since I haven't done anything much at all today, I'm hoping I might be able to get a good segment of something recorded, and piece it together into a whole over the next few days.

Thursday, July 17

If that's your boyfriend...

I managed almost half of *Night on Bald Mountain* for Zan yesterday and then Kaoren and I both slept till what would count as about 4 am in our current sleep cycle, when he woke from a minor nightmare about the hairy roamer space. He seemed very glad I was there, and we enjoyed the luxury of not having anything at all scheduled until the afternoon, when Kaoren had arranged to take his sister out into the city after meeting me. I'm not allowed out without a really large escort now, and that's not going to change in the near future. I was working on not being grumpy about that.

We ate leftovers and chatted briefly about music (it doesn't surprise me that what music Kaoren does listen to is the Taren version of classical), but again we didn't do much talking. Kaoren is a lot less stingy with words privately than he is when he's on duty, and has so far answered every question I've asked him. But I still haven't recovered from my tendency to kiss him.

Around mid-morning Maze sent us the next episode of *The Hidden War* to review, which distracted me enough to stop for breakfast.

"Would you watch this if Fourth Squad hadn't been pulled into it?" I asked, as we settled on the couch with mugs of hot soup.

"I have for years, though not so devotedly as Eyse and Ferus. It shapes the way we are viewed too greatly to ignore, as well as being well-written. A distorted mirror." Kaoren tilted his head at whatever expression was on my face, then gave me one of his barely visible smiles. "If my squad would stop taking it as a direct insult, Lastier would be a source of endless amusement. Some of the things he has said were very much what I was thinking."

He keeps surprising me. "I guess I was very dirty."

"No, 'pathetic creature' would be closer there." His smile faded, then he took my mug and put it and his own on the floor then pulled me properly onto his lap and gave me an image out of his personal log – a closed but not opaque pod on the *Diodel*, with the me from months ago lying inside, freshly scrubbed and deeply unconscious. In the medical tunic they'd given me after I'd been rescued I looked painfully thin and bruised. "I was mildly surprised that you'd managed to survive, composed my report, and didn't think about you until we found you being trained by Namara. Yet I kept that image."

He recovered our mugs (Telekinesis is so useful) and we watched the episode quietly, waiting till the end to talk since there were no ads. It was the first time the show had been primarily from 'my' point of view since I was rescued. I find it odd the things which they show out of order, or which were hugely important to me which are left out altogether. Like my reaction to having my interface expanded, which did after all nearly kill me, and hurt like hell and had me throw the only real tantrum I've managed since I got here. And they'd skipped me going into the spaces with First Squad, which I'm pretty sure was somehow linked to me being able to go home on my birthday (after all, that's hardly the first time I'd been desperately homesick).

As I'd expected the episode started out with me bored and locked up. Even kitten-me was looking sulky. Then the TV equivalent of Maze came in and copped a serve about being transparently manipulative (though since they hadn't shown First Squad taking me to lunch, I felt the impact was rather muted). But it seems they were catching up on some of the things we missed, since after my release from medical they showed First (or Squad Emerald, rather) taking me out into the Ena, and then Nori (Zan) and Faer (Maze) and another Squad Emerald person, Shim, doing more enhancement testing with me and promptly making me collapse when the three of them touched me at once. It switched to Nori's point of view after that, to show the Setari being all shocked and guilt-ridden while they waited around in medical to see whether I had brain damage. Shim (who is male but not at all like Lohn) talked about how Faer had only just decided my language difficulties were because I really was from a non-Muina related planet, and fretted and paced about, but Faer was being silently white-lipped. Then the good news, that I should recover completely, and Faer told Nori she could go and it closed on her looking back at him watching me through an observation window.

"Guess setting up love triangle reason why this out of order," I told Kaoren, pulling a face. "Don't see why can't just stick to the actual story."

"You're refusing to look if you haven't seen how strongly protective Surion is toward you."

Kaoren didn't sounded bothered by this, just pointing out a technicality. I guess Place and Sight Sight is going to spare me any misplaced jealousy.

"Maze has never once made me feel he was interested in seeing me naked," I said. Fortunately. "Was thinking more of Zan. She doesn't need any more aggravation because of me, and this show kind of puts her in a love triangle with me and Maze."

"You're very attached to Namara."

"Zan – that first week when was training me, I wasn't enjoying it, and she get all this hassle because of it, and she was never impatient with me despite all that. I was an assignment, and she very private person, but she let me in a little. And for a while was only person I saw except the ones sticking needles in me," I added equably.

Something in this conversation – either Maze or Zan or needles or the reminder of me being an assignment – put Kaoren into a thoughtful sort of mood, and he touched my cheek lightly, then suggested that we meet at the canteen for lunch, and went to get changed for going out into the city.

I know that Kaoren, in his reasons for not wanting to be with me, didn't really underline what might be the main one, worse than enhancing his Sights in sleep. So long as he's a Setari, I'm an assignment. And to the bluesuits me jumping into bed with Kaoren isn't a problem, it's an opportunity. If a situation comes up where they need to control me, they'll absolutely try and do it through him.

I arrived at the canteen first, and hesitated in the doorway, trying to decide where to sit. Kaoren and I eating lunch together on our free day isn't precisely an announcement, but I didn't doubt it would be noticed. Worse, my least favourite person was there with her squad.

Forel isn't silly enough to be openly hostile to me, so she smiled and nodded as I walked past. Her squad followed her lead, and I said hi, but didn't hang around chatting. I don't think moving from being a valuable stray to a planet-unlocking stray has changed Forel's opinion of me. I couldn't quite hear what she said as I walked on to the servery, but I definitely caught Els' name, and Tsennan laughed.

In the end I sat where I usually sit, because finding the most sheltered corner wouldn't hide me any, only make me all the more conspicuous. A couple of people from Eleventh came in, and then Kaoren, in a dark green pullover, and charcoal grey pants. It was almost disconcerting to see him in ordinary clothes, though they didn't make him look any less dangerous. Or a fraction less hot.

I'm not the only one who thought so, either. Forel followed him up to the servery, the rest of her squad vanishing – totally ordered to go away (and Tsennan looking less than happy about it). All she did was talk to Kaoren while he was waiting for his food, looking all very professional and serious, but she touched his arm, which is such an impolite thing to do to a Place Sight talent. And then I had to laugh at myself for lighting up in outraged fury, and had a sudden mental image of me as Daffy Duck, clutching Kaoren and shouting: "Mine! Mine! Mine!" I'm pretty sure Kaoren can handle whatever she was trying to project at him, and at least she left looking not quite pleased with herself. Forel might count as the resident mean girl, but all that achieved for her was being put on a list of squads I won't be assigned to.

It was a quiet time in the canteen, so only part of Eleventh Squad was around to give us curious looks when Kaoren sat down with me. It's not as if our conversation (about Tare's history) would give us away, and I don't think Kaoren's ever likely to be at all demonstrative in public, but we did leave together, so I expect there's a bit of talk going around now. By that time I was less bothered by the possibility of people knowing because I was caught up in the prospect of meeting Kaoren's sister – who is obviously very important to him – and worrying about how she was going to react to me.

We went to the area I'd waited in during the stickie lockdown and she was already there: a small, thin figure in a long skirt and a white shirt with a blue flower pattern. I hadn't been entirely certain what to expect from Siame Ruuel, but I'd been thinking of her as a younger Taarel – a proud and commanding goddess, all antelope limbs and grace. Siame is slight and delicate, with a sweet little rosebud mouth, a wispy-short haircut, and a very straight and upright stance. She has Kaoren's eyes though, black on black, coolly evaluating me.

Kaoren had obviously told her he was bringing someone to meet her, but not who, since there was just a moment's surprise as she recognised me. She looked from my face to Kaoren's as he introduced us, then nodded her head politely (Tarens don't shake hands) and said: "It is very interesting to meet you." Siame's voice is soft and a bit 'little-girl', but she is only fourteen after all (well, forty-four according to Kaoren, but I just can't think in those terms). She's also incredibly self-possessed and went on in a perfectly even voice: "Why do you want my brother?"

I at least had expected directness from someone related to Kaoren, and think I handled it reasonably well, for all my face went very hot. "There never simple answer to that kind of question," I said. "Other than 'because he is Kaoren'. Best I can say is because he didn't ask me if I was so very selfish." I looked at him, feeling rushed and exposed because I'd been finding it easier to keep our conversation away from deep-and-meaningfuls. "And you didn't tell me to hurry, either. Thought about you differently when we back from Earth near-space, anyway."

Because I glanced at Kaoren, I missed Siame's initial reaction. She was only looking thoughtful when she said to him: "What about Meer?"

"Meer and I have never had this kind of relationship," Kaoren replied, not apparently annoyed by the question. He bent and kissed my cheek, which I think may have been meant as something of a message to his sister, and said softly: "For me it was when you handed over that improbable pet of yours, covered in bruises and insisting on giving it a name. I've had to fight against you ever since." He straightened, adding: "I'll see you after dinner."

Siame nodded a farewell, though she'd gone rather white, and they headed off for the exit gate I'm often tempted to walk through, just to see what would happen. I didn't find Siame at all an easy person to read, but I suspect Kaoren was perfectly correct: she's not going to like me.

Speaking of which, Meer is Taarel. I always think it's a funny name for her, because she'll never be a 'mere' anything. However I want to interpret 'this kind of relationship', it's obvious that even Kaoren's sister considered them to be together. I wandered up to the roof (*not* properly dressed for it) to have a bit of a sulk at not being allowed out into the city, and to chew over 'what about Meer'. And be amazed that Kaoren seems to have fallen for me while I looked like a panda. Awfully pleased, though, that it's been so long for him. It was at the coldest part of the long night and windy so I gave up on sulking (still too many champagne bubbles for a proper sulk, anyway) and came back down to my room to play my game, making a heap of progress. I'm feeling really sleepy now, but guess I should go get dinner

Still no sign of Ghost.

Friday, July 18

Pressed

Mara spotted me heading for dinner last night, and brought me back to her apartment to eat with her and Lohn. Lohn was very funny, teasing me about "coming up for air", but also a bit pink and embarrassed about it all. He and Maze are used to thinking of me as a child to be looked after.

We'd barely settled down to eat when Maze brought all of First into channel, along with Kaoren, to warn us that my Kalasa projection and details of the platforms were about to made public. Again KOTIS was pre-empting leaks from Kolar, and were a few minutes from a press conference.

"It will be a very full disclosure," Maze said. "All the scans of the projection barring that from the drone stationed at your test point, scans of the Chamber of Passage, and some less complete information regarding your injuries and what it is you're able to do. Setari images are not being blocked. There'll be a half kasse delay before the transmissions from Kolar are released, and they are the reason there is no point blocking Setari images. We are reaching the point where the image bar, at least while in uniform, is becoming pointless."

"Is – are they going to talk about the Cruzatch?" I asked.

"Yes. It's inescapable – the building they fled through is sealed, guarded, and it's no secret among the expeditionary force why. There has been some considerable debate as to how to handle the release of information about what it is becoming difficult to regard as anything but a direct enemy. There has always been a certain comfort derived from Ionoth being essentially unorganised. The Cruzatch not only pose an intelligent threat, but their appearance in Kalasa and use of the green stone lends itself to explanations no-one likes to credit. It's been settled that we will disclose almost everything we know of them, barring only the trap apparently laid for you. Half-truths on this point aren't likely to improve the situation."

"We may see another response from Nuri," Kaoren said, and the upshot of that is I'm now not allowed to go up to the roof by myself. Super annoying.

Press conferences on Tare are just mass channels with three tiers of participants – watchers, talkers, and the moderator who controlled who got to speak. Tarmian, the husky-voiced woman who'd been handling the Nuran's visit, was acting as KOTIS' spokesperson. The reporters could barely decide which questions they wanted to ask her, they'd been flooded with so much new information.

The discussion about the Cruzatch was the thing that interested me most, and the first thing the reporters latched onto, asking if Muina's initial disaster may have been due to them, rather than the Lantarens – that it may have been an attempted invasion from the Ena. Tarmian wouldn't be drawn into speculating, repeating that KOTIS was continuing to search for answers in both the Ena and in the written records found in Kalasa. She happily announced that they continued to uncover references to the construction of the Pillars, along with a wealth of information about the Lantarens and their philosophies. She even looked a little teary about that, adding that over the coming months Muina and Kolar could expect to access translations of these documents, to at last start reclaiming their cultural heritage.

That switched them on to me, of course, and the projection of the Lantaren ceremony. Taren histories flip-flop about Lantarens. They were a ruling class, incredibly powerful psychics, and they not only broke the planet, they brought Ionoth down on every planet in this area of space. So they're usually depicted as foolish, or greedy, or outright evil. Images of Kalasa at its height, and all those kids with flowers, messed with the way people were used to thinking about Lantarens.

"Is this a true glimpse of the past?" asked one reporter.

"As best as any of our experts can judge, yes," Tarmian replied. "We of course cannot say with absolute certainty the ceremony occurred, but examination of the fallen structure of the bridge, for instance, has verified that it once functioned as a waterfall – a thing certainly not obvious from a simple survey of Kalasa in its current state. We've cleared the central pool, which was completely covered by fallen stone and tarnish, and found the mosaic pattern visible in the projection."

"Then doesn't KOTIS now have the key to revealing the truth about the Breaking? Have you other visions of Muina's past?"

Tarmian shook her head. "This projection, of less than a joden, left Caszandra Devlin in a coma for two days. The exact nature of her talent set is still being discovered, and even if we come to understand it, and she to control it, the energy cost is dangerous in the extreme."

"What exactly does KOTIS mean by a tangible illusion? Is it true Caszandra previously injured herself?" Most of the media here dropped my surname pretty quickly – I'm 'Caszandra' unless they're feeling formal.

"Illusionists create images. Caszandra Devlin can create projections with not only a visual and auditory component, but substance. If Tsa Devlin creates a projection involving heat, it can burn her, as we unfortunately discovered. She is undergoing an intensive training course to strengthen her health and her control over her abilities. No decision can be made on whether we can risk her until she is completely recovered."

They stuck with talking about me for a while, since the nearly full story of my security pass and how it had finally been transferred to everyone else took a fair bit of discussion and explanation, even with the press release laying it out in nice, sequential order. The whole thing made me sound like a really persistent weed, cropping up everywhere no matter how hard you tried to kill it.

Kaoren arrived in the middle of this, and though we stayed in-channel, we went back to my rooms for the rest, settling into my window seat to enjoy the slow shift to dawn. Kaoren's sister's opinion of me was a good deal more interesting to me than the press conference, so I asked him: "What do you and Siame do when you go into the city?"

"Visit exhibitions usually, then shopping and dinner. Siame is torn between our parents' belief that the most important thing any person can do is create, to express, and the role her talents have brought her."

"Isn't it possible to do both?" Zan had managed to find time to learn how to play a musical instrument, after all.

"Do, yes. Do well?" He shrugged. "Our energy is divided enough as it is."

"Did she decide I'm a threat?"

"You are. I will spend less time and thought on Siame because of you. The question is more whether what I gain is worth what it costs her, and she can't judge that yet." He was giving me one of those half-lidded surveys, as if he was trying to decide himself, looking very serious. "She does not want anyone to be more important to me than she is, and she will hate you because of that, perhaps for years. But she will recover."

I didn't know what to say to that, but Kaoren curled his fingers through mine, and that made me feel a lot better.

"The Kolaren transmissions are being released now," Maze said over the interface, as the press conference began to wind down. "They don't add anything in regards to information – simply images."

We said goodnight to First Squad, then dropped out of channel. I had great fun undressing Kaoren, rather than him simply telling his nanosuit to go away, and he was being particularly intense. I waited till we were ready to go to sleep to record some more music for Zan, since I knew that would knock me out completely, and didn't even bother to look at the Kolaren images until today. Lots of pictures of Kalasa, and tons of the Setari. Very few of me, for which I'm glad, though I could have lived without the little movie someone had made of a greensuit being given the duty of carrying me when they were rushing me back to Pandora after the projection. Not flattering.

There's an earlier shot of me looking over my shoulder, wearing my beanie and my newly drawn-on coat, which seems to be the media's new favourite image of me. And one picture of Kaoren, a really beautiful one with him standing in the central Kalasa circle looking down, which for some reason has sparked immense speculation among fans of *The Hidden War* over whether he's the model for Lastier. And hordes of them are salivating over him, which doesn't surprise me at all.

I've been stuck in medical all morning, having more brain scans and a new round of needles (tons of blood samples, which hasn't put me in the greatest of moods), but at least they've taken my blue bandages off again. My legs still don't look normal, but they're a lot less uneven and seamed.

Joint training with First and Fourth soon – they want to try some two-team enhancement strategies. Not that it ever seems likely I'll be sent out on rotation again.

Strategy session

Pretty straightforward combat training yesterday afternoon. I'd asked Mara beforehand how she dealt with being all on-duty professional with Lohn, and whether there were rules about it. She showed me the decorum-in-uniform rules, which are common sense, and I ended up behaving pretty much as I always do in these kind of sessions, the only difference being that I smiled at Kaoren when I arrived, along with all the other people I usually smile at.

After the session, Maze and Kaoren went off to have meetings as captains always seem to do – Kaoren arranging with me over the interface to meet at his apartment for dinner – and I spent a while sitting on the benches along one edge of the test room with the rest of Fourth discussing my projections, and Kalasa, and all the other news which had been released the previous day. All of the first four squads are now very well-documented, and I asked how they felt about the possibility that the image ban will be removed from in-uniform Setari.

"Given that almost all our appearances in uniform are in KOTIS facilities or in the Ena, it won't make any substantial difference," Glade said. "We've had this kind of commentary since we were Kalrani, since the 'gate-spotters' log everyone of around the right age coming out of KOTIS headquarters. And obviously image-blocking on Muina isn't doing much."

"Is it correct that you are reviewing episodes of *The Hidden War* in advance?" Halla asked. She usually keeps quiet around me. Not because she's a quiet type like Par: I think she's just very cautious of what I represent. Or of second level monitoring.

"Maze is, but I asked if he could show them to me. Get them the day before."

"You'd be able to say what happens next even without that," Mori said, giving Halla a look I couldn't interpret.

"Not really – they keep showing things out of order. Skipped couple of weeks in Setari facility before I went Earth's near-space."

"What would come next? If they resumed telling it in order?" Sonn, too, didn't seem to be asking just out of curiosity.

"Given a lot more interface rights, and an apartment rather than being locked in room in medical between training. Trained with First and Second Squad and then went on Unara Rotation with First." I paused (I was flipping through the images of my diary which I've recorded on my personal log). "Depends really on what's in my leaked file. Next thing I'd consider important was that Zan told me what second level monitoring was, which no-one had bothered to mention to me before. I guess she or Maze might have filed report about that. After that – Lights Rotation, enhancement testing with Eighth, then Maze Rotation and I met Ghost."

"That's the Ionoth cat?" Glade was watching me with a quizzical smile, but not quite looking happy. "Were you really locked up in medical?"

"Yes. They got pretty close to what I said to Maze – kept in box and taken out for tests." I shrugged. "After Maze Rotation, tested with Third Squad, then Castle Rotation. Then there was the stickie lockdown and Ghost showed up again. Then Seventh Squad, then Bridges Rotation, then Fifth Squad." I wrinkled my nose. "Then Pillar recovery, which is next time I had anything to do with Fourth, which I guess is why you're asking. You were all unconscious by the time I got there, but I expect that episode will show what happened before that. Not likely script will follow all that anyway."

"We've been trying to work out a strategy to counter this," Mori said, giving Sonn a quelling glance. "All very well to be told that everyone here knows that it's fiction, but when the interface is full of pictures of Tsee Ruuel, speculating over whether he is the template for Lastier–"

"What could you do?" I asked curiously, while trying to decide whether this would be a good or extremely awkward moment to mention that something rather major had changed.

"At this stage, gnash our teeth loudly and complain," Glade said.

"We can't do anything," Halla said flatly. "You can."

"This isn't the right way," Par told her, while I was busy looking surprised.

"You mean make statement to press or something?" I asked.

"No." I think Sonn and Mori had been arguing on a private channel – or just frowning at each other at random moments – but Sonn went on to say: "If you're being given these episodes in advance, then object to this slander. Not just the most obscene excesses, but all of it, everything not true."

"Isn't it too late?" I glanced at Mori, who was biting her lip but not quite objecting. "First thing Lastier said about me set the character, and is too well established now that even if stuck to exact truth and stopped sneering at everyone, would still be evil Lastier."

"She's right," Glade said. "What would you suggest, Caszandra? I doubt talking to the press is going to be encouraged, but I swear if another person mutters 'filthy creature' to me I'm going to be up on a fighting reprimand."

"Wait two weeks," I said, and stood up, well aware that I'd gone red. I really hadn't wanted to talk to the rest of Fourth about Kaoren, not so soon.

"What happens in two weeks?" Mori looked very worried, which isn't surprising since part of Fourth's job is making sure I don't get too upset.

I spoke quickly, face hotter with every word. "Given how little real privacy I have this planet, and how quickly gossip seems to spread, two weeks about longest I think will take before producers of *The Hidden War* frantically order rewrites to scripts and start trying to make Lastier more sympathetic. Maybe they'll get me reform him?" I shrugged, not able to look at any of them when I added: "Don't see how else they'll reconcile evil Lastier with the fact that I'm sleeping with Kaoren."

I walked off immediately, wishing it was not such a long way across the training room, and was very relieved when I heard Glade burst out laughing. And Mori sent me an apologetic email before I'd reached my room, not saying very much and managing to express astonishment with every word, but at least not seeming angry. But I know, could tell, that she's not going to be quite the same with me.

I sent Kaoren an email, just saying that Fourth had been talking to me about Lastier and I'd ended up telling them we were together. His response was "Perhaps they'll start enjoying him now."

I hope Mara was right about them adjusting.

Saturday, July 19

Chink in the armour

Last night Kaoren asked me if I'd read my diary to him. He'd been in a quiet mood, barely speaking, which isn't as upsetting as it sounds because it makes him very physically expressive. Just as I was drowsing off to sleep he asked me, then added: "I know it's not a small thing. Particularly because I would need it to be complete. If you censored parts I would know, and that would truly distract me."

I'd gone very still and surprised, and was well aware that he'd know my reaction wasn't exactly positive. "Whole thing?" I asked after a moment.

"I cannot learn your world as you have been learning mine. And I have – my Sights drive me to understand – everything I deal with, but most particularly you. Don't decide immediately–"

"It's okay." I propped myself up on one elbow, looking at him through the half-light. "Reading diary be embarrassing in bits, but can live with that if really important to you. Though will make me sound very whiney. Hope you have high tolerance for entry after entry about how much I wished I could stop thinking about you."

There was a lot of kissing after that, and when we did go to sleep he kept shifting so I was trapped underneath him, which is something he seems to do when he's upset. I don't think either of us are regretting getting together, but we're still learning what we're like, and one thing I have to keep in mind is how much Kaoren's life is driven by his Sights, and what those Sights mean for the future of our 'together'. I *think* that I'll be able to cope with a relationship without secrets, but that's the kind of optimistic thing I can tell myself right up until I have something I don't want to admit.

My diary, at least, isn't that big a stumbling block. Not that I didn't spend a lot of today flipping through what I've written and imagining Kaoren's reaction. And I don't know if I'll be able to write in exactly the same way, knowing one day he'll hear it. I've kept half-starting and stopping writing this and wondering whether I'm leaving bits out that I'd normally say. Especially about what happened this morning, when I wandered out of Kaoren's room mid-morning and ran straight into Eeli and Meht from Third.

Eeli started to smile at me, then stared at the door I'd come through. And then her eyes went huge and round, and she said: "How could you?!" and sort of wavered in one spot and then ran back into her room.

Meht, who I haven't had much to do with at all, but who is about as stolid as Eeli is high-strung, shook her head and said: "There goes today's training session," and got an abstract 'talking over the interface' expression while I was busy being all mortified, and then Taarel sent me a message saying: "Come talk in my room for a joden." The door to her apartment – which is just opposite Kaoren's – slid open and, wishing I was anywhere else, I went in.

Taarel was wearing her hair in a long braid down her back, which made her look totally not herself (and eerily like Zee). And she has a big lighted terrarium full of plants, which would have swallowed a lot of my attention if I hadn't been so nervous about having this particular conversation. Of course, I didn't expect her to be nasty or anything, since she's not that kind of person at all, but I'd been spending a lot of mental energy on "what about Meer".

"Don't mind Eeli," she said, gesturing for me to sit down on a black couch covered with a dark green throw. "She's long enjoyed all measure of romantic dreams about Kaoren and I, and I should have prepared her for the reality."

"Dreams not entirely without basis, though?" I said, or asked, since I still wasn't a hundred percent certain.

"Kaoren hasn't talked to you about this at all, has he?" She sat across from me, faintly exasperated.

I shook my head. "I could have asked, guess," I said. "But felt that most probably he would have said something if you were – if there–" I broke off, feeling the heat from my face spreading all the way down my chest. I seem to do nothing but blush lately.

"If you'd stolen him from me," she finished comfortably. "Very true, he would have. But taking the position that it's no-one's business won't spare you reactions like Eeli's. No, Kaoren's never been mine, or I've never been his or however you want to view it. We've been very...convenient to each other, but it was never deeper than that."

I found this just as clear as Kaoren's "never had that kind of relationship", and said doubtfully: "Friends with benefits?"

That wasn't a Taren phrase, but Taarel's very smart and saw what I meant straight away. "Yes, you could call it that. Allies. He is not what I want, and he has never wanted to distract himself with anything serious. But we have a level of trust, and understood each other well enough to give each other an occasional physical outlet. An arrangement which, quiet as we have kept it, has been assumed as far more."

I chewed my lip. "Don't think Eeli be happy to give up idea. Or necessarily believe."

Taarel looked amused. "Eeli will believe what I tell her. And then she will apologise very prettily to you. And then she will want to know all about how you and Kaoren decided for each other, and whether he manages to be at all romantic or if he simply tells you exactly what he wants you to do." That, of course, made me practically go purple, and she laughed. "Kaoren and I would never have survived as a couple. We both enjoy being in charge far too much. And on that note, I think I shall borrow you for the morning. My squad has swimming practice, and I want them to learn this style you taught Namara."

And to show that she is completely undisturbed by anything about me and Kaoren. Taarel really is a spectacular person. Eeli behaved exactly as predicted, and the swimming lesson went very well. The rest of Third only looked at me a little strangely, but since they adore Taarel they behaved toward me as Taarel wanted them to. I swear the woman could conquer a country in an afternoon.

I felt like saying something about Maze to her, but decided not to. It's not nice to prod weak spots.

Sunday, July 20

Expansion

It's going to take me several centuries to read Kaoren my diary since he asks so many questions – every second sentence seemed to contain a place name or a concept he wanted explained. We started off with a long discussion on swear words, since swearing was about all I wanted to do, stuck on a hill in a forest. So I've now learned several interesting Taren words which no-one else would explain to me, and Kaoren can use Earth's most flexible (English) swearword as noun, verb and adjective. An important first step in our cultural exchange.

Then we moved on to Eloise. Tarens and Kolarens don't use middle names, and I'd never brought it up, so my middle name came a bit out of nowhere for Kaoren. He says it is after all a piece of me, and I think was more upset about not knowing part of my name than he wanted to admit. He knew, though, that the Tarens are misspelling Cassandra, and wasn't at all surprised that I haven't corrected it simply because I think it's funny and sounds cool.

I managed to read through my first day, and that was the longest conversation we've ever had. I think I'm going to enjoy reading to him.

Other than training with Third, yesterday was how a normal rotation day would be for us. Kaoren read reports before going into the Ena, came out tired, had to write up a bunch more reports, and was ready for sleep in the late afternoon. I had 'free training' in the morning, then my projection training in early afternoon, and fell asleep curled up against him while he was finishing his last report. We both woke up starving, caught up on news while we ate, and then got very non-verbal for a while. And then diary reading, kissing, and sleep again.

I'm using up what little free time Kaoren used to have, and getting worried about whether he's going to end up needing a holiday to recover from me. Though he has been sleeping deeply and well, so isn't wandering around looking all shadowy-eyed.

This morning was stretching and weights with First Squad and Fourth Squad, which I was nervous about. But no-one in Fourth acted cross. I think they were trying to behave just as usual when I came in, and Par smiled at me, while Glade was looking highly entertained, and they all pretended they weren't watching in fascination every time Kaoren spoke to me – though they'd have been disappointed if they'd been closer, since he was mainly telling me the same stuff Mara does about not bending my knees.

After the training session Maze, who watched me and Kaoren fairly closely as well, but seemed satisfied with how we were, told us all that First and Fourth would probably be posted back to Muina again in another couple of weeks, after the second phase of the larger squad trial. And just now (now being me in the middle of another uncomfortable session of work on my legs) they brought all the squads into a virtual meeting and announced that two senior Kalrani will be temporarily assigned to each squad, and join training sessions for a week before working with the squad on rotations.

"If eight-strength squads are successful, the assignments will be reviewed and made permanent," Maze told us. "No decision has been made as yet on what to do regarding accommodation, but the most likely options are to expand to the far side of the lift well, as with Devlin's quarters, or to shuffle every squad upwards to make room. Either way, a second lift is being considered to facilitate urgent movement."

I've been reviewing the assignment list, checking out the names and talents. First has gained a guy and a girl – Kian Farn and Az Norivan – who are strongest with Ice and Water respectively. Basically rounding out primary talents they didn't already have. Fourth gained two guys, Rada Dae and Sael Toren; Fire and Ice. Morel, the only Kalrani name I recognised among the assignment list, is part of Third, which I suspect he'll be pleased about.

I hope they're people I'll like.

A store is selling copies of my coat, the one I drew the pattern from Kalasa's door on. I'd have to save for weeks to buy one. And beanies have become extremely fashionable. The thing I resent most is that whoever did the coat they're selling is a far better artist, and the pattern doesn't look nearly so amateurish and uneven.

Monday, July 21

Pay day

That was the last major session of work on my legs for a while, which I'm glad of because they always leave me feeling a bit odd – they have a nanite which eats scar tissue and then a different nanite they've cultured from my skin which replaces the scars. The medics tell me they couldn't just do that to start with because it's much slower, and the initial focus is on getting the patient to not die, not making sure the patient's legs are sexy. [Well, they didn't say it in those words, exactly.] Anyway, these cosmetic sessions involve lying there having bits of my legs eaten by nanites. No wonder I feel blah afterwards.

Since it was the night before a rotation, I went and curled up in Kaoren's room, finishing off one of the books he recommended, then wondering whether I should buy more clothes and keep some in his rooms. I was contemplating the small amount of money I had left from my allowance and feeling very grumpy about the number of people making big profits off of me without even saying thanks when – almost as if he were psychic! – Tsur Selkie sent me a channel request and said: "At what point were you going to mention that you continue to receive only the Displaced Aliens Stipend?"

He sounded genuinely curious, so instead of telling him 'next time I met an intrepid girl reporter', I said: "When I needed to buy something I couldn't afford."

"Is that cultural?" he asked, surprising me by not saying a few crisp words and breaking connection. "Some kind of taboo regarding receiving payment?"

"In a way, a bit," I said, having not really thought about it. "If passer-by see someone in trouble, and saves their life, very crass to ask for a fee. I would be very strange person if turned around and say that because I unlock Muina, expect to be given lots of money. But working with Setari – whose job it is to save people – different situation. And helping fill in Rana Junction Gate, completely different situation. Be embarrassing asking to be paid, but would have pointed out eventually that if going to treat me like an employee, very mean not to give me a wage. Waiting to see if anyone notice."

"The administrative body of the Displaced Aliens Fund noticed, and have requested a refund of payments received since you were returned to KOTIS."

I had to laugh. "Tarens very stingy people."

Selkie had reverted to being a bluesuit, though, and simply said: "You'll be classified as captain for salary purposes," and broke connection.

So I'm now an actual employee of KOTIS, more or less – and have an awful lot of money, since Setari captains seem to get paid plenty and I had more than a Taren year's worth built up (minus repaying my stipend, and a whole bunch of taxes). Kaoren, when I told him about it, said that the things I find funny are liable to drive Selkie insane.

He also told me to check my schedule, which had been updated. First and Fourth are going to take me into the Ena for my next few testing sessions, using the opportunity to break in their new members by clearing Ionoth in near-space. This dual-purpose use of time was typically Kaoren and I laughed and told him that if I ever wanted to drive him insane I'd just force him to do something, anything, inefficiently. He went unexpectedly intense in response, and kissed me really hard. I guess I probably already drive him insane.

We haven't pushed each other yet, haven't had an argument or done anything guaranteed to irritate the other, but this – he and I – has been working better than I could have hoped given that he's a driven perfectionist and I'm, well, a stop and smell the roses type. I'm finding myself unexpectedly settled rather than plagued with doubts.

We didn't make love last night, though; the first time in the eight whole days since we got together. Kaoren could tell my legs had left me very queasy this time round, and I think his Sights mean that unless I'm truly into it, it's not going to happen. No faking allowed. Instead we watched one of Kaoren's favourite movies (this incredibly sad and smart and beautiful story about a woman outwitting a mad AI), and then I read more diary and we talked about the schoolies week and going to high school in Australia, and then experimentally eating things to see whether they kill you.

My first four days on Muina. I was so alone.

I had a nightmare later: not one of the Sight ones, just dreaming of walking along that river and never being found. I cried a little, when Kaoren woke me up, because I really don't care that much about not being allowed out into the city, or the size of my pay packet, or anything but not being so scared and isolated. And this growing confidence I have about Kaoren just underlines to me that, despite how nice people were to me, I stayed being scared and isolated long after I was rescued.

Nearly time to go into the Ena.

Under Observation

Maze introduced me to the new squad members (both First's and Fourth's) before we went into the Ena. They were all around my age and being extremely correct and proper, as you'd expect for Kalrani who'd suddenly found themselves joining senior squads.

Kian Farn, joining First, was too guarded for me to get any real impression of him. He's around average height (given that most people here are tall), he said practically nothing, and he was very watchful and expressionless, measuring everything that was happening around him. Az Norivan has a wonderful curling smile, and although not nearly at Eeli-level seems to be a fairly 'up' type of person.

Rada Dae, Fourth's new Fire (plus Telekinesis) talent, and Sael Toren with a primary of Ice, are absolute stereotypical fire and ice personalities, except Dae has dyed his hair dark blue with frosted white tips, which is a complete failure to conform to the 'Fire' colour scheme. But Dae is all energetic and enthusiastic, outgoing and chatty, while Toren is coldly reserved and very down-to-business, so otherwise they slot right into their pigeonholes. Toren will probably appreciate being in Fourth because Kaoren's so very focused and efficient. Oddly, he doesn't remind me of Kaoren at all – Kaoren is more detached than cold, while Toren was definitely of the 'coolly superior and does not think much of you' cold.

Though none of the new squad members were being nasty or grouchy, I didn't get the impression any of them were at all pleased to be placed in First and Fourth, which confused the hell out of me for a while. I don't usually ask Kaoren about 'staffing', since gossiping about the people he supervises isn't something he's likely to do, but interrupted his report writing just now to say: "New people all captain candidates? Appointments to First and Fourth only temporary?"

"It will be interesting to see how long it takes them to reach the same conclusion," Kaoren said. "We're not ready to form additional squads, let alone send them out raw to face the increasing numbers we're having to deal with. After a year working actively in the Ena, most of the additional squad members will be considered for reformation into Fifteenth and Sixteenth. Some will remain, and perhaps become part of Seventeenth and Eighteenth in turn. Eight-strength squads give us an opportunity for advanced training."

"Why not tell them that beforehand?"

"Nothing has been firmly decided. And all captains must learn to follow the lead of their seniors." He shifted me a little closer to his side before going back to his report writing. He isn't at all keen on me being out of reach just now, and that's the Nurans' fault. If I end up having a permanent guard assigned to me even while I'm in KOTIS, I'm going to be severely annoyed.

The testing session itself was very interesting. Maze brought a drone and a scan-chair along, and both squads went up to the roof to a spot where they'd apparently stuck a drone in real-space as well. Zee, Alay and Halla stayed with me while First and Fourth separated and went hunting over the massive-pile-of-blocks expanse of Konna. They rarely have to hunt out over the water, since the Ionoth tend to drown if they come through out there. Even the flying Ionoth gravitate toward the land masses, which only makes sense because Tare's storms helpfully rip them apart if they don't find some level of shelter.

Zee had me start out making projections from memory. And that was so much easier than it is in real-space I could scarcely believe it. I did a few minutes of the first episode of a favourite of Mum's, a BBC documentary called *Planet Earth,* and then took a break, but was nowhere near to passing out as I would have been in real-space. A quick sprint, stop for a rest, then fine to go on.

"Try an object now," Zee said, putting her breather down in front of me.

This was harder to achieve. Projecting images takes a bit of mental effort to start off, but it does work a lot like pressing 'play'. Making the breather is different in ways it's really hard to put into words – kind of like those magic eye puzzles where you have to sort of unfocus your eyes, but I needed to unfocus my mind. I find it easier when I close my eyes and someone starts reading out a long description, guiding what I'll project.

Still, after a bit of frowning – and nearly making a mug of hot chocolate – I produced a breather which Zee could pick up, but which went away as soon as I stopped concentrating on it. And yet my origami cranes are still going strong. My talents seem to me very contradictory.

Since I was still feeling fine – no headache, just a bit of an elevated heartbeat which went away after a rest – Zee had me go on to visualising a room she described. This was a restaurant, a fancy one which seemed to be at 'shift change' – closed for a half-kasse for a thorough clean and refresh. Five people were moving about, whisking fresh cloths over tables, setting out table spices and long blue heated centrepieces where platters of food would be set to keep warm. Two of them were chatting about whether one of the girls should go out with someone, briskly continuing their work all the time. They didn't seem able to see us, but when Halla picked up a glass they noticed that immediately, and pointed, then asked each other which of them was the Telekinetic. But they could more or less see Halla's shadow, now they were looking directly at her, and came and crowded around her, talking excitedly.

I let the projection lapse then (to Halla's relief, I suspect), and shrugged when Zee asked me how I was feeling. "Could do with a bit of a rest," I said, then opened a private channel to her, and Maze and Kaoren, who were distant but within range thanks to the drone's relay.

"There's someone watching us," I said. "On the roof just above. They came during the last projection."

"The Nuran?" Maze asked, while Zee looked down to stop herself from looking up.

"Not Inisar," I said. "It's no-one I know. I looked right at where they're standing but I couldn't see them."

"Does not register with Combat Sight," Zee said, moving so she was standing within touching distance of me. I took out my water flask, though I could tell by the way Alay was frowning at me that I wasn't acting particularly naturally.

"Warn Annan the moment you detect any movement," Maze said crisply. "Ruuel, your squad is closer. We'll hang back in case this is an opening of communication." He brought us all into the one channel, saying: "There's an unknown at the test site. We're returning, but do not attack unless signalled."

"Halla, enhance and scan the roof above with Place," Kaoren said, voice as calmly even as if we were all in one of the training rooms preparing for a test session.

Halla, with just the faintest hint of confusion, moved close enough to brush my arm with her fingertips, then stood gazing upward. I was watching her face, and saw her lips part slightly, then she said, "Streaming," over the interface, and we all got to look at the barest blurry echo of a shape standing gazing down at us.

It was pretty hard to tell, but I thought it was a woman. There was a bump by one leg which could have been the hilts of two swords worn in the same way as Inisar's.

"Is invisibility a talent all on its own?" I asked Zee, since everyone staring upward made pretending we didn't know the woman was there pretty pointless.

"It's Illusion-casting," Zee replied, not shifting her attention away from the place the watcher occupied. "Very few Illusionists can manage it."

I was briefly distracted wondering if Nils could, and if he crept about being invisible, but found I was annoyed and said flatly: "Nurans don't have very good manners."

Zee put an admonitory hand on my shoulder, and I sighed, then tried to remember what it had felt like when Inisar had spoken in my head. The figure above us shifted as Fourth Squad rose up through the gaps in the half-formed buildings below us, and I tried mentally saying: "Not allowed to talk?"

There was no reaction. I decided not to push it, since for all I knew I could be revealing things which would endanger Inisar. And then Fourth was there, spreading in a semi-circle behind me, Kaoren at my other shoulder.

Zee dropped her hand so Kaoren could enhance, and then she said: "Caszandra has a point. To watch, hidden, is hardly courteous."

All this achieved, though, was to make the Nuran leave.

"Teleported," Kaoren said, and Halla and I both nodded.

That killed the testing session. Maze took me back inside with First as an escort while Fourth tried to track the Nuran. Zee and Alay stayed with me until Kaoren returned, and I suspect if I wasn't handily sleeping with Captain All-the-Sights, I'd have Halla on my couch. According to Maze, it'll be a while before a decision is made about whether to go ahead with these sessions. That the Nurans can shield themselves from Combat Sight is something none of the Setari like.

KOTIS sent a ship to Nuri after Inisar first showed up, and were basically "escorted off the premises" by a couple of very uncommunicative Nurans. I can just picture tiny flying samurai staring down the *Diodel* or even the *Litara*. I bet Inisar could pull that off.

Whatever the Nurans want with me, they plainly don't intend to start cooperating with Tare, which no-one thinks is a good sign. Kaoren's really bothered by today's (non-)appearance.

Tuesday, July 22

Crack

A day which started mildly, with nothing but training with Fourth scheduled. Martial arts in the morning – everyone pairing off and trying to hit each other. I was paired with Sonn, and Kaoren left me to her while critically watching everyone else. Toren and Dae were paired to start with, and Kaoren didn't seem to pay any particular attention to them, just swapped them out after a while to fight Glade and Mori.

I still can't tell how good people are at fighting – certainly not when they're practicing rather than quickly taking their opponents down. Toren and Dae didn't seem to me to be obviously better or worse than Glade or Mori, but the way their expressions changed – Dae acting intense and determined and Toren going all grimly quiet – I guess there must have been some kind of difference. Kaoren spoke to them briefly – five terse words – during a rest break and both of them looked like they wished they were anywhere else.

Most of Fourth Squad are twenty (I refuse to think of Kaoren as sixty), while Toren and Dae are a couple of years younger. You can't actively serve as a Setari until you've hit fifty – nearly seventeen – which is the 'qualifying age' on Tare for trying to pass the adulthood exams. Most Kalrani aren't promoted until they're closer to eighteen. Toren and Dae no doubt knew Kaoren's reputation, and Fourth's generally as a squad which focuses on close combat, but I think they were expecting less of a gap.

Still, with me around they never had to worry about being the worst in the room. I was genuinely trying, and I am a little better than before, but I always seem to make absolutely the wrong choice in response to an attack, and I think Sonn was having to spend a lot of effort to not wipe the floor with me.

The best part of martial arts training for me is seeing everyone in the martial arts training outfits. They apparently wear these because the nanosuits give too much cushioning, and can sprout weapons. They do training using the nanoliquid blades as well, of course, but work on the basic combat moves separately. Mori seems to be the best fighter in the squad beside Kaoren – or at least he sparred with her seriously toward the end of the session.

After that we changed and jogged over the stairs. I dropped far behind, unsurprisingly, but Kaoren stayed with me while the rest of the squad went ahead, and fortunately he didn't turn into a drill-sergeant, letting me rest halfway up the longer flights of stairs. I told him it would be a great workout for him if he carried me, but he just asked me deadpan if I thought he wasn't getting enough exercise.

"Am I going to be babysat for long?" I asked. "Haven't failed to notice that Halla keeping close to me even when getting changed."

"That will depend on the Nuran," Kaoren said, not bothering to pretend I'm not under full-time guard. It was pretty obvious I'd been switched to training with Fourth because it has two Place Sight talents.

"Would Nuran really have any chance of wandering about undetected inside? Doors wouldn't open, elevators wouldn't work."

"And scanners are harder to guise against. But shielded rooms won't necessarily keep a teleporter out, though it increases the risk." He tucked a straying strand of hair behind my ear, adding: "Very likely we will be relocated to Muina ahead of schedule, since even Nurans would find the Ddura an insurmountable obstacle. And, yes, that won't change the fact that you are going to be constantly guarded for the foreseeable future."

"I don't like that it was a different Nuran than Inisar," I said, sighing at the thought of constant guarding – for all that a large part of that constant guarding is going to involve just me and Kaoren and probably not a lot of clothing. "Do you think they found out he gave me that book?"

"It's a possibility." He asked whether my legs hurt, and we had a brief, serious discussion about the conflicts between supervising me and sleeping with me. Kaoren prefers my training to be with First, but that I be assigned to Fourth whenever I go anywhere risky. I'm fine with either, just so long as no-one decides to station us on different planets again.

The afternoon was mixed combat training with Fourth and First, with Nils from Second along to make illusions for everyone to attack. He was being oddly quiet again, and didn't even tease me about Kaoren, though I could tell he knew by the way he watched when Kaoren was talking to me. Surprisingly, I don't think the gossip has spread very far. Other than Kaoren and I having lunch together one day, we haven't been seen out publicly, and I guess those who know haven't been telling.

Even Toren and Dae aren't in that loop. Fourth Squad have been politely welcoming toward their two new members, but weren't being relaxed and 'themselves' during break times with them. They were well aware that Toren and Dae didn't like that they'd been assigned to Fourth, and naturally they weren't pleased with that. Or it could be they were still being quiet and non-chatty on account of me sleeping with Kaoren, but I don't think it's quite the case. Sonn seemed a little more like I was an accepted part of the team than she usually is, and I even had a bit of a conversation with Halla about Nurans and what they thought they were achieving by not joining forces with the other ex-Muinan civilisations.

And then, halfway through the two squad training session, the swoops Nils had been projecting abruptly disappeared. The look on his face, when we turned to find out why, was such straightforward shock that First and Fourth reacted by gathering as if to fight off an attack, but then Ketzaren said: "Unara."

I was a beat behind everyone else checking the news feeds, and the first channel I went to only seemed to be showing me a waterfall. A waterfall and a chair. That was from a scanner, but the feed switched almost right away to someone's personal vision. They were in a triple-tiered atrium full of plants and there was water pouring down from a gash, a long, wide crack, in the whitestone ceiling. And there was a woman hanging down, tangled in, I don't know, some kind of cable, with the water pouring past her.

It had only just happened, too recent even for the bluesuits to have worked out any orders, but First and Nils ran anyway, so they'd be ready at the nearest lock. Kaoren said: "Take lead," to Mori and she, Par, Glade and our two Kalrani went, while Kaoren, Halla and Sonn stayed to protect me from

Invisible Nurans. I had a couple of moments' angst about that, then realised that they probably wouldn't have been sent anyway. Sight talents and Lightning wouldn't be very useful when what you were fighting was Tare's weather.

It's only now, hours later, that any sort of clear exterior view of the damage has been available. It doesn't even look like that much, just a tiny crack in the endless blocky meringue of Unara. Other than some falling injuries, it's likely that it wouldn't have been anything like so bad, except this is Tare, and the daily mega-storm was dumping half an ocean on Unara's roof.

I called the crack tiny, but it exposed over two thousand Unaran apartments to one of Tare's full-scale storms. Bad enough, but add to that the countless gallons of water draining over the vast expanse of the roof, some diverted into water collection channels, but most following whatever was the easiest course down to the ocean.

In the first few minutes after the crack opened, a lot of people evacuated, thankfully. But others moved to inner rooms, or were stopped by exit corridors split in two or elevators not functioning. The Unaran authorities, finding corridors and atriums suddenly awash, had little choice but to seal the area as best they could. And the person who was transmitting on the news channel I'd linked to – it was a teenaged kid named Konstan Trabel – drowned.

Tarens can't swim. There's no lakes on Tare, no rivers or beaches, and the only swimming pool is in the Setari facilities. When you live in permanent air-conditioning there's no particular drive to get wet as a form of recreation, and Taren cities don't really have the space to spare for lots of water-sports. I'm not sure many people could have successfully swum out of a room filling with furniture and pot plants even if they'd been raised in the water.

Back when the 2004 tsunami hit I remember staying glued to the TV, watching over and over sequences filmed from balconies, of walls of mud and village sliding past. Knowing that people had to be in that churning mass, glad not to see any, unable not to look. On Tare, the interface lets those people transmit direct to their families, or social network, or news channel, and unless they block you, you can watch and hear and shudder until the images fill with grey or wriggling sparkles of light, and stop.

I switched to a channel which wasn't live-streaming death.

It didn't take very long for the Setari squads to reach Unara. The biggest delay was getting from their entry space to the particular 'suburb' being flooded. The Telekinetics and Teleporters and the Levitation talents joined various drones and emergency rescue workers and a handful of middle-strong civilian talents working to get people out. Every Ice talent KOTIS could send went to the roof and, with the strongest of the Telekinetics bracing them against the gale, formed dams and channels and barriers to route the water away. That was immensely frustrating to watch, knowing how much quicker they could do it if I was there.

Still, they got it done, and the ice held more or less despite the driving rain. There's four squads still stationed at Unara, helping with the job of putting up a temporary seal before the next storm hits.

Far fewer people died than during the Dohl Array attack. But Tare is – I don't know how to put this – *wounded* in a way which it wasn't when the problem was a massive which the Setari could fight and kill. Because the crack was caused by a gate. Not even a huge gate. A gate the size of a car tyre.

Even though the Tarens have refined their whitestone nanomaterial so that it can take a lot of weight, Unara is still a huge, heavy place. I got a bit lost among Taren terms more complex than 'load-bearing' and 'distributed force', but the diagrams made clear enough that far bigger parts of Unara could split or collapse if only a relatively small part of its core structure was damaged. The news channel I was watching had a fine old time showing projections of what would happen if gates opened at dramatically critical points. And then there was the question of air routes, the possibility of one of the tanz clipping a gate, and countless graphs plotting the increase in gate openings, and estimates for what Tare would be dealing with in ten, five, even one Taren year. Open statements on every channel that within four Taren years life here will have changed substantially, and that's not even factoring in the continual increase in Ionoth numbers.

It's like Tare has abruptly woken up to a nightmare which has been happening all along.

Kaoren is a wreck – Sight Sight had shown him way too much, and he's been off talking with Mori, who had a person die just as she was teleporting him. We've been discussing our own anti-nightmare strategy, just to get to tomorrow, and after I've finished writing this up we're going to watch the next preview episode of *The Hidden War* together, and after that hopefully we'll both be too exhausted to stay awake. Then we'll step through a Sights exercise together, and I'll try not to drown us both in my inevitable reaction projection.

Wednesday, July 23

Keep on keeping on

They've moved up our departure for Muina to the day after tomorrow, whether because of the Nuran or because yesterday pushed them into being not so reluctant to use me. I think everyone's looking forward to heading back, overwhelmingly keen to do something, anything, which might result in a solution. It'll just be exploration at first, and I'll probably actively work with First and Fourth.

What I need to focus on is no more meltdowns, no more injuries. I can't do anything about being irreplaceable, but at the least I have to stop putting myself in medical.

Despite all that went on yesterday, First and Fourth went ahead with their scheduled dual eight-strength squad rotation today. Kaoren warned me ahead of time that they'd likely be out for a long stretch – one of the huge advantages dual squads give exploration teams is the extra Ena manipulation to ensure gates are locked, so they can go further without tiredness making it too dangerous. If they'd been able to get permission they would have taken me with them, since I represent the ability to cast very deeply into the Ena, and Kaoren's hoping that some time in the future they'll be able to work with me again, attempting to locate Pillars. But no go.

They were out most of the day, too – nearly six hours, which is an immense amount of time for Setari. I was 'adopted' by Third again for the day, since Tol Sefen has Place Sight. Taarel kept us busy, and the conversation away from Unara, but there was a level of stress sitting under everything. It's not like anything's really more urgent than it was two days ago, but it sure feels like we can't waste any more time training.

Third were a good group to distract me, though. Third's two new members, Shin Morel and a girl called Elory Tedar, plainly can't believe their luck in being made part of the squad and are quite ready to worship at Taarel's feet, which of course means the regular squad members consider them people of taste and discernment. Eeli continued on with being totally fascinated by the idea of me and Kaoren, and though she did try not to pry too openly, she really really wanted to know what drew us together. I don't know what Taarel said to her, but she seems to have completely accepted that Kaoren isn't someone Taarel wanted a romance with.

It must be so weird for Taarel, defending the girl who made off with her convenient lover. Although, if she really is in love with Maze, then it might have come as a relief to her to know that whatever people have been saying about me and Maze wasn't true. No-one's actually told me that there was gossip, but I've started to realise there must have been some, that the direction they're taking in *The Hidden War* is what some people thought was happening. The episode Kaoren and I watched last night follows my first rotation with First Squad, and it's again hinting that the Maze-equivalent character is feeling all conflicted about me. I'm pretty sure Maze has never even considered it.

After lunch, since Third was scheduled to do elementals training, Taarel assigned Tol and Eeli more obviously as my babysitters and we went back to my apartment to find a huge pile of packages waiting – the result of a post-getting paid spending spree.

Tol thought it hugely funny that I'd been getting the equivalent of pocket money, and the mood lightened considerably. I think babysitting me, helping me unwrap packages, was a handy distraction for them as well.

Fortunately I'd opted against buying a whole heap of racy nightwear. I could just imagine Eeli's reaction to that. Along with clothes I'd picked up another couple of blank books, and a big pack of imported Kolaren permanent markers, which I spent a lot of the afternoon putting to good use on my coat while we chatted. Tol had seen the copies of my coat for sale, and asked if that was why I was altering the pattern, but it was mainly that I'd never finished it in the first place because my permanent marker had run out of ink. I extended it about halfway down the back and a little onto the arms, and although it's not perfect I do like it.

When Kaoren walked in we were all three sitting on the floor around my coffee table, me trying to even up the wobbly bits of my coat's pattern, and Eeli and Tol trying to write their names on pieces of paper. They both hastily got to their feet, though I suspect Eeli was mainly hoping for a better view of Kaoren's expression, but he simply told them they could go and waited till they had.

He brought dinner, and after eating made a valiant attempt to finish off his reports, but has fallen asleep on the couch.

Thursday, July 24

Getting serious

There was a fantastic thunderstorm last 'night'. I turned down all my lights and watched it while Kaoren slept, and eventually fell asleep myself. It was still going when he woke me with kisses in the pitchy dark, and we undressed each other between flashes of lightning. That was impossibly intense, overwhelming, and I was shaking afterwards and clung to him.

And Kaoren said: "You need to spend more time on your studies."

"What?"   A whole world of incredulity went into that word, and he wouldn't have needed Place Sight to tell him exactly what I thought of him saying something so...so prosaic right after something I'd found so amazing. I don't remember ever being more furious.

To my shock he laughed, a surprised spurt. "That sounded very out of place didn't it?   The tail-end of my thoughts." He paused, and lightning showed me his expression, a combination of dismay and amusement and something rather more. "I can't marry you unless you pass the adult competency exams," he explained, and then moved forward so he was talking directly into my ear, his voice soft and completely serious. "Are you certain yet, Cassandra?"

"Yes." I was breathless, dizzy with the sudden reversal of fury, but totally sure. It hasn't even been two weeks, but all the past days have done is confirm what I've felt for months.

My Mum would be silently screaming about now, and working out how to convince me that getting married at eighteen is a terrible idea, and that really I need to spend a lot more time before I could decide if Kaoren and I are a permanent thing, and that both of us were probably just reacting to the drama at Unara, and should take things much slower.

But this is Tare.

Tare doesn't have an equivalent to Vegas. To get married, Kaoren and I both have to have passed the adult competency test, and then register an intention to marry, and then live together for five Taren years before applying for permission to hold a commitment ceremony.   And if we break up temporarily in the middle of that, we have to wait longer. I'll be twenty by the time we can consider arranging for the ceremony.

So, yeah, super-romantic place, Tare. The Paris of the stars.

It was late into our shift when we stopped to shower and eat, and then Kaoren spent a while celebrating our not-quite-engagement by finishing his reports. Even with he and Maze sharing the work, going into new spaces means he has a ton of post-rotation work. I spent the time researching what the adult competency test involved. It wasn't an ultra-brainy sort of test, more like social studies: knowing laws and customs, and basic biology and health care. Not very much in the way of sciences, but some history. The laws and customs are the ones which are most likely to trip me up – Tare has a by-law for everything, particularly about babies and who can have them. All the red tape about marriage and so forth is designed to delay when people have babies. There's just not enough room on this planet. Which makes them sensible laws, I guess, but they're also irritatingly weighted toward smart, talented people. People like the Ruuels, or Isten Notra's family, are more likely to be given permission to have second and third children.

This got right up my nose. I can recognise the *reason* for it, but I kept wondering about all the people I knew who wouldn't exist if Australia had a law like that, and furiously resenting the idea of ever having to apply for kids myself, even though I'm sure the Supa Speshul Magick Gurl will be encouraged to have lots and lots of babies, even without counting the value of Kaoren's Sights.

At least Mum would be pleased to know that I'm planning at least ten years of pouncing on Kaoren before even thinking about interrupting our sex life with kids. After reading all those by-laws, I'm considering doubling that to twenty.

Once I stopped being irritated I continued ploughing through the recommended reading for the test, getting a little distracted by the laws for when two men or two women want to have babies, and how advanced genetic engineering can open up lots of possibilities. And then I watched a hysterically funny documentary called: "No, We Will Not Raise The Ceilings" from back when Tare first began to make real advances into genetics and the first thing vast numbers of people did was tweak their kids for 'taller'.

After he'd done with his reports, Kaoren asked me to read some more of my diary to him. It's becoming an important ritual between us, and doing wonders for my ability to speak Taren – my grammar is improving, though my pronunciation is still bad and I miss a lot of the nuances of word meanings. That session, though, I felt so small describing how horrible I'd been to Mum, and I'm really not looking forward to reading out a few of the things I know are coming up. We went off onto a tangent, though, circling around Kaoren's relationship with his own mother. He says all his family are too alike not to recognise the same fault in each other. An awareness of superiority. He curled the words off his tongue, sounding amused.

"It's an easy trap to fall into. Sight Sight can make the preoccupations of others seem such useless things. My mother, my brother, taught me what it feels like to have what is important to me dismissed. It's a lesson I'm glad I learned, but I am not likely to forgive them for it."

"Yet you keep your brother's pictures in your room."

"He made them for me." Kaoren took a deep breath. "For a long time Arden was to me what I am now to Siame, but he was furious with me for choosing to treat being Setari as my art. The pictures are an apology of sorts, since he has come to see that doing this is something I value. My parents continue to push me to resign once I have served the minimum tenure."

Kaoren is not very detached about his family, and seems to deal with it by having little to do with them. And a lot to do with Siame, who he has taken out into the city again because he won't see her for a while. He wants to tell her in person that we're going to get engaged. I'm not sure if he's going to even tell his parents, and doesn't seem keen on introducing me to them. I'm not going to push.

I was hoping I could study during the morning and take the adult competency exam while he was gone, but I did a run-through on a mock exam and while it's not hard – I nearly passed – the random and broad nature of the questions means there's a big chance I won't pass if I try and rush into it, and I can't take the test again for a full Taren year if I fail. I'm not sure if I can take it on Muina, or apply to get married while I'm there, for that matter.

I know it's silly to be impatient. All getting engaged immediately would do is get me a bunch of people asking if I really want to rush into things. I think I just want everyone to know that he's mine. Very shallow.

I've been stuck in medical all afternoon with Jeh from Second being babysitter. Jeh doesn't have Place Sight, which I guess means they're getting more relaxed about the Nuran. My legs look almost normal. There's some faint patchiness, but they're going to give me a break before doing any more work on them, so that the new skin can settle. The new patches are obvious because they're hairy – baby-fine hair though, which is good since the medics tell me I can't use the depilatories on them yet.

Tons of brain scans and needles, which never puts me in a good mood. And–

...

Back in my room now. Maze dropped by medical to visit me and take over being babysitter. He was looking outright exhausted, his mouth dragging down at the corners, since unlike the rest of First and Fourth he hadn't had a free day, and had been attending meetings and working on balancing squad assignments for the push forward on Muina.

I haven't really talked to Maze for ages. I was glad to see he's his normal self with me, and answered my questions about the things First and Fourth have been assigned to do while on Muina – and which ones I'll be allowed to participate in. Then I asked him if he thought I'd be able to take the adult competency exam while I'm on Muina, and he spent a few minutes researching that, and said no, not yet. Because it involves a secure environment hosted by a particular government department (basically child welfare), it can't be done within Muina's environment.

Maze paused after he told me, because there's not many reasons why I'd suddenly want to do the adult competency exam, then gave me one of his super smiles and said: "It's been good to see you so happy, Caszandra. And you have until we reach the gate tomorrow to do the exam, if waiting until we return from Muina seems too large a burden."

He spent the rest of the afternoon chatting to me about Tare's laws, coaching me in questions I was likely to encounter on the test. I think he was glad to concentrate on something other than Unara, and tearing gates and hordes of Ionoth, and whether we'll find any way to fix it all.

We leave for Muina late morning tomorrow.

Friday, July 25

Making it official

I passed! I did the exam during the pre-flight preparation and take-off. It was a bare pass – I hit a run of questions which I couldn't even guess what might be the right answer – but I still passed.

The exam environment makes it so you can't receive any communication (even almost completely blocking what you can see or hear in real-space) and it took about half an hour to complete. When I opened my eyes I could see Kaoren sitting on the seat beside mine, watching me steadily. I think he watched me the entire time, reading my body language to see how much trouble I was having.

It takes about five minutes to get the result, and since we were alone I snugged myself next to Kaoren. We didn't say anything at all, but he was unusually tense, and when I got the email with my result, he knew straight away from my reaction and half-crushed my hand before he leaned down and kissed me – something he's not done before anywhere there was a chance random people could see us. I wasn't the only one all impatient.

The complete absence of squads was kind of suspicious – you're allowed to go to the lounges during flights, but it's common for at least a few squad members to just hang around on their pod-seats. Still, the interface would have told everyone I was taking an exam, if not which exam, so they could have left just to give me some quiet. But I suspect Maze.

Kaoren sent me the link to the form we had to fill out, and since the interface knows all the form-filling stuff about me already, I only had to read through the getting engaged version of 'terms and conditions' and choose 'Yes' a few times and then Kaoren and I were engaged. A far cry from a fancy ring, but certainly more official.

We went and told everyone then; a rare occasion for Kaoren to bring his personal affairs into discussion with his squad. It's really embarrassing to do things like that, though everyone seemed pleased and not particularly surprised and I was hugged a lot, and Kaoren's squad at least briefly treated him like a peer and congratulated him. We got into an interesting discussion on different types of ceremonies, and then Lohn started laughing and said to check the news and of course my name showing up in the intention to marry register hadn't passed unnoticed for more than a few minutes. The best headline was "Devlin to marry Lastier!"

Good timing for the trip to Muina so I can start ignoring the news again. Almost through the rift. Eager to get things done.

New digs

Muina's first set of Setari quarters have sprouted since my last visit, with accommodation for six eight-strength squads (or eight six-strength squads, as originally planned) and a few spares, as well as support staff accommodation, kitchens, medical, training areas, and common rooms. Someone's plainly been having fun playing architect. Instead of yet another big white box, they've produced a round step pyramid with windows and balconies everywhere. It's built into the hill at the southernmost tip of Pandora, and I mean that literally. The hill is still there, but with expanses of whitestone and glass between the grass and trees – or snow at the moment. It reminds me of a cross between a hobbit hole and Parliament House in Canberra (no giant flagpole though). All this in less than a month. Nanotechnology is amazing – they basically injected a building into a hill, no digging required.

The structure is the easy part, and they've had people installing fittings and big pumps and generators (I don't in the slightest understand the technology behind Taren power generators, except that it's not fossil fuel based) and the like so that there's power and water and lights and heating. It's still missing windows and equipment in a lot of places. The *Litara* brought a massive amount of cargo with us, including the first shipment of furniture for the Setari quarters, and when we arrived late afternoon Pandora-time the Telekinetics helped unload the ship and then everyone carried furniture and stores and supplies about, and moved in.

The pinksuit in charge of the fit-out really annoyed me by being shocked because I picked up a box. She really expected me to sit there and watch everyone else lugging stuff around. I told her that it was a requirement of my culture to help, heh.

The main common room is fantastic, with the most incredible view west out over the lake, and glimpses north and south thanks to this huge curving patio and floor to ceiling window/doors (though doubled-glass 'airlocks' and way too cold to want to have open at the moment). Once we'd unpacked the furniture and had something to sit on, we all (First, Fourth, Twelfth, Fourteenth, and Squad Three from Kolar, who have been traded in for Squad One) sat about having an informal meal and chatting, catching up on the latest developments of three planets, all the while watching a gorgeous wrap-around sunset.

Squad Three has one guy (Noran) and five girls (Brez, Olan, Mittaha, Tuse, and Turian). Turian's their captain, and comes across as amiable and polite, but not quite ready to be friends with a bunch of Tarens. But it wasn't a bad atmosphere. Compared to the recently-promoted Kalrani, and Squad Three, Zan was relaxed and talkative. Of course, Twelfth and Fourteenth weren't exactly casual, except for Lara, who is always chilled out. Even Fourth, working with First so closely lately, is still a bit 'on duty' when sitting about chatting with them. I've come to realise Maze and Zee are basically the junior Setari's peer supervisors, and First sets the standard for the other squads, so they're really caught up in not making a fool of themselves in front of them.

And Kaoren, for all he accepted a further round of congratulations, is never going to be casually social with vast hordes of people. He just isn't interested, I think. But, still, it was a nice meal (a sampling of local plants mixed in with the standard fare, product of the greenhouse) and everyone ended up looking pleased and upbeat, the shadow of developments on Tare finally lifting. Like me they're eager to get back to hunting solutions.

Picking out rooms came next, and was fun. There's several circular floors' worth of quarters around a central atrium arrangement – accessible by both stairs and elevators. Those with Levitation or Telekinesis really like this because they just fly up to the floor they want to get to.

Not all of the rooms have balconies – those poke out of the lakeward face of the hill, but the hill itself rises a little higher than the building and joins up with other hills to the east, and on each floor there's a couple of rooms with no windows at all, for those Tarens who just aren't comfortable with having so much outside in their living area. These went pretty quickly, after the squad captains chose floors. Fourth ended up second floor from the top, mainly because I liked the trees which flanked the balconies up there. Kaoren and I have just the one room, since we're now officially cohabiting.

Like on Tare, a good deal of the furniture – kitchen benches, wardrobes, the baths and showers – is formed directly out of the whitestone, and just need doors and things added. The beds are indents in the whitestone walls – huge nooks – and the mattresses are nanotech responsive ones which try to mould themselves around you. Building the beds into the walls apparently makes it easier to accommodate additional shielding, on top of that already on the living areas.

I'm propped up in the corner of mine, waiting for Kaoren to come back from all the captains being summoned to a meeting by the bluesuit in charge of Muina, Tsaile Staben. I think I was introduced to Tsaile Staben when Pandora was first established, but I can't for the life of me remember anything about her, and I'm too lazy to go searching through my log. It must be quite something to be put in charge of an entire planet.

The meeting is about what the Setari will be deployed to do over the next few months, and I was surprised to hear that a lot of that will involve settlement work rather than exploration. There's a huge demand for the Setari here, even with the standing about guarding duties mostly being performed by greensuits now. Tsaile Staben isn't shy about using them for anything which will make the job quicker or easier. I know Kaoren wants First and Fourth to go hunting Pillars, but it sounds like the Setari are mostly going to be working in real-space.

Research-wise, KOTIS is gradually making progress, though very slowly because the paper records found in Kalasa are so incredibly fragile, and turning a page without destroying it is a real challenge. Zan told me that Twelfth has been spending a lot of time going room to room locating anything and everything that looks like writing and doing all these complicated preservation procedures to try and stop the documents from crumbling on sight (or breath, usually). Still no handily-complete explanation of how the Pillars were built or the best way to get rid of them, just tangential mentions.

But tons of books about being psychic. *Telekinesis 101. Reading Minds for Dummies. The Psychic's Guide to Finding Your Inner Self.*

The Lantarens seem to have had a very spiritual approach to their powers, and as Kalasa was a teaching city for the talented most of the books there seem to relate to philosophy and techniques for psychics. Kaoren is understandably fascinated by this, and has been devouring the translations which have yet to be released even to KOTIS on Tare. The translations I've read have all sounded a bit Zen, and it looks to me rather as if the psychic is supposedly drawing power from nature, not simply generating it themselves. 'Embraced' by Muina. That's totally not how the Tarens approach their talents.

There's more than two thousand people living on Muina now, a number which does my head in. And they're planning a big expansion as soon as they've finished some of the larger infrastructure projects around Pandora, like the major recycling and waste facilities going up in the hills to the east.

Tarens are seriously into recycling and have the nanites to really make it work. I can't get over the astonishing pace of it all.

The Setari squads will likely stay the same for a month or so. Twelfth is one floor up and First one floor below. I can pretty much tell where everyone in the building is now, if I push myself, despite all the shielding.

Before their meeting, Kaoren and Maze double-teamed me for a Serious Discussion (having both of them tell me was deliberate to push home that they were *really* serious) about my security arrangements. Given that I'm now being guarded from random monsters, random people, Cruzatch, Kolarens *and* the Nurans, there's not a lot of scope for me wandering around freely. Kaoren's my main security detail, of course, but there will be two other Setari assigned as backup at all times. When Kaoren's not with me, and I'm not in the Setari building, they'll go into full babysitter mode. In the Setari building, though, they'll simply be available nearby rather than sitting on top of me, so long as I have no hesitation using my alert.

The challenge with that, of course, is the Kolarens, who I don't officially need protection from. Being engaged to a Taren does make it unlikely that the Kolarens will think they can buy me, and Maze doesn't think it very probable that they'd try and force me to work for them, but of course we can't be absolutely sure. At least the Ionoth situation on Kolar seems to have improved, and the Ddura means that the Cruzatch and the Nurans aren't a threat so long as I'm in Pandora. But they'd rather be safe than sorry, so I have to make sure I have a Taren with me, or stay in my room.

Pandora's day ends later than the sleep cycle I was on, so it's not even sunset and I'm already beyond tired, but no sign of Kaoren. I haven't actually been asleep when he's not there since we got together, and I'm starting to get all fretty about it – and annoyed at myself for needing him there to be comfortable going to sleep. I think I'll go bug someone rather than get all worked up.

Saturday, July 26

Southern Expedition

Long day today, but a good one, and I feel far more settled than I ended up yesterday, when the evening turned into a severe downer. I hadn't wanted to bug anyone from First and Fourth, since I knew they'd be as tired as me, so went down to the main common room and was chatting with Dess Charn from Twelfth and Pen Alaz from Fourteenth when I fell asleep and had my first projective dream for ages.

The problem is I'm aware of people around me when I'm asleep, so falling asleep while talking to people meant I wasn't immediately aware that I was asleep. And I dreamed that I was in the common room talking to Dess and Pen when Dess' Combat Sight alerted her to a threat, and Pen stared upward.

Strands of black were descending through the whitestone ceiling, growing longer and longer while Pen stared up at them, and it was only when the forehead emerged that it was clear that it was hair. Then the face came through, a woman, upside-down. Eyes closed, she looked calm, beautiful, but then she opened them, black pits, and smirked.

I think it was from a scary movie I saw once. Or manga. I half-recognised the scene anyway, and that made me realise I was dreaming, and I woke myself up. And Dess and Pen were both on their feet, combat-ready and staring at the exact spot on the ceiling, and then everyone nearby with Combat Sight swarmed to the room, and even though I explained, they still immediately informed their captains. Unlike the Cruzatch, this projection was completely visible in real-space, and registered very strongly as a threat, and I really hate the amount of fuss I can cause just by falling asleep.

Plus I felt that everyone was looking at me differently, some understanding for the first time what a problem I might be.

Maze and Kaoren both spoke to me to make sure I was okay, and Zee took me back to her room until Kaoren returned. I put a good face on it all, apologising and being wry and annoyed with myself, which Zee didn't challenge, opting instead to give me a shoulder rub for the short time until the strategy meeting finished. Kaoren took very much the same approach, distracting me with a hot shower and then stroking my back after we curled up together.

I understand more and more why Kaoren would avoid a committed relationship with anyone, let alone an enhancement talent. When he's holding me he can't completely block what I'm feeling, but he wanted to comfort me, so last night became a demonstration of the price he's going to pay for being with me. It didn't help that I kept trying to force myself to not be upset because I knew it was keeping him awake, and failing only made me more upset.

I felt like it was my fault for letting my guard down, and I hate *having* to be on guard about something as straightforward as sleeping. And I hate being the cause of fusses, and especially making Kaoren feel he can't go anywhere without me immediately having a drama. But, most importantly, it meant the bluesuits would think I hadn't gained enough control, and make them more doubtful about using me in missions.

After way too long of neither of us getting any sleep Kaoren gave up, obviously deciding it was better to talk it out with me: "You're upset because you didn't immediately recognise it as a dream?"

"Thought I was past this," I said, trying not to sound whiny and failing. "All this training, all the time everyone's spent helping me avoid this, and I had half the building running the first time I stopped paying attention."

He raised the lights a little, enough to see my expression, then touched my cheek. "Cassandra, I have been trained to prevent my nightmares since I was fifteen. Yet I still have them."

"That's–"

"Different?" He leaned forward to kiss my forehead. "I don't see how. While your nightmares have the potential to do considerably more damage, they are a product of talents you are still discovering." He paused, then added: "You're now capable of waking at will, so the issue is those times you don't recognise that you're dreaming. The simplest solution would be to attempt to wake yourself whenever there is an attack, or unusual phenomena. To assume, at least momentarily, that anything could be one of your projections."

I liked that idea, and he could tell, and smiled. [I'm collecting his smiles. I've built a little image gallery out of my log. A very small gallery.] Then he took me through a visualisation exercise, which was effective in sending me off to sleep once I stopped feeling guilty at the touch of croakiness in his voice which underlined how much he needed to sleep.

Kaoren and I talked it over when we woke this morning, while we were waiting for it to be dawn. Whether it would be better to have separate beds, or for one of us to sleep on the couch sometimes. Neither of us are keen on that option, but given how dangerous it is for him to be tired, we're going to have to consider it. That discussion somehow segued into whether he would change his name to mine, or I would change my name to his, given the conflicting customs of our planets. We're probably just going to leave our names alone. And we talked about children, and how we aren't opposed to the idea, but aren't in a hurry to have them, especially not while we're so very much under the control of KOTIS – and not when I'm potentially facing situations like enhancing large groups during massive attacks, where my system gets so stressed out.

I'm really engaged to be married. It feels very odd to have discussions about when to have children, and to watch Kaoren's reaction. He said he finds the idea "interesting in theory".

Today's assignment was exploration and greysuit escort duty, and while the expeditioners were assembling I had the opportunity to drop in to see

Isten Notra and say hi to Shon. Isten Notra's looking very well, eyes sparkling and full of life. And whether or not she really had thought about setting me up with Shon, she seemed genuinely pleased for me and Kaoren – and said one or two things to him that I couldn't hear which made him develop a faintly wry expression.

Islen Dola and Islen Nakano (the greysuits in charge of flora and fauna research) were leading a joint expedition to Mesiath, which is the platform city in the southern hemisphere tall forest. Mesiath is the old Muinan name for it – one of the discoveries made at Kalasa was a number of maps, and all the 'correct' place names have been adopted. The old town at Pandora has been renamed Aversan, and the lake is Tai Medlar (tai is old Muinan for lake).

It was primarily a sampling expedition – seeking out plants and animals and bringing them back for cataloguing, tests, maybe even cultivation. They don't bring back lots of animals – they capture them, take images and tissue samples, then let them go, unless they think it's a really interesting specimen. A huge number of people were going – about a hundred – most of them belonging to flora and fauna, but also greensuits, a small group of archaeologists, device technicians, geology, survey. Mesiath has been designated a primary site, which means they're likely to establish a settlement there, partly because it's on the opposite seasonal cycle to Pandora, but mainly because it has a platform, but isn't a pattern-roof village.

My job was a mild variation of 'poke Devlin at it': I was simply to let the Setari know if I saw or felt anything unusual. And enhance if necessary.

I gave Islen Dola and Islen Nakano the couple of minutes of the *Planet Earth* documentary which I'd recorded during my last testing session since I'd worked out how to subtitle it. The consequence of this being that I spent half an hour being minutely cross-examined about mass migration, something which a non-seasonal planet doesn't really see – at least not in the numbers shown in the documentary. Of course, they want the entire documentary now, which I'm quite happy to do, except being something like thirteen hours long it's going to take me an age to reproduce it.

I guess this makes *me* the psychic space pirate? No-one tell the BBC's copyright department.

Today was by no means a particularly dangerous expedition. It was overcast, and drizzled briefly at one point, but it was a gorgeous forest and full of birdsong and little scampering animals. Because there was a platform, the area was clear of Ionoth, and since the Ddura was one which is used to Muinans, it even shut up pretty quick. There were still native Muinan animals which might be a danger, particularly poisonous bugs, but otherwise it was a nice outing. I stayed with Fourth, who were helping the archaeologists hunt out significant locations. It was a very spread-out city, with little which was undamaged. The trees had had centuries to work on the whitestone – we were lucky the platform was intact.

First Squad was working with survey and geology – soaring up for aerial views. Every so often the fauna group would get a Setari to come capture an animal for them – Telekinesis and Levitation make that ridiculously easy. A complete lack of drama day, and since Mesiath is in a time zone a couple of hours behind Pandora, when we headed back in late afternoon we arrived just as sunset was fading.

The structure of the new Setari building really makes for a very social set-up, especially when everyone gets back from missions at roughly the same time and sits around the big common room to chat and eat and watch the lake. I belatedly gave Zan the bit of music I'd recorded for her, and quite a few of us watched the latest documentary about the Muina settlement ('latest' as delivered that afternoon by the several ships which are basically on daily shuttle duty between the Muina, Tare and Kolar).

I think I might avoid the news for a while again. My engagement is still all screaming headlines, and there was some annoying talk about undue influence and whether Kaoren was really who I would have chosen if I wasn't kept on such a tight leash by KOTIS. And some irritating 'expert' saying getting engaged was a symptom of my isolation and loss, and that I'd no doubt fixated on Kaoren as a saviour. That was rather balanced by a lot of people thinking it terribly romantic, and there's an increasing number of Kaoren Ruuel lust-sites. I learned a good deal more about the Ruuel family, and saw pictures of his parents and brother.

There was also a lot of discussion about what I could do, and what I should be allowed to do. The Kalasa projection was interesting to a lot more people than historians, and plenty of people were pointing out my potential as an industrial spy.

Devlin. Cassandra Devlin. Shaken, not stirred.

Kaoren fell asleep while I was reading him my diary, thanks to all the exploring after a not particularly good night with me. I've got to figure out a way to not work myself up over things.

Sunday, July 27

Nature documentary

Another day in the forest. Gloriously sunny – which in a forest that tall means incredible columns of light beaming down. Mesiath is a very peaceful place. There's apparently some cat-type predators busily hiding from us, but nothing else anyone's spotted which might think of actively hunting humans.

The city edges on a lake (it's pretty hard to find a city which doesn't edge on a lake on this planet), and I stayed with First and Twelfth Squad today while they did a little landscaping in preparation for 'seeding' a settlement, since even with Zan's level of Telekinesis, enhancement really helped deal with trees that tall. Meanwhile Fourth hunted down gates and explored in near-space.

It was not at all what I'd been picturing that we'd be doing, but managed to combine practical work with a balm of wonder. Everyone was enjoying themselves, glad to be away from the snow, and to see more of their home planet, and Alay disturbed this cluster of butterflies (rather like Monarchs, but with more red and gold) which spiralled up around her into one of the columns of light and she stood in the centre of them, lips parted and eyes bright. I felt like I'd never seen her happy before, and the Unara crack felt like centuries ago, lost to sunlight and iridescent wings.

And then the butterflies settled down over everyone and that was a different kind of fun. Tarens and bugs don't mix, and it was hard not to laugh at the greysuits ducking and scattering.

On a less entertaining note, much of what we were doing was being recorded for another documentary, part of the increased 'openness' demanded. I avoided the scanners as much as possible, especially when anywhere near Kaoren. I don't know if documentaries will lower the number of people sneakily capturing images of us, though.

Monday, July 28

Prescribed privilege

I met two other strays today, people from a planet called Solaria. Despite the name, Solaria's apparently an icy world, snowy everywhere except at the equator, and the two Solarians – who've both been on Tare for over twenty years – had been brought in to give advice and feedback on cold climate living. Very sensible of the Tarens, since my dim memories of a skiing holiday really haven't been very useful.

Solaria's another planet without a marked 'seasonal tilt'. Can seasons really be that unusual among habitable planets? The Solarians were called Denasan (a really wrinkled, white-haired man) and Purda (a woman in her thirties). I spent quite a while chatting to them, learning about their planet, which was in the throes of industrialisation when they were displaced, and asking about their experiences after turning up on Tare. The technological differences were of course the biggest adjustment –more so for Denasan than for Purda, since Purda was only fourteen at the time. Interestingly, the Solarians' Muinan origin has been overtaken by a creation myth involving an ice-god. Stories of Muina are still told, but 'Homeworlders' are persecuted by the priesthood of the ice god, and a lot of Solarians don't believe Muina exists.

Denasan really misses his home planet, and loves being on Muina because it reminds him of the region south of his home on Solaria (at least currently, while Pandora's still having buckets of snow dumped on it – Spring never comes on Solaria), and he's really struggled with living on Tare and pretty much hates it, so far as I could tell. Purda's much more 'typical Taren' and adjusted. She worked on the Solarian version of a farm and even though she was only a teenager when she found herself on Tare, she remembers a whole heap of agricultural information the technicians seem to be interested in.

Although Earth is a good deal closer to Tare technologically, it was pretty clear that without being a touchstone I would have faced a lot of the same issues the Solarians have struggled with, trying to make a 'normal' life as a stray on Tare. The average Taren really does think everyone not from Tare (including, quite possibly, Kolarens) is just a bit slow. Adjusting to a different dialect, and all that advanced technology, makes it very hard to get out of 'Base Level' (which is a Taren term for subsistence living via social security).

There's also a 'stray network' called Tare Displaced Channel which get together for mutual support and complaining about Tarens. Denasan and Purda gave me a formal invite to one of the get-togethers. The Channel apparently has tried to invite me before, and Denasan was rather huffy about it. I explained about me not getting mail from people outside KOTIS, and not being allowed to go out on my own, which I think may have changed Denasan's attitude toward me a little. To the 'average' stray I must seem hugely pampered.

I hadn't really thought about the impact of the opening of Muina on other strays. Suddenly skills which were completely irrelevant on Tare are becoming valuable, and Denasan and Purda aren't the only strays being recruited.

Tuesday, July 29

Urban Design

KOTIS is seriously gearing up settlement preparation. Today we skipped Mesiath and instead all five Setari squads spent the day assisting in the seeding of entire suburbs for Pandora, deep into the hills east of the old city and then along the lake to the north. Five squads of highly-trained killers clearing snow and lugging vats of whitestone 'seed' and computer-constructed models and bits of equipment and chasing off hungry native wildlife.

I was along for enhancement, and learned all these details of urban planning and design which I'd never really thought about. It's not just a matter of plonking houses and streets down. For the past five months, ever since they worked out that people could survive here, a fleet of technicians back on Tare and Kolar have been designing the city layout in terms of water and power and food production and drainage and waste and hospital services and fires and police and schools and transport and industry and shops and entertainment and defence and – my head just starts reeling when I try and think through the whole process. They're preparing initial infrastructure for fifty thousand people, and have expansion plans for long into the future. I just can't get over the idea of fifty thousand people living here.

Before the snows came the survey and geologist types had had a pretty thorough go at mapping the topography of Pandora's surroundings. They selected sites for factories (an industrial hub inland along a river which lets out north of here) and the residential sections will checkerboard with farmland, which in the very long run will probably become parkland. The bit north where all the sheep live is going to be a particularly farmy area since it also brushes along the northern river – the sheep are being 'redomesticated' and already have their personal set of highly technological shepherds – lots of Kolarens involved there, since Kolar deals with animals far more than Tare does. The old city (Aversan) is going to be part historical site and part working gardens. They don't want to pull it down or alter it greatly, but it is a biggish chunk of land, so they're going to use all the gardens either for produce, botanical research, or as a wildlife habitat for animals that they want to study. The plaza/piazza areas will be used as exactly that by the inhabitants of the wider area, and certain selected buildings will be converted to functioning use, particularly around the amphitheatre.

I'm very impressed by their plans. I would never have expected the Tarens, with their closed-off and blockish cities, to switch so immediately to creating a sprawling park with balconies. Given the pictures I've seen of Kolar, the Kolarens have definitely been a big influence – because of the heat, Kolarens sink their buildings, and only have parts of them out in the sun. Like the Tarens, Kolarens lived in caves when they first evacuated from Muina, at least in part because water on Kolar either drains underground or evaporates very quickly.

The Setari building is a prototype of what the buildings of this phase will be like, though most of them will be larger, built to accommodate dozens of families. No individual houses at this stage, just half-buried apartment blocks. The Kolarens and the Tarens have had to work together a great deal on this, both to avoid the Kolarens feeling excluded again, and because neither of their planets really fit the Muinan environment.

Back on Tare and Kolar they're having huge arguments ('discussions') about who gets to move in to all these buildings we've just planted – they've been having them for months, struggling over the big questions raised by two distinct cultures trying to settle the same home world. Is Tare or Kolar in control? Is KOTIS the right group to be leading the settlement? Will there be separate Taren and Kolaren settlements? A unified planetary government? Whose laws will be used? Which dialect? Whose technology? Do they build for complete interface integration, or actually step back in terms of technology? If all settlers have to have the interface, will it be the interface on Tare's terms?

There are plenty of people on Kolar not keen to have the 'internal policeman' which the Taren interface represents, and they find many of their laws horrifying. Of course, Tarens don't think much of some of Kolar's laws either.

Tare is winning a lot of the arguments, though. Nanotechnology is a difficult advance for Kolar to turn down, and it at least sounds like the Tarens are getting rather less anal about sharing their technology now that Muina can offer them the resources they're currently dependant on Kolar to provide. Part of what they're deciding will be temporary, just an initial structure so that they can get moving.

I just realised that all this rush and hurry mightn't be down to population pressures or being so keen to embrace their home world. Tare and Kolar might be thinking of Muina as an ark. Because the Ddura will protect the platform towns even from massives, and a gate in the wrong place on Muina won't bring a city tumbling down.

At least, not unless the gates get bigger than cities.

If that *is* the reason, they're not saying it out loud. All the news stories about Muina are extremely cheerful and upbeat, and so are the KOTIS staff concentrating on getting whitestone seeded and design models placed. Over the next few weeks, with only a bit of monitoring from the technicians (who need to be sure the growing buildings don't run out of readily-available 'food'), a small city will quietly be reproduced. Lacking all the glass and fittings and furniture and energy generators, but with the bulk of the work done. Whitestone even extrudes certain metals and minerals, rather than absorb them. They don't even have to dig to lay the connecting pipes. They're going to grow a subway system.

I definitely chose the right name for the settlement. This isn't a box I can close. I think all the Setari assisting were overwhelmed as well. Happy, though. Maze, particularly, really loves doing positive things rather than endlessly killing Ionoth, and it showed in everything he did.

Kaoren's getting his way about returning to our main mission though. Tomorrow First and Fourth will take me into the Ena for a combination of me doing more testing and them trying to find Pillars. The fact that we can settle this world, that the Ddura will protect the sites, hasn't removed the need to fix the tearing of the spaces, or found the reason why the Ddura started killing Muinans, and what exactly the Cruzatch have to do with it all.

The fact that they're intending to go ahead with the settlement without answering the question about the Ddura scares the hell out of me.

Wednesday, July 30

Back on Track

Kaoren's very pleased. First and Fourth took me on the Ena mission he wanted (having stolen Fourteenth's strongest path finder, Sanya, as well) and they all enhanced and immediately detected a Pillar.

Since they were under strict orders not to take me into combat, but also had the advantage of the immediate near-space and connecting spaces being wiped clear by the Ddura, they could take me along partway, tracking through two gates before they encountered a space which was populated. They then sent me back to wait by the gate with Zee, Halla and Mori as escort, and I got to do tests while the squads pushed on.

A very simple test today – Zee told me to project remembered music or television until I could project no more, and they would measure how much that cost me. I recorded another piece of classical music for Zan (this rather pretty thing done with recorders, slow and spiralling, no idea who it's by), and then a song for me, and then I did an episode and a half of *Planet Earth* which I now get to subtitle. I couldn't do all that in one go – I have to rest every few minutes – but it's nothing like so difficult a task as doing it in real-space. I stopped when I was totally wiped, and spent much of the afternoon asleep, carefully doing a visualisation exercise before going to bed. Zee stayed in the living room of my apartment, but I managed to not have a nightmare.

When I woke up it was late afternoon, and Kaoren still wasn't back, but I was determined to stay drama-free and asked Zan and Dess if we could go for a walk along the lake. That wasn't bad: we chatted about parts of Muina we've visited, and then built snow sculptures on the very top of the Setari building/hill until, finally, First and Fourth came back, exhausted but whole.

They'd had to travel ten spaces to get to the Pillar, and had run up against a few tough battles which made them glad they were dual-squadding, especially since the Ena manipulation talents had had to stabilise an awful lot of gates. Par was levitating Sonn, who'd passed out. They sent Squad Three and Fourteenth out to place a couple of drones, and put some extra stabilisation on the gates, and they made it there and back in about an hour and a half. Kaoren and Maze both waited until the other squads were safely back before getting some rest themselves – working their way through dinner and getting a start on their reports. Kaoren pretty much fell into bed once we got back to our room.

I like these bed nooks. The beds themselves are ever so slightly cup-shaped and the nanomaterial mattress makes sleeping on rock a lot more comfortable than you'd expect. Need more pillows, but the walls are great for propping yourself against.

Kaoren gets restless if I'm not in contact with him. I probably shouldn't be pleased about that. I probably shouldn't keep experimenting to see how he reacts when I move my leg away.

We've only been together two and a bit weeks. It was a shock to flip back through my diary and realise that. I've stopped being so wary of doing or saying the wrong thing.

Thursday, July 31

At the movies

All of the Muina-stationed Setari, except for Kiste and Halla who are babysitting me, are back in the Ena today trying to do the tests which had been planned for the last Pillar. The mood was mixed when everyone left: they've been wanting to properly study a Pillar for so long, but given what happened last time, no-one was exactly cheerful. And, even though the aether isn't fatal to them any more, it does make them drunk, which is not a good state to be in any part of the Ena, let alone areas frequented by far too many deep-space roamers. So today's a serious day.

It's the Cruzatch which are the biggest concern. It's all too possible they might try to sabotage the mission again, so the squads plan to use a drone to lock the outlet levers before they venture close to the Pillar themselves.

At least Kiste and Halla are in the exact same boat as me, worrying about their squads. Though interestingly calling each other Tahl and Charan when they think I'm not listening. Kiste's elbow is almost fully healed now, but he says he's facing a lot of training to get it back to former strength.

It was a nice day outside, so I decided to see how tolerant they'd be of me wandering about. There'd been a big dump of snow the previous night, but the skies had cleared, and there was no wind. Snow drifts did make it a little hard-going in spots, but I figured this could count as me getting some exercise, and tramped my way all the way in to the old town, up to my old tower, only to find I couldn't get in. They really have preserved it as a historical site, fitting shields over the windows and doorways.

Annoyed by this, I headed back to Setari quarters and told Kiste and Halla that I was going to spend the rest of the day working on subtitling. So I'm in my bedroom being sore from forging through snowdrifts, and taking a break from translating David Attenborough.

Hm, the *Litara* just arrived with another massive supplies delivery, and also Third, Eleventh and Thirteenth. More squads here than on Tare at the moment. I guess this is because of the Pillar.

--

Yep, they're going to have all these squads here for a few days. They don't quite all fit in the Setari quarters, but along with the supplies were a bunch more mattresses and couches, so people are sharing apartments. The Pillar experiments are going to be performed in shifts because there's one gate which they aren't going to be able to hold for more than five days, and they can't tell when, if ever, it will come back. KOTIS wants to get as much information as possible before they lose the path.

Why the Lantarens couldn't have stuck these things somewhere easier to get to I don't know.

The Pillars team returned not long after the *Litara* showed up, having had to kill a fair number of roamer Ionoth, but not otherwise troubled. No Cruzatch. They'd successfully sent a drone into the Pillar and obtained bunches of useful scans, and positioned it to block the levers from moving. I don't know if the scans will really tell them anything – ancient Lantaren devices seem to me more on the level of magic than science. They certainly haven't figured out how the teleporting platforms work.

Still, everyone's very pleased that there's been no disasters so far, and the afternoon involved more helpful unpacking and lots of chatting and, since Third is here, great bursts of Eeli excitement. Eeli is totally overjoyed by the new Setari building. A big central socialising area is her idea of heaven, and the sunset over the partially iced lake was glorious enough to brighten the eyes of even the most serious of the Setari.

We had a big group meal, bringing down the new couches out of the apartments to fit the extra people. It was a full-on banquet – the pinksuits are having a great time experimenting with making meals out of some of the plants they've been cultivating. And there were a few different meat dishes courtesy of one of the hairy sheep. Slow-cooked mutton. Kolarens are used to meat, but the Tarens had to be careful. Their regular diet includes some seafood, but red meat is an exceptional luxury for them, like a $1000 bottle of champagne. Eeli was horrified when I told her that people from Earth usually eat the baby sheep.

Then Zee insisted I do a 'screening' of *Planet Earth* with the subtitles so that she could make sense of what she'd seen during the testing session. And the channel she created to watch it kind of snowballed to all the Setari, and then our resident support greysuits and pinksuits, who told their section heads about it, which meant Zee was asked if other people could watch, and then practically everyone in Pandora was. It's pretty disconcerting to suddenly be throwing a video party for three thousand people.

I should have expected the interest. Earth is not only an alien planet, but it's also (relatively) similar to Muina, which is the main focus of research for most of the expeditionary force. Since Zee had control of the channel, she shifted it into two groups – people who could text me questions (Setari and a few of the department heads) and people who could watch if they wanted. I tried to ignore all the extras and pretend it was just the people in the room with me.

Eeli was fun to watch, round-eyed and delighted most of the time, though there's a scene where a wolf hunts down this baby caribou and Eeli was so upset when it caught it. And didn't much like sharks eating seals, either. The first episode is a really useful one to have done, because its subject is seasonal change, which the expeditionary force is particularly interested in. Fortunately it mostly explains itself. There's a short mini-documentary at the end of each episode, which I'd included (since I'm basically just recalling the DVD set Mum owns), and even though I'd only gotten halfway through the next episode, Zee played it too because there were a couple of bits she'd particularly wanted to ask me about – namely how freaking huge the mountains on Earth are, what was the burning red stuff (lava) and what was with all the snow knocking down trees (an avalanche).

That caused some excitement, and I was bombarded with questions by the section heads when I ran out of subtitled recording. Earth's geologic instability is something none of their planets have, which means their mountains are more worn down (if they exist at all). Muina does have mountains, but I don't think they're at Everest level, and there's no sign of flowing lava. I fumbled my way through explanations of continental drift, the Ice Ages and dinosaurs until Isten Notra (although very interested herself) eventually called a close to my inquisition and said that the discussion could be continued at a later date, as could further helpful documentaries.

It was, Kaoren said, a useful demonstration that no matter how much I thought I'd described Earth, it was too large a topic to ever assume a proper understanding. I hadn't properly explained dinosaurs before, apparently, and the avalanche got them all worried about the settlement at Kalasa. Both the Solarians knew about avalanches too, but hadn't mentioned it because they were very rare on Solaria (again, a fairly flat world) and nobody had asked exactly the right question.

Kaoren wasn't absolutely exhausted tonight, only tired. It was nice to have a night when he didn't pass out.

AUGUST

Friday, August 1

Cleared

Another test day for me – I'm scheduled for every second day to avoid overstressing my system. It was only a repetition of the projections we'd already run through on Tare, and then I finished off the rest of the 'Mountains' episode of *Planet Earth*. Zee wouldn't let me push myself to exhaustion this time, since the idea is to get a better understanding of my powers, not churn out BBC documentaries. Still needed a long nap afterwards, though. But I'm doing well. Fewer headaches, better control, and it's just so incredibly much easier to do this in the Ena.

The good news is that I've been stable and injury-free long enough that the bluesuits are willing to move on from David Attenborough. My next session will be a controlled attempt to look into Kalasa's past – visualising a single room.

The Setari have divided into a morning shift and an afternoon shift to perform experiments on the Pillar, examining the inflow of the aether and trying to work out what the Pillar does with it. No sign of Cruzatch still, fortunately, although they were having real issues with deep-space Ionoth, and are debating whether it would be safer to send fewer people in the hopes of attracting less of them. A couple of minor injuries for Eleventh.

Twelfth got to spend the entire day carting stuff about, which is what Zan gets for being the strongest Telekinetic. They've seriously stepped the construction and deliveries up a notch, and there are now four ships (the *Litara*, the *Diodel*, the *Wharra* and the *Luim*) devoted to daily ferrying of equipment. Kolar and Tare didn't have a bunch of spare interplanetary ships lying about, and couldn't simply abandon all the trade currently established, so it's taken a little time to get up to four ships devoted to Muina, and they're fast-tracking construction of more. I still love watching them land, though apparently they intend to construct some kind of airbase well inland past the industrial complex. They haven't quite finished designing that, though I'm not sure how hard it can be to design a big flat plain of whitestone.

This afternoon after he'd recovered somewhat from his session in the Ena Kaoren and I watched the latest episode of *The Hidden War*, which was me being idiotic during Maze Rotation and patting Ghost. The episode continues to build the idea of Faer developing some feelings for me, but otherwise is generally accurate in terms of me looking and feeling bad.

Saturday, August 2

End of Winter?

Ouch – combat training with Third this morning. And also a bit of friction between Squad Three and Eleventh Squad. I don't know the exact cause of it, just noticed the atmosphere. Since Eleventh is injured, they're not involved with the Pillars today, while Squad Three is on the afternoon shift. Endaran took the non-injured members of her squad out on a training run (it would be a training flounder, given the snow, but they've a strong Telekinetic and she had him to clear a path to the paths already cleared by machinery and they jogged around the settlement) until they were totally ragged and far too tired to even care that Squad Three existed.

I think it might be warming up. The snow's looking a bit slushy.

Kaoren's been having his post-Ena nap and now that I've finished my day's subtitling (carefully just making the damn episode available over the interface rather than having a video party), I'm going to wake him up and ravish him.

Monday, August 4

Looking in the wrong place

I was a little keyed up for my visualisation exercise yesterday. Wanting to prove myself, I guess, but trying not to show it. Eeli, part of my guard escort, was a useful distraction, and I could see Sefen of Third and Wen of Eleventh suppressing a couple of smiles in her direction. She always lifts the mood, as excited about watching my projection as she has been going to study the Pillar.

My projection tests have all been held just a little way inside the gate to near-space (not too close or my projection might react with the gate) and Zee brings both a drone to record, and a sense-chair for me to lie on. I settle in and then Zee reads out a description of what she wants me to project.

Yesterday it was a room in Kalasa, a small square with no windows and a single door, where the floor had cracked and dropped in the centre, and all the furniture had tumbled and jammed into it. Everything was smirched with grot and tarnish and mould, the way most of the uncleared rooms in Kalasa are, but this one was extra-damaged thanks to water leaking through the equally cracked ceiling, leaving a total rotten mess. The most obvious shape was a big, formerly solid desk, and I could make out a couple of chairs, a brazier, ornaments. Lots of books, or at least the remnants of their covers.

The projection was no more difficult than any other I've been doing in the Ena, and after Sefen and Wen confirmed I was projecting a single building rather than the whole of the Kalasa Valley, Zee said:

"We're starting with this room because the Place Sight talents marked it as important and worth investigating. Now that we've confirmed the energy cost of projecting it, we'll try to reconstruct it as it was before the Breaking."

"How?" I asked. I hadn't made any effort to look into the past last time, and had been asleep, which is when weirder stuff always seems to happen to me.

"I'm going to redescribe the room as we believe it looked before it was destroyed. It's very important that you try to confine the visualisation to this room, or at least this building."

I shrugged, willing to give it a shot, but not entirely convinced it would work. It seemed more likely that what I'd produce was a fiction of the past, since they were making up the details.

Zee began describing the room again, and I closed my eyes and tried to picture what she was talking about, although the image of what I knew the room looked like now kept creeping in and it was a long time before I got any result at all. Zee ran out of her pre-prepared script, but just started again and on the repetition I managed to focus and could properly see what the room looked like, and felt the extra energy cost kick in. Not too bad, but it was obviously taking more out of me than the current-time projection.

When I opened my eyes the room was crisply real, with bonus people. A guy in robes just in the act of spreading out this big piece of paper and weighting each corner. He was looking very worried, and having a discussion I couldn't make sense of with another robed guy. The most I could figure out of the Old Muinan was something had gone wrong, and things were unbalanced. The language experts have provided a translation, though, and it seems he was talking about the tearing of the gates into real-space and the incursion of Ionoth and how it didn't make sense and that there had to be some extra factor they hadn't calculated for, something which was pulling everything out of alignment.

Zee stayed by me, keeping an eye on my vitals, but gestured my escort guard forward to get a better view of the piece of paper. Eeli and Sefen were both practically leaning over the table to get a full look at it, and the two Lantarens were kind of noticing their shadows and being startled.

I was already starting to tire, and when Sefen and Wen picked up a couple of the books on the desk and flipped rapidly through them, recording the contents, I noticed another jump in my energy output. The Lantarens looked thoroughly freaked out, but still couldn't quite properly see us.

And then – it's really hard to describe, but I felt suddenly like my brain was being pulled out of the back of my head, and it was as if there was a really bright light somewhere nearby – I think the best analogy I could have for it is a neighbouring sun had gone supernova and was turning into a black hole. The two Lantarens – and Sefen – also reacted as if something major was going on. The nearest Lantaren ran to the door and threw it open, yelling something about madness. Zee was yelling too, telling me to stop, shaking me. And then she slapped me.

I did some face and chest clutching then. Face because Zee hadn't held back – my eye's still a bit swollen – and chest because it felt like my heart was trying to kick its way out. I gasped and shuddered, convinced I was having a heart attack, and Zee kept telling me to take deep breaths, which reminded me of Kaoren and the last time I'd nearly killed myself. It was pretty close, I gather – my system had gone far beyond its tolerances and I was shaking and dizzy and had a horrendous headache, but Zee had snapped me out of the projection before I'd done any real damage. I'm not allowed to do any strenuous exercise for a few days, just as a precaution, but at last I've managed to come through one of my dramas without any major injury.

It wasn't till Zee was ready to move me that I noticed that Wen, Sefen and Eeli were all clutching books. I'd made them tangible, though not nearly as well as the origami cranes, since they started fading even before we were back to the gate, and there was a pause while the three Setari madly skimmed through them, capturing visuals of the pages to be translated later. Two of the books weren't related (one was a book of poetry), but the one Sefen had picked up was the latest volume in a meticulous set of observations regarding the activation of the Pillars.

The greysuits are most excited about the piece of paper, though, since it was some kind of hugely complex metaphysical map of the placement of the Pillars. I don't even begin to understand what they're talking about when they start foaming over it – it sounds as comprehendible as the Fifth and Sixth Dimension to me (perhaps quite literally?). This and the journal have produced some ecstatic reactions.

When we went through the gate (Wen was levitating me) absolutely everything in real-space was blurry, which produced the usual needle-to-the-brain sensation. I spent a while barely able to pay attention to anything until my first dose of painkiller, which is when I realised that the settlement had been in an extreme flap when we returned. Zee was staying with me, and told me sternly to calm down when I realised that she'd sent the second shift of Setari to check on those at the Pillar. But she let me clutch her hand until everyone had returned safely.

I'd started projecting the event which wiped out the majority of Muina's Lantarens. And when that happened, every platform in real-space reacted with a huge power surge, as did the Pillar. I hadn't killed anyone, thankfully, or caused the Ddura to stop recognising people as Muinan, and very interestingly the drones stationed with the two malachite marbles detected a power surge from them as well, suggesting that they're somehow linked. I'd given the settlement a big scare, though, for all that the greysuits are overjoyed at the information recorded from the projection. Even the power surge is considered overall a good thing, because it's a clue to what happened, and they got lots of interesting readings from it.

Kaoren was very quiet when he got back, and though I had my eyes shielded at the time, I could hear the way he was being remote and super-polite to people when he did talk at all. Zee apologised to us both for not seeing the implications of the test, which I found embarrassing, and I wish I'd thought it through more myself, because it seems obvious in retrospect that the room as it appeared just before the disaster wasn't a very safe thing to try and project. It took me a while to work out that Kaoren was angry at himself, and when I finally talked everyone into letting me rest in my own room and got a chance to ask him why, he said it was because he hadn't read more than the outline of my test, that he'd let himself be distracted by the investigation of the Pillar.

It didn't help at all that for the rest of the day I couldn't open my eyes without seeing a completely blurry world and getting insta-crushed by the headache from hell. I completely refused to let them hold open my eyelids and shine lights at my pupils after the first bout, thank you very much. Maze told them to tape shut and bind my eyes, and to hold off further examination till today and fortunately this morning they were back to normal, with just very occasionally the faintest quiver out of the corners of my eyes.

Kaoren had Fourth shifted to babysitting duty for the day, and is making me sit somewhere he can see me while he trains his squad mercilessly into the ground – combat training where he actually fights each of them. He's not beating them up or anything, but he's forcing them to look deeply at any of their combat weaknesses and really strain to correct them. He's trying to regain his focus. He had nightmares all last night, and kissed me madly when I woke up this morning and could see properly again. And then went and had a cold shower, heh.

I shouldn't laugh. Worrying about me could get him killed.

Tuesday, August 5

Sturdily fragile

This will be the final day of Pillar investigation. One of the gates won't last beyond tomorrow. I spent much of the morning over at the sciences building, answering questions about cheese-making and tidal waves (and sealing wax and string?) and then I had lunch with Isten Notra and Shon (and Sefen and Chise from Third). Isten Notra tried to explain what she thought the Pillars were doing, which took a bit of work since the terms she was using kept going into the 'does not compute' box. But eventually I sort of got where she was coming from. Because they're called Pillars, and look like towers, I'd been thinking of them as columns propping up the 'roof' of deep-space. But they're more like segments of a single long needle piercing a series of folds in the Ena. Not an artificial wormhole. The Pillars stop deep-space from moving about completely freely.

So it's not so much that the Pillars are holding deep-space open, as that they're holding it in a certain alignment. Deep-space itself sounds terribly complicated: a space shaped like a huge drifting fishing net of teleporting portals. The Pillars make it relatively easy to cross because although there's still a lot of shift further away, in the more 'central' areas around the Pillars everything wobbles only slightly. It's funny: I've been picturing the crossing of the rift as involving a short, straight flight, but really the crew of the *Litara* and *Diodel* have been following this precise and complicated course around all these 'reefs' of gates. And figuring out what's through the gates involves going through them. Wormhole lucky dip. No wonder they have little real hope of finding Earth, especially since it's away from this central 'line' and thus everything moves and shifts about, just as the spaces do.

The main thing Isten Notra wanted to talk to me about, though, was precisely what I'd felt when I'd recreated the disaster. She showed me an interesting simulation – a map of Kalasa, and the location of the room which I'd been visualising. Then she included the scan of the testing session, aligning my test chair up exactly on the map. I hadn't even realised that when the test had gone bad I'd started staring off to my right, back and forth between the people in the room and one of the walls.

"That's the direction that it was coming from, yes?" Isten Notra said. "The heaviness?"

"Ye-es," I said, rather doubtfully. "I think too big to have a real direction, like asking what direction the sky is. There was–" I paused, struggling to pull together any kind of proper impression, because nothing really quite fit what I was trying to say. "Is like that's the nearest part. Like a massive was walking over the top of me, and that was the closest leg."

Isten Notra did something to the simulation, drawing a line in the direction I was looking, and then moving back to a city-wide aerial view as it continued to extend. It crossed one side of Kalasa's circle, and a little down, and landed squarely on the barricaded building with Kalasa's malachite marble.

"Green balls were what was pulling Pillars out of balance? Is what happened next planned, do you think, Isten Notra? Everyone dying and the Ddura not recognising anyone? Or did it all go wrong for whoever built those things as well?"

"Major questions. Particularly regarding the Ddura. One thing we have not yet been able to test is whether the Ddura properly treat Cruzatch as Ionoth. Although their conspicuous absence from any Ddura-guarded settlements suggests an answer."

The rest of the day I've been with Kaoren – we went for a short walk, and then have been curled up in our room being overly mindful of the fact that I'm supposed to avoid strenuous exercise. We talked a lot about the Pillars and what Isten Notra had shown me, and what the Cruzatch might or might not be – and about deep-space physics, which he understands far better than I do. He's recovered fairly well from my latest near-death experience, but made me promise to be more cautious.

I read a great deal of my diary to him, and we're almost up to the point where I get rescued. It wasn't at all fun reading about my adventures in kissing-guys-while-drunk, but Kaoren was more interested in whether I missed being able to drink. He's never been drunk – and I suspect would find being at all not in control of himself horrifying – but he wanted to know if I resented the restriction. The aether tests put me off even the thought of drinking for a while, but I don't really like KOTIS being able to say I'm not allowed to drink.

I miss chocolate FAR more.

Most of the teams are being sent back to Tare tomorrow afternoon, after being suitably worked into the ground helping with the settlement again.

Wednesday, August 6

On the Menu

The first of today's ships – a Kolaren delivery – arrived while a group of us were sitting around the big flat steps outside the common room enjoying a patio breakfast and the increasingly warm temperatures. Lohn, who always keeps up with the news as the ships come in, said: "So that's why they're rushing getting these buildings done."

The Kolaren news feed was full of the prospective end of the months-long negotiations over the resettlement agreement, the complete detail of which would be made public at the official signing ceremony to be held in two weeks – at Pandora. Something which seems to involve everyone really important from two planets coming here for a big stickybeak. And lots of press.

Maze did some private communing with those in charge, then said: "The Council of Tare and the Rukmor. The Ormon of Nent, and the three Southern Ancipars. And their entourage and guests, estimated to be some two thousand people in all. A thousand various other dignitaries and a mere five hundred or so press. Arriving over two days, then the formalities and a grand celebration."

"Quite the timetable," Taarel said. "Do we take the role of guard or guest?"

"Tourist attraction," Lohn said, and grinned at me. "Hope you packed a pretty outfit. I'd wager you're listed as the main course."

"I'm going to be sick that week," I said firmly. They thought I was kidding. Well, Kaoren didn't, but I think he's waiting to see whether I get used to the idea.

The Council of Tare is the mayor (and some sub-mayors) of every major island. The Rukmor is kind of like the designated heads of a bunch of scholastic fields (Dean of Sport, Dean of Performance Art, Dean of Physical Sciences, except planet-wide). Together the Council and the Rukmor have a weighted voting system to make planetary decisions. The Ormon of Nent is the king of Kolar's north pole country, and the Southern Ancipars are the three elected leaders of Kolar's south pole country, which was only established after the Tarens showed up and raised Kolar's technological level enough so that they could travel past their burnt-toast equator.

Much unpacking of ships and hauling of cargo followed. KOTIS does have machinery which can do all this, but it's hard to beat the speed, versatility and flexibility of Telekinetics and Levitation talents – and everyone else treated hauling the small stuff about as weights training. The expansion is roaring along. It's quite something to look out over the growing streets of the settlement, and see balconies emerging in an eerie accompaniment to the fleshy green plants Eeli found poking through the snow (daffodils maybe?). The earliest buildings seeded will be ready for fitting-out by tomorrow.

The ships took away the extra squads, though Twelfth Squad's assignment here has been extended purely because Zan's strength is unmatched and she's considered too useful for the construction effort. I asked her if she minded, but she pointed out that it's giving her squad the opportunity to be involved in things like the Pillar missions. And she really loves it here. She hasn't exactly grown all chatty, but she seems far less separate and closed off and set apart than when I first knew her.

So, First, Third, Fourth, Eleventh and Twelfth now, as well as Squad Three.

Thursday, August 7

Forest rest

Back to Mesiath today, joining the exploration and sampling there. Just with Third and Fourth, while the other squads continue to assist with construction.

Friday, August 8

Part of it all

Breakfast is becoming the big group chat time – most evenings the squads are a bit too worn out to want to hang around chatting. The hot topic of discussion the past couple of days has been the translations of Lantaren teaching material. Everything they've found goes on about the connection with Muina, becoming one with Muina, feeling the world as a primary necessary first step to strengthening your talents.

This is completely not how the Setari learn how to use their powers. Their strength is something they develop in themselves. They've been having endless debates about whether the idea of feeling the world is simply a philosophy, or truly has an impact. I'm pretty sure every single one of them has had a shot at trying to establish some kind of connection, just to see. I know the idea is taking up an increasing amount of Kaoren's spare thoughts – it's hitting him both in his perfectionism and his Sights' drive to understand.

This morning Maze wanted to know whether I felt any connection with my surroundings when I was visualising or projecting, but I'm really not aware of anything like that and said so.

"It could explain the large variance in results, though," Zan said. She was sitting cross-legged on one of the individual chairs, looking incredibly petite as she tucked into one of the huge breakfasts Setari need to fuel themselves when they're expected to haul containers half the day. "Especially the effects you've achieved in sleep. If in sleep you are achieving a greater connection to – well, not the planet, but to the Ena or the universe or however one wants to term it – that would explain your sometimes disproportionate achievements. Particularly travelling back to your own world's near-space."

"That one I think I know how I did," I said, and wrinkled my nose at the way everyone around me went still for a moment, then tried to hide any reaction. I know that KOTIS doesn't truly want to find a way for me to go back to Earth, not in the near future. And the Setari really, really don't want to be in the position of being my jailers.

Kaoren was sitting next to me, and he'd reacted the same way, because I hadn't discussed this with him, but then he relaxed. He knows damn well what 'certain' means. "How?"

"I think I must have made an Ionoth," I said, turning to look at him. "If it was possible for me to fly, I'd be flying by now because that would be so cool, and believe me I've tried. I know I can't do that. So something which can fly must have carried me."

"That makes sense," Kaoren said. "Do you remember dreaming of being carried?"

"No. Don't remember dreaming at all. But isn't the Ena the source of psychic powers? When I first got to Tare, I was sure I was told that all strays have a strong connection to Ena, and that's why end up getting displaced."

"Ena manipulation or Gate sight, perhaps," Taarel said. She was perched on one arm of the sofa Eeli was using, looking regal as usual. "Those are very common talents for the displaced to exhibit. But there's no established link between, say, elementals and the Ena."

They had a long discussion on whether they really could be channelling some form of external power rather than producing it themselves, and just not be aware of it. I talked it over with Kaoren much later, when we were taking a lunch break at Mesiath. It's really frustrating him, to simply not be sure, to feel he's missing something.

Mesiath's such a gorgeous place, just starting to edge into Autumn as Pandora lets go of Winter. We were sitting on some shattered whitestone which had fallen into the lake, paddling bare feet into the cool water. Most of the trees are pine, but there are a lot of the broader-leaf trees which are just starting to think about changing colour – much taller, grander ones than those at Pandora. Masses of birds and animals, and the lake incredibly deep, cold even in Summer.

"That's what you're doing freezing out on the balcony at dawn, right? Trying to channel your talents through a connection to Muina?" I only knew he was doing this because he comes back inside, chilled through and all wound up, and makes himself feel better by carrying me off into the shower.

Which at least means we both feel happily relaxed when we go down to breakfast.

"It may be something the younger Kalrani can learn, even if we cannot," Kaoren said, philosophically. "I am only fracturing myself, trying to take a different approach to using my talents."

"Pandora isn't the right place to try and be all connected anyway," I said, leaning against him. "Since the temperature makes you want to lock yourself inside, to put on lots of layers of clothes. Plus, first step supposedly is to be connected, not to do anything with powers. We should just go skinny-dipping here, enjoy the world."

I had to explain what skinny-dipping is – definitely not a word Tarens have – and was surprised when Kaoren nodded and acted like I'd made a good suggestion.

"Perhaps not entirely without clothing, but you make a good point. I'll talk to Surion about scheduling."

That made me laugh at him, that he would schedule skinny-dipping, and he surprised me again by kissing me. We were in a relatively sheltered spot, but not completely out of sight, and Kaoren is so not into public displays of affection. I think it's a sign of how stymied he feels by the Lantaren teaching tracts.

Maze thinks swimming at Mesiath a reasonable idea as well – whether to attempt some sort of connection, as training, or simply for a fun break. He's said anyone who wants to can take a lunchtime swimming break there during the next week, but of course set a bunch of safety rules about not going off alone and not going too far from the main expeditionary force.

I think all the squads are planning to go tomorrow.

The part of my diary I read to Kaoren today was about what 'Cassandra' means. I could tell he thought that 'she who entangles men' was very funny, but he focused more on the prophecy stuff, of course. He said Symbol Sight hadn't shown him any precise significance to my name, and we turned over how my strange Sight seems to let me see everything *except* the future. And then whether I should try and see the future, which I said I'd probably refuse to try to do. Mainly because I just don't want to be able to do that, but it does also seem to be a far more dangerous thing to do, since I might end up seeing bunches of possible futures.

He asked if it would bother me if he reported the meaning, and I said "Yes," and I think he's going to leave it at that. I'm glad he asked.

Saturday, August 9

Quadrangles

I am increasingly convinced that it's a requirement to be in love with Maze if you're a female Setari captain. All the squads went to Mesiath today, and had a very good time away from the main expeditionary force. Zan came, but didn't swim, and fell asleep tucked against a rock on the bank and Maze found her still asleep and carried her back. She looked really tiny and young against his chest (and I got the impression that her squad wanted to rescue her).

Endaran, the captain of Eleventh, went really thin about the mouth and got ominously quiet. Taarel handled it better, just saying, "She's being overworked," to Maze, and nodding when he said he'd rearrange Twelfth's scheduling. But later on, after only Third and Fourth were left to continue assisting the sampling expedition, I saw for a moment that she looked very alone. Whether Zan woke up before Maze put her to bed, or if anyone told her, I don't know. Maze was looking pretty damn tired at dinner tonight as well.

I'm feeling very lucky to be me today. We had a really gorgeous day. Long walks in the forest, with just a bit of side-fuss due to the swarms of greysuits which need herding. Then swimming before lunch – very easy to get rid of the arms and feet of the nanosuits and set the cloth to a thinner, finer texture. After some initial noise and splashing, we spread out in a side-branch of the lake where we'd found all these drowned and shattered whitestone buildings mostly submerged, and everyone either sunned themselves on sticking-out bits of stone or floated on their backs in the water.

The day was very warm, and floating on my back in cold water with my eyes half-closed looking at the beams of sunlight was really the best way I could imagine spending my time. I have to admit I wasn't really trying to do any of this connecting with the world thing, just enjoying myself and trying not to distract Kaoren. Place Sight and Sight Sight make this complicated for him, but he was very thoughtful about it afterwards and said at dinner that he felt that it was a valuable exercise and one worth continuing. All the captains seem to be in agreement about that, whether because they think it a good thing for squad morale or whether they were succeeding in feeling all connected I can't tell. None of them were yelling Eureka, anyway.

Endaran was being ever-so-slightly catty toward Zan. Channelling her inner Forel.

I ravished Kaoren most forcefully after we went back to our room – I don't take the lead in bedroom very often, but I have great fun when I do –

Kaoren seems to find it maddening and incredibly arousing at the same time and I love watching him trying to control himself. I read some more of my diary to him – all of the day I was rescued – and he's very amused that he made so little impression on me.

I love watching him sleep.

Sunday, August 10

Productivity

Today I was swapped to enhancing the Telekinetics lugging things about – assigned generally, but with Lohn and Mara being my bodyguards.

KOTIS has an assembly line of epic proportions underway to finish the handful of apartment blocks which are going to house the new guests. Each building is inspected after it's fully formed, cleaned of any residual muck and gunk, and then the primary installations are done: power unit, water system, and the really complicated nano-waste facility. The pipe connections are double-checked, and then they start on outer doors and windows, and the heating and air-conditioning and lights and the building's 'brain' (main node for the interface), followed by kitchen and bathroom fittings, inner doors. Then everything's cleaned again, and furniture placed – couch, rug, mattresses, pillows, blankets, kitchen utensils, waste baskets. There's a team for each separate stage, trailing each other from building to building, and once the ship unloading was done and I wasn't needed for enhancing I joined the furniture team and helped lay out rugs and mattresses and made beds and things in the first building cleared for them to work on.

The end result is sparse and samey, but of course that doesn't factor in the Taren interface public space. They're still designing those, but one of the technicians showed me some of the early designs, which are based on the decorations around all the windows and doors in the old town. It's really pretty.

While most of the buildings are exactly the same layout, they're really made different by the amount of ground which covers them – some are almost entirely aboveground, and some are almost completely buried by the rise of the land (must remember to ask why they don't get balconies opening out into the dirt for those ones). There are one, two and three-bedroom apartments, and a small section in each building which is more communal living with individual bedrooms but shared bathrooms, kitchens and lounges. The city layout is also very variable – they worked the placement in with the existing hill scape, rather than trying to keep to a grid structure, and the roads are rather winding. It looks like people will mostly be expected to get about by underground rail. There's even a huge underground warehouse near the HQ block.

Nanotechnology makes building so ridiculously easy for the Tarens. Ninety percent of the work is in the planning, and once they've done all the designing, they use nanotech to produce the model and then nanotech to transform the model to life-size. Whitestone is very strong and adaptable to almost every design, and if they make a mistake they can turn a section back into goo and adjust it. Most of the construction effort and expense then comes with the fittings.

Before heading to Mesiath, Lohn, Mara and I met up with the rest of First Squad to explore an area which will be called Desza Tohl (Moon Piazza). This is an open area designed to be the city centre, north of the science buildings, forming a crescent shape at the eastern base of the amphitheatre hill. The whitestone paving of the piazza is patterned – someone apparently spent months designing the model segments, which represent the light of the moon streaming down from the old city. Each radiating segment shows scenes of Muina's past and present and hoped-for future, and has incorporated the swirly floral designs which decorate Kalasa. It's really, really huge, and the pattern is interrupted by space for banks of grass and raised gardens, and these great whitestone benches which scoop up under your legs. There'll even be a couple of pool/fountains and a sunken performance area. I could have spent all morning wandering about looking at the design if it wasn't still mostly covered by snow, and Maze told me that if it hasn't melted by the time of the big party, he and the other Fire talents get to hurry things along.

Two sweeping balustraded ramps have grown up the side of the hill to the amphitheatre and they dance across each other to continue the theme of the piazza. They're going to put a 'vertical garden' and a statue in the gap in the centre (Lohn was teasing me saying it was going to be a statue of me), and there's some small buildings which will sell food and so forth tucked against the hill. And some elevators off to one side, which go up to the top of the hill, or down into a currently extremely empty underground whitestone cavern which is going to be a hub of the subway system when it's installed.

It took me a while to work out what the buildings on the inner rim of the piazza reminded me of – this place in England called Bath. A solid row of buildings stretching along the massive outer curve of the crescent. The Earth version has more vertical and horizontal lines, if I remember properly, while this swirled and flowed with the stylised outlines of trees (even etched onto the glass which had just been installed on the hotel parts). These buildings are going to be museum, hotels, some kind of theatre, galleries, shops and restaurants. It also extends underground, and most of it is empty whitestone shell without windows, except for the hotel, which is getting close to furniture and fittings stage.

Maze sat on one of the benches looking very at peace and using Telekinesis to brush away the snow so I could see more of the piazza's pattern.

"You really like all this, don't you?" I said, sitting down with him after I'd peered at everything in range. "Putting up a city."

"There's a great deal of satisfaction in making things, even if all I'm contributing is the heavy lifting. I'll miss the sense of accomplishment once this stage is over. Are you ready to go to Mesiath?" He smiled when I nodded. "You've overcome your issues with swimming."

"I guess." I'd forgotten I had them. "Everyone's there, so it doesn't feel the same at all. Do you really think it's useful? That there's something to talent training which has been missing?"

"The training I can't be sure about. Clearing the mind, getting some physical exercise – both are worthwhile, quite aside from whether we achieve further results." He looked wry. "At least that's what I told our training coordinators, who consider this whole approach unscientific."

"Did you feel at all connected to anything yesterday?"

"That's hard to say. I found myself very aware of the larger world, of the forest. Particularly when we all quieted down. Whether having an appreciation of my surroundings can make the slightest difference to my use of talent I don't know."

We gathered together and headed back to Mesiath – which was having a minor drama because one of the technicians had been bitten by a spider and his hand had swelled up very painfully, but Auron took him off to Pandora and everything soon calmed down. Another nice swimming trip. Kaoren was glad to see me, but most of his attention was caught up by puzzling out possible approaches to being 'connected', and I told him I was going to paddle about in a particular spot where everyone could see me and left to avoid distracting him. There were these fantastic miniature weasel creatures lurking about the roots of the trees along the bank and I had a great time with Zan just watching them. I think Earth has something like them, but I can't remember what they're called.

Tsur Selkie arrived back on Muina while we were doing this, and came and looked at all his highly-trained killers lolling about in the sun. He doesn't seem to have objected to the experiment, though, and Kaoren is definitely planning to continue. He says that he's having trouble compartmentalising the challenge though, and is struggling to keep focus outside the swimming trips.

All the captions are at a meeting with Selkie and some other bluesuits at the moment, and I am at least going to make sure that I don't cause any dramas.

Monday, August 11

Hunter

Ghost is here!

I was snoozing in my room after a morning testing session in the Ena (under the watchful eye of Tsur Selkie), and she woke me up with her purring and walking all over me and seems pretty damn happy to have found me. I could hardly believe it, and was so glad to see her, and petted and played with her while I decided what to do.

Not that I really had any choice. Kaoren would be hurt if I tried to keep her secret from him, and I had a snowflake's chance in hell of actually doing so. Not to mention that she was sure to materialise abruptly in front of someone. Kaoren is at Mesiath today (I slept through lunch-time swimming), while Maze is playing construction crew, but the new satellites mean I could send a channel request to both of them which said: "What's the Taren word for déjà vu – the feeling you get when you feel like you've done this before?" and streamed visual of Ghost sitting in my lap.

I think I managed to render Maze speechless. Kaoren laughed, and told me a phrase which means the same as déjà vu. After a bit of speculation on how she managed to get here, and double-checking that I was sure that it really is Ghost, they decided there really wasn't a great deal they could do since I wasn't willing to hand her over for experimentation ('testing'). Not that they're exactly keen, even when I pointed out that she was a great stickie detector.

Second Squad seems to be here, so I think I'll go down and introduce Ghost to them.

Filling up

After a bit of wide-eyed surprise, Second Squad (and Zee, Sefen and Eeli) proved to be a good start for Ghost. They were careful not to be too loud (even Eeli), and followed my instructions for introducing yourself to cats, and soon she was winding her way between their legs and allowing them to gingerly pet her. It's very weird for them, though, since she is an Ionoth and even the ones they don't kill they take good care to avoid. Eeli was in ecstasy, of course, but I noticed that not wanting to scare Ghost meant she was well able to stop herself from being noisy. Ghost, in turn, decided to adore Nils. She purred herself silly and ended up sitting on his shoulder poking her nose in his ear.

Second Squad found this hilarious, and teased him about being irresistible, but he just smiled and set Ghost on his lap and played with her until the other squads started drifting back and she went off and hid in one of the unoccupied bedrooms. Nils is still being unusually serious and subdued, but doesn't seem unhappy or anything. Totally non-flirty, though, which is probably a good thing given that the two Kalrani assigned to Second, Nala and Joen, are taking turns going bright red or drooling whenever he's anywhere near them. They seem like okay people despite that – even when Nils is being mild and polite he just oozes smex in a way which is hard to ignore, so I can hardly blame them for being flustered.

I wonder if Nils and Zee have had some kind of huge argument? They weren't ignoring each other or anything, but just didn't have much to do with each other. I'm very curious, but don't dare ask anyone. Zee's made it clear that I should stay out of her private life.

I did an entire episode of *Planet Earth* during testing – Tsur Selkie ran me through a simple visualisation and then had me tire myself out making TV – but because I spent so long sleeping and chatting and playing with Ghost I didn't get any subtitling done. I also did some random requests – dinosaurs (excerpts from *Jurassic Park*, mainly) and more populous bits of Earth (I did that ad for Qantas where all these kids are singing *I Still Call Australia Home* in different places, and then just random fragments of bits of movies which show famous buildings).

We sat around in the evening talking about the signing ceremony. Just one week away, with people starting to arrive from two days before. It's an insane timetable, even with Setari doing the heavy lifting and a thousand or so people (greensuits, pinksuits, greysuits) working on the actual fitting out of the buildings. All the main Telekinetic and Levitation talents are going to be devoted to construction and construction alone from now until then, although they're still allowed to go swimming at Mesiath or back to their rooms to rest at lunch, since a long day of heavy talent-based lifting is really bad for their health. Their bodies can't keep up with the energy output. The rest of the Setari will be doing what I was doing – helping out with whatever.

They're planning to cycle all the active squads through Pandora again to make sure all the extra members have their security clearance. Eleventh will head back in a couple of days, and then they'll have three staggered cycles of squads coming through, each staying a week. [Which means Fifth will be here soon, but I guess I'll survive. Twelfth will go just after the signing ceremony and be replaced by Sixth, and then Third will be replaced by

Seventh, Second by Eighth and so on. First and Fourth are the long-term Muinan assignment for the moment, mainly for the cause of keeping me somewhere it seems the Nurans can't go.]

I asked what would happen to the agreement if the Nurans changed their minds about wanting to have nothing to do with us, or some other Muina-descended group showed up and wanted to live on Muina. Which of course is something no-one can answer, since it all depends on circumstances. The Nurans still have knowledge KOTIS wants and although Inisar's history book showed they don't have any more idea than we do on what went wrong, they might be useful with suggestions on how to fix it. But nothing Tare's done has convinced them to even talk about it. Tare made another attempt to send a diplomatic vessel through the rift to Nuri, and again some of Nuri's strong psychic talents showed up almost immediately and made them turn around, and wouldn't say anything to them except variations on "Leave now or be destroyed".

People from other Muinan-descended planets are something no-one really wants to see right now. Of course, the Ddura would try and kill them all, so the Tare-Kolar alliance is pretty safe in that regard. But saying "No, we were here first, go away" is an attitude which opens up an ethical minefield. Muina itself is so enormous and fertile and welcoming that they can't really argue that there's no room for other groups of descendants. Hell, if you transplanted the entire population of Tare, Kolar, Channa and Nuri to Muina, it would still be mostly empty. Channa only has about one million people (drifting about in nomadic tribes, suffering more and more from Ionoth attacks) while Nuri's this tiny moon with maybe between two and four hundred thousand people. You could move all of *Earth* here and there'd still be room.

But it sure would get complicated.

Tuesday, August 12

Open your mind

I liked this morning a lot more than this afternoon.

This morning was more 'instant town' work, with Lohn and Mara as my guards. Lohn and Mara are always worth spending time with, full of energy hauling mounds of mattresses and sheets and pillows everywhere (up all the stairs, since the elevators weren't operational yet) and making beds. I lost count of how many beds we did, and it was amazing how tiring something so simple can be, but it was fun too. KOTIS personnel everywhere, really busy, but cheerful with it, and they get a real kick out of seeing Setari carrying about mounds of pillows. And I seem to have turned into the village mascot (which I don't particularly like, but it's hard to resist how pleased most people seem to be to see me).

That was this morning. This afternoon has been brain scans and people being all 'you did it once, try harder to do it again'. And blood tests, because I needed more needles. So not in a good mood right now.

For all that, I guess it's worth it, since Kaoren is very happy. Not understanding what the Lantarens meant about connecting with Muina was really getting to him, to the point that when we all went to go swimming today, he came along since I wanted to go, but decided he was going to take a break from attempting to puzzle out the meaning. Which was very fine with me. We went swimming about together, exploring the tumbled and drowned city. I don't know what happened to make the lake rise to cover that part of Mesiath, but it's a really neat place to swim through – especially when you know that there's nothing lurking in the shadows of the buildings which registers as a threat.

We found an excellent ruin which was sheltered on all sides, and where the stone was just the right level to sit half underwater while still enjoying the streaming sunlight. We dozed in the sun for a while, until I got curious about – well, mainly I was curious as to whether Nils was anywhere near Zee – so I pushed out with my knowing where people are sense to find them. But Nils was with Lohn, Mara and Ketzaren, while Zee and Alay and Jeh seemed to be chatting. I amused myself tracking where everyone was, and then finding the little weasel things, and then all different sorts of animals, and the fish in the river – some right underneath where we were lying – and then there were birds and snakes and bugs and these large windy spaces which I eventually realised were the trees and it was really very enjoyable and relaxing doing that. I felt incredibly calm, and very pleased with myself, but then I noticed that more and more of the bright, sharp presences which were the Setari had gathered around Kaoren and me, and so I sort of drew back to myself and looked up at them.

"Can't be that interesting to watch me daydreaming," I said, annoyed. Finding a dozen people staring at me isn't my idea of fun.

"What were you doing?" Kaoren asked. He was sitting cross-legged just out of reach of me, and his eyes were open very wide. It was a bit disconcerting seeing him with that expression, because it's what he looks like when he's trying to contain himself, which he usually doesn't need to do. Most everyone was wide-eyed.

"Just seeing how many things I could sense, and how far. If I push out really far even the trees start to be there for me." I wrinkled my nose. "And, yeah, I guess that does sound like this connecting to Muina thing that everyone has been trying to do, but it doesn't explain why you're all here staring at me. I don't feel like I was pouring out a lot of energy or anything."

"It's the mechanics of your enhancement." Kaoren made a brief, meaningless gesture with his hand – a sign that he was almost beside himself with excitement, since he rarely moves without purpose. "The technicians have yet to find any physiological explanation for how it operates. What you were doing then – deepening your connection to your surroundings – resulted in a considerable increase in the strength of your enhancement. I called Surion and Namara so that I could study how the increase was effecting them."

While he was enhanced himself, of course, and the rest of First Squad had come along to watch, along with Taarel, Regan, Endaran and the Squad Three captain, Turian.

"I could clearly feel the shift," Maze put in. "The best I can describe it is that you don't feel the air around you unless there's a wind." He held out a hand to me and when I moved in response, brushed the tips of his fingers against mine. "Even when your enhancement is at ordinary levels, there's a sense now of the shift."

"Why is being able to feel when I'm enhancing you so amazing?"

"Because it's still there when the enhancement wears," Zee said. She smiled, with just a hint of wonder edging into her eyes, which is not what I'm used to from Zee. "What you're doing is increasing something already present. We are – we think that we have all already been connected to the Ena, all along, but our awareness – it's like when you have worn a scent every day. You cease to be able to smell it, unless it grows stronger."

"When you enhance us, you are not channelling power to us," Kaoren continued, with the certainty which told me that this was something which had come from his Sights. "It is more that because you have such a strong connection with the Ena, contact with you causes our own connection to come more into focus, to align correctly. You aren't increasing our powers, you're triggering a state which we should be able to achieve on our own."

The upshot of which is that I got to spend the afternoon in the medical building, trying to reproduce my expanded state under clinical conditions for the benefit of the technicians. Only Kaoren, Maze, Zan, Zee and Taarel had touched me while my head was off among the trees, and they all continue to be aware of this 'scent' or 'breeze' or whatever, even if they haven't figured out how to focus it. Naturally I haven't been able to come anywhere close to doing it again, have just been giving myself a headache pushing myself to be able to detect everyone in Pandora and getting increasingly irritated at the group of people in the next room having a meeting about me. I can't hear what they're saying, I just know that they're there. Kaoren and the other people I extra-enhanced at least were stuck having lots of tests too.

He's so tremendously happy just being able to understand what he was missing, even if he can't reproduce the effect (yet). We've been having a sporadic discussion over the interface about the implications, which are good for me in the long run, but suck in the short term, because every Setari on two planets would naturally appreciate having their connection to the Ena pointed out to them in the same way. Lots of pressure for me to get into whatever you'd call today – a trance state, maybe? Broadening of the mind? They've decided the best thing to do is to have me repeat as much as possible of today at Mesiath to try and trigger the expansion.

I call that taking all the fun out of it.

Thursday, August 14

On Schedule

I surprised myself by being able to get all trancey again without a whole heap of frustrating days of trying. Of course, Kaoren knows me more than well enough to work out the best way to achieve the result he wanted, making sure that I spent the morning doing more carting things about so that by the time it was lunch I really wanted a rest, and then getting me to locate and show him the miniature tree-weasels, and then chatting to me for a long while back in our secluded nook before telling me that I should attempt to locate all the Setari, but if I started getting the headaches and stress I was feeling yesterday afternoon to just stop – that the further expansion was quite possibly something I'd only be able to do on an infrequent basis.

Him and his psychological training.

At any rate, making beds and swimming about, and the early Autumn heat and sun had left me very drowsy, to the point where I almost fell asleep leaning against Kaoren's shoulder. But – especially since I had really *liked* the sensation of being all expansive – I began looking about for different animals, and found it not at all difficult to follow the same route to expansion. For a while I got caught up trying to sense smaller plants than the trees, but then just pushed out as far as I could.

I didn't exactly find a limit. I felt I could keep going further, but I started to lose any awareness of what was happening immediately around me, which was a sensation I didn't like at all. Kaoren and Maze had been staying with me the whole time, calling up squad members two at a time, and I got really confused when it seemed to me that I'd been left alone. I had to kind of push back toward myself, and was relieved when my perception of my immediate surroundings came back. Kaoren and Maze were still with me, along with Halla and Tsur Selkie, who had come along a little before I'd gotten confused.

Drawing back into myself made me realise I was really tired – and there was something on my head. Maze had been talking – and it occurs to me to check my log, because second level monitoring does record sounds when you're asleep – Maze was talking about whether to try and move me, but broke off when I suddenly lifted my hand and patted at this sensor pad they'd fitted on me. "Tricky," I said (unhelpfully in English) and promptly went to sleep until midday today.

There's this increasing list of things I can do which they're too scared to let me do. This one because I stopped registering any higher brain function, and my breath and heartbeats were coming further and further apart. They're planning another cautious expansion experiment, but not for a couple of weeks.

When Kaoren told me about the postponement of testing, I had to ask: "Is there some kind of order which says 'don't let Devlin do dangerous things until after the signing ceremony'?" and he told me "There is now."

He was looking terribly tired – he's sleeping on my lap at the moment. Even after I came back to myself, I was showing abnormally low amounts of brain activity, so he sat with me until I woke up and had been cleared by medical – he says he had a backlog of reports to review anyway. All my good intentions to not worry and stress Kaoren out aren't making any difference.

On the positive side of things, all the Setari on Muina are now aware of 'the wind of the Ena' or whatever analogy they're using at the moment. They'd brought a drone along (without telling me) and were getting what readings they could off me and the Setari while I was trancing out. The 'extra' enhancement only lasts while they're actually in contact with me – if they move away it drops down to the normal enhancement for the usual period. The extra enhancement is also a bit too much for the Setari – it's not something they can endure for very long at all, and they think it might be dangerous for them to use high-energy talents while enhanced.

And I'm feeling really quite good. No headache, very well rested. Caught up with the latest episodes of The Hidden War (it's funny that Ghost showed up on Muina about a week after the episode where Ghost arrived in The Hidden War). This new episode aired a few days ago and Mori had already warned me what was in it, but I'd not got around to watching it yet. It was a big double-episode covering everyone getting knocked out by the aether at the Pillar, the retrieval mission, Ghost showing up in my hospital room, and then Kaoren asking me what I'd meant about aether being moonlight. I think these were meant to be separate episodes and they were just showing them back to back because the timing ties up very conveniently with the signing ceremony. The next episode, which will almost certainly be the Muina mission where I give the squads with me security clearance, airs on Tare in two days, which happens to be the day when everyone's supposed to start arriving here.

It's only four days until the signing ceremony. And, urg, I just had about a million things added to my schedule. Lunches and dinners with people, tours of sites, an open-air concert, and then the signing ceremony and the celebratory banquet. I pulled my sickie a few days too early, though I suppose I could have a shot at 'experimenting' with mind expansion the day before the signing and then getting to spend the day in bed. I get the feeling just pretending to have a sore throat isn't going to be enough to get me out of this.

At least, looking at his calendar, they've had the sense to schedule Kaoren to be with me all the time. And Maze, it seems.

Bleh, and Fifth Squad's just arrived.

Friday, August 15

Comedic Set Piece

Woke up just before dawn because I could hear the Ddura making the hunting noise. And then Ghost came pelting out of nowhere, dived under the covers and tried to hide underneath me, all shaking and trembling. When she reached me the note of the Ddura's call changed, to the confused sound it makes when it's puzzled about new arrivals and their faked security passes.

I hadn't even thought of that, when Ghost showed up. That the Ddura would hunt her. I could tell Kaoren had, by the complete lack of surprise he showed when I woke him, and the faint hint of relief that I hadn't had to watch my cat get slaughtered. I asked him why he hadn't warned me, so I could have sent her back to Tare, but he pointed out that it was more a matter of warning Ghost, since they had little chance of preventing her from simply returning, even if they managed to get her to leave.

Kaoren and I wrangled over whether it was a good idea not to warn me about things I couldn't do anything about (not an argument – we've managed not to properly argue with each other yet – we really don't want to). Then I checked and found that Nils was awake, so opened a channel and explained what had happened, and asked if he could take Ghost back with him when Second returns to Tare. He said 'Of course'. I think he was really worried about her – she'd been sleeping on his stomach, and woken him up in a total panic and then bolted off.

I made an attempt to reconcile Ghost and Kaoren, but she was very busy trying to hide in my armpit, and didn't seem at all interested in forgiving him for levitating her. Before this morning, Ghost wouldn't stay around at all when Kaoren is with me – she goes and rides around on Nils instead. She's with him now, but she stuck with me obsessively while we were out and about today.

She also made morning smex a little impossible, so we went down and had an extra-early breakfast with Nils and went out into the chill to look at the patches of grass and plants poking through the snow. No flowers yet. Since the guests for the ridiculous party were due to start arriving from tomorrow, everyone else got up early too. Not all the prep work was finished today, either – they'll be completing the last few buildings even as people start using the first ones.

Kaoren's very good at making beds. He has a bright career in hotel service. It was really funny watching Sonn watch Kaoren make beds. Like she thought it would be beneath his dignity or something. Not that I didn't get a big kick out of it myself, especially because he can't help but figure out the most efficient way to distribute boxes of mattresses, pillows and linen from the entrance of the building so that we could make them with the least amount of tromping back and forth.

Next we went out to Moon Piazza to meet Maze and Ketzaren. Even though the day was turning out nice and warm, they had decided to clear the thicker drifts of snow off. The signing ceremony is going to be there, and they'll be setting up the day after tomorrow.

Ketzaren enhanced and created this massive howling windstorm to push the loose snow together (using Telekinesis over such a vast space would be way too exhausting). Maze, Sonn, Kaoren and I sat with her on one of the curving tiers of the vertical garden walls and watched (well, I was theoretically assisting by enhancing). It's really rare that Ketzaren uses her wind powers, because there's only a few spaces where it's useful and she produced a truly spectacular gale (which caught a few greensuits unawares) sending all the snow flurrying upward. We were out of the main force of the wind, but Ghost still hated it and hid inside my coat.

Maze went and melted the big piles Ketzaren had made, and did a tour about finding pockets which had been blown under benches while the rest of us wandered about looking at the fully revealed design. Lohn and Nils showed up (they're really good friends and I can tell Lohn's sorry that Second won't be staying long), and they both teased me mercilessly about the sections of pavement which show my arrival at Pandora, and then the Setari around the platform and its unlocking. And also the massive battle, which surprised me. Then it moved to settlement and discovery images. I didn't mind these images, because they're pretty stylised and abstract, and could be any random girl really, but Lohn kept insisting that he really meant it that there was going to be a statue of me, and Maze finally confirmed that there was going to be some kind of group statue which would include me. He didn't know the precise details – there's supposed to be a grand unveiling on the day of the signing. It's by one of Kolar's most famous sculptors. I can live with it if it's a group statue, I guess, but I'm still not very keen on the idea.

Looking like he found my reaction very funny, Maze suggested we break for lunch, but then another ship came in and he had to go help with the unloading first. Kaoren went to fetch lunch, while Sonn, Ketzaren, Lohn, Nils and I climbed back up onto the tiered garden and watched the greensuits, who had arrived to plant up the garden beds out on the piazza with alternating white and pink and blue flowers. Lohn said that they were the same plants which were coming up everywhere at Pandora, but from further south, where it was a little warmer.

Ghost got busy seducing Sonn, who couldn't quite manage to not pet her, despite really wanting to be all proper about Ionoth. It occurred to her that the Ddura might hunt Ghost, and I explained what had happened that morning and how Nils was going to take her back to Tare. Kaoren came back with the food and we were unpacking it and having a really serious discussion about how strange it was to be protective of an Ionoth, when I felt some people take the elevator down from the top of the hill and follow the wall of the piazza.

Two girls, three guys, the black Setari uniform making them stand out against the whitestone paving. One of the guys was saying how big a waste of time it was to go running around blindly.

"I want to talk to her," said the girl who was tromping along out in front. Se-Ahn Surat, the actress who plays me in *The Hidden War*, trailed by the show's lead actress, Lanset Kameer (Nori), and then the actors who play Faer, Lastier and Nori's best friend (and the guy she should be in love with) Searns. All of us on the garden wall froze in a kind of amazed disbelief.

"So talk to her tomorrow, when you're scheduled to meet her," said Eyle Sured (Faer). "You'll delay the shoot running off."

"You and Lanset have all the first scenes," Se-Ahn replied. "And being at the same dinner with Caszandra and a hundred other people including the Rukmar of Performance Arts is *not* a conversation. The only way I'm ever going to get any idea what the wretched creature is like is to corner her somewhere."

"And how will you convince her to talk?" asked Teral Saith (Lastier). He, like Roak Larion (Searns), was lagging behind, distracted by the patterns in the paving. "She's refused every interview request so far."

"I'll think about that when I find her," Se-Ahn said, pausing to survey the long curve of buildings. "And given how painfully wrong your portrayal has been, I don't see why you don't want to do a little research yourself."

"A little late for me to strive for accuracy. I'd rather keep the character as consistent as I can after all the script-butchery." Teral (who fortunately looks less like Kaoren in real life) shrugged. "Besides, it's perfectly possible for him to be an arrogant bastard and get the girl. She might suit him perfectly – I find it hard to believe Caszandra can be as improbably sweet and heroic as you're playing her, at least."

"Either way you're going to have to follow the script," Lanset Kameer pointed out, sounding annoyed and a little upset. "You think we're not curious as well? Fifteen years we've been asking to meet the Setari, or at least tour the KOTIS facilities. Tomorrow we'll finally be able to talk to some of them. Unless you get us banned from the site trailing aimlessly about. You don't even know which direction to go."

Maze and Par chose this moment to fly past in the distance toting a couple of big cargo containers. All five actors fell silent to watch them drop down out of sight well to the south-east.

"You'd never get there and back in time," Roak Larion said. "Not walking."

Lohn, by this point, was close to swallowing his own hand trying to restrain himself. Sonn had gone all tight-lipped and was looking daggers at Teral. Nils and Ketzaren were leaning against each other shaking with silent laughter. Kaoren had almost shut his eyes, which he does when he's angry, or when he's very pleased with something.

Since it takes a hell of a lot more than comments from actors to get him angry, and because I was feeling a bit sorry for Lanset Kameer, I called down: "They won't stay very long at the warehouse. They'd be gone before you got there."

The frozen disbelief this produced was enough to send Lohn rolling. Kaoren brushed his fingers against mine, then lifted all five of them up to the metre-thick wall. That was a bit of a challenge for him – he can use Levitation and Telekinesis at the same time, and enhanced can lift up to four hundred kilos with each, but five separate objects at the same time is difficult for his strength level.

"Not improbably sweet," Kaoren said. "I won't try to gauge the level of bastardry. Sit down."

Instant obedience. Kaoren's such a captain, even when he's indulging his sense of humour. But these were very famous actors, and recovered quickly enough, and there were introductions and questions, some of which we answered. Maze came back, and was rather resigned about it all, but very nice as he always is. Lohn and Nils were extra-charming and held off on the teasing, and even Sonn unbent a little. Ketzaren took them away after lunch, and Kaoren, Sonn and I went back to making beds and, as Kaoren pointed out, would now hopefully not have to worry about avoiding being cornered anywhere. Except for the several thousand other people who might try the same thing.

Avoiding Fifth Squad is another issue. It's not that they're being rude or hostile or sneering or anything – not with Maze around and Tsur Selkie prone to turning up unexpectedly – but I don't feel like sitting around the common room chatting when any of them are there. Not that that's really a problem, since Kaoren and I enjoy a lot of private time.

The actors were okay people, but I'm really not looking forward to the next couple of days.

Tuesday, August 19

All Eyes

Finally over with.

It's been three days of breakfast with group one, tour with group two, lunch with group three, meeting with group four, dinner with group five. Too many names and faces and endless questions to politely squirm out of answering fully. Two mini-concerts and some talks given by the scholarly types on the discoveries which had been made. The concerts and talks were a bit of a relief, because no-one was asking me questions during them. And yesterday afternoon the signing ceremony, and the unveiling of the statue, and endless speeches and announcements about Muina's future, and then an afternoon banquet (they couldn't have it at night because there's no prepared rooms big enough for that many people, and the temperature is still dropping too drastically at sunset for an outdoor meal). Then, I'm told, there were bunches of alcohol-fuelled after-parties and a hell of a lot of networking and deal-making and discussion because after all how often do so many important people get together?

Kaoren was with me almost all the time, with Maze, Zee or Zan providing secondary back-up. I'd been wondering if someone would show up with a dress and tell me to wear it, but fortunately we didn't have to fuss about clothing and could just wear our uniforms, even for the party. Black goes with everything, after all. I would have liked to have seen Kaoren in those strange Taren formal outfits though.

I hardly remember most of what was said to me, and have been reviewing a few of my answers in my log. Scads of VIPs who wanted to know how much of *The Hidden War* was true (my stock answer was that the events were for the most part correct if a little out of order, but the people were very different), and who wanted more details about this or that or the other part of my 'adventures'. Bunches of VIPs who had questions about Earth. More than a few VIPs who wanted to know very personal things. Three or four VIPs (or, mostly, their adult children) who made almost openly suggestive comments even with Kaoren there and looking at them in his most unimpressed way.

Only a few parts stand out for me. The Rukmar of Performing Arts was this very funny little man, all mischief and delight, and totally wanted to know everything about Earth musical instruments. I hadn't paid a lot of attention, but of course the episodes of *Planet Earth* which I've been subtitling have been transmitted back to Tare and Kolar – I'm practically a cottage film industry. The Rukmar didn't care so much about all the animals, as the music played in the background, and wanted to know the names of all the instruments and styles of music used. He adores the violins – the Tarens and Kolarens do have an instrument which involves strings and a bow, but it's this tall, kind of wibbly-sounding instrument which sounds totally different.

Since that was at dinner, and I could go to bed after, I made a projection of an orchestra for him, showing people using the usual sorts of instruments, and then did a projection of the instrumental version of *Eleanor Rigby* for him. He was just skipping with delight, and was a lot of fun to talk to.

Ghost caused a bit of a fuss, since so many people arriving meant the Ddura kept turning up and so she wouldn't let me out of her sight. Lots of strong reactions from people, but mostly positive, even though she's an Ionoth. She is terribly cute. One of the Rukmars had brought her kids along (a pair of twins around ten years old), and they positively stalked me because not only was Ghost a very appealing cat, she was one which kept turning invisible.

I sat between Isten Notra and Kaoren for all the formal speech-making and watching of the signing, and Isten Notra told me on a private channel how they'd decided on a paper signing for the Kolarens' benefit, even though many of the Tarens had had to then learn how to physically sign something. Isten Notra made the whole ceremony easier to get through.

There was one speech – one of the elected leaders of Kolar's southern pole talking about how she'd grown up believing that the people who had fled Muina had a shameful past, that there was little to gain in constantly looking back. It was only when she'd seen the projection of the ritual at Kalasa that she'd felt that there was more to the story than overweening pride and death, that there was something to be embraced. She had tears in her eyes. So did Isten Notra, who patted my hand. A lot of the speeches were pretty mortifying for me, but at least they let me stay sitting down.

The statue, which arrived the day before yesterday, wasn't as bad as it could have been. It was basically a huge white column with a slanted top (more moonbeam imagery) made out of some kind of quartzy rock growing out of a base of dusty-looking grey stone which kind of made you want to stroke it. There was a hazy outline of a figure inside the column, tall and androgynous and meant to be Muina. Sitting at the base of the column was me, in slightly darker dusty grey. Someone had obviously given the sculptor an extract of the mission report from my retrieval, because it was the exact image of me from Sonn's log – sitting wide-eyed, ill and alone on a rock, my school bag held against my legs, my uniform looking worn and tattered. Standing to my right, though, were Kaoren and Sonn, again in darker stone: incredibly cold and professional and upright. And to my left were Shaf and Nalaz from Kolar's first squad – Nalaz was gazing all far-eyed into the distance, but Shaf was looking down at me with the faintest hint of a smile. Bit of a Kolaren bias there. Still, not being the only one represented makes the statue relatively tolerable for me. Especially because Kaoren looks particularly gorgeous.

Lots of big announcements along with the signing. KOTIS is going to continue to be in ultimate control for twenty Taren years – military rule – while Muina's initial stage of settlement is underway. After a Taren year after the signing, all the residents and citizens of Muina will be asked to nominate a provisional ruling council to begin ratifying Muina's system of laws and government, which are likely to end up being a compromise between Tare's and Kolar's. The biggest announcement was the opening of the application process to be a Muinan colonist. There would be certain requirements (psychological testing for being able to stand being outside for Tarens) and lack of criminal convictions and desired skill areas, and obviously being young and healthy and talented with dozens of degrees and an artistic bent helps, but it sounded like it would be possible to just get lucky for some applicants, which is nice. It's going to be really weird when people start calling Pandora home. Isten Notra and Shon are both going to become permanent Muinans, and at least half of the staff already on-site at Pandora are predicted to apply to bring their families here. The Setari aren't allowed to apply, as yet.

I'm having a very quiet day – almost everyone has a leave day now that they're done playing escort to VIPs – and Kaoren and I stayed in our room all morning, except for a dawn trip downstairs to grab breakfast and also some stuff to take away for a picnic lunch. The only other person I've spoken to is Nils, who came in with Ghost riding on his shoulder – he said he likes watching the mist which has started rising on the lake recently. We talked about Ghost while Kaoren was looking for something to put the food in – I double-checked whether Nils really was okay with taking Ghost with him, but he absolutely is enjoying having a pet. I was glad, and said he'd seemed kind of down lately, and he gave me an amused look and said Ruuel made me far too scary a proposition to flirt with. But then was more serious and told me his father had died recently, so he'd been a little preoccupied, but there was no need to worry on his account. And then teased me about being in danger of being overly sweet.

I'm glad Ghost decided to adopt Nils as her human.

Since the Ddura was still in the area, we took Ghost with us on our picnic, flying down to the otter stream a bit before lunchtime. They're still there – I'm so glad about that. And glad that I can tell where living things are, since they were hidden away in some kind of burrow and didn't show themselves for an age. We ate lunch and enjoyed the peace and quiet and the views, and now Kaoren is practicing sensing his connection with the Ena and trying to focus it without me touching him – something which he's found impossible to attempt the past few days. Everyone's still diligently working on this when they get the chance, but hectic mandatory socialising doesn't exactly make for the best atmosphere. I'm writing this up while watching Ghost explore, and Kaoren says we have to jog back to Pandora later (and has been talking to Zee about amping up my training, bleh).

Double bleh – a bunch of people just flew overhead gawking at us. It'll be a couple of days before all of the tourists and news reporters have been shuffled back to Tare and Kolar, though most of the really important VIPs are already gone. But soon there'll be people actually living here – non-KOTIS people, I mean.

Wednesday, August 20

The best laid plans...

Overwhelming day. The only good thing I can say about it is that I've continued my run of not being seriously injured.

It started when Tsur Selkie woke me and Kaoren up hours before dawn and asked us to come down to the common room where he was waiting. He'd been reviewing the logs from the last time the Tarens had sent a ship to Nuri and been turned back, and wanted to enhance and also for Kaoren to enhance and review them as well. I'm not sure if he was actually reviewing all this stuff at 3 am, or had maybe been having the kind of insightful nightmares that Sight Sight talents suffer from.

I looked at the logs as well, but all I saw was some fields and trees and a guy dressed like Inisar floating in the air in front of what I guess must have been a hovering spaceship.   He didn't project telepathically, just kept repeating in a stern voice that they had to leave or be destroyed, which the ship fortunately had the external sensors to pick up.   Kaoren and Selkie watched it three times, then Selkie said: "Your evaluation?"

"There is an overlay of...constraint." Kaoren was frowning, looking very puzzled, and shook his head. "A reading from scans rarely works for me with Sight. Symbol shows a guard turning away an intruder, implacable rejection. But still, there is a hint of something more.   And – I have a sense of urgency."

Selkie nodded, all curt and intense.   "This is similar, a stronger impression, to what I saw with the one named Inisar. There I interpreted the sense as disobedience, twisting orders to suit his own purposes when he provided that book. Yet here I have the same sense, on a far stronger level. It is almost as if this Nuran is acting against his own will."

"Mind control?" Kaoren said, doubtfully, while I said, "Geas?"

They both gave me that wide-eyed and still reaction which means one of their Sights has triggered, then Selkie made me explain what the word meant. "Just myth and fiction," I said. "A kind of spell put on people to make them perform a particular task. But – Inisar was obeying strictly to the letter of his orders, yet able to work around it, and that's how geases are said to work."

"Have you been able to visualise using an individual as point of focus, rather than a place?" Selkie asked.

"Have had real dreams of Kaoren a few times," I admitted, going all hot and embarrassed. "Haven't tried to do that when I'm awake, though."

"Ever while on different planets?" Selkie asked

I shook my head.   Kaoren caught and kept hold of my hand while he watched the logs again.

"Constraint," he repeated. "And urgency."

"Very well," Selkie said, and brought us into a channel, then sent override requests to the captains of all of the other squads on-site – First, Second, Third, Fifth, Twelfth, Squad Three and Squad One (who had been sent to attend the ceremonies) – and also Zee, who I've started to realise does a lot of captain-duties in a kind of 'senior female' capacity.

Selkie's override message said: "Prepare for Ena mission, channel members only, secure event." Which means they couldn't tell the rest of their squads. Kaoren grabbed a bunch of energy drinks from the kitchen, and I hit the ground floor bathroom.

As soon as everyone was awake (and presumably able to process what he was saying), Selkie went on to describe Inisar's second visit (something which I'm pretty sure only Maze and Kaoren knew among the Setari), then went on to say: "Sights indicate that there are critical developments on Nuri. We are going to attempt to use Devlin to visualise the situation there."

I'd hate to be a Setari captain, woken up in the middle of the night just to watch me. It was finding out that there'd been events they hadn't been told about which would be the bigger issue, though. But they didn't comment, or show more than a crisp readiness to get on with the job – even Kajal was totally proper.

We went to the same spot I'd previously been testing in, hauling along the usual drone and medical monitoring chair. Selkie told me to attempt to visualise without projecting until I had some idea of how much energy it was going to cost me, then stepped back to let me try on my own.

I closed my eyes to do it, picturing Inisar as I'd seen him last, but not getting anywhere. Deciding that he mightn't necessarily be dressed the same way, I just began repeating his name to myself. And saw him, not the tall, proud samurai, but a filth-smeared man sitting chained to a wall, wrists held above his head by glossy white manacles, face swollen and bruised, chest covered in burns. Shock made me open my eyes, and I found that as usual I hadn't managed to just visualise. But the projection of a single room isn't really that much extra energy for me, and being in the Ena had made other-planetary visualisation not nearly as hard as the first time.

"Nuri leaders not very nice people," I said, after a horrified moment. Inisar had been seriously tortured.

"Those burns–" Maze said, voice flat.

"Cruzatch." Selkie looked at me. "Are you able to move your focus point?"

I tried, but it made me feel queasy. Regan and Taarel were at the projection's door, a very solid white slab. "Nothing we couldn't break," Regan said.

"It's likely the projection continues outside the room," Kaoren said, then moved forward and cautiously touched the projected Inisar's shoulder with a gloved hand.

The Nuran's unswollen eye flickered open, and he looked up at Kaoren, then turned his head and looked at me. Even so very battered he still managed the same look-right-through-you expression he'd been wearing the first time I'd seen him.

"Child of Gaia," he said, voice a hoarse whisper, then looked toward Selkie (who doesn't let being short stop him from being the one obviously in charge). "Nuri is lost," he continued, totally without inflection. "Betrayed from within. They will hunt the Gaian child, for she is valuable to them. And a threat. As you have become. Guard your people."

"How has Nuri been lost?" Selkie asked, then paused when I stood up – which was really not an easy thing to do – moving and projecting at the same time made me totally dizzy.

Fortunately he was only a couple of steps forward. I knelt down and put the back of my hand to his cheek – the same gesture Kaoren had made for me once. His skin felt cold.

"It's a projection, Cassandra," Kaoren said. "Aiding it will not alter the Nuran's situation."

"But isn't everything connected?" I asked, and pushed out as I had been doing at Mesiath, not to sense the living creatures around me, but to follow the link which had to exist for me to be able to see what was happening to Inisar. That was a weird moment, as if I'd moved out of a tiny box into a cathedral, except I felt like I was being smothered, like I was surrounded by glue. The projection faltered, but it was like when I was in Earth's near-space talking to my family, and I could see Inisar still, a greyed-out image of him, and just vaguely feel his skin against my hand shifting as he woke and looked at me and his unswollen eye went very wide.

It took everything I had to lift my hand to the funny-looking seal thing which fastened the chains of his manacles to the wall above his head. Moving was harder even than projecting a seal which was cracked, was shattered, broken, falling to dust. There was a moment like being at the bottom of a pit and having an ocean drop into it, a thooming resettling of whatever I was holding out of the way and then I was just kneeling in Muina's near-space, dripping with sweat and shaking.

Kaoren, keeping himself out of touching distance just in case, moved into my line of sight and I flapped one hand to show I wasn't about to have a heart attack. He nodded, then said to Selkie: "Those manacles were more than a physical restraint. Whether freeing a badly injured man will make any difference to Nuri being lost I cannot see."

I couldn't tell if Selkie was angry that I'd gone and done my own thing, but obviously the news that Nuri had apparently been overrun by Cruzatch (or something) was an overwhelming development, and he ordered us back into real-space, upgraded Muina's security status, and sent the *Diodel* screaming off to Tare with the news. After that was a nail-pulling delay because it's a kasse to reach the rift on Muina, in addition to the time for a return trip through deep-space. Once the *Diodel* reached Tare they just waited at the rift until they had return orders. Kaoren said that one thing we obviously need to do is ensure that there's a ship stationed at all times near the rift on Muina so that there's less delay in sending urgent messages. The small Arenrhon settlement is closer, but unfortunately there's no working platforms there (and apparently even with security clearance standing on the Arenrhon platform takes you nowhere – I hadn't even known they tested that).

Naturally I spent most of this time in medical, having scans done (and sleeping, since I was pretty tired), but did manage before falling asleep to talk with Kaoren about my occasional tendency to be impulsive. He admitted he wasn't exactly happy that I'd done that without any warning, but nor did he feel that he could ask me not to do anything like that again, since that would amount to asking me not to try and help someone who had tried to help me, and neither of us would be happy to be in that situation.

It was just after dawn when a response finally came back from Tare that they were going to send a ship to Nuri to investigate the situation. Setari squads were deployed to active guard at Kalasa and Pandora, and personnel withdrawn from Arenrhon and Mesiath. The remaining squads had been ordered to rest, though I'm not sure if anyone managed it. I woke up about an hour after this, and quietly fretted about the whole idea of three planets being put on security alert because of something I'd projected. And fretted more about how I'd feel if the ship didn't come back, if it was destroyed investigating. Kaoren had me released from medical and we ate breakfast, then had a shower and lay down together to talk and rest more. We were both really keyed up, and though lying together in the dark helped a little, neither of us could pretend to be anything but really worried. It was mid-morning when a ship brought word of the Nuri investigation, and we were both beyond stressed out by then.

And Nuri was gone.

The investigating ship had recorded very odd readings from the Nuri gate and chosen not to fly through it – and lost three drones before finally succeeding in getting one to go into Nuri real-space and return. It came back incredibly damaged, its scans showing what looked like an asteroid field. No-one had expected that, and everyone's seriously freaked. Even massives pale in comparison to moons blowing up.

After we heard the news I kept finding myself on the verge of making comments about Death Stars, or a million voices crying out at once, and despite being hugely upset I couldn't get my mind off not-funny things to say.

Nuri isn't a place I've been, and so most of the people there weren't more than an abstract idea for me. But Inisar was real, and tried to help, and was tortured for it. And whatever I did wasn't enough.

There was a kind of frozen patch during the middle of the day where we were waiting to hear more orders, and no-one had any real suggestion about what we could do other than fret and watch ships take off, hastily ferrying more officials back to Tare and Kolar. Except for a handful of people who refused to return on the grounds that Muina was safer because of the Ddura. Orders finally came through after lunch, recalling most of the Setari squads to their home planets, with just First and Fourth remaining here with me. All Setari were given an overriding mission of finding the Cruzatch's home space – the best defence being a good offence approach.

But the captain of the *Diodel* – the ship which brought the orders – completely threw everything askew again by announcing that on the trip back they'd seen people, hundreds of people, in deep-space. It had only been a glimpse, and deep-space is incredibly weird, but the ship's scanners had recorded it. They think it might be survivors from Nuri, and all the Setari on Muina, and me, have been sent to investigate. Not long to the rift now. The big party seems like forever ago.

Thursday, August 21

Fallen

We went in three ships – the *Litara* and *Diodel* and one called the *Chune*. The idea was that if there were survivors in deep-space, we might just be able to cram them aboard. If there were too many, one ship would be sent to bring more ships while the Setari helped protect them.

Deep-space is hellish to navigate. Visually it's white with rainbow washes, and it's full of gates which are only visible from certain angles. It does have a kind of 'ground' but the level of it – and angle of it – is unpredictable. It's an Escher drawing where all the lines have been erased, and going off course could result in a collision or unexpected emergence in a dangerous part of real-space. And, of course, it's where deep-space Ionoth come from, although it's so vast and weird that ships rarely encounter them. The *Diodel* went in lead to the point where the people had been sighted, scanning madly, while the other two ships lagged well behind. Third Squad was on the *Diodel*, with Eeli trying to path find.

The rest of the squads were on the *Litara*, and Kaoren went off to have a captain's discussion about how to deal with going outside ships in deep-space. It's not totally full of aether, fortunately, but aether tends to collect around the rifts and even though it doesn't hurt 'Muinans', it's still not something they want to fight in. I sat with Zee and petted Ghost (who I couldn't risk leaving behind and who was really twitchy and unhappy). Nobody was talking. Ever since the report of the Nuri investigation had come back, everyone had barely seemed able to put two words together. The discovery that the problem had reached the stage of Cruzatch invasions and moons exploding – despite the Nurans being the most talent-rich settlement – made it all seem beyond discussing. Everyone was drained and grim.

The fact that I'd been brought along at all was a sign of how desperately KOTIS wanted more detailed information. Only by properly understanding what had happened to Nuri could KOTIS make a real evaluation of the current threat level, and what steps it would need to take to prevent the same thing happening to the worlds it protected.

We were all in mission channel, though the only people talking were Taarel and Eeli giving feedback on path finding on the lead ship. I'd only been half-watching the output from the *Diodel*'s scanners, and started when Taarel said crisply: "Massive sighted."

I checked the multiple 'screens' of feed to see not only an enormous, spindly, vaguely humanoid, um, scratch figure, but also accompanying swoops – and a huge fireball taking them out. It wasn't a very good view – the massive kept vanishing as bits of folded deep-space got in the way – but it was a pretty sure bet that where there were fireballs there were survivors. The *Diodel* changed direction and began working out how to reach them, and we trailed along behind, achingly slow.

When we finally got a proper glimpse of the survivors, I wasn't the only one who caught her breath and stared to confirm what Taarel (rather less crisply) said: "Survivors sighted. Thousands. Children. It's almost all children."

I'm willing to bet Taarel practically never lets her voice shake like that. The Captain of the *Litara* immediately ordered the *Chune* to go on to Tare and report, and then Maze began talking everyone through how we were going to go about fighting, once we were able to get within range. The navigation tools were going to be overlaid directly into the Setari's channel, making a visual representation of the landscape we couldn't properly see. The roof of the *Diodel* would be the staging point. Wind talents would focus primarily on any encroaching aether. Par was going to be my toter. Squads were to stick tightly together and, if possible, draw the massive's attention away from the survivors.

I tucked Ghost in a pod when it was time to go outside – not that it would hold her, but I was hoping she would get the message. We paused on the roof of the *Litara* and Kaoren enhanced to start with, and took the opportunity to give me a long survey, very much in captain mode. I was feeling a bit weird – like I'd been on a boat and had come ashore and was still feeling the waves – but nothing major. Deep-space, like all of the Ena, is uncomfortably cold but unlike the spaces it feels particularly strange and wrong.

As the *Diodel* and the *Litara* took up a hovering position as close as they were willing to go, another fireball took down another cluster of swoops, but the massive was leaning forward, reaching down a...well, not so much a hand as a hand-shape. That massive was the weirdest thing I've seen yet – a three-dimensional humanoid shape, but formed out of scratchy nothingness. It wasn't even solid – it was like cross-hatching around a pearly-white mist.

"Light will be best," Kaoren said. "All others to lesser effect. Sound may usefully disorient. We need to open the chest and use Light within. Avoid physical contact at all costs."

"First we'll draw it back to the marked position," Maze added, as the massive's hand was knocked aside. He signalled for enhancements to begin while he outlined a quick plan of attack.

I was staring at the Nurans, ignoring the quick succession of hands touching me. There were so many kids, all in a single huge mass with just a few figures flying above them. I couldn't count how many. The younger ones, huddled in the centre, looked tiny: three or four years old.

More and more information about the area ahead was appearing in the channel's simulation, including a big circle outlining relatively clear ground to the right of the massive. Maze's plan for getting the massive's attention involved a strafing run up the length of it and over its head, trying to draw it toward that area. I wasn't involved in that (and couldn't even bear to watch it). A second group had been assigned to getting rid of the swoops and, after they'd enhanced, my small guard group (Kaoren included) carefully followed the massive as it turned.

The thing looked so fragile and intangible. But that was half the problem – it mightn't move quickly, but attacks seemed as effective as shooting arrows into a haystack. Worse, another cluster of swoops lifted into view, right where the main attack force had been headed and the leading edge of Setari suddenly found itself in close combat and in disarray. I saw people fall, and closed my eyes.

"Throw the swoops at the massive's chest," Kaoren ordered, which has to be one of the odder tactics he's come up with. But it seemed effective – particularly since two of the swoops were encased in blocks of ice – and the cross-hatching was ripped away to expose pearly interior. Maze immediately gave the order for the Light talents to blast, and the thing reeled, and covered its chest with an arm.

"Group two, gather up the swoops you're fighting and hit it from behind," Maze said. "Light talents circle to join them. Second, Squad Three, continue the frontal assault to keep it oriented."

My group paused, then joined up with the Light talent group so they could re-enhance. I saw Lohn's face – stiff and white-lipped – and realised Mara was one of those who'd been caught by the swoops and injured. When the next order came for him to attack, he did so with a furious anger, putting everything he had into it.

The thing fell – the quickest massive fight so far, but the one with the highest number of injuries I'd seen. Only Grif Regan and Alay from First and Second hadn't been hurt. Mara was bleeding badly – a swoop had flown right into her, raking and biting and she'd used her arm as a shield against its teeth. Combat Sight apparently doesn't work very well when you've got a massive on one side of you emanating overwhelming threat. And when it had crumpled and pitched over, a lot of the forward group had barely avoided being crushed, and been jolted with agonising pain which had left them all weak and sick and meant that a few of them fell hard because the person levitating them abruptly stopped. Best I can tell it was like instant radiation poisoning – though fortunately something they started recovering from once they'd moved out of range.

Maze was temporarily out of it, but Regan took over command without more than a moment's pause, getting the Levitation and Telekinesis talents to let their squads down at the nearest edge of the vast stretch of Nurans, and then take the worst of the Setari injured straight up to the *Litara*.

There were eight thousand, seven hundred and sixty-nine Nurans.

Or, at least, eight thousand, seven hundred and sixty-nine Nurans were how many there were when we got them to Pandora and counted them. There might have been more during the fight, but I don't like to think about that since it really was almost all kids. Only six hundred or so adults. We only got that figure this morning. Coming down from the air, all I could think was what had happened to their parents, and I guess Regan was wondering the same thing since, as soon as three of the Nurans who had been defending the survivors dropped down to join us, he asked: "Are there other groups we need to look for?"

"This is all of Nuri," said the woman who stepped forward to talk. She was basically a female version of Inisar – same hairstyle, same clothes, same upright calm – except absolutely exhausted, and her eyes were red-rimmed. It was the woman who'd been watching my testing session back on Tare. I could tell that because of my weird people sense, and I searched about for Inisar as well, but couldn't make him out among all the other Nurans and felt rotten, though it turned out that he was there, just badly injured and unconscious.

Regan and the woman quickly got down to practicalities, postponing any explanation of what had happened to Nuri in favour of sorting out the injured and getting them and the youngest kids on board the *Diodel* and *Litara*. And bringing down everything the two ships had in the way of supplies, since the kids had been walking for hours in the cold without food or water. They were at least reasonably dressed – Nuri mustn't have been a shorts and Singlet kind of place – but most of them were dropping from exhaustion.

I don't know if there was any argument about whether to take the Nurans on to Muina, or to Tare or Kolar instead. Still, even though Muina isn't exactly set up to look after thousands of orphaned kids, anyone who knew anything of Nuri wouldn't doubt what planet the Nurans wanted to be on. They'd walked almost the entire way there.

While the *Litara* and *Diodel* were being loaded, the captains gathered together with the three Nurans (with an audience of a few hundred more in earshot) and talked over whether to continue the trek through deep-space or wait in the same spot, weighing up the threat posed by the Ddura once they'd reached Muina compared to the almost certain attack by more deep-space Ionoth. It was Taarel who suggested that people be sent to all of the platform towns, to call the Ddura to them. That way they'd be certain no Ddura would be scouting the area around the rift, giving KOTIS a chance to ferry everyone to Pandora by ship.

By the time they'd decided to push on, the *Litara* was crammed full of children. The Setari who'd been sick after getting too close to the massive had recovered (more or less, they looked pretty grey), and Maze and the lead Nuran, whose name was Korinal, discussed the route, then distributed the Setari squads to each corner of the huge mass of children.

Nuran kids are very quiet and obedient. Or maybe it's just that they were all dead on their feet, too tired to even cry any more. They ranged from toddlers to nearly my age, with a smattering of adults, and seemed very wary of the Setari and the ships, but didn't put up any fuss about being taken away. The only other question Maze asked Korinal before the *Litara* and *Diodel* started off was whether Kolar, Tare and Muina were likely to be under imminent threat. The short answer was no, which was a huge relief.

The long answer had to wait for another couple of hours, until we had reached and cleared the rift gate, since too much attention and energy had to be given to navigating deep-space's weirdness, with pauses to fight Ionoth (no more massives fortunately), deal with aether clouds, and untangle snarls of children who had reached the point of dropping in their tracks. Most of the work for the Setari was in preventing drift off the back of the pack, and more than a few of them had to divide their time between fighting and carrying some of the remaining smaller ones.

I had one of those, and a flower, a tiny deep purple daisy, bruised and wilted but still jauntily floral, presented to me with great solemnity by a girl of four or five about twenty minutes after we'd started out. I think it had taken her that long to work her way to the front where I was walking behind Korinal and Maze. She was a very pretty girl, her hair in a long, thick black braid, and her eyes were confident not frightened when she held the flower up to me. After I'd accepted it, she lifted her arms up. A very imperious little creature, the demand to be carried totally clear.

Since she was white with exhaustion, I couldn't not do it, though my cousins long ago taught me that kids are fun to carry for about five minutes and then they're wriggly little torture devices. Kaoren looked at me, then past me to two other kids, a curly-haired boy and a short-haired girl both around twelve years old, who were giving me basilisk glares as the girl wrapped her arms around me, sighed once, and fell immediately asleep.

"Your sister?" I asked.

They didn't answer, instead glancing at each other as if deciding on a way to rescue the girl. I figured that Tarens have a pretty bad rep with Nurans, which is going to make this whole mess even more complex.

Kaoren just said: "It will be easier if you adjust your suit into a harness," and I experimented with this for a while, keeping an eye on the worried reaction of the two twelve year-olds to black suit-goop suddenly oozing over their sister. I was also keeping an eye on Kaoren. Walking through deep-space wasn't easy on him – I could see that he was having trouble blocking his own Sights while remaining on alert for attack. I managed okay carrying the girl – the harness helped a lot and she slept limply collapsed. Not that I didn't deposit her in the first dry patch of grass I could find once we were through the rift gate, leaving her to her close-mouthed siblings.

Getting through the gate was a challenge in itself. Third went ahead with all the available Wind talents, who worked up a gale to blow it free of aether while Third searched real-space for predators. But there was just a meadow studded with rocks, and goats, the whole thing slushy with snow melt. It quickly turned to mud as an endless stream of Nurans flooded out across it.

That became complicated, because the kids would rush through the rift gate, blink at all the sunlight and sky and grass and goats, and promptly sit down. After the first few mass tangles, all the Telekinetics and Levitation talents began picking up batches and flying them a short way across the meadow. The other Setari set up a loose perimeter, while the goats sensibly ran away. Then we waited.

Tare sent every available ship as soon as the *Chune* brought word, but even though some of these were larger than the *Litara*, it was hours later, approaching sunset at the rift and well into evening at Pandora, before the last ship was loaded. Most of the Setari remained until the final flight so that, if a Ddura showed up, they had the option of taking everyone still there back through the Rift.

During the long wait the Captains had plenty of opportunity to work down the list of Things We Wanted To Ask Nurans. As soon as everyone was safely through, and the guards sent out, we all gathered around a trio of the Nuran Setari (for they are, apparently, Nuri's version of Setari) on a high pile of rocks with a good view of the meadow. The Captains were streaming the conversation back to Pandora, and to their squads, while clumps of Nurans – mostly teens – gathered in a circle below us to listen, even though we were speaking in Taren. The one called Korinal, my watcher from back on Tare, was designated spokeswoman since she could speak the Taren dialect, though with a very strong accent.

"We have not been unaware of developments on your world," Korinal began, and didn't sound like she was going to go into just how they knew. "As you ventured into the Ena, we saw an increase in the number of Ionoth, and there was much debate as to whether the change was linked, and what damage you might cause. This anxiety only increased when it was reported that you had gained access to Muina, and the reports made it clear that you had done so through a touchstone."

"What does Nuri know of touchstones?" Maze asked. "And of Gaia, for that matter. Tare and Kolar retained no information of either."

"Of Gaia we know only that the path to it had been lost, but that it was once deeply tied to Muina. Of touchstones..." Korinal turned her head and gave me a long look. A really strange look, as if I was something wondrous but deadly, which fascinated and repelled.

Okay, yeah, that's probably reading a *little* too much into it, but she did stare at me for an uncomfortably long time, and made me glad that Kaoren was at my side.

"It is rare for a touchstone to exist," Korinal went on. "One born with a profound link to the Ena, a focus connecting all that is to all that once was and all that could be."

"That is–" Maze began, and stopped. Which was his polite Maze-ish way of going: "Wut?"

"You have been experimenting with the abilities of the child of Gaia, have seen that this connection can, in a limited way, be used to create objects, even small spaces. And you have seen that the great devices on Muina draw upon the aether. You have not understood the potential of a device powered by aether, and a touchstone."

Machine component. As job descriptions go, that one is probably the worst so far.

"In truth, we barely understand it ourselves," Korinal went on. "The device makers died with the Shattering, and we retained little of their craft. But it is known that a touchstone existed at the time of the Shattering, and we believe that touchstone was used to create the Ddura." Korinal glanced back at me, expression closed, evaluating. "Among my people, there are those who believe that that touchstone was responsible for the Shattering."

Kaoren slid his hand into mine, though my reaction was delayed trying to unravel her accent. Once I understood, I immediately wanted to change the subject, so I said: "What are the Cruzatch?"

"That we do not know," Korinal said. "We have encountered the Ionoth known to you as Cruzatch in two separate spaces, and also as travellers. The behaviour of those generated by spaces is distinctly different to those which travel through the Ena. We suspect that the Cruzatch linked to spaces are memory-imprints of the travellers, while the travellers–" She paused. "There are a number of theories, but it appears that the traveller Cruzatch are active in real-space, possibly on multiple worlds."

"Active how?" asked Raiten Shaf, moving a little closer. The Kolaren squads had followed the Taren squads' lead during the battle, but as Senior Captain of the Kolaren Setari, Shaf had been biting his lip holding back questions. "Were they active on Nuri?"

"That – my senior, Inisar, spoke of them when he released us, but there was no time, and I could not–" Korinal paused, and I could almost see her push back what had to be overwhelming horror and shock, struggling to regain the detached tone she'd been using. "If they were, we did not suspect it until this day," she went on. "But for some time Inisar and others among us have been trying to unravel strange dealings on Nuri. Our people have been fractured by differing opinions about the strain within the Ena, and underlying that has been a strong sense of deceit. We thought it political, a struggle between the two with the greatest chance of succeeding to the leading House of Nuri, and when word of the touchstone on Tare arrived that impression strengthened. The urgency of the command to retrieve the touchstone, and Inisar's return empty-handed, brought many arguments. Inisar was sent again, this time only to observe, and did not return."

"So you were sent," Kaoren said. "And yet, there was some aspect of constraint."

Korinal nodded. "A Command. Created by a device of the Lantar brought from Muina during the evacuation and formerly rarely used. To place one under Command indicates a lack of faith, a cause for distrust. We were told that the divisions of opinion made it necessary, but it was a grave insult."

She stopped speaking, looking past Maze at the field of Nurans: those watching and listening, and those clumped in sleeping piles, curled on grassy tufts, tucked against tumbled stone.

"We did not look hard enough, allowed ourselves to be distracted by immediate concerns, even when among our own ranks there were those whose behaviour would have required investigation in less difficult times. Constraint. Yes, that is a word for it. Perhaps they, too, were under a Command. I returned to Nuri when it became obvious the child of Gaia had been removed to Muina, and found my people hard-pressed by Ionoth. And then the Dazenti – a type of Ionoth which has periodically plagued us in recent years: small, swift-moving, attacking in swarms, and capable of phasing so that even walls could not keep them out. The swarms have been growing more frequent, of ever-greater numbers, and though we were equal to tracking and dealing with them, the number of deaths among those we protect had become so excessive that it was necessary to create shelters. When the alert was given, all not capable of defending themselves evacuated to the shelters, and the walls charged with a shielding we had only recently discovered–"

She broke off, because half her Setari audience had reacted: a scatter of quickly-controlled movement and murmurs.

Maze, a muscle jumping in his cheek, said: "What you describe seems to resemble a place we found on Muina: an underground installation, the walls shielded, and many people trapped within, who died suddenly."

Nuri's spy system plainly hadn't passed on details about Arenrhon to Korinal. Her head went up and back, confusion plain, and she looked away from Maze, staring again at the clumps of children all around us.

"Were there large stones in their depths?" Taarel asked. "Dark green, smooth, perhaps two persons' height in diameter?"

"The shield generators," Korinal said, exchanging a glance with her two fellow sword-wielders.

"The Cruzatch use the stones as gates," Taarel explained. "We have found two on Muina thus far, and do not know whether the Cruzatch were involved in their origin, or merely take advantage of them."

Korinal, after a long moment, simply went on with her story. She doesn't seem to be a type who likes to speculate.

"A swarm warning was called this morning in First Home, our oldest and largest city, during the preparations for the yearly March of Dawn. We oversaw – our first duty is to protect the evacuees into the shelters, and then we hunt, clearing all the Dazenti. But Timon, one of our own, he–" She paused. "I will hope he was under a Command. I prefer that to thinking he betrayed us. He lured us into the smallest of the shelters, claimed it was breached. And sealed it."

She let out her breath, as if she had passed some hurdle she had dreaded. "It is not possible to teleport through the shield, and we could not reach the generator. But then there was Inisar. He was burnt, starved. Filthy. But he was outside the shield, able to activate the release we use when the swarms are over. He ordered us to open all the shelters, to get everyone as far as possible away from them. He said they were a trap.

"We had barely begun – only a handful of shelters were open when we found the releases wouldn't respond. There was a rising, overwhelming, sense of danger, and we concentrated on racing those in the open shelters to the surface."

"And then the end," said one of the other Nurans. "The death of Nuri." He was speaking in his own dialect, but it wasn't too hard to work out.

"The shelters exploded," Korinal continued, her voice thin. "All who were in them – there could be no hope. But it did not stop there. The sense of danger only increased, and the explosions did not cease. Stronger, deeper. We could see the far reaches of the city...vanish, dropping downward. The rift was the only place to go, and only those from the nearest of the shelters had any hope of reaching it. We sent them running, carried who we could. The ground began to open – we lost hundreds within a stone's throw of the rift – they were still pouring through and I was one of those just within trying to keep the movement flowing when it all – when – no more came through."

Someone was crying, down below, and luckily a new ship arrived to distract us all from thinking about what happened on the far side of Nuri's rift gate, to all those running people. I've never been so close to so much loss, and felt inadequate and overwhelmed, and was glad when Maze only asked a few more questions after the ship was loaded.

The explanation for most of the survivors being kids turned out to be the ceremony I'd seen at Kalasa. It's called the March of Dawn, where all the children of the city carry flowers to symbolise the new year's blessing. The Nurans hold a form of the ceremony on the anniversary of their arrival on Nuri, and they'd just been preparing to march when they'd been sent to the shelters. Korinal didn't know if the timing was deliberate, or if there'd been any purpose in having all the children gathered in one place.

I keep picturing a trail of crushed flowers through deep-space.

When the captains had run out of immediate questions for Korinal, I asked Kaoren to take me to find Lohn, who I felt a great need to hug. Mara had been treated in plenty of time, but the wounds were deep and her arm's badly broken and if she'd been a fraction slower the swoop would have had her neck.

Lohn was so upset. Everyone is, shocked and jumpy and made small by an event so large, but Lohn's fear for Mara was something I felt more equal to approaching. He didn't say much at all, but he half broke my ribs squeezing me back, and Kaoren and I stayed with him being perimeter patrol as ship after ship came and left, until the *Litara* finally returned from Pandora to gather up everyone who remained. I was tired out by then, and dozed off sitting beside my favourite seat in the packed common room where most of the Setari had gathered, only to be woken by my flower-giver climbing into my lap.

She latched her arms around my neck, and it was the weirdest sensation because she was shaking as she hid her face against my throat. Not sure if she'd had a nightmare, or was just reacting to the day's horrors, I looked about for her two shadows and found them coming into the common room. That gave me another strange jolt, because the pair – who had been so silently possessive of the younger child and spent most of the walk through deep-space glaring at me when they thought I wasn't looking – were barely recognisable. Eyes down, faces blank, hands and shoulders held so that – it's hard to describe it – like they were trying to be completely *nothing*.

They were followed by a boy a year or two their elder, half-heartedly herding them and looking like he wished he was anywhere else. And bringing up the rear, one of the adult Nurans, a plumply pretty woman who looked about anxiously, then said something sharp and soft to the two kids in front.

I was on my feet so quickly I might as well have levitated, despite the not-inconsiderable weight latched around my neck. In another second I might well have teleported across the room. I never thought the way someone was *standing* could have such an effect on me.

Fortunately the woman spotted me, took one look, and simply turned and walked away, quickly followed by the unhappy older boy. And the younger boy and girl became people again, heads coming up, shoulders straightening. They didn't exactly look pleased to see me holding the younger girl, but they picked their way across the room without hesitation, and my new neck ornament let go and clutched them instead.

Kaoren, and the conscious parts of First and Fourth, had watched this mini-drama in silence, and shifted so the little trio had a corner to tuck themselves in, where they promptly pretended to be asleep. But the interface means you can always talk about someone right in front of them, with no worries about them overhearing.

"Pandora is about to become extremely...complicated," Lohn said, in the channel we made.

"There is a great deal we do not know about Nuri," Maze agreed, and added to me: "We'll flag this trio for a higher level of monitoring. Although–" He paused, then said to Lohn. "Complicated is an understatement. It was a struggle to get Kolar to accept the interface. Nuri...traumatised Nuran children...that's not an issue we can force."

KOTIS' well-oiled colonisation plan has gone out the window. "Was that woman related to them?" I asked Kaoren.

"I don't believe so," Kaoren said. "Since we are likely to be hosting most of this last ship-load in the Setari facilities, we'll have a day or more to establish some form of oversight, even without the interface."

He was right about that. There weren't nearly enough completed buildings at Pandora to house over eight thousand Nurans, even squeezed in together, and all the Setari ended up with guests on their couches. Given KOTIS' usual efficiency, it'll only be a day or so before they bring in fittings for some of the scads of windowless buildings waiting to be completed.

The language barrier isn't too bad. None of the flower girl's trio has said a word to us – or to each other that I've heard – but they follow instructions quickly enough to show that they're catching the meaning when we speak Taren. While Kaoren was fetching food, I showed them all how to use the bathroom, and Kaoren and I gave them (terribly oversized) clothes to change into and after they'd eaten settled them on our couch for the night. Three of eight thousand orphans.

We left our bedroom door open in case they panicked in the night, and when I woke around dawn, hours before anyone else seems inclined to get up, both Kaoren and the flower girl were sleeping on top of me. I had to wriggle out from beneath them for some quality time with my diary.

I don't know what to do about her. Why does she keep coming to find me?

She's sweet, in an imperious little princess kind of way, but the most I can do is make sure that she's "flagged for monitoring". With my hospitalisation rate, it would be stupid to try and keep some kind of connection with her, or her frowny sister and brother.

Assimilation

When Kaoren woke this morning, yesterday caught up with us in a big way, and we locked ourselves in the bathroom for an extra-long while. Kaoren is struggling with all that his Sights are battering him with, and I don't even want to think, let alone talk about the suggestion that it was a touchstone who was responsible for the disaster on Muina.

Three pairs of eyes greeted us when we emerged: one curious, one embarrassed, and one scornful, but at least we were primly dressed in our nanosuits. And then my flower girl presented herself, arms uplifted commandingly. I had to laugh.

"Sweetheart, you're going have to tell me your name if you want me carry you about all the time," I said, picking her up obediently.

"What sweetart?" she asked, wriggling about to see my face.

I still drop the occasional English word into speech unconsciously, so translated, pleased to have proof she was capable of speaking, though her shadows reacted with stifled shock and displeasure.

Kaoren handed each of the shadows a mug of juice, and stood considering them. "Not siblings," he said. Which was news to me. All three of them – like the majority of Tarens and Nurans – had black hair and brown-black eyes and though they were by no means identical it hadn't occurred to me that they weren't family, since they so obviously came as a set.

"Ys and Rye," my flower girl said helpfully.

"And you?"

"Sweehart?"

"Sentarestel." The boy said it, pink and unhappy. He's proving more a blusher than a glarer.

"Someone got all the syllables. I call you Sen, okay? Name of girl in one of my favourite ever stories. You three can call me Cass." I put Sen down on the couch, and noticed the girl (Ys) immediately helped steady the mug of juice Kaoren handed the younger girl. Relative or not, she was very used to playing Sen's minder.

I was debating little speeches to make to them when I heard a familiar "Hhhiiiiii" and stiffened. "Ddura is hunting," I told Kaoren urgently.

He immediately started speaking to someone over the interface, while those three pairs of eyes watched us curiously, widening in astonishment when Ghost came tearing out of nowhere and leapt into my arms. I'm relieved about that in retrospect – I'd forgotten I'd left her on the *Litara*.

"Not Ghost it's hunting," I said, feeling sick when the cry continued. "They missed someone security clearance." But just then the Ddura made the query noise, then stopped. "Gone."

"Signalled to a different platform. Someone will be posted to keep calling it there, but you need to report immediately if you hear it again." He gave Ys, Rye and Sen another evaluating look. "There will be a general assembly of all of Nuri at the middle of the day. Until then, you will stay with the group in this building. Do you understand?" All three of them nodded, though I won't guarantee they had more than a vague idea of what he'd told them.

After they'd dressed, we took them down to the common room, where a communal breakfast had been arranged, and asked two of the Setari who were helping out to keep a special eye on them since Kaoren and I had to go off to a meeting of the senior bluesuits.

It was a big meeting – not just bluesuits, but Isten Notra, the senior Taren and Kolaren Setari, and all nine of the surviving Nuran Setari, along with a half-dozen Nuran adults who had been suggested as representatives. We met in the fancy hotel, and the first person I saw was Inisar – obviously ill, but rested and clean and dressed in what looked like part of a greensuit uniform. I was very glad to have it confirmed that he was alive, and he gave me one of his ultra-formal nods in response to my relieved smile.

It was a breakfast meeting, and Tsaile Staben had everyone collect food from a buffet arrangement, then gave a short speech about what KOTIS had been doing on Muina in terms of settling and trying to uncover a solution for the tearing spaces. Korinal translated this for the Nurans, and I got enough of the gist of what she was saying to be fairly relaxed about talking to Nurans without a translator – it's not as if every word of Nuran is completely different to the Taren version, though there's going to be a lot of guesswork for a while.

After that, Tsaile Staben introduced 'her side of the table' very briefly (including me as "Caszandra Devlin of the world known as Urth or Gaia) and Korinal introduced the Nuran side of the table. Two of the Nuran representatives were 'landholders' (so far as I could tell this is a particular type of moderately wealthy farmer), one was a scholar, one a smith, one a cook and one what I'd call a (very young) priestess if Muinan planet-reverence used the word.

There probably wasn't a single one among them who hadn't lost almost everyone and everything they cared about, but only their red-rimmed eyes gave it away as they listened intently.

After introductions, Tsaile Staben said: "Both Tare and Kolar are of course willing to aid you as much as possible. But it is from you we need to know which direction to take. We need a decision, for your people, whether to remain as a group on Muina and become part of the colony at Pandora, or to be sent to Tare and Kolar to be housed with host families."

That got an immediate and very definite answer: Muina was their home world and it would now be their home, and there could be no question of splitting up the survivors of Nuri between other worlds. But one of the landholders, equally as definitely, objected to the idea of Pandora.

He wasn't nasty about it – he actually came across as one of the nicest people there – but he spoke really eloquently about the differences between the Nuran and Taren/Kolaren ways of life, and how becoming part of the Taren/Kolaren settlement would mean abandoning being Nuran, as well as risking becoming a lesser, subservient underclass. That though they would be grateful, of course, for temporary shelter, the best thing for them to do was choose a relatively safe part of Muina and create a settlement of their own.

Even though I don't think the bluesuits liked the idea of a Nuran-only settlement at all, Tsaile Staben simply nodded and asked the other representatives if they agreed. And it was clear all the Nurans were far from keen on living with Tarens, and wanted nothing more than to go somewhere Tarens weren't. But the idea fell in a heap when they even began to think over the practicalities of eight thousand children and six hundred adults trying to build a settlement, no matter how much outside assistance they received.

The cook, a woman named Eran, let the others talk back and forth, then summed it up by saying: "No matter what we want, how fair is it on them? Even if we treated the oldest as adults, we would be raising ten youngsters each. And *they* would be the ones doing most of the work." Then, after Korinal had translated, she turned to Inisar and said she wanted the Setari's view.

Inisar's voice was still really ragged, making it obvious why Korinal had been doing all the talking for the Nuran Setari. But croakiness didn't undercut the power of his words: "We are at war."

Korinal took over, very briefly pointing out that both the increasing fracturing of the spaces and the machinations of the Cruzatch were active threats which could not be ignored. That whatever decision the people of Nuri made, all the Nuran Setari's energies must go into fixing the bigger problem. And that while they might settle at a platform town with the protection of the Ddura, Ionoth were far from the only dangers a Nuran settlement would face on Muina. Even the landholder who had initially objected had to concede when the cook added that it was better to try to retain some sense of identity as part of Pandora, to contribute to what kind of people would be known as Muinan, than to be dead.

Once the representatives had made a unanimous decision to stay at Pandora, Tsaile Staben moved on to the question of leadership, and whether the rest of the Nurans would accept further decisions made on their behalf by the representatives in the room, or whether some kind of election needed to be facilitated, or if there was a person or group of people who leadership could be expected to devolve to. This was another twisty question for them to answer. Nuri had a ruling class, but most of them were dead. Of the representatives only the scholar and the priestess were these elite 'Zarath', and neither of them had been close to actual leadership. A small percentage of the children were Zarath and while there were no members of Nuri's last ruler's immediate family, there were a handful who would debatably be 'next in line for the throne' – though they hadn't had a chance to work out exactly who was among the survivors.

But, even though everyone who had reached Muina had been together in the same shelters, it was clear that now the initial shock was passing there was a lot of anger growing about who on Nuri had been working with the Cruzatch. The representatives very much doubted that a Zarath-dominated leadership would be accepted.

"There is only one who I know all would follow," said the cook, again cutting short the debate. "Because we have followed him already, to keep our lives." She bent her head briefly in Inisar's direction.

"No."

Inisar's very good at being absolute. The most they could budge him was that he would advise the council when necessary, and eventually the council decided to temporarily keep the current group as representatives, until some form of election could be held.

That settled, Tsaile Staben moved on to the agenda for the rest of the day: first to gather all the Nurans in Moon Piazza, announce the provisional representatives, and have them explain the decision to stay at Pandora. Once that was done, the Nurans would be grouped into temporary 'residences', distributing the adults first, so that every apartment had at least one adult. And their ten kids.

Everyone needed to be shuffled for a second time through the platform room to try to ensure the whole group had security passes. There would be information sessions on screens set up at different parts of Moon Piazza to give Korinal-translated statements of what had happened on Nuri and what was going to happen over the next few weeks at Pandora. Supplies had been urgently sent from Kolar and would hopefully reach Pandora in time to be distributed, so that everyone would have a couple of changes of clothing, underwear, and things like hairbrushes. There would be very cursory health checks. Most importantly, names would be collected in the hopes of matching surviving family groups back together.

And that brought us to the big sticking point. When Tarens find strays (which I guess is kind of what the Nurans count as), they immunise them, put them on birth control and, unless they're Kolaren, inject the interface. Birth control they weren't going to worry about at the moment, but the immunisation had to be mandatory, which meant explaining what immunisation was. But it was the second needle which was going to divide Pandora in two.

It's hard to live in a Taren building without the interface. You can use the bathrooms, fortunately, but you can't even turn the lights on or off. Before the Tarens agreed to give the interface to settlers, the Kolarens had had to use handheld devices to do everything – respond to alerts, locate rooms, get through doors.

Tsaile Staben wanted the Nuran representatives' advice on how to best approach explaining the options – which in itself involved a great deal of explanation and you could see that even with a bunch of people selected for calm leadership qualities, none of them thought "a machine in your head" made any kind of sense.

It would make life infinitely easier for KOTIS to have the Nurans accept the interface, but I don't think Tsaile Staben thought for a moment she could convince the representatives, let alone the rest of the Nurans. She just wanted to make option two – injecting an 'identity trace' in one hand – seem like a bearable alternative. A barcode below the skin, so KOTIS could track where all the Nurans were.

Isten Notra, sitting next to me, stole Ghost from my lap and quietly played with her while the conversation went back and forth, and eventually said: "Perhaps Caszandra can share her experiences. Although her reaction to the expanded interface was asymptomatic, her introduction to it might give you a better idea of what to expect."

Given that the interface has nearly killed me twice, and I had thrown a temper tantrum over it, I didn't consider myself at all the right spokesperson. The Nuran representatives looked at me doubtfully, and the cook asked apologetically to be reminded who I was (I was dressed as a Taren Setari, after all).

Inisar spoke up at that, his ragged voice cracking from the effort as he said: "Caszandra Devlin is the touchstone who made it possible for Muina's children to return to this world, and the one who freed me. She is the reason you are alive, and here."

Even the other Setari looked shocked at that – I guess he hadn't had a chance to explain *how* he got free. Tsur Selkie super-briefly explained about Sight Sight leading him to ask me to try to visualise Inisar, and the questioning of the projected version of Inisar (something which made Inisar's eyes widen rather – he hadn't known about that), and then me reaching out and breaking the real Inisar's chains. And then Selkie noted that when I'd been first discovered on Muina no-one had known I was a touchstone and so I'd been processed as an ordinary stray and given the injection we were discussing.

It's really hard not to hide under the table when people are staring at you like you have two heads.

"My language very different from Muinan," I said cautiously. "So I had not an explanation beforehand. Implanting the interface, they use a rounded metal tube pressed against my temple. It stung, and then was bad headache worse and worse over the next days. It tapered off after third day and then I start seeing things – the basic controls of interface."

I paused, considering how very unattractive that had all sounded, then pushed myself to say clearly: "Have you noticed how people here keep glance at that wall?" I gestured to my right, and saw that the Nuran Setari at least nodded. "That's because the interface let us see map display there, show all of Muina, and track the ships come here from the rift. Is like an illusion only people using the interface can see. I can use the interface to talk someone on other side of planet, or read any book Tarens have ever written, or look at what goes on outside, or watch everyone fight that scratchy massive, to see if I miss anything. The interface monitors my heartbeat and sends alert if I'm hurt or ill, and I can use it to call for help if someone attacks me. You said before that you were worried that by staying here the Nurans would become underclass. If you stay here, and don't use the interface, you guarantee that. It would be like – like not learning to speak."

I don't think "it's going to give you an awful headache" really sold them on the idea, but the representatives dutifully went off to talk about how to try to explain the choice to their people, and I had another meeting with just the Setari (and Isten Notra and Tsur Selkie). Tsur Selkie wanted to know everything which had happened to Inisar, who told his story via Korinal. I guess he can't talk telepathically to groups of people.

Unfortunately he didn't have a great deal to add. He'd reached Nuri, gone directly to report to Nuri's leader, and was in some kind of waiting room when his Sights told him he was in danger. But before he could identify the source, or teleport away, he'd passed out. He thinks it was something in the air.

When he woke, he was chained to that wall, and someone called Torenaltelasker (one of the two likely heirs of Nuri) had questioned him several times about what Inisar had told me – using the Command device but still not believing the answers. The last time he'd been questioned, a Cruzatch had participated, burning Inisar but never speaking.

"There was communication between them," Inisar said, speaking directly. "Mind-to-mind. Torenaltelasker...fawned. Even without my Sights it was clear that he bent his pride not from fear or respect, but in pursuit of some gain."

Sadly, this Torenaltoomanysyllables hadn't read the *Villains' Handbook*, and totally failed to gloat, or explain his evil plans, or let slip any clue about what the hell they were trying to achieve with their underground bunkers. Inisar couldn't even guess whether the explosions were a sign that it all went wrong, or if that was meant to happen.

After that the Setari exchanged details of encounters with the Cruzatch, debating the idea that there were two different kinds of Cruzatch. No-one can decide if the Cruzatch are some kind of 'natural' creatures with their own planet, or Muinans made into Ionoth – let alone why anyone would want to be made into a Cruzatch. All the Sight Sight talents – Tsur Selkie, Kaoren, Inisar, and a Nuran woman named Elemnar – say that the idea of the Cruzatch being former Muinans feels right, but wrong to them.

The current plan is for the Setari of all three worlds to try to track the Cruzatch's home space – or at least one of the spaces which forms Cruzatch as memories, like the "Old West" one which had Cruzatch pinned on frames, or the space called "Columns". And if any Cruzatch are sighted anywhere, the Setari are going to try and capture one.

Inisar started looking exhausted again, so Tsur Selkie called a halt, and I went down to Moon Piazza with Maze and Kaoren to watch the mass processing and be part of a non-obvious cordon around the area to intercept any Nurans who tried to wander off. I brought my diary, and have been able to write all this and it's still going. We're sitting on the tiered gardens below the amphitheatre again, and the Nuran festival clothing has turned Pandora into a sea of cream and blue and violet. It looks like total chaos, but is apparently progressing to schedule. They've even managed to roughly outfit another of the big apartments, so the overflow won't need to be crammed into the Setari building.

I'm not looking for my flower girl trio. Really.

Friday, August 22

Lord Vetinari

Yesterday, I'd finished writing up my diary when Nils and Keer from Second came to take Kaoren and Maze's place in sitting about watching, since they had to go to a Captain's meeting. Both Nils and Keer had basically landed on their faces when the massive fell, and were looking extremely disreputable. Nils had been unconscious for most of the day, which I'm glad I didn't know about at the time. He's got a broken cheekbone and arm, while Keer somehow managed to achieve a broken nose and leg. Since they're Second's Telekinesis and Levitation talents, they can only blame themselves for their fall, and were teasing each other in a comfortable kind of way when my flower girl came down from the tier above us, walked right between Nils and Keer, and climbed into my lap.

"Head hurt," she said, sounding very pitiable.

As much pleased as dismayed, I rescued the cloth bag of clothing and personal items she'd discarded in favour of sitting on me, and looked around to find her shadows still on the stairs from the amphitheatre (also carrying bags). They looked, as usual, cross and reluctant. Each had a faint pink mark on one temple.

"Did you three agree have interface install?" I asked, disbelieving. It had come as no surprise as the medical checks went on that the Nurans didn't want anything to do with the interface. Even the identity trace had been a big point of contention.

"Ys, Rye want learn read," my flower girl said. She wriggled about in my lap, trying to get comfortable, then noticed Ghost in Nils' lap and held out her hands demandingly. Nils, looking very amused, handed Ghost over obediently, but Ghost doesn't tolerate hasty introductions, and vanished.

"You can meet her properly another time," I told Sen, then introduced the three children to Nils and Keer, and motioned Ys and Rye to come sit closer.

Nils complimented Ys and Rye for braving the interface, and gave them sympathy in advance for the headache they were going to suffer, but as usual they completely ignored friendly overtures. Ys fixed me with the basilisk glare which is obviously her speciality, then I think elbowed Rye, since he started, then asked: "Why is there a statue of you and that other one here?" [At least, I'm fairly sure that's what he said.]

"Because I was first person come here since Muina abandoned," I said, struggling not to notice Nils' hugely entertained expression. "And Kaoren and Sonn were Tarens who found me. This place is commemoration of re-opening of Muina."

Again this was ignored, and the pair sat down cautiously on the bottom of the nearest stair, watching with close-mouthed resignation as Sen decided the beginning of her headache wasn't as interesting as Nils and Keer's injuries, and began inspecting them. Nils tolerated the bruise on his cheek being fingered, but must have asked someone else whether rogue children needed to be chased off, because the garden wall was abruptly made fuller by the addition of Kaoren, Tsur Selkie, Korinal and Inisar (obviously just up from a nap).

"Fiionarestel's daughter," Korinal said, after a moment's consideration of the self-willed imp giggling as Nils lifted her with Telekinesis so he could stand up. "Last of the strongest-Sighted House of all Nuri. This one was given to the care of Kimirenar after Fiionarestel fell to an attack some years ago." She glanced at Inisar, then nodded decisively at Tsur Selkie and Kaoren. "I agree. There is at least a double handful of children from strong lines who have survived, and who will need particular guidance whatever their chosen path. It would be dangerous not to collect and mentor them."

"Teaching methods can be discussed later," Selkie said, watching impassively as Sen retreated to attach herself to my leg. "An addition will be constructed on the Setari building to serve as quarters for children identified."

I was watching the two older kids, who had stood at Inisar and Korinal's arrival and 'assumed the position' – eyes down, arms held limply at their sides. Empty. But as Korinal spoke, the pose faltered, horrified eyes lifted and dropped, and though they managed to almost regain that blank expression, I could see them going white.

"We'll use the apartment next to ours to house these three until the school is ready," Kaoren said, and I was so grateful to him for that, for having been perfectly aware that there were two kids there who mightn't be from this strongest-Sighted family, but so clearly dreaded being separated from Sen, and hadn't expected to be taken into consideration at all. Sen showed her approval by switching from clutching my leg to clutching Kaoren's.

"This will bring many of the Zarath together in one place," Inisar said. "Protection should be arranged for any others until feeling is not so high."

They moved down the stairs, discussing whether to collect all the Zarath in a single location. Kaoren detached Sen and followed them, and I gave the older kids a reassuring smile. As soon as the Nuran Setari were gone they straightened up, still far from cheerful, but markedly different as Sen bounced up to them.

A pair of greensuits came trotting down the stair from the amphitheatre – having discovered three escapees from their group – but Nils obligingly intercepted them and then Kaoren came back.

"They've gone through all the processing," he said, scooping up Sen's cloth bag. "Shall we walk?"

Waving goodbye to Nils, I opened a channel to Kaoren as we pointed the kids in the right direction.

"You guessed that she would find me again?"

He nodded. "Her Sights are driving her to you."

"But why? Does she know something about the Cruzatch?"

He gave me one of his fractional smiles. "I doubt it. All her energy appears focused on the two older children. In you I think she must see a way to elevate their status."

"She – what?"

"Inisar explained that names such as Ys and Rye would signify that they are not members of this Renar House – of the family – but instead belong to it. A kind of property."

Slaves. Or maybe what would be called bond-servants.

"It is likely Sentarestel's care was their duty – that they are the ones who have been raising her. In return that child is absolutely determined not to be separated from them."

"And so she–" I stared at the three ahead of us and met Ys' eyes as she glanced suspiciously over her shoulder. And Sen looked back as well, thoroughly pleased with herself.

"Little Miss Machiavelli!" I said out loud. "You think you're going to wrap me around your little finger do you?"

I spoke in English, but she obviously had no problem understanding the tone. And laughed, this utterly delighted little crow, then took the hands of the other two and skipped, showing no sign of her headachy crotchets. I had to wonder if it was even true that they wanted to learn to read, or if she'd just said that because it was like shooting an arrow to the heart of all I think right and proper.

"Were you like that at her age?" I asked, staring after them.

"No. Perhaps. Sight Sight is very clear in the early years, then becomes more difficult."

"And I was thinking about having children with you," I said, more than a little appalled, and he laughed in turn, which was really nice to hear. The past couple of days have been hard for him to handle.

"It will be difficult to deflect Sentarestel from you," he said. "But it is possible, particularly if we locate a stable family for the three of them, satisfying her primary aim. We need to decide soon whether we want that, to limit the uncertainty they're experiencing."

Caszandra

He was looking ahead, one of his typical gazing-off-into-the-distance with Sight expressions, except this time his eyes were fixed on three kids. I am still learning so much about him.

"Are you saying you want to adopt them?"

"I am saying I intend to teach those two not to hold themselves as if they had no worth," Kaoren said, with all the distaste someone raised in a mostly-meritocracy could manage. "There are a number of ways we can approach that."

"But–" It was such a completely unexpected thing for him to want to do. Especially given the whole busy-saving-the-universe thing. Not to mention the huge dint it would put in our sex life.

There's no way to make a decision like that in a moment, so instead I asked Kaoren why he thought they behaved so differently toward us.

"I suspect they class all non-Nurans as outside the hierarchy," he said. "You also told them your name was 'Cass', which matches the name form of the Houseless." He touched my arm reassuringly. "As I said, there are a number of ways to see about their future. The construction of the school gives us time to decide which one we prefer."

Of course, he would never have raised the idea at all if he hadn't already worked out what he wanted. I still don't know how to respond. Despite Sen being a cute little monster in the making, and how much I want to give Ys and Rye reasons to never stand like that again, I just can't picture myself playing Mum. I'm eighteen! I have years of gallivanting and sleeping till midday to go yet! And I don't see how we can work it, not when our lives aren't really our own, and we have so little time to ourselves already.

Kaoren, being ever-efficient, had not only asked Sonn to move rooms before we managed to walk back to Setari quarters, he'd sent a technician to make a doorway from our lounge into the bedroom of the next apartment – something which only took about ten minutes to do. So now we have a bedroom for the kids and a bedroom for us and two lounges and bathrooms.

Along with being extremely suspicious of me, the interface injections and a long afternoon out in the sun meant the kids just wanted to lie down. Which, after Kaoren oversaw food and baths, left me free for an evening ping-ponging between thinking I'm a selfish bitch, resenting the hell out of Kaoren for suddenly deciding he wanted this, and wondering if he was doing this because I'd spent the afternoon fretfully trying to spot three faces in a crowd.

The problem is I think I want to do it. I just don't know if I should.

This morning my head had stopped being on permanent spin-cycle long enough for me to decide I needed to talk to Mara, so while Kaoren took his squad out for some serious catch-up training, I dragged my three subdued charges to medical, where I knew there would be at least one spare greysuit in the Setari medical section who could check them over more thoroughly than the basic glance the medics were giving each Nuran yesterday.

Mara was sitting up, very frustrated at not being allowed to move about, and in the process of sending Lohn off to get a proper rest. Once I was sure she'd recovered enough to be bored, I explained as best I could about Ys, Rye and Sen.

"Do you think KOTIS Command would let us do?"

"It's possible." She sounded dubious. "If the youngest truly is a strong Sight Sight talent, it makes a certain kind of sense. But – are you certain you're not simply finding them a useful distraction?"

"Distract how?"

"I've listened to the explanation of what a touchstone is, and the suggestion that one was involved in the Breaking. Are you focusing on these children because it's easier than examining that possibility?"

I went hot, then felt a little angry, and shook my head. "They're definitely *distracting*, guess. But I would be just as tangled even if Korinal hadn't said. And–" I shrugged uncomfortably. "I don't particularly like idea being plugged into machine, and don't want think about, but kids not help me cope with that any better. I just – I keep telling myself more sensible find someone else do this, but if I did, how could be sure they okay?"

She studied my expression, then made an equivocal gesture. "I don't see an ideal choice here. Given the last few weeks, even sending them to Tare might not necessarily be a safe option. But you are far from a stable–"

We were interrupted by the greysuit – Ista Temen – who'd been examining the kids.

"Interface developing within normal guidelines," she said, crisply. "Generally healthy, with no immediate issues. Exceptional talent set for the younger girl, but only above-average potential for the others." She paused, looking mildly offended, then added: "The older two have scarring indicating repeated beating with some kind of cord. No sign of such treatment on the younger. I can schedule cosmetic work to remove the scarring, but there is a considerable backlog of procedures building."

I shook my head. "Only if they ask for," I said, and thanked Ista Temen for fitting the kids in, asking if I could at least use icepacks to help with their headaches – and you can, which makes me feel really ill-treated for my own interface ordeals.

"You weren't surprised by that at all," Mara said when we were alone.

"They don't trust anyone," I explained. "You haven't seen how–" I stopped. I mightn't have been surprised, but I found it hard all the same, and had to wipe at my face so it wouldn't show when Ista Temen brought the kids. Mara reached out and squeezed my hand encouragingly. She clearly doesn't think adopting Nuran orphans is a good idea, but she quite understands being upset about them.

The three wan children who filed into Mara's little observation room had plainly enjoyed medical exams even less than I do, but even Ys could barely summon the energy to glare at me. Their interface headaches are shifting from background pain to major concern, and tomorrow is likely to be rough.

When I took them back upstairs they retreated into the second lounge room, to turn over the small selection of picture books and pencils which had been tucked in the bottom of the Kolaren care packages they'd been issued. They seem to be enjoying that, but also restless. I think I'll see if we're allowed out for a walk.

This Kimirenar isn't among the names of Nurans rescued, but there may be other people from that House, and I feel like yelling, and hiding, and argh.

Saturday, August 23

Assemble family

Dreadful night. The kids' headaches had fully kicked in by dinner, their interface installation progressing faster than mine – apparently the older you are the longer it takes. Sen became incredibly clingy, wanting to be held all the time but also to be kept as still and dark as possible, and she wouldn't stay resting anywhere but my lap. Ys and Rye, once they'd given up trying to coax Sen to stay with them, just lay limply on their bed, hurting too much to sleep but too exhausted to do anything but try.

Sen finally dropped off and Kaoren and I left her on our bed and sat together on our couch, half-heartedly debating one of us sleeping while the other sat up. I ended up reading some more of my diary to him over a private channel – describing past-me just recovered from her own headache and released from KOTIS – but there was a part coming up (about Sean J) which I didn't want to read out, and I'm sure Kaoren sensed that I was all over the place still emotionally – tired, worried, and underneath it all feeling put-upon and resentful.

He took my hand while I was hesitating at the beginning of the next entry and said in-channel: "I was too efficient."

That was a seriously unusual thing for him to say – being efficient is one of Kaoren's basic drives. "About?"

"These arrangements." He nodded at the doorway leading to the kids' bedroom. "I could see that you were reacting to them in much the same way as I, but I progressed through the tolerable responses before you did."

He has the funniest way of apologising, and I had to hug him. "Maybe just a bit. I certainly wouldn't hold my hand up to adopt if someone ask. I just, I can't stand idea of sending them off and not be sure they're treated way I want them treated. So, I guess caught up with you. I don't feel equal to be someone's...parent, but that doesn't mean don't want to try. But I'm − something Mara said to me today, asking me if I was trying distract myself from what Korinal said about touchstones. I don't think I am, but all that − I'm all over place because I do want to be involved, but how can I if so dangerous? Or so in danger?"

He didn't answer right away, then lifted one hand, long fingers apart, giving me a chance to remind myself how much I like his hands. Then a curving spur of Light sprang out of his arm, making me jump.

"We're all dangerous, Cassandra. And we're all in danger. You are too strong to be paralysed by what *might* happen."

He looked like he was going to say more, but abruptly frowned at the darkened doorway into the kids' apartment. We got up to investigate, and found Ys and Rye in the bathroom piling their sheets and blanket into the bath. Ys had thrown up all over herself and the bed, and I hated, hated, hated how she and Rye went still and stood eyes fixed on their feet when we showed up. Waiting.

Kaoren, of course, just told them to leave the sheets and put Ys in the shower with the water nice and warm to wash the vomit off, then took Rye off to the other bathroom so he could use that shower, telling me he'd bring some clothes back. Ys was in bad shape, exhausted and scared and shaking. I couldn't think of a single thing to say to her, so as soon as she was a little cleaner I got in the shower with her, sat down and pulled her onto my lap, ignoring her attempts to get free. She stopped poking her elbows into my ribs eventually and just leaned limply against my chest.

Kaoren came back and left some clothes (my lab rat nightshirt for Ys, heh), telling me that occasionally the interface install does cause nausea, but that it was usually a sign that it was coming to an end, and that he was going to get some clean sheets.

Rye had fallen asleep on the couch by the time I was done making sure Ys was properly clean and dry, and Kaoren had finished fixing the bed (fortunately it's pretty impossible to soil a nanotech mattress), so we settled them both back in their room, and brought Sen in to join them. Kaoren and I sat on the side of the bed, and I held Ys' hand until she finally fell asleep. She was too tired to resent me for it.

I was totally wiped myself by the time I could curl up with Kaoren. Since he has circles under his eyes, I guess he only let himself have a few hours sleep, but the rest of us were out of it until nearly midday, when Sen woke us all up with the wonderful discovery of a floating dot in the centre of all the rooms. Since none of them can read (and Sen is so young) they're going to have a very different learning curve with the interface, but it was fun to show them the room controls – Sen adores turning lights on and off – and after Kaoren and I brought them back from the medical section they spent the afternoon mesmerised by the wall display when I set it on random scenery and pictures.

Imagine an entire *room* as your first experience of television.

Tomorrow Kaoren and I have assignments scheduled, but he had with typical efficiency already cleared the initial hurdles with KOTIS Command – and even arranged babysitting – so after dinner we sat the kids down on the couch for Serious Talk time.

They made a curious set, all three wearing clothing sent from Kolar – shirts and long, loose pants of a light, off-white 'cotton'. Sen was calmly cheerful, her thick hair neatly braided thanks to Ys. Ys on her left had barely bothered with her own short hair, and her jaw was set with a determination not to give anything away. Rye, just a fraction shorter than Ys, had tried but failed to tame his riot of curls, and kept lifting anxious eyes and then dropping them.

"Tomorrow Cassandra and I will both be away," Kaoren said. "We work for the organisation which is in charge of resettling Muina and dealing with Ionoth, and it is only on occasional days that we will not both be called away for part of the time. For the next few days, when we're away you will be supervised by colleagues of ours, and after that the new school should be ready."

He gave them a moment's study, then added: "We've seen how important it is to you three not to be separated, and in order to ensure that, Cassandra and I have asked permission to continue to care for you. You will attend the school while we work, but return to us when our work is done each day."

Rye's response was the strongest, his head jerking up, eyes wide and disbelieving as he looked from Kaoren's face to mine, and then he dropped them again and took a breath so deep he almost bounced in his seat. Ys, through sheer force of willpower, managed not to react, but looked across at Sen. She still hasn't uttered a word in our presence and makes absolutely clear that she hates how Sen has attached herself to us, but she definitely wasn't going to object to not being separated from Sen. And that self-same little imp was chirpily pleased at how easy it was to pull our strings.

My turn to speak, and I just wanted to hug all three, but knew not to overwhelm them. "Because we've listed this as your residence, doors will open to you," I said. "You can go outside on hill, or down into main room of building if you want, but don't go away from building unaccompanied. When we're away, if something happens that you need talk to us about, you can contact us using the interface."

I created a shared space which showed all the basic interface tools which were currently available to them, which at their stage were some very simple pictorial icons – one for school, one for games, and one for age-appropriate news and entertainment programs. Then I created some new icons for them – ones representing me, Kaoren, and each of the other children – which would change colour depending on our status (out of range, busy, not busy, asleep) – and had them try opening a channel to us and talking over the interface. It was too funny the way Rye jerked upright, mouth a perfect circle of astonishment, when Sen managed to talk to him in his head.

Kaoren took over again and gave the kids the same rules about multiple people touching me which all the Setari have to live with. This sparked a rare question from Rye, and I explained how First Squad had accidentally sent me into seizures and now there were all these rules about not touching me. Kaoren was very serious about this with Sen, since she's so inclined to climb on me, and into bed with us – even though it's the strength of Setari talents which seems to cause me the most problems, Kaoren feels it's safer not to risk group contact.

So we've set up some ground rules for living together, and made clear that we have no intention of separating them, and the main thing we expect from all of them is to be kids, and become part of Muina's settlement. That involves attending the school when it's built, but for the moment they can set their own pace and explore the interface as they like.

Ys and Rye have done nothing but school lessons since. I guess Sen really meant it about them wanting to learn to read. Sen, while she tried the alphabet lessons, was far more interested in opening a channel to me roughly every ten minutes and collapsing into giggles when I answered.

I can look at their interface activity, since I count as a 'guardian', though I won't be able to read their emails and voicemails and so forth, or listen in on personal conversations. I feel so utterly unprepared for this.

I can't even remember reading any books about people being parents – kids always seem to be part of the happily ever after. I've read lots of books about kids without parents, or with parents who need to be avoided. All my favourite TV shows seem to have involved magical pregnancies which are over in a week and then the baby is an adult and trying to destroy the world. The only useful thing I can remember watching is *Supernanny,* and I'm not sure a Naughty Corner will get me far with Little Miss Sight Sight.

I'd love to know what Mum would make of me being engaged to get married AND fostering three children. I really want to ask her. Tomorrow I'm back on my schedule of visualisation testing, and I think I've waited more than long enough to try and visualise Earth.

Sunday, August 24

Behind the news

Tsur Selkie says I can try and visualise Earth during my next testing session, the day after tomorrow. Really excited about that, but trying not to get too worked up.

My visualisation session today was about Cruzatch, and was very unsuccessful. Tsur Selkie supervised me, and wanted me to visualise Cruzatch, particularly the Cruzatch's home space. I wasn't keen at all, and found it very difficult, eventually ending up visualising the space I'd gone to on rotation with First Squad, the Old West town with the Cruzatch on frames. That gave me an awful headache, and took a huge amount of energy. The problem, I think, was that it was a big outdoor space, and I tend to reproduce way too much when I'm visualising somewhere outdoors. And it made my eyes go all blurry, leaving me with another afternoon in medical, all headache and frustration while Kaoren was off with Fourth and Squad One trying to track Cruzatch through the spaces, but finding no sign of them at all.

Lying on the scan-bed with my eyes shut did give me an opportunity to catch up on all the news stories for the last few days. I browsed through them in chronological order, taking a little journey from delirious enthusiasm, teetering abruptly into The Sky Is Falling, and ending up deep into conspiracy theory.

The early stories have tons of stuff about me, of course – every journalist at the signing ceremony seemed to feel they had to give their impression of what I'm really like, regardless of whether they spoke to me or not. They mostly say I'm sweet, shy, cautious, but surprisingly articulate. So still *suyul*. Endless tedious stuff about how Kaoren and I looked together, and how he seemed more bodyguard than partner.

Someone had also interviewed the actors playing us in *The Hidden War*, which brought out the story of their impromptu picnic. They both described how mortified they were to discover how very unlike our portrayals we actually were, and how they'd asked me at the time what I thought about the Lastier character. I'd said: "You don't play him as a Sight talent." Which is perfectly true, and which Kaoren thought very funny, but was perhaps not the strident defence of his good name I should have mounted.

There was one reasonably good impression of us, from someone who apparently spent the entire three days trying to get an interview with me and only catching glimpses of me as I was leaving. The article had a really great picture – one I like enough to keep – showing me and Kaoren through a doorway leading into the back part of the lecture-hall type place where we'd watched one of the presentations on screens so that the Kolarens could see it. We'd obviously just gone through the door, and I was smiling up at Kaoren in open relief while he said something to me, and he'd reached out to touch my hand or I'd reached out to touch his and our fingers were just brushing.

There were quite a few interesting articles about preparation for settlement, for a local currency, a stipend of basic essentials, a local wage system. There were also profiles on certain people who had already been approved as settlers – a couple of expert chefs from Kolar who are going to run one of the restaurants at Moon Piazza, three 'media technicians' who are going to set up a local news service, a couple of high-profile craft-types itching to start making fancy furniture with all the wood which is being cleared aside on Muina – it's such a rare and precious resource on both Tare and Kolar.

And then all the settlement stories are completely derailed by Nuri. I'd had no idea that the fact that Nuri had exploded had leaked before KOTIS had any real idea what was going on, leading to a near-riot in one section of Unara.

Things calmed down a little after Maze had forwarded a preliminary summation of Korinal's story, emphasising that it wasn't an attack which could be turned on us. Not that this really stopped anyone from being frightened, but the lack of shielded underground bunkers made the threat seem less immediate.

Reaction to the Nurans seems mostly sympathetic. KOTIS released some images of the refugees being threatened by the massive, and I read a nice story about how the little care packages were assembled – incredibly quickly – and though there's been occasional suggestions that Nuri contributed to its own destruction, none of the stories I've read lose focus on the terrible betrayal and loss.

I feel bad for laughing at a story that said Muinan settlement "comes with free orphan!", but it's true enough. Anyone wanting to settle here is going to have to be vetted on their potential as foster parents or willingness to adopt. Though, given how many hoops you have to jump through to get permission to have more than one child on Tare, I don't think that's going to be a big drawback with Taren settlers.

Once the medics had cleared me, I found my own orphans on the edge of the common room patio watching Nils – who had offered to look after them for the day – trying to write the Taren alphabet in the mud with a stick. He wasn't doing too badly, and said he was using a tracing program in the interface to show him the best method of forming each letter.

After thanking Nils I took them upstairs for dinner, asking – in approved Mum fashion – how their day had been. Ys tightened her lips stubbornly. Rye blushed. And Sen told me, in glorious and partly comprehendible detail, all about watching the new school building goopily growing, and their walk to the lake's edge, and the bee in the flower, and the little speckled fish in the water, and the duck, and the stick vegetables for lunch, and Nils flying them to the top of the Setari building, and the 'fake lady' called Tsana Dura who wanted to play games in her head.

Tsana Dura still wants to play games in my head, too, though she's morphed into a slightly different fake lady – sterner and less fluffy – as I've progressed through the school years. She shares her lessons with a fake man named Tsana Ridel, and Dura and Ridel are these incredible institutions to Tarens – the entire planet shares the same two automated teachers for basic lessons from kindergarten to the end of high school. They were apparently created by averaging the voices and appearances of a few million Tarens.

There's tons of Dura-Ridel smutfic. Rule 34 never fails.

Monday, August 25

Denied

The Nurans held a memorial service today. Not just for their dead, but for their world, and all that they had built and created for a thousand years. All of Nuri's plants and animals, all their books and art and instruments. I didn't understand the speeches very well, but I felt the raw loss in the voices of those who spoke.

Ys, Rye and Sen, who I've come to realise haven't been as upset as most of the Nurans because all their care is tied up with each other, were still very grave and quiet, and sat with me and Kaoren at the edge of the crowd. Even though I'm furious about Ys and Rye's injuries, I don't want to keep them away from Nurans generally – or let them isolate themselves, as I'm fairly sure they'd prefer to do. I'm not sure if the talent school is the best way to go about it, though.

For the moment my parenting efforts have mainly involved keeping Sen occupied so Ys and Rye can learn to their heart's content. They've been attacking learning to read with such grim determination that I'd been starting to worry I'd have to put some limits on their lessons, but they stayed off the interface for the service, and took a break afterwards, distracted by the paper planes I was making for Sen.

I've still yet to see either of them smile or laugh, but it was the most relaxed they've been with me, totally absorbed by the mechanics of paper airplanes, and reproducing the other origami shapes I created for them. They're tremendously interested in everything, but seem to consider it vital not to show it. Kaoren says they're approaching learning like a starving man gorging himself on food: racing to swallow everything before it's taken away.

Late this afternoon I took the flower Sen had given me, all limp and flopping, and gave it to Islen Dola over at Botany. He was very pleased, and said that even though the seeds weren't fully matured, there was more than enough genetic material to reproduce it. So one more tiny bit of Nuri will survive.

We ate dinner down in the common room this evening, with Sen wandering about charming everyone within reach, and Ys and Rye sitting together enduring being looked at by Setari from three worlds. Since Setari do training with Kalrani, it's not as if they're not all used to dealing with children, but playing foster parent is an entirely different matter, and of course Fourth Squad don't know what to make of the whole thing.

Even with so many orphans needing care, I doubt the kids would be allowed here if it wasn't for the combination of the rarity of Sen's Sight, which Kaoren is one of the few people ideal to nurture, and my involvement. I sometimes imagine the conversations KOTIS Command has about me. I'm mostly shielded from my own uniqueness by the Setari, who treat me with more pragmatism than deference, but I'm well aware that I could trade on my own importance to get an awful lot of things. And that as often as not it doesn't even have to occur to me to try, because KOTIS now watches me very closely and tries to make sure I don't even have a chance to get unhappy.

Today I'm glad of that, and I mean to take advantage of it.

Friday, August 29

Over There

Having to do a bit of catch-up.

Tsur Selkie's been conducting my visualisation sessions, usually with Zee along, and a couple of other people for guarding purposes. Kaoren usually isn't involved, but came for my attempt to visualise Earth, mainly because he correctly expected me to be upset. Lohn and Maze were along as guards, and two Nuran observers as well, Korinal and Inisar. Inisar's recovering steadily – although his burns were painful, his main health issues were due to being chained to a wall and not fed much. He's still not close to fighting fit – or even 'good brisk walk' fit – but he was able to come and watch me having family moments.

And he was wearing a Taren Setari nanoliquid uniform, which was highly disconcerting, but the best thing to ensure he stays warm in the Ena. All of the Nuran Setari are going to have the interface installed, even though they all seem to share Inisar's opinion that it's a "distortion". I find that fascinating – they think it will make them less human, but they're going to have it installed anyway because they know it will make them more effective in combating the Cruzatch. Like someone drinking demon blood so they can fight monsters.

They're taking turns to have it installed so they won't all be out of commission at the same time.

The Nurans were there because they want to observe me being a touchstone, but it was an awkward audience for me while all keyed up and emotional about the possibility of seeing my family. I'd had a lot of trouble sleeping, too, and been fretting all morning while Kaoren was off on another Cruzatch-hunt with Fourth and combined First-Second. I'd nominated a particular time for the session, to coincide with 7.00 pm Sydney time (hoping I was right about it not currently being daylight savings time) because at 7.00 Mum usually kicks Jules off the X-Box and watches the news.

Even though Earth is the furthest I've attempted to look, it was one of the easiest visualisations I've ever done. What could be easier than my own living room? Mum's not exactly into redecorating, either, so the most it changes is more books, different games, and whether she has the ironing board out. She was exactly where I was expecting her, barefoot and dressed in her usual semi-casual work clothes. Jules was a bit of a shock – he's jumped at least three inches in height and gone all gangly. Thirteen's obviously his year for Dad's stork genes to activate.

It took a moment after me opening my eyes for them to react, to notice that more than half a dozen people had appeared in the living room (or, in a couple of cases, in the kitchen – where most of the 'audience' partially retreated). Mum seemed to see only me at first, and then was off the couch and squeezing me to death. I started crying, of course, even though I knew it wasn't really Mum, but a projection of Mum, and when she said: "You're home, you're home" over and over I had to try and explain what was really going on. It's pretty hard to tell something that looks just like your Mum that she's really just a psychic version of a holodeck projection of your Mum.

Fake-Mum, after a moment's shock, thought that was really interesting – which kind of says everything about my family – and then asked me why one of my eyes was a different colour. Jules was busy ogling Kaoren and telling him to make the cool sword come out of his arm again, a demand which Kaoren's Symbol Sight didn't seem equal to translating, so I told Jules I could do that too and made a spike for him, but then introduced Kaoren to fake-Mum and explained that we were engaged and getting married in about a year and a half and that I would try to visit properly but didn't know if it would be possible.

Mum's reaction made me laugh, and I told Kaoren: "Mum says that if she was real she would congratulate us and welcome you to the family, but thinks that should be saved for when she really gets to see me again and instead will give you several pointed hints about find a way for me to visit Earth." Kaoren said he'd try, and then gave me a warning about my energy use, but I gave myself a free extension by expanding my senses – finding it marvellously easy. It made me feel a lot less like passing out, but also infinitely less focused.

I told fake-Mum I didn't have a lot of time, but had a bunch of questions. First, how did I go with my exams? [So irrelevant to me now, but I'd *studied* for them!] She didn't know – she hadn't opened the letter, but sent Jules to get it for me. Second, what did 'aether' and 'touchstone' mean on Earth? Fake-Mum more or less knew the answers, but since she had her laptop, she googled the words for me. It's so weird that she was able to do it, and it really hit me in terms of energy cost, but now I know that a touchstone was a piece of rock used to test the quality of metal, which doesn't match me at all, and that aether meant pretty much what I thought it meant. Next thing I wanted to know was how everyone in the family was. Mum said that Nick had gotten into the uni he wanted, and that I'd missed the Olympics. I was just going to ask what had been happening in my favourite shows and webcomics when a weirdness in my peripheral vision distracted me – and when I turned my head to focus on it properly it distracted me so completely that I dropped the visualisation altogether, fake-Mum and fake-Jules and fake-home fading away in a few seconds.

Kaoren moved forward, concerned, as I turned my head again to see whether my distraction would keep happening, and then I said "Streaming visual," and tried to show them what I was seeing.

There was this whole other world lurking out of the corner of my eye. If I kept up my expanded senses, and moved my head sharply, for a moment I could see it overlaid over Muina's near-space. And yet, it was Muina, just a different version of it. The old town was still there, sprawled along the lake bank to the north, except much larger and grander and not ruined at all, and with this huge beam of light shooting up into the sky from where the amphitheatre is. And big statues of people, including one out in the lake with some kind of temple built around it, and these incredible crystal structures which were glowing with the last vestiges of sunset. No hint at all of Pandora, whose buildings are already well-formed in the area's near-space. It was coming up to night-time in the other world, and lots of the windows were lit, and it looked very sumptuous and busy. We seemed to be sitting just outside one of the buildings, and I had a vague glimpse of a person just to my right walking into the building. Just an ordinary-looking person, dressed a bit like the Nurans.

I'm seriously glad that the interface was able to transmit what I was seeing, because I must have looked particularly weird getting all fascinated with my peripheral vision. The Nurans had to wait until we were back in real-space to be shown what I was seeing.

It was really really tiring trying to look at it, though, especially coming on top of my Earth visualisation, and I could only manage a half-dozen side-swiped glimpses before I started feeling grey and ill and Tsur Selkie ordered me to stop. And of course going back into real-space made my vision go totally nuts from blurriness. I've learned from past mistakes, though and kept my eyes shut, risking only the briefest squint. The headache from that was enough to send me to the infirmary for the rest of the day. I gather that they were worried that my interface was going to start growing again, because it was giving the equivalent of 'feedback'.

It's taken two days for my eyesight to stop being blurry, which has meant two days of being blindfolded. That's not as impossibly inconvenient as it sounds, since they gave me a little portable scanner which I could wear like sunglasses to use to see instead. Totally weird seeing the world that way, because all the colours and my depth perception were ever so slightly different. It exacerbated my ever-present blurriness headache to use it for more than a couple of minutes, but at least it meant I could get to the bathroom.

Sen had a wonderful time playing ministering angel while I lay about feeling rotten and reading. It's a little harder to tell what Ys and Rye made of it all, but they seemed to be in the background a lot making sure that Sen's attempts to nurse me didn't end up with me having mugs of juice tipped on my head.

I'm feeling a lot better today. The headache only properly went away when the blurriness did. They haven't even begun to decide what, if anything, my peripheral world means and what they might want to do about it.

Aspiration

Kaoren seems to have cast a spell on the kids while I wasn't paying attention. We went down to have lunch on the common room patio to celebrate me being able to see normally again, and while Ys and Rye are still all quiet and wary, they constantly look at Kaoren to check his reaction to everything. The rest of Fourth, who were the only ones about for lunch, watched with intense amusement and Mori told me later that it was only to be expected.

Mori and the rest of Fourth Squad are only just beginning to relax with me again. They never reacted really negatively, but for a long while stopped gossiping and sending me comments over the interface. There'll always be a level of constraint, though, I think, but as much because of my increasingly weird position of touchstone as because of the idea of "Tsee Ruuel + snuggles".

Of course, Mori has an added level of complexity since she's sleeping with the captain of Eighth Squad, who seems to be Kaoren's closest friend. Mori was more than cheerful when Eighth (and Seventh and Squad Two from Kolar) arrived today, but from my point of view it wasn't good timing. Exhaustion, headaches and children have meant a relatively chaste engagement, and I'm not in the mood to watch Forel purring over Kaoren. Even though I know he doesn't want her to, I still can't stand it when she puts her hands on him – while congratulating him on our engagement, no less.

I'm so going to ravish Kaoren when he gets back from his training run.

Kaoren's given Ys and Rye a schedule of things they have to do other than lessons, and also set achievement expectations for their spelling tests. I think that might be what won them over. Not only allowing them to learn to read, and taking an interest, but requiring they do it well.

Going to ravish him a lot.

Stories

Kaoren ended up having to go off to a Captain's meeting, and came back really tired and not a candidate for ravishment. I'd spotted the meeting being added (I've learned to keep an eye on his calendar), and so I managed to shrug off being disappointed about it. I don't want our relationship to always be him supporting me and never the other way around, so I just gave him a foot rub and wasn't surprised when he fell asleep almost immediately. He spent a lot of time with me when I was all headachy and trying to sleep, and so got to be headachy and unable to sleep as well. Except he didn't get to spend all day in bed to make up for it. I'm going to have to revive the sleeping on the couch discussion.

I distracted myself waiting for him to come back by asking Mara for some recommendations for children's books, and browsing through them to pick one to read. Kaoren had also set bedtimes for the kids, and to reinforce that with Sen (who is very difficult to keep in bed) I decided story time would be a good addition to the routine. I think that worked well, particularly since Ys and Rye could treat it as a continuation of their lessons. Not a bad story, either – it's called *Caves of Nonora*, and is set back in the underground era on Tare, where a bunch of kids finds a huge hidden kingdom of blue people beneath their island. A chapter conveniently seems to be Sen's staying-awake limit, putting her to sleep nicely, while Ys and Rye were totally fixated.

I've spent my whole life reading books. I vaguely remember Mum reading to me in our own bedtime sessions, and our house is practically a library. The way I think, the way I act, most of that's because of the books I've read. *Caves of Nonora* is Ys, Rye and Sen's first book and my voice was a little shaky reading it because I kept thinking about that, and about all the books which were important to me that I don't have to read to them.

The talent school building is at habitable stage, and they're going to move in children they've identified tomorrow morning, then hold an orientation session in the afternoon. It's not going to be anything like so controlled an environment as the Setari school – the idea is not to turn them into Setari, it's to make sure they have enough control of their talents to not accidentally set buildings alight – and if they have family their family will be living with them. The school will be connected to the Setari building through the medical section and kitchens, and is set further back from the lake, with its balconies looking mostly toward Pandora.

Since almost all of the Nurans have refused the interface, school is going to be a major part of Pandora for a while. KOTIS Command is hoping that eventually Tsana Dura and Tsana Ridel can take over, but until then it's going to have to be face-to-face classes, which will take up a lot of resources.

I'm worried about the school, unsure how Ys and Rye will be received. At least, because they're using the interface, Ys, Rye and Sen will attend only the physical and psychic classes, and will simply be supervised during the day while they do interface lessons.

Saturday, August 30

Away team

Fourth and Seventh were assigned to go Cruzatch-hunting in the Ena today. They started fairly late, well after lunch, but still aren't back. I was trying not to be fretty about it, but knew they were officially overdue when Lohn and Mara showed up to sit with me. It was nice to see Mara out of medical, and I talked to them for a while, but I was just fretting too much and asked if they minded hanging about while I wrote. They're watching a movie.

I'm climbing the walls, of course. Fortunately I didn't start to get really worried until after story time was over – there's no way I could hide the way I'm feeling from Sen. Ys and Rye are awake, but snug in bed lost in their virtual classroom.

This has been a day which began well, but slowly went downhill. Kaoren and I started out very happily making up for lost time, then having a fairly unresolved discussion on what to do when I'm sick to prevent him from having to suffer along with me. Neither of us wants to sleep in separate beds, but Kaoren said he'd think about a row of pillows in between us.

During the morning we had technicians in to reshape the kids' apartment so there's three largish single beds and a bit more privacy for them, but keeping them still in the one room. It cost them a chunk of their lounge room, but I think it works out well this way. It was a bit hard to gauge Ys and Rye's opinion of the changes, but Sen remains unreservedly positive about almost everything which we do.

This afternoon, though, after Kaoren had gone on his mission and we headed over to the talent school, Sen stopped being her usual chirrupy self. The identified children and their families had been brought over just after lunch and moved their sparse collection of belongings into their assigned rooms – the school apartments are similar to the Setari apartments, but with two or three bedrooms each. Then everyone gathered into a small lecture room, filling the rows of scoopy whitestone benches. There were more Nurans than I was expecting, about forty in all, a couple of them adults.

Nils, bruises fading, was playing my escort. I'm not altogether sure if I'm required to have a guard even in the talent school, or if he just tagged along out of curiosity. He seems to find the kids endlessly entertaining.

When we walked into the room there was a little flutter of suppressed reaction, but that was nothing to do with Ys, Sen or Rye and all about what I've started to think of as The Nils Effect. The squads are relatively used to him, but anywhere Nils goes – among civilians or KOTIS staff who don't see him day to day – The Nils Effect produces a mass wave of Profound Awareness of Nils. Even wrapped up in Kaoren as I am, there were a few times today when my heart suddenly started racing because Nils had leaned forward, or brushed my arm, or done entirely innocuous things which triggered PAoN.

The pinksuit in charge of the school handled her PAoN very well – glancing at us as we came in, going an interesting shade of purple, then carrying on as if Nils wasn't in the room. Except purple. We sat up back, with Ys and Rye between us and Sen between them, and all three were quiet and tense, not even paying attention to Ghost, curled in Nils' lap.

One of the Nuran Setari, a man called Serray, spoke first – all in Nuran, which I struggled to follow. But he was just explaining how this residence was different, that the primary focus was one of controlling their stronger talents. Some of the older children might already have received training within their houses ('house' seems to have been the major social structure on Nuri), but they would be given a review and further training to verify they had full control of their abilities. They weren't being trained to be Setari, but skilled talents would be useful in many aspects of Muina's development. Those family members who were here who did not have strong talents would also be offered talent training, if they so chose. All at the talent school, as with the rest of Nuri's survivors, would be receiving language and skills training, to allow them to find a role in Muina's settlement.

A girl down in the front row stood up then (this seems to be the Nuran equivalent of raising your hand) and when Serray looked at her, asked could they learn to be a Setari if they wanted to be. Serray (who doesn't have quite the same gravitas as Inisar, but is still a commanding type of person) told her that it was not the current intention, and that Setari must begin their training at a very young age to truly attain that status.

The whole question of what a Setari really is and how inadequate the Taren and Kolaren version might be is something everyone's danced around. Best I can tell, the Nurans approach the role of Setari from a spiritual viewpoint, and also start out with the focusing the connection to the Ena step which the Tarens and Kolarens skipped, and are now (so far without success) trying to relearn. The Nuran Setari don't seem to think adults have much chance at all of learning how to do it.

The first part of talent school orientation was to divide the Nurans into age groups for their physical classes, and take them on a little tour of the facilities, and then they all had appointments for individual assessment.

Dividing into age groups was where we hit our sticking-point. Everyone was supposed to rearrange seats so that the youngest were in the first row, next oldest in the second, the third would be Ys and Rye's age group, and the next the oldest of the kids and the adults. Sen latched on to Ys and Rye's arms and wouldn't go down and looked very much on the verge of a temper tantrum until Nils leaned over and whispered something in her ear. To my shock, after an uncertain look, she let go and obediently trotted down the stair.

As Ys and Rye followed, I asked Nils what he'd said, and he told me: "That she can't protect them forever."

Sen plumped herself down in the front row and immediately turned around to watch, a miniature mother hen all fluffed up as Ys and Rye reluctantly moved forward.

Almost immediately a girl in their age group saw them and said loudly: "Lianzrenar, aren't those servants from your house?"

I could only see the back of the head of the boy who turned to look at Ys and Rye, but I recognised him when he hunched his shoulders. It was the boy who'd been following Sen on the *Litara*.

"There are no servants here," he said, barely audible. I searched about for the woman he'd been with, but didn't find her.

"Are they supposed to be exceptional talents?" the first girl asked. "Or are they in the wrong place?"

"Ys, Rye, mine," Sen said, in a loud, annoyed voice.

The boy called Lianzrenar mumbled an explanation I couldn't properly hear and the (very annoying) girl who had started the fuss turned to Serray and the Taren pinksuit who was trying to clear up the confusion and said in an obnoxiously helpful voice: "They're in the wrong place. Just servants set to watch Fiionarestel's daughter, not family at all."

Of course, by this time I was down the stair, and dropped a hand on Ys and Rye's shoulders. They were so tense, and had adopted "the pose": hands deceptively loose at their sides, eyes fixed on nothing. Posture designed for absolute neutrality, neither cowering nor aggressive. It made me so angry.

I could see the pinksuit didn't need any explanations – I'm sure Ys and Rye's files have big flags on them because of their connection to me. I looked at the annoying girl, reminding myself that the kid had just lost her entire planet, probably most if not all of her family, and had no doubt been raised to believe that people really could be 'just servants'.

"Ys and Rye are here because they're my wards," I said. "There's no mistake."

The girl was disconcerted by this, but not ready to give up the fight, saying: "But–"

"You're the person whose statue is in the parade ground," interrupted another girl, the one who had asked about becoming a Setari. The Nurans' ID trace injections will show name and location, and told me the second girl's name was Karasayen, while annoying girl was Zelekodar. Karasayen seems remorselessly incisive, which wasn't exactly convenient for me. I've no idea exactly where she stands in the Nuran hierarchy of importance, but she was pretty totally certain of herself.

"One of them," I agreed, resignedly. I'm liking that statue less and less.

"They say that it was you who saved us all, but I don't see how."

"I saved Inisar. Inisar saved everyone else." Which is the most credit I'm going to accept for that whole situation.

"I'd heard Sentarestel was with the Setari, that her talents required special care," Karasayen continued. "And you're taking on her servants as well, to keep her feeling secure? That's very kind of you."

I shook my head, to stop myself from roaring at her for putting it that way. "No. I was simply very impressed by these three." I glanced down at the tops of Ys and Rye's heads, well aware that they hadn't relaxed at all at my arrival. "Practically alone of all who've come here, they had the intelligence to recognise the interface for the tool it is, and the courage to have it installed. I admire that a great deal." I looked back at the pinksuit, a woman named Truss Estey. "Sorry for the interruption."

"Not a problem." Estey took charge, telling everyone to sit down, and I gave Ys and Rye's shoulders a squeeze and went back to my seat. I probably would have stayed the entire afternoon, watching anxiously, but Nils steered me out of the room soon after, since I had another of my apparently inescapable medical appointments.

Nils didn't tease me, as I'd half-expected, but suggested I give the school a week to see how it goes, then left me to my blood tests.

There were no reports of upsets, and Ys and Rye seemed as usual when they returned. I've found Sen is a useful barometer of how the people around me are feeling, and her recovered chirpiness was a good sign, for all that Ys and Rye apparently wanted to not even be in the same room as me when they got back. They weren't able to resist the next chapter of *Caves of Nonora* though.

And I told myself that by the time I finished writing up what has happened today Kaoren would be back, and I was wrong, and I can't stand this. I'm going to ask if I can try visualising him.

Sunday, August 31

Overclocking

Maze and Tsur Selkie agreed to me attempting a visualisation, and the combined First and Second Squad and Tsur Selkie went out into near-space with me.

Nils tells me I'm going to have to start paying him babysitting, between the cats and the kids, but he was just teasing. Ys and Rye had at least gone to sleep – they're sidestepping the bedtime Kaoren set them by getting up really early and ploughing through a thousand lessons before breakfast.

Visualising Kaoren was easy, though it took more energy than I was expecting. I'm not sure if that represented the number of spaces of distance, the size of the space he was in, or another factor. It was some kind of river valley, with high rocky walls, and so large both Fourth and Seventh were travelling together – it looked like they were in for a long tramp. Still whole, though, and I sagged with relief even as fake-Kaoren turned to Maze, more urgently intense than I'd ever seen him on mission.

"Surion, we were drawn away and a gate sealed behind us. It's a trap, but not for us."

"Do you have a solid path?" Tsur Selkie asked, while First-Second Squad went all tensely alert and started scanning in every direction.

"None yet," fake-Kaoren said, and looked at me. "Drop the visualisation."

I was being a bit slow to understand, but have learned by now that he only uses that tone on me when he really means it, so reluctantly dropped the visualisation.

"Back to base, no delay," Tsur Selkie ordered, but at the same moment Maze said: "Threat," and so did Zee, and Regan added: "Multiple directions."

They'd been waiting in the surrounding spaces, at strategically chosen gates with a view of my testing area, and didn't emerge until they saw the visualisation. My people-detect does kind of work through gates, but not very well. Combat Sight doesn't at all, so there was no warning before there were dozens, maybe fifty, thickest around the gate back into real-space, but quickly zooming forward from every direction. Cruzatch.

"Caszandra, try to increase your connection to the Ena. Quickly." Maze was using his most even-toned captain voice, pushing me down to kneel beside my test chair even as the Setari contracted in a defensive formation around me, quickly enhancing in turn. "Kettara, Norivan, Light walls at first and eighth mark. Regan, Dolan, Fire at fourth and tenth."

The Setari snapped into action, setting up a hasty barrier of elements to slow the incoming charge. Cruzatch are very fast though, and most avoided damage, though at least couldn't go straight through. But there were still others coming through the gaps which couldn't be covered.

"Missiles," Maze said, as the nearest drew back their arms. "All Tel-Lev repel. Regan, bracket us with Ice, thick as you can manage."

I'm not terribly great at speedy reactions, especially trying to quickly do something which I usually need a calm state of mind to manage. The most I could do was close my eyes as the Cruzatch began throwing things at us, and send my senses out further and further, not trying to be calm, but just trying to sense anything alive out beyond the Cruzatch, as quickly as I could push it. It wasn't a good way to do it – I felt forced, as if I'd pulled a muscle – and the things going on immediately around me kept trying to pull my attention back – Maze's voice steady, flashes of heat and chill right near me. The Ddura hadn't been called in the last few days, but the near-space was still very clear of Ionoth, and I was really glad when I found a lone swoop. It felt like ages away, and then it just felt like one of a world of points of life, and I stopped properly being aware of what was going on around me, and only vaguely noticed that most of the points of life around me abruptly vanished, and then I got incredibly dizzy and had to draw back to myself and found myself still kneeling next to my test chair, but in a pool of water, and I felt like I was going to pass out and was coughing because of some acrid smelling stuff which Ketzaren was trying to blow away even while she was coughing herself.

Almost all the Cruzatch were gone, vanished, and only Ketzaren, Tsur Selkie and one of First's Kalrani spares, Az Norivan, were still on their feet. Regan and Lohn were unconscious and the rest had fallen, and were choking on the gas worse than me. Maze was right next to me, shaking and gasping and looking like he'd run a marathon. There were three Cruzatch still moving, hanging back at long distance, but unfortunately in the direction of the gate.

Ketzaren managed to get up enough of a breeze to move the gas away, but that didn't help with the dizziness, and Zee passed out instead of recovering.

"Spel, Norivan, we three will advance as quickly as possible and attack," Tsur Selkie said, after a quick survey of the Cruzatch. "If they split and attempt to make for this point, Norivan and I will return. Spel, you are to head as quickly as possible to the gate and call for reinforcement. Go."

His fingers brushed me as they went, and he blurred ahead of the other two, running all-out. Ketzaren followed, levitating Norivan along with her. As Tsur Selkie had predicted, the little cluster of Cruzatch split, one remaining to attack him while two came circling toward my location. Ketzaren dropped Norivan down to run back and obediently continued on toward the gate.

Enma Dolan from Second levered herself shakily to her feet as the two Cruzatch came at us, flying far more quickly than Norivan could run. She used Lightning, which was a mixed blessing since the enhanced ball she produced arced and spit so randomly that while one of the Cruzatch was zapped like a bug, it also meant that Norivan had to make a major detour.

Maze kept trying to get to his feet next to me, spiked out a nanosuit weapon, and then collapsed. I was feeling dizzier and dizzier – we'd obviously all had enough of a dose of the gas to be knocked out: it was just a matter of how long it would take for each of us. Setari trying to fight or use their talents while being all dizzy and on the verge of passing out are not safe people to be around, as I discovered when Norivan desperately threw a Light wall into the path of the remaining Cruzatch, and the thing appeared horizontally directly above us. She was damn lucky Dolan had collapsed by then. She did get the Cruzatch, though.

I guess the way my breathing slows down when I'm expanded is the reason I held on longer than everyone else. As Norivan dropped, I poked my head cautiously above my test chair and saw that the Cruzatch Tsur Selkie had been fighting (he has no elemental talents or nanoweapons, so had basically been kickboxing the thing) had decided to ignore him and come back and get me. Tsur Selkie fell down, and there I was, the only person still conscious, with one Cruzatch remaining.

I knew I had no chance of outrunning anything that flies, so straightened and formed one of the suit weapons. And the damn thing grinned at me, one of those Cheshire Cat smirks stretching over excessive amounts of its face. Annoyance briefly overtook terror, and I set my feet and tried to remember everything Mara has taught me.

Then I passed out.

But I got to see the cavalry arrive, right before I dropped. I'm glad I missed the next bit. The Cruzatch apparently grabbed me and made for the nearest gate – giving me yet another set of minor burns, this time from being slung over its arm. Fortunately only Cruzatch claws are super-hot, and so my nanosuit was able to mostways cope with the heat. Arad Nalaz from Squad

One saved me by simply using Telekinesis at the extent of his range to grab me back.

The gas kept us all unconscious for a couple of hours, but Maze, Tsur Selkie and I were the only ones actually injured. Tsur Selkie and me with minor burns, and Maze from the side-effects of using his Fire talent all-out while being extra-enhanced by me, which put a huge strain on his heart and caused some bleeding and swelling in the brain. So he gets lots of scans and monitoring for blood clots, and won't be on duty for a while, but I suspect he found some level of satisfaction in crispifying all but three of the Cruzatch in a fiery maelstrom of ultimate doom. The Ice he had Regan make was to protect us from him using his talent like that, the first and probably only time anyone's going to dare use an elemental while my enhancement is at max.

Fourth and Seventh couldn't find a path back to Pandora at all through the spaces they'd been lured into, but eventually managed to work their way to a different part of Muina. Fortunately there's much better satellite coverage now, so they could simply signal their location, and a ship's gone to pick them up. They should be here by dawn, and other than being really tired are completely fine.

Kaoren opened an interface channel to me as soon as he was in real-space – not a channel request, but using his Captain privileges to not have to wait a moment longer to say: "Are you injured?"

"No – not much," I said, and after that we could barely talk to each other. A few more short sentences and then we've just kept the link open and streamed our visuals to each other so we can see and not try to put anything into words.

And there is no doubt left at all that the Cruzatch badly want to get their hands on me. KOTIS Command has ordered the Ddura be kept in constant attendance at Pandora until they decide what to do (which means Ghost is in constant attendance on my lap). I'm sore and very tired, even with my drugged-out nap, but there's no way I want to sleep till Kaoren's here. Not long now. Zee's agreed to spring me from the infirmary.

SEPTEMBER

Monday, September 1

Reasons

Nils was asleep on my couch when Zee brought me back to my apartment, but she shifted him to the couch in her room, and I'd love to know what he felt about waking up there, or why Zee didn't take any of the many other couch options available. Zee is way too good at not giving anything away.

While she was gone I checked on the kids and found that Sen had climbed in with Ys, but they'd otherwise slept through. Zee came to look at them too, and told me she'd arranged for Mara to come make sure they got breakfast and off to class so Kaoren and I didn't have to worry about getting up in the morning.

I think I'm proving a pretty inadequate foster parent, and asked Zee if she thought I would do the kids more damage than good taking them in when both Kaoren and I lived such weird and dangerous lives.

"I should hope you asked yourself that before now," she said, but not harshly. "Would it have been better for them if you made clear that you were too caught up in other matters for them to be a priority? Have you discovered why Sentarestel was being pursued?"

"Korinal and Inisar think it likely that her Sights make her valuable enough to want to control – that some remnant of House Renar wanted her to regain part of the status they've just lost. Though at least she's apparently not anywhere near what would count as next in line to the throne of Nuri. The main candidate for that *is* in the talent school, along with one of the children from House Renar, and–" I sighed. "Anyway, I'm sorry First Squad has had to pick up my slack."

"Don't be – you're not alone in seeing something in that trio. And it's a refreshing change to deal with children as children rather than Kalrani."

I think the conversation made Zee sad, but I'm glad she sat with me and helped me stay awake until Kaoren arrived. A couple of months ago I would have been firmly encouraged to go to sleep, or kept sedated in the infirmary, but they've worked out that I've got a better chance of nightmare control if I wait.

Zee mentioned that it was lucky Seventh was the squad with Fourth and I guess that's so – whatever else Forel might be, she's determined to do her job well, and her squad has a massive amount of elemental firepower. Thanks to Seventh's strength, Fourth and Seventh paid for their marathon in the Ena only with exhaustion.

Kaoren ate and showered on the flight back and spent the rest of his time listening to me talk to Zee and getting through a fairly epic report so he was free to come straight to our quarters to kiss me breathless and examine the blue jelly bandages across my stomach and side, and let himself for a few minutes just be really upset that I'd been hurt and he hadn't been there.

Kaoren's such a very decisive and in-control person, and after he'd guessed what reason the Cruzatch would have for cutting off their path back to Pandora, he hadn't been able to do anything about it. For all of the long journey searching for a path through the spaces he'd had no way of knowing whether I'd been brought out to try to find the missing squads, and if there'd been the ambush he anticipated, and whether I'd been taken. Even once we were back together he couldn't properly speak to me. He'd had to stay cool captain in charge for all that time in the Ena, and he'd done that, but he'd wound himself so tight inside that he started shaking when he finally could hold me.

Neither of us were in a state to do anything but clutch each other, and my burns made it awkward even to snuggle together properly – they're comparatively minor, but I'm going to have to sleep on my back for a few days. We rearranged pillows, and Kaoren propped me up against his chest, and finally relaxed enough to pass out.

I'd only been asleep a couple of hours when repeated tugging on the hem of my pyjamas dragged me awake. I felt like complete shit, headachy and heavy and itchy hot and tender about the middle, and I'm sure Ys and Rye now have a very strong impression of me as not a morning person. It was Ys doing the tugging, while Rye stood behind her at the door, and I squinted at them blearily for a long moment. It was the first time they'd ever sought me out, so I wasn't about to just send them away, but I could have asked for better timing.

"You okay?" I asked – not very coherently.

"It wasn't true, what you said," Ys said. Firm statement, though with a suggestion of sword-at-throat. The first time she's spoken to me.

"Which thing that I said?" I asked, struggling a little more upright while trying not to disturb Kaoren. It's not often anyone could walk into our room without waking him.

"We had the machine in our head because Sentarestel told us to," Rye said, chin high. "Not because we understood what it meant. Not because of what you said."

I really wasn't up to two kids making what they seemed to think was a firing-squad confession. It took a bit of processing time, which I covered by glancing back at Kaoren, and discovering that my stomach really wasn't liking me doing anything stretchy. Then with some more cautious levering I managed to sit up.

"Do you always do exactly what Sen tells you to?"

"Sentarestel only ever tells us right things."

"So she told you to get the interface install because would let you learn how to read, and because you trust her Sight you did?"

They both nodded, as if it was a great admission of guilt.

"You were intelligent enough to trust Sen's Sight, and brave enough to do something new and strange on her word. How was I wrong?"

Ys looked stymied, and Rye near tears. "It's – you shouldn't–"

"I think I should," I said, standing up gingerly, but deciding it was a bad time to try hugging. "I see you and want you to feel you're safe and you belong. It's not complicated thing."

I headed into our lounge-kitchen, and set out breakfast just in time for Mara to show up. She gave me one of her assessing looks, and summoned a greysuit to give me a nice dose of painkiller. Kaoren half-woke when Mara sent me to bed after the greysuit's visit, but just rearranged us and went back to sleep until late afternoon.

I'm back in medical for a stomach inspection and entirely unnecessary brain scan, and Kaoren's off at a meeting which he tells me is about what to do about me. Lohn is keeping me company, and I guess I'm always going to have someone keeping me company from now on, even in the Setari building.

Having fifty Cruzatch come after me has made being babysat seem like a very minor thing.

I hope I said the right thing to the kids.

Tuesday, September 2

Settling In

One bit of good news Kaoren passed on when I was released from medical yesterday afternoon – they were able to find their way back to Muina because Par had succeeded in focusing his connection to the Ena. He's only able to do it in short bursts, but he can reliably enhance himself now. I went and found Par and hugged him, and he gave me one of his slow smiles, knowing exactly what I was thanking him for.

Kaoren's other bit of news was that my projection training in the Ena has been cancelled till further notice, which was no news at all. The possibility of ambushes, and the discovery that the Cruzatch can mess around with the gates, means that even the doubled Setari squads are going to be limited in the kind of missions they undertake.

Eighth and Squad One and one of the Nuran Setari went out to examine the gate which was blocked to try to figure out exactly what happened to it, and brought back a bunch of readings but no clear answer. The Ddura is going to be summoned to Pandora three times daily on a random schedule in an effort to prevent ambushes in the immediate area, and some greensuits will be permanently stationed at the amphitheatre to call it on a moment's notice. More drones will be set into near-space, to try to track any Cruzatch movement, and they're looking at some kind of breather which can be used to counter another gas attack (unfortunately our underwater breathers don't work out of water).

The dealing-with-Devlin meeting had been argumentative, with the senior KOTIS representatives disagreeing about what to do next.

"We have more pieces of this puzzle," Kaoren told me, "but as yet no way to put them together. Without any direction, we are left reacting instead of acting."

It's rare for Kaoren to let himself sound so frustrated, but a going-nowhere meeting on top of yesterday had really got to him. We are all pretty much running about like headless chickens, not even able to see a way to a solution.

The rest of the day was a complete contrast – determinedly focused on the business of resettling a world, which has been powering on despite the plots of burny floating people. When we took the kids down to the common room for dinner, the chatter was all strictly kept to the expedited intake of some of the approved settlers from Tare and Kolar, including a small group who are basically the newly-created 'Muina Broadcasting Corporation'. They'd arrived that morning and lost no time setting up, and even did an evening broadcast which the Setari all watched and discussed.

To a degree the 'MBC' is going to be a mouthpiece of KOTIS – they have some strict rules they have to follow while the settlement remains under military command – but they're otherwise independent and took a friendly, chatty sort of approach to their stories, which were mostly about the school structure and housing set up for the Nurans, and the progress of the construction of the industrial complex, the completion of which will truly make Muina independent, because so long as it's operating, technicians can with time, care and nanotech produce pretty much anything.

The MBC crew had also done a series of interviews with the people who had been selected for early settlement, and it was fun to see the mix of joy, ambition and nervous excitement the new arrivals brought.

I particularly enjoyed an interview with a family of Kolarens who were related to one of the greysuits working at Pandora, and were going to operate a store at the edge of the residential complex, close to Moon Piazza. It will be a mixture of café and trading post and luxury import service. Their hugely excited teenaged children seem to be founding members of the Raiten Shaf Fan Club, one of the girls announcing that he and all the other Setari (but especially Shaf) would always be given a free cup of fahr (a treacly tea) whenever they dropped by.

Of course all the Setari found this very funny, and teased Shaf about needing to take a bodyguard with him to save him from his fans. Kolaren Setari don't have an image shield, so are much better known on their home world.

After dinner Kaoren and I played an interface game with the kids. Many Taren games, particularly for children, have a big physical component – necessary when so much of their lives can be conducted sitting down. This one was a spelling game which created an overlay of plants and statues in our lounge room, and then hid letters all over the place, which you had to hunt and touch to spell words.

It gave the kids appropriate challenges for their learning level (basic letter recognition and 'cat' and 'dog' equivalents) and Kaoren incredibly complex polysyllabic words which he collected without an error, and me moderately advanced words which I kept almost spelling right but not quite. Even Sen beat me.

Ys and Rye are trying to return to not talking to us, but Rye slipped a few times, caught up with the game. After they were settled in bed, Kaoren and I sat on the grassy slope outside our balcony, listening to the sounds of the early evening out over the lake, and just being glad to be alive and together.

The kids are aware that I've been injured (Sen unceremoniously lifted my shirt at breakfast so that she could inspect my bandages), and we've been trying to set up systems to cover the times our routine is interrupted by emergencies. Kaoren created calendar icons and stepped the kids through viewing and interpreting our schedules. This was a pretty large conceptual leap for children from a sundial time system. Sen followed in only the most general way, but it was some measure of Ys and Rye's capacity that they were able to interpret the blocks of colour to discover that I had an appointment this afternoon (more medical), that Kaoren had morning and afternoon sessions (squad training) and that tomorrow both Kaoren and I are booked for almost all day (going to Kalasa). They can't read the explanations yet, but Kaoren showed them how to run a text-to-sound facility, producing a kind of frozen amazement as he put entries in their own calendars for school, story time, and bedtime and the interface obligingly read them out.

He also showed them how to use the Taren dictionary function – which combines nicely with the text-to-sound facility. Hard to imagine being so tremendously excited about a dictionary, but it briefly broke Ys' control: she was obviously delighted at having a book which told her the meaning of all the words.

This afternoon, after my medical session and Kaoren's training is done, we're going to go for a walk along the lake (with Lohn and Mara and Nils and Ketzaren, since Kaoren's not allowed to take me anywhere alone any more). I also want to take a trip up the river to see if I can work out roughly where I arrived from Earth, and Kaoren is going to try and arrange that, but says there might be resistance.

Wednesday, September 3

Cattiness

Really enjoyed the walk yesterday afternoon, although Lohn and Nils started asking me questions about my arrival here (ten months ago!), and then took great delight entertaining the kids with a highly coloured history of Cassandra Devlin. Ys produced some marvellously incredulous looks.

Mara hates being injured. Even Taren science won't let her shrug off massive blood loss, bite wounds on arm and side, and crushing fractures. During our mild walk I could see her tiring, and getting frustrated with herself, and Lohn watched her like a hawk, all the while pretending not to, so I guess he's under orders not to fuss. Sen provided a useful excuse to fly back – which is a pretty spectacular thing to do at sunset beside a lake. We endlessly confused a flock of ducks, and since Rye seems to be fascinated by animals, Nils kidnapped the kids to follow after them for a while, and brought three very pink-cheeked children back for a goodbye dinner for Second, who returned to Tare today. Nils took Ghost with him, and I'll miss them both rather a lot.

I can just imagine the reaction of those ducks. *Whatthehellare- Fly faster! Fly faster!*

I'm enjoying our new evening routine – we played a maths game this time, which was far easier for me than spelling, with Kaoren only just edging me out of first place. If I ever do beat Kaoren in one of these things, it won't be because he let me win. I told him I'd own him in a game of *Pictionary* and he had me describe what that was and that's what we're going to play later today.

I also dug out some of my bubble bath, which made it impossible to get Sen out of the bath until I pointed out that it would mean we wouldn't get through a whole chapter of *Caves of Nonora* before she was supposed to be asleep.

Ys and Sen bathe in their bathroom, while Rye uses ours. I generally leave them alone for it, but noticed today when I offered the bubble bath that Ys was being very careful not to let me see her back. It's hard to decide whether that's out of shame, or distrust of me, but it did mean I had to go into the lounge and take a lot of deep breaths.

Most of today Kaoren and I were at Kalasa for a multi-purpose assignment allowing the various recently-arrived Setari to be 'judged by Muina', and for me to do a very minor visualisation, and also to let this latest batch of Setari enhance while my attachment to the Ena is increased so they become aware of the mechanism.

The first task scheduled, though, was to bring down the shielding on the malachite marble building so they can run a new series of scans, and since they currently don't want me near it, I was given permission to go outside the city valley until they were ready to move on to the enhancement rounds. It's early Spring at Kalasa, and while Kaoren was with the group staring at the Green Stone of Possible Doom, the rest of Fourth took me out the valley gate, which opens high above the lake with a view down over sweeping slopes still patched with snow, but otherwise totally covered in wildflowers.

Snow and masses of flowers side-by-side were a new thing for me, and Fourth Squad were as interested as I was during the short walk along a newly-worn path to the research building which has been named after me. The mass of colours didn't have as strong a scent as I'd expected, but tremendous variety.

'Caszandra' (or 'Kaszandra') is an iceberg. A few small blocky buildings providing entrances, and quite a large complex below ground. Iskel Teretha, the pinksuit who was the head administrative person for the research station, took us on a tour, chatting happily about all the particular challenges they faced there – the island gets far worse weather than Pandora, and doesn't have a Ddura which can be summoned, so Ionoth are a regular occurrence. So they have all this gorgeous view but live underground and have to have an escort of greensuits to go outside the buildings, even with a Setari squad periodically coming out to sweep the island and near-space.

I spent the entire tour thinking in terms of Underground Science Complex = Evil Lair and trying to decide if it was more James Bond or Zombie Infestation. I did check out escape routes, but managed not to ask if the building had a self-destruct sequence, just as I manage (if only barely) not to say "You killed my father, prepare to die," on the rare occasions I get to introduce myself these days. It still bugs the hell out of me that all the jokes I'd worn thin with repetition back home are completely inexplicable here.

Though I have a cunning plan about that, which I must put into operation sooner rather than later...

Anyway, after a brief consultation over whether the greysuits had found anything poisonous about the flowers, I received permission to pick myself a glorious bunch of them (some of which I later gave to Mori, who looked like she wished she could be all non-professional on duty and pick some too).

My visualisation test was located in the empty building the technicians are using for headquarters down near the platform junction. They wanted me to increase my connection to the Ena, and then try to visualise the room at the time of the March of Dawn – and absolutely not the time of the disaster.

Having a bunch of people come and paw me while my mind is elsewhere isn't something I'm all that comfortable with, even with squads I don't dislike. I'd never discussed her with him, but Kaoren knows perfectly well that I could do without Forel, and that's probably why he told me beforehand that he'd be with me the whole time. And it looked to me like he sent the captain of Eighth (his friend Ro) to make sure all of Seventh stayed at a distance until my senses were fully expanded and I wasn't focused on how little I liked Forel around – and instead on the discovery that there's lots of little furry animals like lemmings or guinea pigs living in burrows on the island.

After attempting a little furry animal count, I followed flocks of birds until I started to feel vague at my centre, and withdrew back to myself enough to notice that a greysuit, Maze, Inisar and Kaoren were sitting with me, which was the signal to switch to trying the visualisation. For a few moments it felt like I wouldn't be able to do anything – my mind was so hard to focus – then instead of dipping into Kalasa's past I ended up creating a projection of the weird squiggly power things I'd seen while I was sleeping. I did it across the entire city for quite a while until I noticed that I had developed three greysuits instead of one, and it occurred to me to stop. I felt fine, but my brain activity, breathing and heartbeat had really slowed again, which means I get to spend all afternoon having blood tests and scans.

But the projected squiggles pleased the technicians, and overall it was considered a good result day. All of the Nurans passed Muina's judgment, which didn't surprise me at all. And Forel passed, which I guess is a good thing, since it was neither nice nor sensible of me to hope that she'd be the first Setari who failed.

But, bored in medical, I played back what the interface had recorded while my mind wasn't paying attention, and got an earful.

Kaoren had as promised stayed with me the entire time, and the Setari visited me in pairs to spend about a minute each touching my arm or hand and having the mechanism of the enhancement made very clear to them. Forel was the last to come, and shifted from a neutral, surprised comment about the mechanism to saying how much she admired Kaoren's ability to keep me calm, and that he was doing a fantastic job with me.

All Kaoren said was: "Cassandra manages herself very well."

"I have to admit I was surprised you went into this," Forel added, being all confiding and secretive. "Though you always were one to put the mission above all else."

I wish my eyes had been open so I could have recorded the expression on Kaoren's face. "If you've finished exhibiting your complete ignorance of who I am," he said, "it's time to move on to the next stage of this outing." Cold, irritated, bored. The very arrogant person he prefers not to be, goaded into making clear his disdain for Forel. She didn't say anything else, but laughed as she left, very smug and purry.

I don't know if she hoped I'd hear, or if she really believes Kaoren has been ordered to sleep with me. It's made me think a lot – not about Kaoren being in love with me, because I have no doubt that he is – but about how he behaves with other people. How he used to behave with me, when he was trying to keep me out. I remember that I used to think he wasn't a very nice person – not nasty like Kajal, but hardly brimming with kindness and goodwill toward all. There are very few people he takes a personal interest in, and for the rest he is either very professional, or doesn't care about at all.

I would be very much in the mood to do interesting things to Kaoren right now, except the medics bored with blood tests and started fooling around with the burns on my stomach again, and have given me a shot of something which makes me want to vomit.

Thursday, September 4

Into each other

Kaoren can draw. Really well – quick, effortless lines which immediately capture what he's trying to portray. I should have expected it, given what he'd told me about his family, and what I'd seen of his brother's work. When he chose to put all his energy into becoming a Setari instead of following his family's lead, it wasn't out of lack of artistic ability.

I was being very laid-back after dinner, thanks to floaty drugginess mixed with queasiness, and so reacted to Kaoren's skill only with a variety of pleased wonder, much as the kids did. Kaoren had had Ro Kanato create a random list of words which people from three different worlds and wildly different age groups would have a chance of drawing and guessing. It was a fun game, and Rye wasn't able to not laugh. Ys will be the hardest to crack, but she tried very hard with her drawings, and spoke when guessing Kaoren's, and when she and Kaoren won she went very pink (and extra-basilisky) when he told her well done.

It was only later, when we were trialing stuffing a large number of pillows between us (which lasted about half an hour until Kaoren decided queasiness was not enough reason not to curl up with me), that I worked my way around to asking him not only about how he felt about drawing, but also about Forel's comments.

"Do you think Forel really believes you've been ordered to sleep with me? Or was she hoping I'd hear and get upset?"

He went still a moment – his usual reaction to me saying something he didn't expect – then leaned forward to look at my face. Then leaned back.

"If I believed that comment was intended for you, she'd be on report right now, but it was very likely her attempt to rationalise a situation which unsettles her." He reached across the barrier of pillows to touch my hand. "You didn't feel a moment's uncertainty, did you?"

Kaoren looked rather wry when I explained that the possibility had occurred to me our first night together, but agreed that it would have been a particularly stupid move on his part. He wanted to know why I'd been so thoughtful all evening, if Forel hadn't upset me, and I told him I'd been thinking about how he behaves with the kids, and whether I'd changed him, or just given him an opportunity to be more 'himself'.

He wasn't really sure which better fit about how he felt with me, but he knows he is behaving in unexpected ways.

"I haven't drawn for years," he said. "I stopped completely during a home visit when I was thirty. That was such – it caused the rift between

Arden and I. But I needed to put it aside to follow this path, and I've not done more than take Siame to exhibitions since. Yet when you suggested that game, so sure that it was something I couldn't do—"

"Had to prove me wrong?"

"Anticipating your expression made producing a handful of sketches a strangely minor issue. I'm finding myself capable of more than a few things that I thought I could not devote time to, and I suspect what you've changed is my sense of proportion."

That was about the point he decided there were too many cushions.

Nothing much happening today – Fourth is out jogging again. But the medics tell me they'll leave my bandages off today. My stomach has this big silvery band of crinkling skin curling around my side. Tomorrow another trip to Kalasa.

Lessons

When the kids came back from 'school' today Sen was a bit hyper and over-energetic, so I asked what she'd been doing and found that since all the other children were having classroom lessons, my three were doing interface lessons in a study room all day (except for lunch). Ys and Rye are fine with this, but Sen has the Sights to be completely aware she isn't playing with real people, and thus isn't as responsive to the interface teacher.

I went and liberated a couple of balls from the Setari training rooms – a variety used for dodging practice – and though they were a little zingier than a tennis ball they were fine for handball. We played on the patio, marking a line with a scrape of mud. There was just enough room for a four-way battle, or two two-sided battles. I doubt I would have played there if Seventh were back from their Kalasa patrol, but it was just parts of First Squad in residence, and Sen really loved it when Maze played against her but down on his knees, especially since he always seemed to manage to hit balls she had a chance of returning. Lohn had a match with Rye and Zee played Ys. When the kids were tired out Zee, Maze, Lohn and Ketzaren had an amazing all-out battle. I've been playing handball since primary school, and they were all better than me in about five minutes.

When Fourth returned from jogging (all sweaty and tired – Kaoren's pushing their fitness again), Sen insisted Kaoren and Maze match up, which is something Kaoren would normally refuse, but even Kaoren isn't immune to Sen.

Maze and Kaoren were pretty evenly matched – both with similar speed and both with Combat Sight – and put on a spectacular display of blurring motion and long rallies. Maze had the advantage early on, but Kaoren eventually pulled even and probably would have taken the game if they hadn't decided to call it quits at ten points each. The extra anticipation Sight Sight gives him makes him very hard to fight.

Though I guess Maze is still recovering from mass Cruzatch burning. I hadn't been planning on dinner downstairs because Seventh would be back, but Zee opened a channel to me and asked me to keep the kids down. I wasn't sure why till I saw her watching Maze with Ys and Rye. Maze has been under so much stress lately, and I realised then that I hardly ever see him smile at all these days. Some things are worth putting up with Forel.

And it was hilarious watching Sen work the room as the Setari arrived back for the day. She thoroughly enjoys having lots of people around to charm – and she pleased me no end by seeming to avoid the people in Seventh who I'm wary of, but picking out the few who seem reasonable to introduce herself to. Her big thing at the moment is to go around introducing herself and trying to read the name display of the person she's talking to – she mangles their names pretty spectacularly, but almost deliberately I think.

Maze was far more successful at chatting with Ys and Rye than I've yet been, for all they still act like they expect to be punished for speaking in public (I have a horrible feeling that's because they *have* been punished for speaking in public), but you could hear the sheer pleasure creeping into their voices as they told Maze all about dictionaries and how you can look up an explanation of every word you heard, and the interface would even read it out to you. That the interface would read out whole books to you and that there were so many books in there that they hadn't even been able to reach the bottom scrolling down the first letter when browsing the list of them.

After dinner we played the spelling game again – and even in the past few days Ys and Rye have improved to the point where they know all the Taren alphabet and can manage most two and three letter words. After the game tonight Kaoren told them if next time they played they got a better score then they could ask for a treat of their choice, and they practically turned inside out trying not to look pleased. Though, given that the interface seems to be the greatest treat imaginable to them, I'm not sure what treat they might ask for.

Since they're able to use the interface to read for them, I was half-expecting them to have finished off the book I'm reading Sen, but whether they have or not they still listened as keenly. Sen's gone very snuggly, seeming to know that my burns have ceased to require pain meds and care, and insisted on two bedtime hugs during her story, and more from Ys and Rye between bath and story time.

I don't think they're ever likely to think of me as Mum, but they're starting to believe they're allowed to be here. I feel all over the place at times, jumping back and forth between world-saving and fumbling attempts at parenting, but in a way Mara was right – the kids are a great distraction for both of us – certainly for me, because not wanting to be all upset in front of them has lent me a certain amount of calm.

Friday, September 5

All Around

Rotten dreams last night. Over and over being kidnapped by Cruzatch – not too-real dreams, just straightforward nightmares, which are a lot harder to force myself awake from. Kaoren had nightmares too – probably communicated by me – and we figured we were most likely having a delayed reaction to the ambush. At dawn we gave up on bed and walked down to the lake (which is not strictly permitted for me at the moment, and I suspect even such a short trip meant Kaoren had to tell whoever was on watch that we were going).

It's not Kaoren's style to pretend that bad things won't happen, or that he has the power to make everything okay, and so we had a short discussion about wills and making arrangements for the kids in case something happens. He thinks it's important that they don't end up with his parents.

KOTIS Command will probably stop quivering in a corner soon and go back to more dangerous experiments, but today's trip to Kalasa was another attempt at visualising the past in the same room. Exactly the same result as last time, but I had the distinct impression that the device technicians really wanted me to make all the light squiggles anyway, since they were all having excited discussions about it when I came back to myself. One of the things the technicians had particularly wanted to see was how the light squiggles reacted to the malachite marble, and they found that the marble has its own set of squiggles, and seems to 'eat' any Kalasan squiggles that come near it.

It's pretty solidly accepted now that the malachite marbles were some secret construction related to the Cruzatch. Most of the technicians are of the opinion that the marbles interfered somehow with the platform and Pillar infrastructure set up by the main body of Lantarens and thus are the major cause of the tears between spaces. A smaller group argue that the platform and Pillars themselves would have still had the same effect on the Ena.

Plenty of theories, but no-one's come up with any solutions.

On the good news front, this afternoon Kaoren and I held a quiet celebration over the fact that he's started to be able to enhance himself. He can't do it as reliably as Par, yet, and has only told me. He says he suspects he's not the only one who's reached this stage, but because it's such a sensitive issue for the Setari, few are talking about their own efforts. He doubts all Setari will be able to achieve the enhancement – certainly not in the short term – but he thinks he knows why Par achieved it first. Just as my connection with the Ena grows stronger when I concentrate on everything surrounding me, it was the key Kaoren used to discovering how to focus his own connection. Path Sight and Combat Sight are a big aid.

Tomorrow is a rest day, and Kaoren plans to spend the morning off on one of the islands working on enhancement. But he's going to come back at lunch and take me and the kids (and a suitable escort, I guess) off to visit Pandora's first ever café.

Saturday, September 6

Out and About

I asked Raiten Shaf to be one of my escorts to the café, on the theory that the Kolaren family who runs it would be so distracted drooling over him that they'd not pay any attention to me. I don't think Raiten's very keen on being fawned over by fans, but he thought the idea of playing distraction was funny enough, and I ended up having an all-captain escort of Kaoren, Raiten, Maze and Ro. It still bugs me that I can't just go for a walk into town by myself, but it's getting better now that I'm on a first-name basis with almost everyone who gets assigned to guard me.

Ys and Rye had been in an odd mood all morning – pleased not to have to go to the school, I think, but also having some sort of argument whenever I wasn't around. Sen obviously didn't know what Ys and Rye were discussing, which put her out of temper with them, and she insisted on playing a game alone with me. I cheered her up by braiding her hair with ribbons, which she adored (and finally gave me something to do with them – Nenna had given them to me and I'm not a ribbon person and had just stuffed them in a pocket of my backpack).

It made Sen forget she was annoyed and she ran and fetched Ys and made her come and have her hair done the same way. Ys has quite short hair, a bit ragged and neglected, and I couldn't possibly do it in two long braids like Sen's, but I went and borrowed a pair of scissors and tidied it up a little and then did small, ribbon-bound braids holding back the sides. Ys endured this, and wouldn't even look at the result in the mirror.

Rye's hair I just neatened a little, and I did my own in a French braid ('assisted' by Sen) and found a Summery dress and felt good about myself. I've ordered more clothes for the kids, but am still waiting on delivery – and even with my lush wage I had to wince at the shipping charges, which are deliberately discouraging.

Still, we all looked very neat when Kaoren arrived back, and he obligingly changed to one of the few non-uniform outfits he brought with him. The other captains were also dressed not to stand out and I have to admit that I was almost as excited as Sen. Going out to the shops for lunch – something so normal and unremarkable for me on Earth – is more unusual for me now than flying, fighting monsters, or meeting world leaders.

Moon Piazza is quite a long way away from the Setari building, which is the far-flung southern point of Pandora, and so we had a nice walk to work up our appetites and arrived after what would count as the 'lunch time rush'. We had the option of walking through the science buildings (the university, as I keep thinking of it), or looping through the old town, and decided to go through the old town to gawk at the changes which were slowly being made to it. A small team of archaeologists had never stopped working, even after much of the attention had been diverted to Arenrhon and Kalasa, and now that the snow was finally gone the botanical types were having a field day exploring the gardens, so we'd walk through patches that looked exactly as it had been when I first explored the place, and then a stretch of houses where all the gardens and buildings had been painstakingly restored and preserved.

Today wasn't the 'weekend' for just the Setari, but for most of Pandora, since the settlement has shifted to a four days on, one day break cycle, and so there were people – children – everywhere. The old town drew them like a magnet – the other major point of interest being Moon Piazza, which had lots of kids playing ball games – most groups had some kind of adult supervisor and there were some rather harassed-looking greensuits patrolling in an effort to keep the more adventurous out of any of the uncleared buildings. It wasn't just Nuran children, but the long-serving KOTIS employees and the first wave of settler families, nervously picnicking on the lake's bank.

Not wearing our uniforms was reasonably effective at muting attention – though walking around with four seriously fit guys isn't exactly the best way to keep a low profile. Some of the gawking was down to me, some to Setari recognition, but much was down to ogling. Most of the Nuran kids, at least, had no idea who any of us were, and the Tarens and Kolarens simply stared or waved. Sen went into puppy mode, bouncing about, scampering off the path and bringing things back to show me or Kaoren. I ended up weaving all the flowers she kept bringing back into a little coronet for her, which she has yet to take off, crushed and wilted as it's become. Ys and Rye continued to act seriously worried about something, paying a good deal more attention to Kaoren explaining to the other captains his theories on enhancement than on the beautiful day around them. I didn't notice when they separated Maze out from our group – it was a quick sharp glance from Sen which tipped me off.

Sen is very much a sweet and joyful girl, but that doesn't stop her Little Miss Machiavelli moments. Rather than go and find out why Ys and Rye had dropped behind, she held up her arms demandingly and when I picked her up kept taking peeks over my shoulder. I exchanged glances with Kaoren, then decided to pretend I hadn't noticed. Ys and Rye's conversation with Maze took a good hunk of our walk, while I tried to decide whether it was a good thing they'd decided to talk to someone, or a bad thing that they didn't feel they could talk to me or Kaoren. It says something about how innately and obviously nice Maze is, that the brief conversation he'd had with them the other day had impressed them enough that they were willing to open up to him.

They looked inordinately relieved when they finally decided to catch up with us, took a few sidewise glances at me, then finally started paying attention to their surroundings. Sen wriggled to the ground and went and tucked herself between them, and I gave Maze a 'really need an explanation' look. He opened a channel with Kaoren and I and asked: "Have you looked at the news feeds this morning?"

I hadn't, but immediately looked, and could hardly miss the feature article titled: "Killing Caszandra Devlin". It was actually a pretty good article, discussing KOTIS' dilemma in trying to use me to find solutions to problems both major and minor. Because my talent set and connection to the Ena is so little understood even now, and yet so useful, they're torn between 'poking Devlin at it' and the repeated close calls I've had. The reporter had pieced together a pretty accurate summation of the injuries I've received since being rescued, which was impressive in a single list, and discussed the morality of almost inevitably getting me killed for the greater good.

"When did Ys and Rye get access to the main news services?" I asked, embarrassed not to have known. "That seems a little complex for the filtered, age-appropriate information the technicians described."

"It would fall in the 'challenging content' area for children in their early thirties," Maze said, shrugging. "It's the language differences which were causing most of the problem here – using a reader for a complex article in a different dialect. They wanted to know if the article meant that the leaders here were planning to kill you, and if you knew and had any chance of getting away." He gave me a wry smile. "They seem to have not wanted to ask you directly, since being marked for sacrifice would obviously be an upsetting thing for you to talk about."

"They don't yet talk to Cassandra because they fear that as soon as they accept being a part of our family, we will reject them," Kaoren said, frowning as he studied the kids' backs. "They've been taught that they have no value, and won't allow themselves to trust anyone treating them as important. But it's a good sign that they're becoming protective of you," he added to me. "For all we can do little to deny the dangers. I've found the steps we need to follow to ensure their care if we're both lost."

Maze, though he looked sad at the blunt pragmatism of preparing for the possibility of us dying, only said: "I suspect that you might find more than a few among First and Second who have taken an interest in their future."

I just wanted to hug them all, but settled for catching up to them to point out the tower I'd lived in – well off to the north – and agreed to take them there after lunch (a trip made much easier by having a Setari escort who could fly us there). We headed down the stairs to Moon Piazza, where many of the buildings in the bracketing half-circle have been completed, and the residential areas just beyond are far less raw and un-lived-in, more like a place which might be a living town. The interiors of the museum and the art gallery were coming together, and some of the fancier shops. The area beyond the Piazza particularly surprised me, since it had just been paths and residences when I'd last been here, and now there were several new buildings in places which had been reserved for non-residential structures.

The biggest change was a school just past Moon Piazza's outer circle – they grew an entire huge school in a week. Maze says there's actually four of them, spaced out among the sprawling residential sector (and that's still two thousand students per school – the closest one was for the oldest students). It's something of an open-air school because they haven't fitted the windows yet, and it follows the circle theme of most of the new structures in Pandora by being a full crescent shape, with rising smaller tiers going up five levels – once again merging with the slope of a hill. The circular school yard and the open part of the crescent face south so it will get a lot of sunlight during the day. Opposite the building is a much lower structure in the same shape – a huge two-tiered crescent around a lot of what will be flat, grassy areas once they finish removing boulders and bushes. This seems to have been designed as a 'youth recreation centre', with sections marked out as courts for different games, a small amphitheatre, lots of whitestone benches and tables, and – the entire reason for our trip – Pandora's first store and café.

The store part was larger than the café part, and still mostly unstocked – just whitestone shelving everywhere. The café had opened two days ago (with plenty of teething problems, but a lot of good-humoured support), and I liked it straight up because it was playing actual music – from speakers instead of over the interface. It just makes all the difference. Whitestone everything does lend a certain sameness to the décor, helped along a little by a gorgeous desert scape filling one long wall in the interface, and some decorations hooked on the wall above the servery hatch. There were also a seemingly random bunch of painted handprints on the other wall, but before I could get a good look at them the fifteen-ish boy (impressive in an ankle-length black apron) who was seating people saw Raiten.

He whooped, reminding me of when I visited Isten Notra's house, then reeled off welcometoMuina'sfirstcaféandpickanytableyoulike in a single stream of noise before turning and running into the kitchen. This was soon followed by a rather large crash. We all had to laugh a little at that, except Ys and Rye, who looked highly suspicious.

There were only a couple of tables which could seat a group our size, and we slid around one, ignoring the handful of other restaurant patrons, who were almost all openly staring. The tables were covered with the thin 'plastic' tablecloths which were the next generation along from flat screen computer monitors – Kolar's current level of technology. Each table cover was running a fancy patterned screensaver, but when we touched it, it shifted to a "Welcome to Café Crescent" message and then showed us menu selections.

Raiten recommended dishes, since most of the choices were Kolaren, and Sen had a wonderful time stabbing random selections and seeing pictures of food come up. I told her her eyes were bigger than her stomach, which sent her into peals of laughter (and Kaoren quietly cancelled most of her selections, and prodded Ys and Rye into picking something). We simply didn't look at the crowd of faces cramming into the servery window, and I appreciated that the staff didn't all come and squeal over us or anything, but instead carried out their usual duties except with a great deal of delight and huge, trembling smiles. The entire family took turns to bring us out glasses of water, and appetisers, and every serving separately.

It was definitely a good idea to bring Raiten along – he drew the majority of the attention, and I was able to concentrate on my lunch, and enjoyed my dessert almost as much as Sen (who enjoyed a bit of *everyone's* desserts). The café staff invited us to put our handprints on their customer's wall and write our names, and I glanced back as we left to see them all clustered around the wall comparing their hands to Raiten's print. He's a serious megastar on Kolar and I think it says a lot about how skewed my perspective has become that it's never even occurred to me to fan girl him.

After a quick glance at my still-sealed tower, we went to look at the island where Kaoren has been practicing his enhancement. It was well out into the lake, and big enough that you would need an hour or more to walk around it. Really nice trees – tall and black-barked with fat flower buds all over them, but no leaves yet.

A tiny waterfall ran from a spring on the small central hill, and we followed the stream which drained the pool at its base, paddling in the shallows. Rye was in his element, forgetting to be shy as he and Sen searched the water for fish, and spotted tiny flowers and the occasional fleeing animal.

A definite holiday day, and all four of my captainly escort were looking refreshed when we flew back to the Setari building. I'm feeling – I don't know – protective. Not just of three Nuran children, but all of them. Kaoren, Maze, Mara, Zee, Nils, Isten Notra, Tsur Selkie, my endless horde of medics. Every squad member. Planets' worth of people. Even Forel and Kajal.

It's too late for us all to skip off into unicorns and roses, crisis solved, no bones broken. Nuri's not coming back. But I just – yeah. I keep seeing the title of that news story. If fixing this means letting KOTIS risk me over and over in the hopes that they'll learn something before they kill me, I guess I'm going to do that. Maybe not the most heroic approach, but I don't have any better ideas.

Training with Mara tomorrow.

Sunday, September 7

Toughening Up

I continue to exhibit my lack of parenting chops by guessing the kids' ages totally wrong. I was reading through a comprehensive report provided by the school and found the age estimates according to their physiological development.

Sen I'd been right about – the estimate is twelve (four). Rye, though, is estimated as twenty-nine to thirty-two, and Ys as thirty-one to thirty-four. Ten to eleven, when I was thinking of them both as twelve. I can't imagine myself at ten (let alone seven or eight) having all the responsibility of looking after a little girl. I so much want to find out more about them, to know how they ended up with only each other, but I think it's going to be a long time before they're at ease enough with me to talk about things like that.

I think they're a bit like I was when I was first assigned to Fourth Squad, starting to feel like I fit in and happy to be near Kaoren, but knowing that I'd eventually be transferred, sure that I was just an assignment to him. Except for Ys and Rye it's a thousand times more uncertain. They do like being read to, though, and the routine Kaoren's established continues to please them.

We finished the book I'd been reading and I've asked Rye to pick the next one.

Fifth and Eighth were swapped out for Sixth and Ninth today, and tomorrow is another starting people with self-enhancement session, and also an attempt to visualise the location of any other malachite marbles. Lacking any clearer direction, KOTIS has decided to make establishing malachite marble numbers and locations their highest priority.

I spent my day at Mara's mercy, while Fourth was off doing more intensive training. Mara's working getting my fitness up into her rehabilitation (and Lohn's given me strict orders to wimp out and have an attack of vapours whenever it looks like Mara's pushed herself too hard). She's a lot better now, though, and could probably have run rings around me, but instead focused back on the basic combat stepping exercises, and then amusing herself throwing balls at me. We had lunch together sitting on the hill roof of the Setari building. It's become a favoured spot already and someone's put a couple of whitestone benches up there under the cluster of trees which survived a building growing beneath them.

Our visit to the café had sparked some questions about the three children who'd been with us, which in turn led to a wide range of news stories, the worst of which was about over-pampered me treating traumatised Nuran children like dolls. And yet another irritating expert talking about my isolation, and coping mechanisms, and how I was plainly trying to create a sense of stability and normality by building myself a family.

Fortunately there were also a lot of broader articles on how the mass of Nuran children were adjusting, the weight of the loss they would continue to feel, and the percentage which had been – officially and unofficially – made part of Taren and Kolaren settler families.

I was skimming some of the nastier articles when Mara said: "Nominate Lohn and I as replacement guardians."

Since Mara hadn't seemed to approve of my connection with the kids, I had to hide my surprise. "Maze told you we're making wills?"

She nodded. "I'd like to pretend that you needn't think about such things, but it's only sensible. And I'm..." Her mouth curved in a wide, bitter smile. "I'm so jealous I could strangle you."

There wasn't any bite to her words – thankfully – so I only panicked a little, then slapped myself mentally and said: "Because you..." then paused, thinking it over. "Would you still be in the Setari if Maze wasn't?"

"No. Or – perhaps. The situation has changed and retirement is out of the question until this crisis is over. But these past few years, since Helese, we've stayed because we couldn't walk away from Maze. Which means putting our lives – so many things – on hold because the cycle of rotations and training and injuries leaves no time or energy for anything else. Even though I'd hardly want to be in your position, I'll take leave to resent you just a little for the way those three have come to you."

"I hadn't even thought–" I began, then blushed and said, "Sorry. And thank you. It really helps to know you'll be there for them."

Then I asked her what the crisis being over – 'winning' – would mean to the Setari program, to all those kids who've been living rigidly strict lives so they could grow up and kill monsters. What would they do if the monsters weren't a problem any more?

Mara just gestured around her and of course the answer was completely obvious. And the way she smiled as she looked out over the lake was a proper Mara smile – warm and thoughtful and sure.

Monday, September 8

Secession

Last night (or just before dawn, rather) about a hundred of the older Nuran kids and a couple of the adults decided to leave Pandora. They took a bunch of tools from the old town gardens, and also a bucket of unformed whitestone, and went off north along the lake.

KOTIS Command knew straight away, of course – even before their ID tags flagged that they'd gone out of the town zone. But they simply informed the Nuran Setari, and Korinal and Inisar went for a talk.

Except for a lone ten year-old who they considered too young to make this choice, and who is now ensconced in the talent school to make it easier to keep an eye on her, the two Nuran Setari made no attempt to bring the group back. Instead they pointed out the Ddura's usual range (which is about four days' walk if you could keep to a straight line, and means I either was walking in circles or was very very lucky) and gave them an emergency beacon which they could use if they wanted help returning to Pandora. Not for if they just wanted to call for help, mind you – only if they wanted to return. It was how the Nurans decided to handle it, and nobody is sure if it's the right thing to do or not.

KOTIS held off making an announcement about it until mid-afternoon, saying its position was simply that it wasn't in the business of holding people against their will.

There was a lot of back-and-forth discussion in the Setari common room about whether the splinter settlement would make a success of it, and why they went (not liking to be told to go to class and learn Taren reading and writing seems to have been a major factor, though it sounds like a few of them would have left no matter what). Muina's a lot easier to live on than Tare or Kolar, but it'll be a huge challenge compared to being looked after in Pandora.

Lohn asked me what I thought, being the resident expert in wilderness survival on Muina.

"Huge disaster," I said.

Inisar (who, like all the Nuran Setari, tends to keep his opinions to himself and just listen to these conversations) asked me why.

"Because you had to tell them how far Ddura's protection extended. Whoever is leading them is idiot if he didn't find that out before they left. And if idiot's making decisions, they'll keep doing silly things. I don't understand point of building settlement a short flight from Pandora anyway. Wouldn't it have been more sensible to demand be taken to one of the other platform villages, and re-establish it? It's like they don't really mean it."

"Their intention was for us to force them back," Inisar said, with the faintest nod. "There are two who wish to have a stronger voice in our decisions. A subsistence existence is not what they desire, nor would it preserve our culture and values as they claim to want. The young among them who are angriest at the new conditions of their lives would have been infuriated if they were brought back against their will, increasing support for those who drove them to this move. We will post one to observe them secretly, although it is not a good use of our resources, and protect them if absolutely necessary. Any return which is not entirely of their own choosing would create a true fracture."

I could see that Maze and Raiten had already known this, and Kaoren as usual looked wholly unsurprised. But even Ys and Rye didn't so much as blink, so I asked them about it later after I'd finished the first chapter of the (long and dramatic) story Rye chose to have read next.

"Some at the school were talking about it today," Rye said, after a glance at Ys. "They said the same thing."

I didn't ask any more, but it's silly how pleased I was that he answered me.

Otherwise, a fairly uneventful day. Rather than go to Kalasa, they had me expand my senses and attempt my visualisation in a test building they've created for me here (a bit inland from the Setari building and well away from any other building). Sixth (the squad who lost one of their members during the Pillar retrieval) and Ninth (all happy and relaxed now Anya's just a bad memory), filed through and then I brought my senses back and tried to visualise malachite marbles. I did that fine, but only the two that we already knew about – easily distinguishable from the KOTIS monitoring equipment.

Since that didn't work they're going to fall back on aerial surveys looking for more installations like Arenrhon, since the book Inisar gave me talked about 'a number of' underground dwellings. The Setari squads and the Nurans are going to scout using Path Sight. Inisar says that his Telepathy doesn't allow him to hear the Ddura from real-space, so I'll probably get to go on these missions to see if I can reproduce my tracking of Arenrhon.

I'm looking forward to the missions – my two fave squads and lots of touring and exploration.

Tuesday, September 9

Wounds

Training with Mara today involved handball in the morning (on a newly-created patch of whitestone specifically marked out for handball games). Mara says she sees no reason why I shouldn't be able to dodge balls if I can hit them, and even though one of her arms is still strapped and healing, she practically had me dodging the balls playing with her – hard, fast games which left me panting.

After another rooftop lunch, and a quick tour of the nearby trees to look at the flush of opening blossoms (mostly white tipped with pink, like the first flowers, but a variety of others, including purple and a vivid orange), all of First worked out in the gym. A really hard session for me – lots of repetitions and different machines to use, but enjoyable in a way because I haven't completely lost what little condition I've gained and so didn't die from it immediately.

Mara and I both had a session in medical after that – me for the first cosmetic work on my stomach (which means I spent the rest of the day queasy and dozy) and Mara to gauge the recovery of the muscles in her arm and side. The tooth mark scars are seriously spectacular, and I could hear the medics giving her a lecture about stressing the recently-healed wounds too much.

Sen, trailed by Ys and Rye, showed up while I was getting new bandages applied, anxious to tell me that all sorts of boxes were sitting on the floor in our quarters. I told them they were for them, just some clothes and supplies, and did my best to act like it was nothing special. Of course, that didn't stop Sen from being giggly with delight, nor Ys and Rye from being extremely withdrawn and doubtful. It was mostly clothes, and a selection of shoes, and some hair things and bubble bath.

I was so out of it from the medicking session that I just lay on the couch drowsily smiling as they unwrapped it all and worked out what was meant for whom. Fortunately Mara had come with me, since I fell asleep until Kaoren woke me.

We ate in our rooms, and then played the spelling game, and since Rye beat his previous score (Ys technically won the game, but came even with her previous score, and Sen was wildly silly), Kaoren told him he could choose a treat and Rye asked if we could go visit the island again, so that's what we're going to do the day after tomorrow and if it's a warm day we'll give the kids their first swimming lesson since while Nuri might have had rivers and streams, swimming apparently wasn't common. Talking about swimming prompted one of my rare recommendations to KOTIS Command, namely that eight thousand children and a lake was going to be trouble in Summer. The bluesuit I spoke to told me they'd look into it.

Since my drowsiness wasn't going away, Kaoren took over story reading duty for the night, and I sat with Sen and fell asleep and now of course it's the middle of the night and I've just woken up.

Wednesday, September 10

The Plains of Telezon

Really enjoyed today, even though we didn't find what we were looking for.

It started out well, too, with Rye asking questions over breakfast – some of which I suspect Ys was feeding him over the interface. They both get up really early and read the news feeds – which sure isn't something I ever did at ten – and there'd been a big story about Mesiath, which led into a nice little discussion about the handful of settlements on Muina.

Sen, after insisting I do her hair, briefly appeared in one of her pretty new sun dresses, but re-emerged later accompanied by Ys and Rye, all three in the standard-issue clothes that all the Nurans have. I should have thought of that – the teachers would let me know if there was any open hostility, but I'm sure Ys and Rye are doing their best to keep a low profile about the unexpected privileges of their new life. The Kolaren clothes work as a kind of school uniform, I guess.

I'd bought Kolaren hats for all of us, and sunburn cream, and presented Kaoren with his during the kids' bath time. He'd tried it on agreeably, but said that the Setari uniform was being reviewed for out-of-Ena work. And this morning, when all the squads met up before the mission, Maze gave us a new suit configuration, one designed for warm-weather travel rather than fighting in the Ena. The black nanogoop obligingly reformed into light cream and grey cloth, tight-fitting only around our feet, chest and forearms (to support suit weapons), with wide hoods we could pull up to keep off the sun. The cloth is a layered loose 'weave' designed to breathe, and the overall effect is similar to the formal robes Tarens wear to weddings.

I knew the nanosuits could simulate different textures, but I wish they'd told me earlier that the nanoliquid can change colour – not to mention I wish I'd thought of a hood when I was in the desert turning into a lobster. The Kolarens have started using the nanoliquid uniform when they're based at Pandora, and seeing all three worlds' Setari in cream and grey made me wonder if they would think of themselves as Muinan Setari, or whether they would have preferred a way to set each other apart.

I had a ton of trouble paying attention to the mission briefing because it had occurred to me to picture the Setari all in a different coloured uniforms, and perhaps flying giant mechanical lions. The possibilities of anime costume transformations opened up to me, and it was only through an Act of Sheer and Implacable Willpower that I didn't drop shrieking to the ground in the middle of the briefing because the mental image of Maze pirouetting gracefully and ending up in a *Sailor Moon* outfit was just...

So, anyway, it's lucky the mission was non-complicated – we were simply to go to one of the platform towns and cast about in a large spiral trying to path find marbles, Cruzatch, other platforms, etc. There's a limit to the distance which Telekinesis and Levitation talents can haul about their entire squads, so if there's no result within their range out of any of the towns they're going to have to do the same exercise using shuttles and just cast further and further.

Muina is, I think, a little bigger than Earth, with the land and water more mixed together, and there's just no way even a dozen squads would be able to effectively scan more than the tiniest part of it. But the platform towns give us a starting point, and it will handily combine with useful survey work, and – mainly – there's no better suggestions.

Since the areas around the platforms are relatively safe, most squads are going single with a Nuran or two to keep them company. First and Fourth are going paired each time, plus Inisar, because they're taking me with them. Maze is back on duty (though Zee was monitoring him for strain) and only Mara was left behind.

Our first assignment was at a place the old maps call Telezon. A rare town not planted on a lake, it was surrounded by golden grassy plains crossed by a winding, twisting river in the centre of the largest land-mass.

The grass had recently set seed in plumes of purple and white which scattered like dandelions puffs whenever the wind took a punch. And all of it was completely seething with small birds and massive dragonflies, as we discovered when we set down for the first time and ten million grass-gold birds took off in a storm of wings to give a Midas touch to the sky.

We couldn't fly about constantly – we went out on a long curve from the village, then set down to walk along by the river so our 'wings' could recover – with some extra recovery time needed for the collective heart attack given by Huge Bird Mass. After that we flew some more and walked some more and found birds and bugs and three different kinds of probably-native predators – including a gold lynx-sized cat which sprang vertically out of the grass to snatch a bird out of the air – but no Evil Lairs.

It was a full-day assignment – we brought lunch with us and left at that time zone's sunset, reaching Pandora early afternoon. All I had to do was listen in case I heard the Ddura in any other direction than the town, which I didn't, so the day was pretty much a tourist trip to me.

Mara was on the patio playing handball with the kids when we all trooped in, sweaty and slightly sunburnt despite our best efforts. We were the second group back and as we headed to our rooms for showers Mara told the kids to help her and the support staff bring out dinner, and I was pleased and relieved when they reacted positively – not as servants, but as accepted members of an extended and very unusual family. Kaoren and I had a cold shower together, and then a hot one, and then we all watched a second sunset.

None of the squads found any malachite marbles, but the day did wonders for my morale. I was, in my usual self-absorbed way, mildly suspicious that this series of 'light' assignments was the result of a few "Stray's mental health" reports recommending a break after the Cruzatch attack, but I overheard Maze say to Zee that he wanted to rotate more of the squads who've been working the rotations on Tare through, and gave myself a mental kick up the ass for overlooking a hundred or so other people who could use a day in the sun.

Thursday, September 11

Family Outing

Today started out with a near-argument with Kaoren, who'd made an appointment for me to go to medical to have my bandages checked. I'm not supposed to get them wet for long periods after a cosmetic treatment, so yesterday's long shower and the idea of a swimming trip had been worrying him. I told him I didn't think it was necessary, and he paused, then said: "It isn't a request, Cassandra."

He meant, of course, that it was one of those times when his job and our personal life were in conflict – he *has* to be bossy about my health, and I knew that but I still snapped "Fine," and stomped off with a complete lack of grace, and then hated myself and sent him a "Sorry, not your fault," text.

He texted back, "~~Improbably sweet~~. :) "

Tarens have immensely complex emoticons and I'm less surprised that their smiley face is much the same as our smiley face than I am that Kaoren would use one. He made me laugh, anyway. Next time I consider having a hissy fit because I've been sent to medical for the thousandth time in the last ten months, I'm going to remind myself that for the Setari, medical has been a constant through their entire *lives*. Years and years of scans, bruises, strains, and broken bones. That's part of what being Setari is: a necessary part of honing yourself into a weapon. All that even before they start fighting monsters.

Of course my good intentions wavered when Ista Temen tut-tutted the idea of going swimming, took off my blue goop bandages and said the new skin was in a fragile state. But I must have produced a particularly effective Sad Puppy Face, because she decided she could 'seal' the treatment so long as I stayed in medical a few hours for monitoring. After a full dose of fortifiers I slept until just before lunch, but then was fortunately cleared to go. My skin is vividly pink and tender, and terribly sensitive to temperature, but no bandage.

Currently Kaoren's not allowed to take me even a short flight away without additional guards – I have to have a handful of Setari within 'immediate response' range – but First Squad made it all a very picnicky kind of guarding. We brought along big hampers of food, and then split up before we ate it – swimming lessons at the central pool and First Squad on the shore of the lake within range of a quick dash. We could occasionally hear the echo of conversation or a splash, but otherwise it did feel like just me and Kaoren and the kids alone on a family outing.

The day was very sunny, but humid and heavy – perfect for wanting to get in the water. We walked about the hill, examining the way the spring welled up, and spotting pippins among the tree roots and some small blue wren-type birds building nests, and then went down to the pool to swim and escape pestering insects. I'd gone for a lycra shorts and t-shirt look for my swimming outfit. I'd just feel way too weird parading about in a bikini, even if I could find one and didn't have a very strange-looking stomach. Similar clothes for the kids, at least in part to avoid the question of exposing the scars on their backs. Like most of the other Setari, Kaoren was wearing the nanoliquid swimming outfit for a just visiting from the Olympics vibe.

Swimming has been a big part of my life, and watching Ys and Rye grasping the basics of dog paddling made me feel like I was on Earth, and I had to work to not look too goopily teary as they swam back and forth between me and Kaoren until they were comfortable enough to keep themselves up without panicking. Sen was the most nervous of the three, surprising me since she loves baths so much and is so generally brave. She wouldn't go out of arm's reach, and a nose full of water sent her clinging to me, but she was happy enough so long as one of us held her.

We moved back into the shallower water to give them a rest, and I told them about how Australia is the largest island on my planet and that most of the people live around the edges of it, and almost everyone learns how to swim there because there's so much coast and it gets very hot. And then I told them about the people who go swimming across the English Channel, all covered in Vaseline, and about scuba diving and krakens and mermaids. Just like when I was explaining volcanos, the difference between what's real and not-real about Earth exists in a strange land of could-be because I'm the only person who's been there. I was highly tempted to try and convince them mermaids were real – would it really be so different from telling little kids Santa Claus is coming? Or tourists to watch out for Drop Bears?

I think Sen would know, though.

That thought made me open a channel to Kaoren to ask how to lie to a Sight Sight talent – or, more to the point, how the people behind the conspiracy on Nuri ever managed to hide what they were doing from their Setari.

"Embed the lie behind a lie," Kaoren said. "While it's not unusual for Sight to reveal that a person is lying, it is rare that Sight can convey the truth behind the lie. The Nurans saw deception aimed at political gain, and very likely were rarely given a chance to closely question the conspirators. Half-truths can also work – the power stones *are* shield generators. That is true enough to hide whatever else they can be used for."

Ys and Rye were the most relaxed with us they've been so far – not totally without their guard up, but Rye is more and more willing to ask questions and Ys at least spends less of her energy glowering. During their second session, paddling about became less of an ordeal and more of an adventure and they had a little dog-paddle race over to the scary deepest part of the pool by the hill, and then back to us. And their eyes went huge when Kaoren said that next training session that fell on a hot day, he'd see if

Fourth Squad could swim from the Setari building to the nearest water landmark, Tupal Rock, which is much closer than 'our' barely visible island.

The pool is cool and shady, all dappled light and the occasional drifting leaf or flower petal, so when the kids started to get tired we went out to the sunnier lakeshore to join First Squad. They'd also been swimming – and were talking about bringing breathers and goggles another time so that they could look to see what the lake was like under water – and our arrival was the signal for lunch, which was tasty and sumptuous, and we all lay about basking on big black rocks to digest and chat and watch the truly spectacular number of birds wheeling over the distant northern bank of the lake. A couple of thin spirals of smoke were visible, further west than our island, and Maze confirmed that the breakaway group had stopped walking on the second day and set up camp near the ducks nesting on the north shore. When storm clouds started to roll in we all felt thoroughly sorry for the Nurans, but of course there wasn't much we could do but collect up all our scraps and head back to Pandora.

It was a serious storm, breaking in late afternoon – it's been a while since we've had any really rainy weather – and we watched the lightning and the sheets of rain with wincing sympathy from the safety of our snug apartment. We've had no specific news on how the Nurans are doing, though one of the Nuran Setari is always off watching them.

Another platform town exploration tomorrow. We'll resume training every second day once the initial survey has been done on all of them, but all-day flying is too energy-intensive to not schedule in lots of rest days.

Friday, September 12

Nursery rhymes and fairy tales

Kaoren woke me earlier than usual this morning, and held a hand to my mouth so I wouldn't say anything, murmuring: "Listen."

So I listened, and heard singing: "Thiz li'l piggy had roass biff. An thiz li'l piggy had non. An thiz li'l piggy wen wee wee wee all the way hom!"

Ys. And then Sen, giggling with hysterical delight, just as she'd done last night before story time when I'd been playing silly games with her. I'd sung it in English first, then translated the words, but Sen had vastly preferred the English version.

"Did she log it?" I asked Kaoren.

He shook his head. "They don't have that function yet. This is from memory."

Ys moved on to 'Inzy Winzy spida', and then 'Rown an rown the gar den', her pronunciation off, but word perfect each time, for all that I'd only repeated each rhyme a couple of times the night before.

"They were beaten for eavesdropping on the lessons of the household's heir," Kaoren told me, and when I glanced sharply at him, added: "A Sight dream. There was no reason for the ban, no law among Nurans that servants should not learn more than how to serve, though it is unusual for them to aspire. The master of the house was cruel, and saw how much they wanted, and so took pleasure in denial. That was my dream – from the master's point of view, enjoying giving the order."

He had to squeeze me for a while, caught between revulsion and fury. It's rare that Kaoren has Sight dreams now, but when he does they're particularly strong, and all day today I could see the shadow of it on him. And he's furious, because the two of them are so very smart, and someone thought it fun to hurt them.

When we made a noise, Ys immediately stopped singing, so we went out and pretended it was just another morning. Over breakfast our explanation for why we'd be later back today led to a discussion of time zones and planetary rotation and we spent a lot of time in a shared space showing them my log of golden plains, and looking at a gorgeous room-sized image of Muina, pointing out the locations of where we were now, where Kalasa was, where we'd been the day before yesterday and where we were going tomorrow. Kaoren showed them how to zoom in to locations, and different interactions they could do with the globe – and then gave them an exercise to locate and view the two other towns we were scheduled to visit, which made me laugh at him and call him such a captain. But the kids loved being able to make the connection between our calendars and the planet, and just looking at different places in the world – particularly the immensely detailed aerial view of Pandora and the live views from numerous scanners which have been placed around the lake and town.

The storm had died away to another muggy morning, but our mission location was Firiana, a town on the largest of a series of small islands in the next big lake to the east. It was cold and raining there, a constant heavy downpour which didn't let up for the entire long day. It wasn't all bad – our hoods were happy to be waterproof and we adapted our uniforms to be partially Taren Setari and partially Muinan Setari and so were quite snug. Just constantly a bit damp.

The islands were home to a lot of long, slender furry seal-things with an odd resemblance to Afghan Hounds. And bigger 'lake serpents' which appear to be the sharks of this world (and fortunately don't live in the waters

Pandora borders upon). They're about ten metres long, furry, and have a touch of Luck Dragon about them. Possibly they're relatives of the seal-dogs, but much larger and toothier. All the Setari developed rather odd expressions when we found the seal-dogs, and when we stopped for lunch Glade told me old Taren-Muinan stories about benevolent creatures called 'surri' which would rescue people who'd fallen in the water, and which they'd thought were mythical. Today would be like me finding a flock of griffins roosting at Bondi.

After a long, wet day we reached Pandora a little behind schedule – past sunset – to find Sen fretful and worked up. She'd refused to let Mara read the next chapter of the current story, though she'd been happy and cheerful up to that point. Ys was watchful and withdrawn, and Rye seemed simply relieved that we were both in one piece. Teaching the kids the clock and calendar means they know when we're late.

My solution was to show them how to send us emails and voicemail, explaining that at least when we're on Muina, if they need to ask us a question then sending an email is a good way to ask without worrying about interrupting us with a channel request. But I should have thought to send them one, before 'late' became an issue. This Mum thing has a huge learning curve.

After story time was over, Kaoren and I had dinner with Lohn and Mara and discussed our mutual interest in the kids. I squirmed a little because it was so clear that they'd both been aching to have children for I don't know how long, and it wasn't till Mara had spoken to me that I'd even thought about their feelings. Lohn is already completely wrapped around Sen's little finger, and proud as any Dad about how quickly Ys and Rye are progressing with their lessons. And relieved, I think, that the kids are distracting Mara from her frustration at being on sick leave.

Despite bedtime fretting, Mara said it had been a good day. "When I checked on them at lunch it looked to be a drama because they'd been playing with the Muina map, only to be discovered by the other students. Since to those without the interface it looked like three children standing in an empty room pointing at nothing, that not surprisingly produced a little spate of mockery." She caught my eye. "And Ys and Rye reacted as you described, that self-erasing pose, not even trying to explain. Sentarestel's attempts to defend them were not entirely intelligible – she has something of a temper, you've noticed? Fortunately Squad One hadn't left yet, so I called down Diav and had her use Illusion to show the rest of the students what Ys, Rye and Sen had been seeing."

Mara's smile took on a wicked edge. "I probably shouldn't have enjoyed their reaction so much, but one of the more opinionated students has been arguing against any suggestion that they consider the interface. What point tainting yourself, she's been saying, when the handhelds will do the same thing? That map is a wonderful counter-argument. The girl did, rather feebly, try to suggest that a bigger screen would produce much the same result. Here."

She gave me a log of the scene, and I can't stop grinning at the image of Rye, pink-faced but determined, lifting his head to say: "It's nothing alike. It's a narf to a tarena. Using those little boxes is like crawling in the mud."

A narf and a tarena are – were – apparently two Nuran animals, the equivalent of comparing a slug to an eagle.

"He sounded sorry for them," Mara added. "I think that's what clinched it. We've abruptly gone from only your three here with the interface installed, to a mere six holdouts in all of the talent school – and by the afternoon the other four schools were logging a handful of requests as well. It's not so big a shift there, but it's the most progress we've had since the initial processing. Those in leadership roles recommending the change didn't have nearly as much effect as pity from what these children consider their social inferiors."

I bet it was that Karasayen girl arguing against the interface.

"Any overtures?" I asked, not very hopefully, and Mara shook her head. I've been bugging the people in charge of the talent school probably a little too much about the behaviour of the other children to the 'servants' in their midst. Other than to try and pry information about me out of them, they're usually leaving Ys and Rye alone. Not unexpected but the main reason why I'm not sure if the talent school is the right place for them.

Sen they treat very differently, and she's cheerfully social in her age group for the sport sessions. Of course, Ys and Rye hardly encourage anyone to talk with them either and at this stage aren't the least bit interested in friends and to tell the truth that's probably the best thing for the moment. Eventually I'd like to see them with friends, but I want them feeling safe and secure with us first.

Another late day tomorrow.

Saturday, September 13

Tiny steps forward

Finally a new marble. Ninth found it, at the very edge of their range out from the equatorial platform town called Pelamath (the old Muinans were very fond of putting 'ath' in their town names). The area is a bit like those plateaus in South America, though not quite as high I think. Very rainy. Up on top of the plateau it's scrubby, all bushes and spindly trees, while down below is jungle. The platform town is up top, and they found the marble (or, rather, another set of boastful doors) buried in a notch at the base of one of the sheer sides of a different plateau.

We heard the news before we even left, since Ninth has been working through the time zones in the opposite direction and thus started out around midnight. The terrain at Pelamath makes it rather more challenging than Arenrhon to set up a base of operations to begin investigating and so far Ninth has only placed some drones there. But the idea is to first locate as many of the things as possible, and then start delving into them in the hopes of finding more information – preferably that elusive book *Our Secret Plan and How to Foil It*.

First and Fourth were assigned to a slightly later time zone to yesterday's, but southern hemisphere and closer to the pole so we had a short, chilly outing. Mostly fir trees with a few massive yellow-leafed nut trees completely infested by squirrel-types with black fur, tufty white-tipped ears, and long curling tails. Packs of dogs, too, though not border collies, and various deer along with my old acquaintance the Mondo Elk. Not quite halfway through Autumn (we think) and already it felt like snow wasn't too far off there.

I made a point of calling the kids when we stopped at lunch, and showed them the different animals we'd seen, and some of the prettier streams and waterfalls. Rye definitely has a Shon-level interest in the natural world, and wanted to know what all the animals would be called – which is really anyone's guess at this stage, although a lot of animals are being casually named for their resemblance to the animals of old Muinan stories. And the border collies are being called border collies, which amuses me greatly.

A channel request to Shon was all it took to arrange a tour of the flora and fauna buildings and a personal explanation of naming conventions. The three of them (and Mara) ended up having dinner with Isten Notra after their tour – and meeting the rest of her family, all of whom arrived just two days ago as new Muinan settlers. I found out about that when Isten Notra sent me an email, warmly amused as usual, but ending up with: "Don't overlook the brittle fragility of the older girl. Even metal of her quality can shatter after years of strain."

Ys is tying herself into knots, used to being the one who protects the others and makes the decisions, so tempted and distrustful of the life we're offering her. She hates that Sen lavishes affection on me, and Rye's deepening fascination with Kaoren must feel like a second betrayal. I spend all my time wanting to hug her and being careful to pretend not to notice when she's excited and enjoying herself.

I'm glad she met Isten Notra.

I'll make sure to contact them during our next mission day after tomorrow. Of the fourteen platform towns, First and Fourth are exploring four, while most of the single squads are doing three, so two more for us – and again the next time zone over, which means sleeping in, leaving in late afternoon and not getting back till after Sen, at least, should be asleep.

It's raining at Pandora again. Inisar says the Nuran splinter group has shelter now, but I bet they're not enjoying themselves.

Sunday, September 14

Day-Tripping

Pandora's day started out hot and sticky again – another storm on the way – and since everyone at the talent school is spending their energy trying to deal with dozens of kids with severe headaches, we took the kids off to our island after what was breakfast for us and taught them to float on their backs, and kicking. Rye did very well at this, Ys less so – she wasn't comfortable with me holding her up while she was floating, but we took a break and tried again and though she was far from relaxed, she did better the second time.

We had Fourth with us instead of First, and Kaoren turned it into a mini training session, leaving Par and Glade (our toter-abouters who he didn't want to tire out) to sit with me on the bank while he took the rest for a short practice swim.

All three kids are highly curious about Kaoren's squad, and Fourth are eternally entertained by the idea of him in a dad role. Glade had a huge amount of fun pretending Kaoren worked them to death and was a heartless taskmaster. Sen was outraged and kept saying "No-o!!" in highly doubtful tones at Glade's increasingly unlikely claims, until she was sure that he was teasing her and then she started giggling madly. Rye, who I think was for a while really furious, finally appealed to me.

"Tough but fair," I said, since my opinion of him as a captain hasn't really changed. "Kaoren expects people to do their best, but he doesn't push them just for fun of it." I had to grin and add. "Admittedly, I train with First instead of Fourth."

"You – is it you are to be a Setari?" Rye asked.

"It would take years – decades – to turn me into any sort of fighter. But the basic training comes in handy because using talents strains the user's system. And, well, you never know when you need some urgent running or swimming. It was definitely embarrassing when Zan – the leader of Twelfth

Squad – had to levitate me because I couldn't keep up with her squad during an emergency."

Before we left I told Sen that she should choose a short story for Mara to read, if she wanted to save the current one for me, and Mara tells me that she was happy with this new arrangement. I'm getting better at this.

Our platform town today was the border collie one, which on the old Muinan map is called Falazen. I asked Maze if I could bring a snack along for the dogs (partially to tease him) and ended up having a rather serious conversation with one of the fauna technicians, who wanted to know more about how dogs are used on Earth. Teasing Maze is not nearly so much fun if the end result is a meeting.

The Kolaren farmer who is in charge of the hairy sheep was also there, allowing me to demonstrate my ignorance of sheepdogs AND sheep. To cover the gaps, I did a short projection of some collies herding as a farmer controlled them with whistles. The technician has been conducting a study of the dogs, observing them through drones, and was full of talk about their intelligence and social set-up, and wasn't very keen on the Kolaren's suggestion that we do a bit of puppy-napping. But they agreed that regularly bringing food gifts to the dogs was a usefully non-confrontational step toward redomestication.

So we took doggy snacks with us (well, a bag of dried chips of vat-grown protein) and laid them out on one side of the amphitheatre under the watchful eye of the two collies which were guarding the place (the technician told me that there's always at least one collie keeping an eye on the place). The chips were gone when we returned at the end of the day, so I guess it was a suitable offering to Falazen's current owners.

It was an uneventful day in terms of exploration. The land around Falazen is very like Pandora, although with a somewhat different selection of animals, and dominated by a pale-barked tree just setting out leaf-tips. Lovely displays of spring flowers below them, too. Other than the mild disorientation of getting up mid-morning and travelling about until late evening, and the fact that the Telekinetics find days like this a strain, I'm still really enjoying this stretch of missions. It was late afternoon for the kids when we stopped for lunch, and I showed them where we were, and pictures of the flowers, and the dogs.

Flying and walking about half the day isn't doing my sex life any good, though. Kaoren usually flies himself, and the effort of that means he's very tired by the time we're ready for bed.

Monday, September 15

Where Now?

Raining a lot at Pandora today, so I spent my late morning playing games with the kids while Kaoren was off at a Captains' meeting. There's an endless array of games available for them to play – some free, but a lot with a tiny purchase fee which either Kaoren or I have to approve – and we played through a heap of trials to decide which ones they wanted. I won some 'Mum-cred' by being better at random games than I am at spelling in Taren, and I made sure Ys and Rye picked at least one game each which catered more toward their own age group, rather than entirely to Sen's tastes. Ys picked what amounted to a junior adventure game, like the historical games I've been playing, so I showed them those games, and warned them they might be a little complicated but that I thought they were tremendously interesting because I'd learned so much about Taren history from them.

Then it was off to the southern hemisphere again, though this time not so far south, so we found deciduous trees all shifting into Autumn – primarily a gorgeous translucent yellow, with occasional masses of orangey-red standing out like beacons. This town was quite close to the ruins of another, larger, settlement, and the whole landscape was quite spectacular – lots of whitestone ruins tucked among sharply up and down hills which had at one time been terraced for farming but now had been overtaken by trees, and also these massive (taller than me) bushes which were covered in a white-gold fruit. Tiny brown and black striped pigs kept shooting out of the undergrowth, and huge flocks of birds were feeding on the fruit and seemed completely fearless, moving away only when we were within hands reach. We brought a few samples of the fruit back for the technicians to test, but no more tangible result.

So in all of the past week, one marble. It's not been wasted effort, of course, since our trips have basically amounted to wider surveys of the terrain about the platform towns which are almost certainly going to form the major hubs of civilisation on Muina. But we've barely scratched the surface, and further surveys will be much harder, since they will be outside the zones reliably kept clear of Ionoth by the Ddura. They're going to trial a low-flying drone to see if they can spot any of the grand doors which have marked two of the sites.

Needle, meet haystack.

Ninth and Sixth flew out today by ship to the site of the one marble discovered, and they're going to support the initial establishment of a research site. Until they're able to access the platform (since there is apparently a platform in there) and call the Ddura, there's going to be a fair bit of Ionoth-clearing involved. We have tomorrow as a break, and I'm looking forward to lazing about.

Wednesday, September 17

Pricing Fame

Kaoren is very sneaky. He'd been deliberately vague about plans for our day off because he'd managed to get permission for us to retrace my course to try and find where I'd first arrived on Muina. This was a good deal more of an undertaking than a jaunt across to our island since it could take us out of range of the Ddura's primary hunting ground (it does hunt beyond the four-day's walk range, just rather unpredictably) and we would need fliers and greensuits and rather a lot of Setari.

And, of course, convincing KOTIS Command that no, really, Cassandra won't leap through the gate back home the instant she sees it.

The trip itself was anti-climactically easy, since Kaoren had planned the route using the information from my diary. We whizzed off along the lakeshore until we reached the river, and then followed it to the easily-recognisable rock in the middle of the river where I'd spent a day being sick (I'm not likely to ever forget it). Kaoren used that landmark as an estimate for how fast I was travelling on foot and we zoomed along the river until the point he'd calculated would be around the area where I'd come out of the hills and then we lifted up and looked for a hillside clear of trees, the old burn-off with a stream where I'd spent the second night.

There was one clearly obvious place, and we set the fliers down there so I could confirm that it really did look like the place I remembered. After ten months they didn't have much hope of Place Sight being able to detect any real impression of me, and so weren't surprised not to find any. Even though it looked different in Spring, I was sure it was the right place – and confirmed that by finding my muesli bar wrapper by the stream. Convenient, though I felt bizarrely guilty to be caught littering.

It was a struggle trying to remember what direction I'd come from, but we took a guess and coasted slowly over the hills until Inisar spoke up to correct our course and guided us straight to a place which from my point of view might or might not be the spot where I first stepped on to Muina, but which everyone with Gate Sight said was the site of an unaligned natural gate.

They couldn't say with absolute certainty how long it would take for the gate to align – Inisar said it was responding to my presence and that was very likely the reason it had opened at all, but that it did not feel even close to aligned to him, and was unlikely to stay aligned for long if it did open. Before the embarrassingly short flight back, we set up a drone which will monitor the gate, tracking fluctuations in hopes of predicting when it's ready to align.

And that was it for the dramatic rediscovery of my way home to Earth.

Most of my energy went into being completely clear that I have no intention of leaving. I'd love to visit Mum and Dad, but I'm not going to risk being trapped away from Kaoren, Ys, Rye and Sen. It's not even hard to make the admission. They are my life now.

To be sure those without Sight Sight were completely clear on that, I kept talking about "sending a letter". If the gate goes to roughly the same area on Earth, I can put a letter in something waterproof and say "Please post me" on it, and the chances are at least moderately good that someone will post it. I have five stamps in my wallet, ready for intergalactic special delivery.

That's something for the future (though I can't help but spend half my time mentally composing letters). The rest of the day we played sports with the kids – I taught them French cricket with a rather uneven bat, and teased them about being the only people in the building I had a chance of beating in handball. A fun, relaxed and mildly silly afternoon in other words, reminding me very much of family holidays back on Earth. Sen has got to be the most indulged child on the planet, and Rye's idea of heaven has become the tiny nod Kaoren gave him when he scored a lone point in their handball match. Ys is still being wordlessly polite and totally guarded – doing a good imitation of a Kalrani among superior officers – but I spotted her enjoying herself once or twice despite her best efforts.

Maze vanished for a while during the afternoon, and when he came back took me and Kaoren aside to talk about *The Hidden War*. The current season had wrapped up recently, very dramatically with kitten-me vanishing after being stood on the platform at Pandora, and production was now on a break. I hadn't actually been reviewing the episodes, relying on Maze to warn me if there was anything upsetting, but now they'd reached the stage of wanting as complete a detail of everything which happened after Kalasa as I was willing to allow.

Maze already had a fairly complete summary which someone had prepared of my assignments and injuries and major Setari and me-related events (lots of Cass having nightmares and having to be babied). The proposal suggested by the producers was that their writers read the summary, and come up with questions for me about more detail they'd really like, and an outline of the direction they want to take each episode, and I either give them information or object to bits I can't stand, and then they write up a proper script and the process goes through again. They're offering me huge amounts of money (even more than the Kolarens were, which is saying something). Money is so weird and abstract for me here, since I have more of it already than I've ever had in my life, and I hardly need to touch it.

Because of the differences between the fictional story and the real story, I'm not sure it's really a good thing to feed them information. There's no way for them to properly portray my relationship with Kaoren, not with how different Lastier is from him, and so to a degree it seems pointless to me to try and help make it slightly less inaccurate. KOTIS plainly wants me to do it, but I've been hanging back on agreeing.

And then there was the extra request. Instead of filming my Kalasa ordeal, *The Hidden War's* producers want to buy the mission tape from KOTIS. To take my log and simply broadcast it, right up until my rescue (or, well, until I passed out before I was rescued).

"Why would I want that?" I asked, shrugging off the prospect of even more money. "Why would KOTIS want that?"

"For KOTIS it's simple – the log doesn't tell anything more than what everyone knows, but releasing it undercuts the belief that we're not being completely open and honest about events. Not that anything other than the more worrying theories are currently being held back, but since the destruction of Nuri suspicion has reached sky-breaking level. There isn't a great deal of motivation for you, other than allowing people to see who you really are."

"I'm not sure all the whimpering and crying I did is how I want to present myself," I said wryly, and told him I'd have to think about releasing the log, but I could live with the other arrangement since it's obvious that a lot of people are still treating *The Hidden War* as the Gospel of Devlin.

It surprised me that the military could sell the right to broadcast its records, and asked Maze whether it would be simpler to just release the summary information direct instead of filtering it through *The Hidden War*. And that's an option. Kaoren is firm on this being entirely my decision. I think he knows that in part I just don't want to look at my log for that period, because it's hour upon hour of me being scared and helpless and right now I'm avoiding scared and helpless.

I might be firm about wanting to stay, but locating the gate to Earth left me with a bad case of nostalgia, so after dinner I asked if I could do some expanded senses projection practice, and recorded some Earth video clips for the entertainment of those squads who were awake after their adventures with time zone adjustment. Just a few songs – Mika's *Grace Kelly* and *Love Today*, and Radiohead's *Exit Music for a Film*. It was the first time I'd projected anything in front of the kids, and they seemed very interested – Sen was particularly interested in the piano in the *Grace Kelly* clip, so I made one for her, and muzzily watched her pound it until I fell asleep, and now it's almost dawn. We're heading out in a couple of hours to assist in the opening of the new marble location.

Mmm

Stinky hot weather during the exploration at Pelamath, worse after the violent downpour during the afternoon, which was soon after we arrived since that time zone's well ahead of Pandora's. There wasn't room in the canyon for a camp to be set up – at least not until they eat some whitestone buildings into the canyon walls – so the base camp and ship (the *Mesara*) was on top of the plateau and the Setari did a lot of lugging people and things up and down because they're so much quicker and more efficient than the fliers, and didn't have to be loaded.

Fourth and First (and me) scouted out two other entrances to the underground structure – from initial scans it seems to be set up in much the same way as Arenrhon, just with a slightly different entrance system – and found ancient stairways built into the walls of the cliffs. All terribly crumbly now, and one of the entrances was buried under rubble until Maze cleared it.

The technicians had had plenty of practice at Arenrhon, and had the shielding for the first door ready to be taken down by the time we'd arrived back from marking and clearing the other two. It looks like this is going to be a repeat of Arenrhon, since the interior of the first level was basically identical. Exploration was uneventful, just sad. So many bodies, desiccated and nameless, and crowded again at the entrance. I could see the echoes of their deaths settle on Kaoren with the gentle impact of an anvil – and Inisar and Halla were equally as white-lipped.

We returned to Pandora a little after lunch, since they've decided not to risk night work, and Kaoren was stressed enough to need me a great deal. We spent a very long time in the shower, and then decided to wander over to the talent school to see what the kids were doing.

Sen was out by the lake with her age-group class of newly plugged-in Nurans, having a dance lesson. That was fascinating to watch, because not only did each child have their own personal miniaturised instructor, but the interface was projecting robes with long, long sleeves which they could whirl about and make shapes and patterns. It looked wonderful, and though I didn't join in the dance, I tried out one of the robes, and discovered the wonderful world of projected fantasy clothing. Projected clothing even feels a little like it's really there, stimulating the sense of touch, though not quite achieving real weight. I am so going to spend hours playing with that.

The day for Ys and Rye's age group is now split into a session of 'self-study', a group class, a talent class, and a sport class. They were also in the middle of their first interactive game when we looked in, but sadly not one involving spinning about in floaty clothing. Ys and Rye aren't at all keen on having more shared classes and likely would have preferred to have remained the only students with the interface.

It was great to see the way Rye's face lit up when he noticed Kaoren. I do think he likes me as well as Kaoren, but he simply worships Kaoren. Ys just ignored us after a long glance. We were a fairly disruptive influence on the attention of the rest of the class, though, so it was a good thing the day's lessons were nearly over. Collecting Sen as well, we walked back via the top of the hill, where I out-squee'd everyone over the discovery of hummingbirds feeding on the tree's flowers. They were very tiny and very amazing – something I'd only seen on TV before.

And I'm finally back for our evening routine, so I don't have to feel guilty about using Mara as a babysitter. She's itching to be shifted back to active duty, and will probably be cleared soon. It was a good evening, especially since neither of us were tired, so after Sen had gone to sleep and Ys and Rye had buried themselves once again in the interface, Kaoren and I had a lot of time to be glad to have each other. We also caught up on a chunk of diary reading, reaching the big assembly of Setari being told about me. It was the second time I'd met Kaoren. It seems like an eternity ago, when he was merely one of the huge array of new people I was dealing with, and I was just a curiosity to him.

Thursday, September 18

I Spy...

Today was a poke Devlin at it day.

We were up early again and off to Pelamath, where they'd already opened the second and third levels and were working on the difficult fourth – the idea being to work our way quickly down to the bottom and turn off the shielding – and then erect a KOTIS-approved shield in a bubble over the top of the marble, so that no Cruzatch can use it to come through.

The place had a different set of 'gods', two men and a woman, another three entries into House Zolen's pantheon. I still can't decide if they really deliberately turned themselves into Cruzatch, or if it was some terrible error. I mean, who schemes to turn themselves into floaty burny things?

There'd been a lot of back and forth discussion about whether I should be involved at all, since it would be possible for the Cruzatch to mount a raid through the malachite marble, but they eventually decided on a brief visit after the power stone had been used to turn off the shielding.

This meant a lot of sitting about for me, slathering myself in the insect repellent which is a particular necessity for the Pelamath area, though we've been using it during our other exploration trips. I had a rotating series of guards, and chatted to some of the technicians I hadn't seen since Arenrhon, who all seemed to want to tell me about some individual discovery they'd made, some piece of information about Muina's past which had touched them particularly. These conversations are occasionally surreal, particularly when people I haven't talked to before stammer or blush or grin madly. I've learned to pretend not to notice but it –

I started to write that it makes me feel as fake as wearing the Setari uniform, but realised that I no longer feel like I don't belong in the uniform. Not since Kalasa, I think, when I was just so glad I had it on.

My involvement at the Pelamath installation was to be limited to a quick trip down to the two lowest levels just so they could record which objects were blurry, and any other random observations I had. Which was straightforward enough – and I'm getting better at handling the blurriness – but then it got confusing because the blurriness started to *resolve*.

I kept seeing the same place, but with all the dust and grime gone. And when they told Fourth to bring me back up to the surface, I kept getting flashes of the other floors with all the corpses gone, and people moving about in a businesslike way (most of them favouring an Egyptian kilt look). When we made it out to the canyon, the stairs looked sharp and clean. The technicians were all fascinated, and had me go back in and tour about the unsealed part of the upper floors until my old friend Pounding Headache showed up and bought me a ticket back to Pandora.

The most popular theory is that the power stones had such a strong impact that it imprinted the past on the area, allowing me to see the place before their activation. But I don't know if that's right, and Isten Notra pointed out that the peripheral vision world I was seeing while in near-space was similar but different.

Alternate reality? As if this wasn't confusing enough.

I recovered quite quickly from my headache, which is an improvement, though I was still sentenced to an entire afternoon in medical for brains scans, and very annoyingly a lot of blood and tissue samples once again. Tomorrow they want to try taking me close to the Kalasa power stone, which doesn't have any sarcophagi, to see whether it will let me have more glimpses into Kalasa's past, since seeing without projecting is far less energy-intensive for me. Well, that's the current plan unless someone in KOTIS Command changes their mind again – they're so wary of using me. But all the news reports today have been about the increasing density of Ionoth in Tare and Kolaren near-space, which has led to more incidents of Ionoth reaching real-space and thus a spate of deaths. I'm guessing Kalasa will be a certainty.

Friday, September 19

Urgent Relocation

Back on Tare. I never cease to find new ways to have a crisis.

This was another dreaming problem. I'd barely gone to sleep the night before last, and was having a confusing dream about being trapped under something heavy, when Kaoren woke me up. I occasionally have dreams about being trapped under things because Kaoren has rolled on top of me, and hadn't really felt anything different about this one other than the fact that Kaoren had woken up instead of me, but he said he was feeling extremely uneasy about me, and that my vitals monitor was showing a slower than normal heartbeat. He wanted me to go sleep in medical attached to the scanner, which I wasn't keen about at all, but I could see he was really unsettled, so I checked all the kids were asleep then went along just to spare him the stress, and felt tremendously guilty about having to wake up Ista Mezan (this week's primary medic) just so he could watch *me* go to sleep. He was very nice about it, but looked so tired.

I was pretty tired myself, so went to sleep quickly, and started having another dream about being trapped under something heavy. It didn't exactly feel like one of my 'real' dreams, and my head felt very vague and I just lay there until it grew clearer, not that it ever really grew clear. There was a mistiness to everything – fog – and I seemed to be in a dark place with a narrow light directly above me, making the thin tendrils of fog glow, and I could make out different pinpoints of light to either side, and some kind of pattern in the ceiling. I couldn't move, couldn't turn my head, couldn't lift a finger, couldn't speak, didn't even really feel like I was breathing. I didn't feel at all like myself.

And there was whispering. Lots of words on all sides of me – or *on* me. It felt like there were tiny incredibly heavy people sitting on top of me, whispering. I couldn't make out what was being said, beyond that it had the zeddy noises common in Taren and the other Muinan dialects.

I didn't like it at all – I felt so small and helpless and constrained – and started trying to wake up and couldn't. I knew it had to be a dream, but the easy ability to wake out of my dreams seemed to be gone. I tried sitting up, and still couldn't move, and tried creating a projection of an Ionoth Kaoren to free me, and nothing happened, and then I panicked, in a futile and unproductive way. I couldn't even feel my heart beating.

The only thing left I could think to do was try and sense whether there was anyone nearby who might help me. I began pushing my senses out, but even that didn't work properly, and I felt like I'd fallen down a well – or up a well – and then I snapped back to staring at the ceiling. That wasn't a very nice sensation.

But it was the only thing I could do, and I was by that time out of my mind desperate, so I kept pushing out, pushing and pushing and falling up this well but I felt like I was a rubber band stretching too thin.

And then I was me again, trying to gasp and choking because there was a tube down my throat. And still heavy, like there was an anchor hooked to my spine. Ista Mezan said something in a high, relieved voice and then helpfully pulled the tube out (horrid sensation) and then Kaoren was in reach and I got hold of him and just gasped and shook for a minute or two. Ista Mezan did his best to get a physical assessment of me without prying me off.

Kaoren's heart was beating really fast, and his voice was even but unusually flat as he explained that my heart rate had slowed soon after I fell asleep, and then plummeted – the time between beats increasing exponentially. So far as they could tell, I'd stopped breathing altogether, with barely a flicker of brain activity. They'd hooked me up to a machine for breathing and tried waking me with an alarm over the interface, and Inisar had tried speaking to me telepathically, and they were debating shooting me full of stimulants when I'd revived as abruptly as I'd gone. I'd been not quite dead for nearly twenty minutes.

Having said that, Kaoren gently detached me and had me lie down so Ista Mezan could take better readings. Another technician, and Maze, Inisar and Zee were in the room, all of them grim and tense.

"It hasn't ended," Inisar said, watching me narrowly. "What did you dream?"

My throat hurt – I really don't recommend tubes – and I had to swallow a few times. Maze brought me into a channel (which had Isten Notra and the settlement commander and another bluesuit in it) and I spoke in there instead.

"I was somewhere I hadn't seen before, a dark misty place, and I couldn't move. I don't think–" I struggled to understand the whole thing. "I don't think I was dreaming. That was nothing like my dreams."

"I'm not finding physical damage, but energy output is significantly elevated," Ista Mezan said. "She's actively using a talent."

"I'm trying not to go back. I feel like there's a heavy weight pulling me," I said, wanting to clutch Kaoren some more. He slid his hand into mine, and I risked a glance at his face and saw that it was like stone, his eyes nearly shut.

"Recommendations?" Tsaile Staben asked, voice very clipped.

"It seems more likely to me that it is a response to the second exposure to a power stone, rather than some form of attack," Isten Notra said. "In either case, distance is the only obvious response. Get her as far from the power stones as possible."

Tsaile Staben told the other bluesuit to arrange a ship, while Isten Notra asked: "Caszandra, can you describe the place you saw in any more detail?"

"Not properly." I thought about it, then: "Can we go outside? I want to try and project where I was, and there's not enough room here to see it."

"But–" Ista Mezan started, but stopped. What could he tell me, after all? That I needed to get some rest?

Maze was looking sick, and Zee's mouth was a flat line, because they could see why I didn't want to wait. Kaoren just picked me up. He knew I wouldn't suggest something like that unless I thought it was important.

The nights are still cold at Pandora, and the sky was very clear. Maze brought along a drone and we followed the path down to the lake's bank. I was struggling with feeling dizzy – moving about didn't agree with me – but at least the dizziness made it easier to resist falling back asleep. The projection was unexpectedly easy to do, and not as distressing as I'd feared since Kaoren kept me snug against his chest the entire time – and this time it wasn't me lying unable to move.

It was a big room, made of blackish stone and lit not only by the balls of light in the ceiling, but the mist which filled it, which I belatedly realised was aether. The stone walls were covered in carvings, reminding me vaguely of circuitry, and there was only one thing in the entire place – an altar or platform or bed – a waist-high carved rectangle of stone on top of which a black-draped humanoid figure – tiny, no bigger than Ys – lay beneath a scattering of round, green stones. Little malachite marbles.

"I think it's her dream," I said, shaking from the effort of maintaining the projection and just...sheer horror. "It's the ceiling I wanted to show you."

"Spread out so we capture as much as possible," Maze said, and he, Zee and Ista Mezan moved, looking upward through the aether. Inisar was staring at the shape of the girl under the dust-fragile black drapery, and

Kaoren knew better than to shift about when I was projecting. They didn't even make it to the far end of each room before I had to let the projection fade. Isten Notra ordered Ista Mezan to give me stimulants and we went back inside.

"Ship will be ready in ten joden," said the second bluesuit, as I was getting another quick examination and a couple of injections. I hesitated over the fortifier Ista Mezan handed me, since they always make me sleep, and Kaoren told me to drink just a little and to bring it with me.

"Let me wake the kids," I said, as Maze and Kaoren sent alerts to their squads, and Kaoren gently lifted us both back to our quarters. I could stand on my own, though it made my bones feel achy, and Kaoren watched me carefully a moment, then went and packed with his usual extreme efficiency.

Ys woke at the slightest touch, and I told her to wake Rye and then sat myself rather heavily on Sen's bed and prodded her gently awake. I think Sen knew straight away – she climbed into my lap and hugged me madly and then was quietly mature in the way she gets when she's being driven by her Sight.

"We're going to Tare," I said, once they were all awake enough to take it in. "Mainly because my talents now acting weird, and best to get me away from Muina until better understand what's going on. I need you three to get dressed and pack belongings – use your pillowcases to put them in – so that we're all ready to get on ship. Can you do that?"

I hated to see Ys and Rye's reaction, all sense of certainty stolen away in seconds, and then their expressions shutting down. But they nodded and hurried to do what they were told. I helped Sen get dressed, and sent her to the bathroom while I packed everything I could reach without having to move about too much. Kaoren was soon there with a proper tote bag to pack their crammed pillowcases in, and his calm and restrained approval swept them along. Mara and Ketzaren showed up and whisked them and our bags away so Kaoren could pick me up again. We flew inland to the flat acres of whitestone which was now Pandora's barebones spaceport. First and Fourth, Inisar, Ista Mezan and a couple of his minions, all together in a hushed and grim group: Mori wide-eyed and dismayed, Lohn with his jaw set, no-one wanting to talk. I couldn't pay a great deal of attention because I was all dizzy again and very nauseous.

The ship was the *Diodel*, and Kaoren took me straight to the small medical section. He let the technicians have me so I could try to explain why I was looking so green, and went to make sure the kids were settled, coming back just before takeoff and dryly saying: "She understands that," to stop one of the technicians fussing about how if just getting to the ship had made me dizzy, ship travel would be worse.

I could tell that they were treating this as super-urgent because the tedious pre-flight checks were cut short to critical systems checks only.

The medical station has two 'sick-pods', and a room to one side with more ordinary pods, but Kaoren and Ista Mezan ignored the 'everyone strap in for takeoff' protocol and stood with me as the ship lifted, paused, then zoomed forward. And I went grey, green, then vomited extravagantly in the well-placed bucket Kaoren had snagged from the medical supplies. I don't remember much of the journey to Muina's rift, given that my brain seemed to be tumbling in free-fall the entire way and I spent all my energy dry-retching and shifting about because I kept having really weird muscles spasms. It did mean that it wasn't difficult to stay awake, but by the time we reached the rift (it sounds like we went at record speed) all I wanted was to be knocked on the head. The whole time I could feel something pulling me down.

Kaoren wouldn't let them close my pod when heading into the rift, and stayed standing with me despite a high chance of getting a dose of aether, which was fortunate because apparently I had a fit and passed out briefly – I don't remember that, just this incredibly awful sensation like my insides were all staying on the far side of rift. By the time I was capable of noticing more than that, the technicians were talking in very relieved tones, and I no longer felt dragged down. Awful in many other ways, but whatever connection I'd established to the malachite marble or whatever the hell was going on with me had been broken.

I was totally drained, and just lay for a while letting them give me injections and take brain scans, but then asked if I could have a shower (I stank of vomit and was mortifyingly sure I'd wet myself as well, which thankfully my nanosuit was containing). Nanosuits are tremendously useful for having medical emergencies in, since the technicians can make bits of it go away and come back so easily. Kaoren came and had a shower with me, which got around the technicians worrying I would collapse and gave us the opportunity to be all scared and upset with each other for a while. He'd had to spend the entire time not showing how frightened he was, and we ended up sitting on the cramped floor of the shower cubicle, squeezing each other and shuddering. We were still in the shower when we went through into Taren real-space, and I decided that, however exhausted I was, I'd rather try and stay awake until we were back at base because I really didn't want to face the possibility of more vomiting.

Ista Mezan (by then looking almost as exhausted as I felt) told me to finish the rest of my fortifier, but I bargained him into fetching me some real food, and Kaoren went to get my hairbrush, so I was (if you ignored the two other technicians in the side-room) alone when Ys found me.

She marched straight up to where I was sitting sideways on the sick-pod (the unsick pod, in this case, since I'd swapped to the one they hadn't had to clean vomit off) and said in this angry whisper: "You have to stop."

"Stop which?" I asked muzzily.

I could see she was shaking with anger, and my mild question was apparently the last straw because she had her own little volcanic eruption, all in the same stifled and furious whisper.

"How can you be so selfish? If you're in danger all the time, why do you keep pulling them closer to you? Don't keep hurting them just to make yourself feel better. You can't just decide to be their family and make them love you, and then take it all away. If you're going to die, then die!"

The enormity of the last one seemed to hit her – she'd gone further than she wanted to say – and she stopped short, gasping for breath. Kaoren, Mara and Maze were standing in the doorway behind her, being very still so she wouldn't notice them. I really wished I could ask Mum for advice, and touched Ys' cheek, but she jerked her face away.

"Every time Kaoren goes on mission in the Ena, I spend entire time convinced he's not coming back. But does that mean I shouldn't love him because he has dangerous job? Would it be better to find someone who lived safer life, even though I like them less? I know that I'm in lot of danger, but if I spend all my time not doing things, not caring about people, because I'm caught up in knowing that I'm in danger, then I'm wasting chance I've been given to live. I want to live while I can, even if it's just for few weeks, or day, or hour."

"Selfish," Ys repeated, voice strangled, and I worked not to look like I agreed.

"I know tonight has been scary. But I don't think I'd be doing right thing by not hugging Sen, just because might be for the last time, any more than I think would be the right thing to not make sure that you and Rye have never-ending supply of books. Do you know, one of the things I've enjoyed most this past week is watching expression on your face when you get explanation for something? It's like the universe is one massive puzzle to you and thing you like above all else is to fit another piece in place."

That made her stare at me, as if she thought I could somehow have missed something so obvious about her. I added carefully: "And I'm very proud of you for always trying to protect Sen and Rye. You'll have to forgive me for being just little selfish about wanting to see you smile. I am trying very hard to avoid dying, but if I can't then I hope all three of you will be able to remember the fun things we did together, rather than just the fact that am gone."

I slid off the over-tall med-pod so I could hug her – which made her go rigid and she beat her fists against my ribs (really hard too) and then briefly clutched at the front of my nanosuit and gulped because she was absolutely determined not to cry. Kaoren came in and put a hand on her head, and told her Sen was looking for her, and knowing him he said just the right things to calm her down a little as he took her off. Mara and then Maze came in and hugged me very painfully (I refrained from hitting them) and I could see that by making speeches about dying I'd succeeded in upsetting both of them rather a lot. Too many of the people they grew up with and cared about have been killed.

Mara made me sit back down and tidied my hair while Maze filled me in on the things I'd missed while I'd been busy vomiting. Isten Notra had begun analysing the images from my projection straight away, and said the patterns on the ceiling were almost certainly related to the patterns we'd seen on the diagram of the Pillar placement. It didn't seem to be, as I had half hoped, a map to the location of all the malachite marbles, but she said it was important anyway.

Ista Mezan came back with a cup of hot green soup at the same time as Kaoren, Inisar and Zee, and I sipped it cautiously as they tried to coax more information about the not-my-dream out of me. I hadn't mentioned the whispering before that, and they're going to try and enhance the drone's audio pick up enough to maybe make out what the stones were saying.

"That another touchstone, yes?" I asked Inisar. "The one think was involved in disaster."

"Most likely. You said you didn't think that was your dream. Could it have been hers?"

I didn't know the answer to that. "It felt like trap," I said. "But she's the one caught in it." Thinking about it, remembering what it was like, started to upset me a lot and I nearly dropped my soup down my front until Kaoren steadied the cup. "She can't be any older than Ys," I said, and was glad when they decided that it wasn't a good time to push me any more.

Left for the moment alone, Kaoren and I sat together on my med-pod, hands locked together, and I opened a channel to him.

"Sen's Sights led her to the wrong person."

"No." Kaoren frowned at me. "For what she wants, you and I are exactly right. It becomes, now, a matter for us to protect you. And for you not to fail her. Promise me that, Cassandra. That you will think, and take care, and not surrender to this."

"Live up to her?" I said, and thought he might as well be asking for himself. And probably was.

"Promise me," he repeated, and I did. And I'll try. But this thing, that room, it scares me. I don't know if it's something I can just push on through.

Kaoren carried me out to the common room, where more hugging was had, and Sen planted herself in my lap and fell straight to sleep. I spent a little while telling Rye (and a highly subdued and stubbornly silent Ys) about how great the storms on Tare were to watch and how the planet only had two types of weather: storming and about to storm. Then I fell asleep, of course, but no dreams or heaviness and Kaoren must have pushed them to not keep me too long in medical because I woke in my apartment – with this heavy weight on my chest, which panicked me a moment until I realised it was Ghost. Kaoren was very deeply asleep beside me, and Mara was watching over the kids and pretty much treated me like one when I stumbled out needing breakfast.

My apartment now has four bedrooms and is even roomier than the Muina version. It's obviously been set up this way for a while: KOTIS thinking ahead. Having a big, strict military organisation trying to anticipate my every need is a very surreal sensation. Sen was loving it, as usual, especially Ghost reappearing, while Ys and Rye have been discovering that the interface is a lot larger on Tare than it is on Muina. It was very funny listening to Rye asking Mara questions about the Song Star Setari program.

The headlines are all full of speculation about me having died, or being near-death, so I guess it's not really possible to take urgent emergency health flights without *someone* gossiping about it. KOTIS has issued a denial, which has only produced conspiracy theories.

Although I was marched back to medical for scans, I had a fun time anyway playing interface games with Sen and doing my best to live up to my own speech.

Saturday, September 20

Ties

Great news yesterday. Lohn and Mara have registered to get married. Mara told me when she sprang me from medical. It's something that they'd always been putting off to 'after retiring from the Setari' (at least in part because of Maze's wife dying, I suspect), but they'd decided that there was no real reason to. They held a little celebration/announcement party in their quarters, with the 'old-timers' of First and Second Squad and a scattering of others (including Kaoren, me and the kids) which was a very cramped affair, making us miss the common room at Pandora.

Because they've been living together for a long time, Lohn and Mara only have to wait two Taren years instead of five, so they'll be getting married in approximately eight months. I noticed everyone kept a weather eye on Maze to gauge his reaction at first, but then relaxed into wedding talk and 'future talk'. Maze just looked happy and relaxed and pleased for them – and spent quite a lot of time chatting with Ys and Rye (explaining Setari squad structures from what I could tell).

Nils teased me about needing to limit my medical dramas – particularly because he'd woken up well after I'd come back and been hit by all these headlines about me having died, which he says totally put him off his breakfast. The persistence of the stories about me being dead or near death is getting a little silly, and we tried to work out why people were more inclined to believe I was dead than KOTIS' announcement that I wasn't. I thought the best solution would be a shopping trip, so I could introduce the kids to the wonders of mall life. Maze and Kaoren weren't very keen, but they did promise to suggest it. Later on Kaoren and I talked rather more seriously about introducing our new extended family to his sister. And then, kids safely in bed, we spent hours having mad, crazy sex, trying to banish the spectre of my heart stopping.

Never one to delay, Kaoren arranged for us to meet with Siame today, cleverly combining it with a trip to the roof to relieve my already-increasing feeling of being locked up. Ys and Rye particularly seemed to find the idea of meeting Kaoren's sister the most daunting thing about Tare so far. Ys dealt with it by spending a great deal of time making sure Sen was dressed beautifully, her hair carefully braided. She spent a lot less effort on herself, though I'm glad to see she's willing to wear the clothes I'd bought now that there was no risk of the other Nuran children seeing her. Rye just looked like he had a stomach cramp all morning.

We lucked out on the weather, which was the second sort – about to storm. The sky was clear above, with a huge black bank of clouds off in the distance, flickering with lightning. Siame met us outside the elevator entrance, wearing her Kalrani uniform. She's nearly forty-five now (fifteen) and looked totally in control and correct, every inch a Setari in the making.

Standing on top of the massive pile of blocks which is a Taren city is enough to take anyone's mind off social awkwardness. So was the full-on wind. I said it was kite-flying weather, and explained what kites were (though Kaoren wouldn't let me create a projection of one – I'm not supposed to use my powers for a while). Rye wanted to know whether there was any 'proper outside' on Tare and was I think less than impressed with a complete absence of visible plants and animals. Since the storm started rolling in in earnest we went back down to my apartment for hot drinks.

Siame's attitude toward the kids was neutral, unconcerned, as she asked them questions about their experiences with the interface, and about living at Pandora. But she didn't say one single word to me. Since she's such a powerfully self-confident person, the impression she gave was of forbearance rather than any upset, and I was surprised when Sen abruptly reached out and patted Siame's hand. It was a clear gesture of sympathy, and Siame broke off in the middle of a question, her face losing all expression.

"Why don't you show Siame your room, Sen?" I asked.

Sen jumped up eagerly – she's very proud of her room and particularly the mound of cushions she's collected from all over the apartment to bury her bed in. Ys and Rye followed, and I kissed Kaoren because he was looking worn.

Kaoren is as protective of Siame as Ys is of Sen, and his long absence on a different planet right on top of him making a major change of his life has shifted her from having a very close relationship to him to being on the fringes. Beneath all that composure she was miserable. He's spending the afternoon with her – giving her some combat training because he's now too well known for a casual trip into the city.

The kids and I watched the storm, which hit very spectacularly, with a lead-up of lightning followed by horizontal rain pounding at my window. That was a lot of fun, with all of us in my window-seat and the lights turned down and Sen pretending to be frightened, Ys forgetting not to speak to me because she wanted to know how lightning works, and Rye wondering how any animals on Tare manage to stay alive. I turned it into a research exercise, with all of us looking up information on lightning, and the small number of hardy surface-dwelling animals of Tare's islands (think armadillos), and the vast variety of cave-dwelling ones, and the efforts the Tarens have gone to to preserve Tare's land-dwelling wildlife once they realised they were in danger of wiping most of it out.

I love it when the kids get distracted and stop being defensive with me. Tonight, Kaoren and I are going to work through the legal documents for making them (and Siame) our heirs and naming Mara and Lohn guardians in the event of our deaths. Not that we're officially their guardians, or are likely to be able to qualify for adopting them on Tare, but it's a step we can make quickly, and next we'll start investigating the process under the provisional Muinan laws – which are having to deal with the issue of adoptions as a matter of priority.

Maze just emailed me an expanded summary of everything that's happened to me, and told me to edit in anything I'd like to include. KOTIS is going to add it to my official biography as well as providing it to the producers of *The Hidden War*.

First and Fourth are back on duty tomorrow (they've theoretically been on holiday these last two days), but it's a training day. It looks like I'll be training with them, but need to check the arrangements for the kids. Not that Ys and Rye aren't perfectly capable of looking after Sen and self-studying, but I want them to be children, not babysitters.

Sunday, September 21

Back and Forward

During my days the kids will be attending the Kalrani training school, which didn't sound like a good plan to me, but Kaoren tells me the school is more than flexible enough to handle them carefully. They'll spend some time in classes with Kalrani, but won't have the pressures or intense training intended to turn children into Setari. They didn't seem upset when they returned today, anyway – Sen is always happy to meet children her own age (or a couple of years older, in the case of the youngest Kalrani) and one of the older Kalrani appears to have been assigned to give Ys and Rye very basic combat training (those stepping exercises), which has delighted Rye to no end. He was so happy when Kaoren told him to show what he'd learned and then spent some time correcting his stance. Ys isn't nearly so interested in combat, but Kaoren put her through her paces as well, and she went a little pink when he gave her one of his tiny approving nods.

I was floatingly tired from the full-on training Mara put me through and declined the opportunity to have my ability to step back and forward corrected. We played the spelling game again, and all the kids are continuing to improve in leaps and bounds, but when we asked them what treat they would like they couldn't (or wouldn't) settle on anything. When it was time for me to read the next chapter of our story I had Ys and Rye each read a couple of paragraphs to start out with, helping them spell out the more complex words, and then finished off the rest myself.

I had to laugh at Kaoren, since I next went and read to him. His response was to have me write him out the English alphabet and start teaching him English as I read. We're reading through more of my period of being Zan's trainee, revisiting my struggles to understand the concept of the Ena and what the hell was going on. And just desperately wanting Zan to like me, since she was the only person I knew. It immediately made me email

Zan and ask her if she was interested in going swimming together some time (possibly with the kids).

Today I have medical appointments again, while First and Fourth are on Ena assignment and I'm trying not to worry about Mara's first day back on serious active duty. I finished off reviewing the little history of me which is going to be made public. It's pretty dry, so there wasn't anything to object to.

Monday, September 22

Day Trip

Score! The bluesuits decided that some kind of public display of me was going to be necessary to quash the conspiracy theories, and so agreed to me going shopping. Probably the oddest assignment I'll ever have – a mall visit to foster public calm.

Maze, Kaoren and I had a sit-down after First and Fourth were back from mission yesterday and talked through the technicalities. It's one thing, after all, to take the kids shopping, but another thing altogether to expose them to the kind of crowds which turned up at Rana Junction. And a large, obvious number of guards would draw attention like a magnet, whether or not they were in uniform.

Eventually they decided on an escort of ten Setari, including Kaoren. We would take a roundabout way getting out of the KOTIS facility, dropping down to the 'basement levels' to a freight shuttle and then coming up straight into the middle of the prime shopping district on the island. Kaoren, Zee and Nils would stay with me and the kids, and the rest of the escort would shadow us in two groups while we shopped, joining up only when travelling between floors and then stopping for lunch. We rather suspected that after lunch too many people would have recognised me for the excursion to continue. The police would be given an hour or so's warning, but not too much because that would lessen the amount of time for word to leak.

I was all for wearing a blonde wig and dark glasses, except of course that would defeat the purpose and sunglasses are not exactly common on Tare. I settled for plaiting my hair in Sen's favourite twin-braid style, since it was a way I don't usually wear it. Mine isn't long enough to be half so impressive as hers, and I skipped the ribbons, but I still quite liked it and Nils said it was different enough that people would need to take a closer look to be sure.

Nils was part of my 'near' escort because he's such a good Illusion caster, and Zee because she's managed to be one of the least-photographed of First Squad. I longed to tease them about it, but since Nils seems to be pretending that he's never been one to flirt with Zee, or indeed with anyone much, I figured it was best to leave it alone. They're driving me batty showing no sign of particular interest in each other – I so want to pry and don't quite dare.

Sen was tremendously excited, of course, and I think Ys and Rye were at least curious. I'd prepared them with a few select kids' shows featuring Taren daily life so they had some idea what it was like. They're used to Taren-style buildings by now, but one of the big multi-level atriums is something else altogether.

I'd told them we were going to pick out some quilt covers for their beds (they all had standard-issue plain blue), and Kaoren had laid out the rules they had to follow in his usual clear and concise way. He offered up a few rules for me as well, and tweaked one of my braids when I suggested a couple for him in return.

With Nils and Zee taking lead, our trip up from the train was uneventful, with no-one spotting me at all – The Nils Effect means that most people don't at first glance notice anyone but Nils, and then they're often busy walking into light poles or rubbish bins. All the double-takes I saw were focused conveniently on him and Zee as we made our way to our first stop, an overwhelming multi-level toy store which stunned even Sen into silence.

"Since you couldn't think of a treat yesterday," I said, "I figured this would give you some idea. Pick something you like." Ys developed a stubborn look, and I gave her a stern one in return. "We can't leave till you do, so best get started."

I'm not entirely certain I would have won the battle of wills, but Sen gave Ys no chance of victory, grabbing her hand and almost catapulting her down an escalator to an endless display of dolls. It was a great store. I found a few toys for myself, and wasn't the least surprised when Sen collected a thousand choices. I made her pick just two, but would buy them the entire store if I had somewhere to put it. She spent a lot of time with these horribly lifelike dolls (and androids!) taller than herself, but abruptly settled on a simple cloth one with a cheerful drawn-on face, and a poseable rainbow coloured thing with long arms and legs and googly eyes.

Rye found a kind of meccano construction kit, which Nils offered to carry (and then sneakily swapped to this humungous ultra-deluxe everything but the kitchen sink version). Ys was very reluctant, fingering a few things when prodded, but still without a choice by the time Sen had finally settled on her two. Kaoren solved this by picking something for her, this ultra-cool crystal statue – about two feet tall – which is made of nanobots and can take on any form you like – either a pre-programmed shape or one you make by treating it as modelling clay. There are hundreds of pre-programmed shapes, some of which sneakily change position when you're not quite paying attention. Ys adores it. And Ghost spent half the evening stalking it.

We made it through the toy store without attracting attention, at least until we actually purchased the treats and found this girl who was on packaging and delivery service (they don't really have checkouts at most stores since you can purchase through the interface at any point in the shop). Nils took them up for delivery, and The Nils Effect thoroughly distracted the girl wrapping the items, but when she saw the address he wanted her to deliver the packages to, she went all extra-awed and looked interestedly at the rest of us – and then stared at me and burst into tears.

It is severely embarrassing to have people cry at the sight of you. Sen didn't like it at all, and attached herself to my leg, and I said some awkward words to the girl, who was apparently just glad I really wasn't dead. Word spread after that, as we headed to a bed-ware store and successfully had even Ys select a quilt cover that she liked. You could see people gathering in little groups to stare at us and, since we'd deliberately left the image-shield inactive on everyone except the kids, our shopping trip was soon a live-streaming event.

We'd chosen the place we were going to have lunch with care – it had a rear exit which was close to the elevator down to the lower levels – and we had booked a nice big table to fit us all and arrangements had been made to let us escape out the back. The place filled up spectacularly quickly, and it was funny to watch us having lunch from a dozen different perspectives. Fortunately we were able to tuck the kids far enough back that they could barely be seen, and of course not recorded. And the city authorities had arranged for security outside, which was a good thing, since an impressive crowd gathered. I felt sorry for disappointing them by sneaking out the back, but not even slightly tempted to go out there.

Sen likes her quilt cover (a seascape) enough to release her hostage cushions, and with the addition of two dolls and the latest in her ever-changing array of colourful public space designs, her room is beginning to look definitively hers. Ys and Rye both set their 'treats' out in their small lounge/play area, and have been sharing between the three of them. Nils told me later that there'd been a lot of private channel discussion over whether the kids would be too overwhelmed if everyone bought them gifts, as our escort had been sorely tempted to do. He said I was entirely to blame for First and Second Squads' sudden excess of parental yearnings, since they'd had all this practice babying me, but he still seemed to really enjoy showing Sen how to 'finger paint' her room's public space and then levitating her all over the ceiling so that she could leave virtual handprints up there. I set our main lounge ceiling to look like stars in response (I need to be careful about what appears in public space in our main living quarters, because it has a big impact on Kaoren's Sights).

Endless amounts of news stories and forum discussions about my brief appearance – including exact details of what I'd bought for the kids. That caused me some angst, thinking that it might cause trouble when we go back to the talent school, but I don't think never buying Ys, Rye and Sen any presents is the solution to the talent school situation. And, although I really enjoy going out and seeing more of Tare – and just being able to do some hands-on shopping – I don't think I'll push for a trip like that again in the near future. People crying at me is dreadfully uncomfortable, and the bigger the crowd outside grew the more I wanted to leave. Today demonstrated the impossibilities of ever giving the kids a 'normal' Taren life, which is especially an issue because right now we don't know if I can go back to Muina.

The theory they're evolving about what happened to me is guesswork held together by bubblegum and sticky tape. On the near-certainty side is that these malachite marbles, most likely built secretly by House Zolen, first unbalanced the newly built Pillar network – causing the barrier between real-space and near-space to start tearing – and then triggered the disaster on Muina. On the mostly-guesswork side, they think that House Zolen was either, incomprehensibly, aiming to turn themselves into Cruzatch, or ended up like that accidentally. And that they used the touchstone who existed at that time, the one who created the Ddura, as part of their malachite marble network. Since the malachite marbles are designed to use a touchstone, bringing me repeatedly near to them attuned me to what would count as the control room of the malachite marble machine. Whether that machine still exists, or I was linking all the way back to a thousand years ago, is still up to debate, as is what will happen if I go back to Muina. I might be fine so long as I don't go into one of the malachite marble rooms. I might be in danger if I go through Kalasa. Or I might drop into another death-spiral of energy expenditure as soon as I'm through the deep-space rift.

Tomorrow I'm scheduled for some very wary projection tests so that they can begin to try and find out whether projection of any sort will give me a medical crisis. They're not going to decide anything more till after that.

Tuesday, September 23

Disclosure

Nothing dramatic happened during my testing session (which was scheduled in the afternoon after First and Fourth were back from another Ena rotation). It was held in the medical section, rather than out at Keszen Point, and I couldn't help remembering my nightmares about the Velcro massive, as well as all the lusting I did after Kaoren.

Kaoren ran the session (with Maze and Zee in the next room), and kept me to a brief song projection. They fed me a mild sedative to get me to nap straight away, but I just slept, and fortunately they decided that I was safe to sleep in quarters (though I have a distinct feeling Kaoren's going to stay up watching me for a while).

He's reviewing the questions *The Hidden War* producers have sent back (which are long and extensive and far more than I want to discuss – revolving mainly around how I felt at every moment, and especially when and why I fell in love with Kaoren). Neither of us like the situation with *The Hidden War*, funny as Kaoren finds the Lastier persona, and we're well aware that by trying to control it we're only giving it added legitimacy.

We're going to fill the questions out together, but we need to decide whether we prefer to tell things which are private, or keep it minimal and have them concoct a romance half the planet will believe is the way things really happened. I still can't decide about releasing the log of my time in Kalasa, either.

Wednesday, September 24

Privacy/Disclosure

No dramas for me overnight, although Sen did wake up from a nightmare and come climb in bed with us. She was shaky and very upset and I think that's the first time I've seen her really cry. I couldn't make much out about what she'd dreamed, but it seemed to be about Nuri's loss, and trapped people. Once she'd calmed down a little, I lay holding her while Kaoren talked to her about controlling the things Sight made you see, and stepped her through one of the visualisation exercises until she fell asleep. She has Sight Sight, Place Sight, Path Sight and Symbol Sight, and an Ice talent, and Kaoren says that unlike Ys and Rye she's more than strong enough to qualify for Setari training, but that the whole Kalrani program is going to need to be reviewed, both in regard to teaching the awareness of a connection with the Ena, and for the program's intensity and volume. We don't know if we can fix the tears, or if everything's only going to get worse, and thus whether the program needs to be expanded or contracted.

Kaoren also gave Ys and Rye a small visualisation lesson over breakfast, explaining to all three of the kids (and me) how Sight Sight and Place Sight tends to develop at Sen's age, and how to help Sen through learning to control her visions. Nightmares upon nightmares. We're going to add the visualisations to story time as a final step, since she's started staying awake until I've finished reading the chapter. Ys and Rye are always very serious about Sen's welfare, enough so that Ys briefly dropped her non-talkativeness to pepper Kaoren with questions. Kaoren also talked to them about learning how to focus their own connection to the Ena, since being able to do that will immensely strengthen their abilities, and had them try picking things up using Levitation/Telekinesis and then try to sense their connection with the Ena. He explained that it was something most Taren Setari couldn't do and he was only just learning, but that he wanted them all to try and sense it whenever they were using their talents.

Another training day, with projection work in the afternoon. We went out to Keszen Point this time, and I recreated the first visualisation I'd done, of the museum Kaoren had described, this time with my senses expanded. Then the requisite nap in medical. Going to sleep in the afternoon and then waking up and being groggy till evening is annoying, but it's preferable to the maybe dying thing. Preferable to the look I've seen in Kaoren's eyes when he's contemplating what they can and can't do if this goes wrong.

I had a swimming lesson to wake me up today, at least. I'd arranged with Zan (who is on a completely opposite shift and so had only just got out of bed) to meet me and Kaoren at the pool to give the kids another lesson. We needed three because that pool has no shallow areas, and I knew the sheer formidable depth of it would make it more than daunting for the kids. Their eyes turned to absolute saucers when they looked down into it, and down, and down. But Sen was okay so long as she could cling to me, while Rye's desire to win Kaoren's approval only grows, and I don't think Ys can stand to show she's afraid of things.

Zan was fantastic with Ys. She's so calm and non-threatening and small, yet very sure and commanding when she wants to be. And, I think, Ys doesn't have such a big emotional barrier built up against anyone but me and Kaoren, so was able to concentrate more on the swimming part and less on not giving an inch to me.

The main thing I wanted to teach them was how to get out of a pool, and then kicking and turning their heads to breathe while we held them. Sen was totally unkeen on being face-down in water, and I didn't push her since she's only young, just had her practice dog paddle again. Rye's gained a lot of confidence in the water, and I think he's enjoying swimming more for its own sake now, and not merely because it's time spent with Kaoren and earns him approving nods.

After the kids tired, we had them sit on the side of the pool and had a race across and back, which Kaoren won easily. Zan pwned me as well –

she's obviously been practicing hard. Still, I kept up, and it was fun, especially because I briefly had the lead because I dive and do the turn better than them both (though, knowing Kaoren, he'll have perfected that before our next swim).

Good timing reading my diary tonight, since we'd reached the point where Zan was doing lessons with me in the pool. Kaoren was both very amused at the way I described Kajal and Forel, and hugely unimpressed with their behaviour. If Zan had been too severely impacted by their bullying, it was perfectly possible her distraction could have gotten her squad killed. We had another of our almost-arguments, since Kaoren thought Selkie needed to know, and I was pretty firmly of the opinion that Selkie already knows what both of them are like and that my world would be even more circumscribed if people felt they couldn't trust me not to replay everything they did in front of me. We're doing okay with our occasional disagreements – probably because we haven't yet hit anything where neither of us will give ground. Kaoren had to cede this one – my diary reading is something utterly private between us, and he won't act on anything I tell him unless I agree to it.

Explaining the Orlando Bloom Meter to Kaoren was about a 7 on the Excruciating Scale, and I was glad to stop reading so Kaoren could catch up on the mass of reports he's supposed to review. I'm going to work some more on the Q&A thing for *The Hidden War*, which I've decided to answer fairly detailed in some things and not at all in others (particularly questions about the kids). But I think I'll make it a condition that they have to release the Q&A to the public after they've made their episodes. And I'm going to have fun writing up how upset I got because someone stole my personal file and turned it into TV.

Thursday, September 25

Gravity

Again no drama overnight, and fortunately no nightmares for Sen. Breakfast was all about Tare's endless sunset, and another discussion of planetary rotation. I find it very weird how the day-night cycle on Tare is so long, yet the year so quick. We ended up deep in explanations of gravity and centrifugal forces and the fact that the entire universe is moving.

Ys and Rye seem less reluctant to go to the Kalrani school than they were attending the talent school at Pandora. Not keenly eager, but treating it as a task like cleaning up after breakfast. They're the neatest damn kids – except Sen, who is mess on legs and has provided me with the challenge of teaching Ys and Rye *not* to clean up after her. Kaoren or I clean up Sen's mess, or Sen cleans up Sen's mess. Theoretically.

I spent the day finishing off the Q&A. There were tons of questions about me and Kaoren, all about when and where and why and how we felt about each other during every single event, and I'm sure that they'll be disappointed that I simply added dates for when I first felt for him, and when he first felt for me, and when we got together.

Most of the other questions I answered a little more helpfully, although there's quite a lot of things I would only go to the edge of (not describing the kids, or other Setari, or certain aspects of my talents). I took considerable pleasure describing how upset and violated I'd felt about my file-napping. Kaoren and Maze and probably a whole bunch of other people will review it before it goes to the show's producers, and I'm sure I'll regret some of the things I wrote down. I thought for a long time, and then agreed to release the Kalasa log as well. I'm not entirely comfortable with it, but I guess it will stop some of the more exaggerated stories about what I did there, and at least it won't be distorted by reinterpretation. It saves Se-Ahn Surat from a complete water-logging.

Today's test was to simply have me expand my senses until my centre went vague, which I did without trouble or incident. Now KOTIS Command is having fun arguments about what the next test should be, and whether they can risk taking me into the Ena, and whether they dare take me back to Muina to see if I can help unravel more of its mysteries. So I'm back where I was before we last headed to Muina, frustrated at not being able to do anything useful, with the need to find a solution only growing more urgent. If there is a solution to be found. First and Fourth had a rough rotation today – a single six-person squad would have been overwhelmed. I'm not very keen to go through all that vomiting again, but having everyone I know fight harder and harder battles until someone gets killed is even worse. I keep checking the news for new discoveries coming out of Pandora, but the most I've heard is that the nanite factory is close to activation, and that more of the Nurans are accepting the interface. There's not even news about the splinter group.

I'm shying away from reading other news at the moment, and have been ploughing through more schoolwork instead. The rate that Ys and Rye are shaping up, they'll end up passing my Taren school level in a couple of years, which would be a little embarrassing. I keep telling myself I've graduated from high school back home, and am about to be paid an enormous amount of money, and there's no need to study geometry during a galactic apocalypse. And, yet, studying.

Friday, September 26

Ball

Weird dream last night. Not the rush-to-medical type, and not a projection, but a bit like when I was dreaming of Kaoren at Kalasa. I was dreaming of a bunch of children playing, kicking and tossing a ball made of cloth (a hacky sack?) to each other. Dressed in 'non-tech' clothes, which could mean Nurans or old Muinans, and most of them the same gold-brown skin, black-eyed, black-haired type as Kaoren and Sen. There was a girl watching them, standing at the top of some whitestone stairs leading to a walkway, and although physically she was far more like Sen, she reminded me so much of Ys – that fiercely shut down expression, the stubborn don't-need-these-people attitude. She was dressed a good deal more formally and expensively than the other kids, and I could see her working herself up, until finally she strode down the stairs and into the courtyard area where the children were playing.

They ran. Abandoned their ball and scurried like rabbits through archways and doors, looking genuinely frightened. The girl pretended she hadn't noticed, and strode chin held high across to another stair, managing to kick the little ball into a muddy patch as she did so. I had to wonder what she'd done to make them so scared of her.

I described the dream to Kaoren this morning, which mainly served to spark a discussion on whether I was supposed to wake myself up from all of my dreams, or just the ones we've established are a problem. He wasn't even sure himself which was the better response to dreams about unhappy little girls, and uncertainty's a pretty rare thing for Kaoren. Then he told me to write a report up describing in tedious detail everything I'd seen, including any decorations, and style of the buildings and types of plants and clothing. I asked the kids whether Nurans ever played with balls made of cloth, and Rye shrugged and said balls were made of lots of things.

Training, training, training all day. I'm far more toned than I ever imagined being. Mara has recovered really well, although she still has a fair bit of cosmetic work to do to get rid of the scars. The skin on my stomach has settled down, although there's a faint difference between the new and old skin. Nothing so bad as to need another session.

Today's test was just another visualisation, with no ill effects, but tomorrow we're going to go into the Ena so I can attempt to visualise Pandora. Four squads as guards, and they've had drones set up out there to scan for any sign of Cruzatch.

We had Siame over to our apartment for dinner. Kaoren wants to have her more regularly involved in our lives to make her feel less excluded. That went okay, I guess – she at least has decided to talk to me now, if only to ask questions about precisely how my talents work, and what exactly was the crisis which sent us back to Tare. That was more detail than I'd given the kids, and I had to be careful not to show any hesitation in letting them know more about what was going on with me. I think it would be harder on them to feel we were keeping the truth from them, than to know.

Sen insisted on showing Siame her spruced-up bedroom. Rye was cautiously polite. Ys was silent unless asked a direct question. I'm hoping things will get more relaxed as these meetings go on. Kaoren's looking worn again – he hates how unhappy Siame is. I think I'll see how he feels about back rubs.

Saturday, September 27

Edge of Drama

I dreamed about that girl again. At least this time I knew to try and spot identifying marks, for all that there was precious little to see. I wanted to try doing a projection of it, which is so much simpler than trying to describe things, but when I suggested it later Kaoren and Maze said to not try that yet. It was duller than the first dream – the girl was in a narrow corridor (possibly even a secret passage), apparently eavesdropping on conversations.

These were muffled – whitestone blocks sound pretty efficiently, and unlike the girl I couldn't press my ear to what I guess were purpose-built listening holes. Besides, I think they might have been talking in old Muinan. The tone of the voices was mostly casual, occasionally intimate. Finally the girl stopped to listen at a room where I wasn't even sure what I was hearing. A group of people, yes, male and female, angry and worried, not quite shouting, but the words sounded like bells and thunder; resonant, strange, inhuman. Then the conversation abruptly faded, a deep voice said a couple of short words, and the girl took off at a run.

I woke up then, and snuggled into Kaoren's side, and tried to decide why I was dreaming these things. The best I could come up with is that I'm dreaming about the last touchstone's life, before the disaster on Muina. She looks about the right height for that small, shrouded figure. That's nothing more than a guess, but Maze and Kaoren haven't been able to suggest any solid alternatives. Of course, if it is the last touchstone's life, then anything or nothing could be important. It's given the technicians something else to argue about, and during the debate about whether I should sleep in medical I considered just not mentioning any more dreams, but I've accepted that enduring medical is part of what I need to do.

The test in the Ena was uneventful. I visualised the café at Pandora, and found it dark – night-time there. It was tiring enough that I didn't mind a nap afterwards, in medical or not, and again had no dramas.

Tomorrow they're going to have me do another projection of the place where I was dream-trapped. Kaoren's not keen on this, and nor am I really, but it is the logical next step. They're bringing Inisar back from Muina to get the benefit of his Sight Sight as well.

Sunday, September 28

Stress

No dream of girl last night. I didn't know whether to be relieved or disappointed. Today the visualisation of the room I'd been trapped in went smoothly, right up until they started talking about lifting the cloth covering the figure. Maze moved toward it, and I said: "Don't!"

My heart rate spiked through the roof, and I lost the projection, and then couldn't explain why I'd felt so panicked. Maybe it was just the idea that they might lift that cloth and the little girl I've been dreaming about would be lying there. Or what's left of her. I earned myself an extra-long time in medical as a result, and then while I was there news came in that there'd been a massive attack on Kolar South.

The Kolaren Setari and military had managed to kill it, but people had died, including two of the Setari. The two who died weren't Setari I'd met, and I feel bad that this makes it easier for me. Everyone's looking seriously stressed out – massive attacks have never been close to so frequent before this. The kids picked up on it – or probably had been reading the news services again, which were full of doom-laden predictions.

I'm pretty sure I'm going to have nightmares tonight, no matter what visualisations I try. I'm just too upset by the idea of more and more massive attacks.

Monday, September 29

Settled

Nice to be right. I kept having projective nightmares, over and over – mostly the Velcro massive dream. I've become very adept at recognising them and making myself wake up, fortunately. I put into effect Kaoren's suggestion to try to wake myself up from anything even mildly disturbing, even when I'm not sure if it's a dream, and am feeling all the better for that working. Otherwise, right now I wouldn't be able to risk sleeping anywhere near other people. Poor Kaoren woke with me each time, and after the fourth dream we gave up and had hot drinks – and then I heard Sen murmuring and fretting, so I went and smoothed tangled threads of hair off her forehead until she settled down. Since she was as usual in Ys' bed, I managed to wake Ys in the process, but I just gave her the same treatment, and she stood it for a full ten seconds before turning her head away.

I was less stressed out by the time we went back to bed, and had another dream about the unhappy girl. She was sitting on a whitestone roof, looking very wan and confused and vague, like she'd been doped up on drugs. I had a good view of the scenery, and divided my attention between the girl (who sat unmoving, even when it started to drizzle) and trying to memorise as much detail as possible of a busy Muinan-style city. It looked like Nuriath must once have looked, although there was a single very tall statue off to my left. It was facing away from me, and dominated the city.

After a good survey I tried to go kneel in front of the girl, but that made me aware that I didn't have a me to kneel with, and so I woke up. All this waking up (and using my talents while sleeping) meant I spent the day feeling gluggy and tired. Despite longing to get things done, I was glad that they decided to make the day a training day instead of another session in the Ena. Not that I felt like exercising either.

Fortunately, Mara toned back her intensity, and we even had time to fit in another swimming session for the kids with Zan. Rye's determination to do well in front of Kaoren at least sparks an equal determination in Ys to not lag behind, so they both made good progress. Sen is growing more confident with the dog paddle, and thus less inclined to cling, and the three of them looked to be enjoying just paddling back and forth to each other (in that so-funny little-kid way which makes them look like frantic frogs). Kaoren's been off in a Captain's meeting most of the evening, and it felt very strange to have dinner without him. I've yet to understand the difference between the meetings he can attend over the interface and the ones he has to go to in person.

Ys is drawing ahead of Rye in terms of reading ability, judging from their attempts with the beginning of tonight's chapter. Taren isn't nearly so inconsistent a language as English, and they're both able to consistently sound out words now, just with varying levels of speed and some distinctly odd syllable breaks. I did notice that they're beginning to shift to a more Taren rather than Nuran accent, which I guess is what you get when you cram yourself full of Taren schooling for weeks on end.

And it has been weeks. That really amazes me to think about. We've had the kids with us for over a month now. The idea of them belonging with us is beginning to solidify into a reality. And Kaoren and I are more certain about each other every day. I've been able to put aside my sense of impending doom to simply be thankful for all the good things which came with the bad.

Tuesday, September 30

Blocked

I dreamed of 'my' girl again. She was sneaking through a series of rooms and corridors, dodging and hiding behind walls, dashing across open spaces. There were a lot of guards about, dressed in cream tunics and carrying heavy, ornate spears. No glowing eye flashes anywhere in this dream, but I did start wondering if I was watching an episode of *Junior-League Stargate*, which is why I'm so uncertain whether these dreams are important.

My girl was very good at sneaking about, although I think she was still drugged or whatever was wrong with her last time. Occasionally she would stop and develop a lost and confused expression, and once was nearly caught during an unfocused moment. When she wasn't confused she seemed upset and frustrated and angry, again reminding me so much of Ys' fulminating determination.

I didn't see the outside of the building she was working her way through, but it seemed to have an awful lot of rooms, and three or four levels. It wasn't until she reached the central chamber that I realised we were in some kind of pyramid. The walls stepped upward in tiers to a small square ceiling which was glowing with a greeny-gold light, picking out glints which might be symbols in a big black...dome tent made of stone. That's the best I can describe it – the shape of a big black cloth which had been pinned to the ground at the corners and then blown upward so that it formed a stone bubble, the unpinned sections curving higher to provide four entrances. It was hard to see what was underneath it – just dark and glints of the greeny-gold light, giving the space an aquatic gloom.

There were guards in the room, and the girl was watching from the uncertain shelter of one of the corridors leading into it. She grew very keyed up and nervous as she watched and waited, and shrank back at the first sign of movement under the stone tent. And then they came out. Eight foot tall, dressed in simple robes, blindingly beautiful. These weren't fit, good-looking people like the Setari; they had an extreme physical perfection which makes me think Michelangelo, or Photoshop. Beyond flawless, honed to an eye-flinching glory which declared their importance, like they had their own personal lens flare.

The Photoshop Gods made me feel small in a way which had nothing to do with height. They just were...powerful. Power-filled. Maze might have called Inisar 'beyond formidable', but Inisar has never made me feel like he could effortlessly squish me like a bug – even if that's true. I swear the air vibrated as they walked past.

All the stern guards either bowed their head sharply, or turned to follow the Photoshop Gods, and that was the girl's chance. She dashed silently forward toward the dome, except the closer she got the slower she moved, like she was trying to walk under water. She made it, though, staggering through into the shadowy light to a place which was full of sarcophagi standing tilted upright like at Arenrhon, except without lids or little nameplates. The sarcophagi were arranged in a circle around a central pillar, and one still had a Photoshop God in it, a man laying all limp and motionless, his golden skin looking weird and waxy in the odd light, and his lens flare turned off.

And there was noise, a low whispering which instantly brought me back to my dream of being trapped.

The girl was heading toward one of the empty sarcophagi, her face all screwed up from effort. But she hadn't gone unnoticed, and one of the guards was already racing toward her, and her spear flashed forward, and my vain attempt to stop it woke me up.

I think – I'm not sure, but I think the spear went through the girl, not in a blood and piercing way, but in a one-of-these-things-isn't-tangible kind of way.

I was still very upset, of course, and though I tried to be all analytical and detached describing it to Kaoren, I ended up bursting into tears and crying all over him. Again it was really hard to explain why I was so upset, beyond that she reminded me of Ys and I felt sorry for her.

"Don't discount the strength of your reaction," Kaoren said. "Whether this just happened, or is the past, or on some level a fiction, it gives us new possibilities to follow."

"Do you think that she might have been a ghost – an Ionoth like my Ghost – or is there any super-rare talent for being insubstantial?"

"You said she kicked a ball in the earlier dream."

"That wouldn't necessarily make her not a ghost. Ghosts are supposed to be able to focus their energy to move things. And that would explain all those kids being afraid of her."

I hope some sense can be made of it all, and soon. No progress during today's test in the Ena, where they decided to let me try and project the last room of my dream, and all I succeeded in doing was straining myself to the point that I started shaking and spent the rest of the day having muscle tremors. They still haven't quite gone away.

I slept in medical, so of course can't sleep now, but at least I can watch Kaoren sleep. I'm working on him getting more rest, and spent a big portion of the evening distracting him with what I'd written about my trip to Earth, and extended hand-holding. He doesn't even remember calling me a stray, and said he was consumed by the discovery of the Pillar, and simply relieved I did exactly as he told me. I had to laugh at him for that. And I've found that if he starts having a nightmare while I'm awake, that if I think about something peaceful which made me happy, and kind of push it out to him, he settles down and sleeps more deeply. The power of positive thinking.

OCTOBER

Wednesday, October 1

Respite

No dreams last night, which meant I spent the day trying not to fret about my dream girl. Fortunately Mara was in the mood to work me hard, which helped me not stress too much about it. My tremors are almost gone, but they decided not to do any testing today, so it was a full day of training.

Fortunately me sleeping through means Kaoren had another good night, and the shadows are gone from under his eyes. At the end of the day First and Fourth had a joint dinner in the canteen, and amused themselves interrogating the kids about what they've been doing at the Setari school. Rye's so cute, drawn irresistibly out of his shell, and really wanting to not make a fool of himself among all these people who think he's worth spending time on. Ys seems resigned to the attention, and is working to hide how much she hates the two people she cares about most letting more and more people into their lives. She reminded me so much of my dream girl that I couldn't resist reaching out and rubbing her shoulder just for a moment. I can't make her be happy, but I can do my best to be sure she's comfortable and not pushed beyond her limits.

They haven't decided what I'm doing tomorrow. Still debating risking returning me to Muina, but currently the no vote is winning.

Thursday, October 2

Big Sister

When I'm curled up in bed drifting off to sleep I spend at least a few minutes noticing the people around me – it's like noticing the noises around you more when you're trying to sleep. And especially when I'm asleep and not dreaming I often am at least partially aware of people moving around me, so I usually know if Sen has climbed into bed with Ys, and when Kaoren moves about. Of course, if my attention is caught up in something I can be completely oblivious to *everything* going on, which Kaoren wants me to make an effort to overcome. I'm getting a little better about it, I think.

Anyway, so long as I'm living in close quarters with people I'm always going to know who is sleeping with whom – certainly everyone within 'comfortable range' distance which at the moment seems to mean all of First, Second, Third and Fourth, and a bit of Fifth and Sixth as well (I'm kind of glad I can't reach Kajal's room without deliberately trying). I can't actually tell what anyone's doing, just where they are, but if there's two people in a bedroom all night it kind of becomes obvious. Alay often sleeps with one of the device technicians, and Ketzaren spends most of her nights with Jeh (I feel so thick for not realising they're a couple). Maze and Zee don't sleep with anyone so far as I can see and, for all his reputation, neither does Nils. Well, unless you count Ghost, who divides her favours between him, me and Rye. Though I guess Nils' reputation isn't about sleeping.

I'm less aware of Third and Fourth's relationships, but still am awkwardly conscious of knowing more about a few of them than I expect they'd be comfortable with. The thing that surprised me today, though, was Inisar and Taarel. Not sleeping together, but just I've noticed them together a handful of times over the last few days.

Inisar's been kicking his heels while my projections fail, so I suppose it's possible Taarel's been assigned to be his native guide – or pump him for information. But they make an interesting pair – she's so kingly and he has such presence. Though since Taarel thought she wasn't a match with Kaoren because they both like being in charge, maybe Inisar's someone she wouldn't consider.

I've been in a very in-love-with-Kaoren mood all day, because when I woke up this morning he just had this look of contentment in his eyes. Being with me makes him happy. Spending an hour with him in the shower in the morning makes Ys give us scornful looks all through breakfast.

I didn't dream of my ghost-girl again last night (which is probably at least part of the reason I'm burying myself in adoration of Kaoren), but on the up side Maze suggested that I try projecting my dreams of her as if it was a movie, and that worked in a patchy, disjointed way because it took a lot of what felt like mental gymnastics. Still, I was able to show them what the outside of the city looked like, and the guards, and that central room of the pyramid. The three Sight Sight observers (Kaoren, Tsur Selkie and Inisar) were extra-serious while examining the inside of the weird stone tent bubble with the one limp Photoshop God slumped in the upright sarcophagus.

They think it's a door. Or a lock, like the metal boxes the Tarens put around gates. Or something. After that Tsur Selkie had me try to reproduce every view of the city's outside that I could, particularly from when I was up on that roof, and they're doing some topographic analysis of the land contours to see if they can figure out where all this happened.

I started getting muscle tremors again, not really severe ones, but that's the last of the experiments for me for a while. A bunch of days of training and medical tests instead, while they try to analyse the jumble of images I'd produced.

Friday, October 3

Close Calls

Siame visited for dinner again. She seems to be swapping through approaches with these visits, first ignoring me, then interrogating me, and now making very polite conversation but looking completely bored. The most she achieved with that was annoying both Kaoren and Ys (who probably thinks she has dibs on being rude to me), and prompting Sen to offer her one of her dolls and then Ghost for cuddling. But Ghost doesn't currently approve of Siame and went off to haunt Nils instead.

Rye was either oblivious to undercurrents, or determined to pretend not to notice and distract us with the latest news from Muina. A handful of the breakaway group of Nurans had returned to Pandora carrying one boy with a broken leg. Who'd had a broken leg for a couple of days. The leaders of the breakaway group had refused to allow anyone to call to Pandora for help, and since they had no skilled medics with them, the poor guy spent a short eternity in agony until finally his closest friends 'rescued' him and tried to carry him all the way back to Pandora. I'm not exactly sure what the settlement's Nuran Setari observer was doing during all this, but I expect he's the reason a group of greensuits in a flier happened across them almost straight away and gave them a lift. Details are sparse, but KOTIS did make a short statement that those who had returned had chosen to stay.

Inisar went back this morning, before the news broke, and more news arrived after the kids had gone to bed that about two-thirds of the group had upped and followed the injured boy's group and started marching back to Pandora. Some more fliers were sent out to pick them up. There's a little under thirty Nurans left at 'Nurenor', which is what they apparently have named their little settlement. The news stories showed some aerial shots of Nurenor, which looked muddy and muddled and dispiriting. I was most interested in the number of hairy sheep that they'd managed to pen up. There's more hairy sheep in that region of Muina than any other animal, I swear. Apparently being butted by one of the rams was how the injured boy's leg was broken.

A reminder to me of how lucky I am.

Saturday, October 4

Two Feet

Still no dream of my ghost-girl. Odds are I was dreaming the last days of her life up until she died.

Kaoren could see I was down, but worked with my mood rather than trying to change it. I wish I could be as perceptive about him in return. I didn't even realise he'd been injured in training until I saw this huge black bruise on his back. The padding covering one of those swinging booms in the Sight training course had come loose when he jumped on it, and that had delayed his jump long enough for another boom to hit him in the back. He said minor injuries were to be expected, and shrugged it off.

Since his Sights make it almost impossible for me to hide that not knowing dismayed me, I just accepted that he would know that I was feeling bad about not even realising, and distracted myself giving him foot rubs while reading him another installation of my diary. I made it all the way up to Unara Rotation, and then he fell asleep and I could let myself freak out.

That boom could just as easily have hit him in the head.

Sunday, October 5

Bruised

Kaoren's shoulder was so stiff and sore this morning, he took himself off to medical. Nothing's broken, just unhappy muscles, and the medicking has helped it along tremendously. By the time he was feeling better, I was stiff and sore and bruised instead, as Mara continues to push my training (including, sadly, dodging and learning how to fall down in clever ways). I am quite fit now, but not a fan of throwing myself on the ground.

Sen had a marvellous time investigating our injuries and playing doctor by applying the green goop the medics give for bruises. We finished our current book at bedtime, and I told Ys it was her turn to pick the next story, and she told me straight away. I think she's been looking forward to it, and for a minute I had to blink at how pleased I was and how much I want her to accept me. In return I asked her if she'd take Sen through her sleep visualisation exercise, and I think that pleased Ys a lot. One thing I can't let myself forget is that Ys and Rye raised Sen, and it upsets them immensely to be in any way sidelined from her life. Ys had obviously paid a great deal of attention to the exercises, and was very calm and measured taking Sen through her favourite.

I was careful not to push it by complimenting Ys overmuch, and I think the simple nod passed her suspicion barriers well enough.

I'm turning into Kaoren.

Monday, October 6

Price of Together

I dreamed of my ghost-girl! She was dazed and non-responsive, but at least didn't seem injured. She was again sitting on the roof of a building, and with Tsur Selkie in mind I made sure to get good long looks in every direction. Then, conscious that last time I'd tried to do anything in this kind of dream it had immediately woken me up, I very cautiously tried to project my voice so she could hear, but I'm not sure if I managed it or not, only that I woke up feeling rather tired and dizzy.

Since I was still feeling rather tired and dizzy after breakfast was done, Kaoren took me off to medical, where I promptly fell back to sleep and dreamed of my ghost-girl again (still sitting on the roof). Kaoren had warned it was probably best not to try attempting communication again, and though I was tempted, the energy level it seems liable to take might be beyond me unless I was asleep in the Ena or something.

I'm scheduled for another experiment tomorrow, and I'm going to ask if I can try manifesting just the girl, rather than the place she's in. It's not something I've tried before – too afraid of making permanent Ionoth which roam free attacking Setari – but I think it's worth a shot.

I guess she really is a ghost though, since she's still 'there' after being speared. I asked Kaoren today whether what Earth people calls ghosts would count as Ionoth. It seems different to me. He's not entirely certain. Tarens do have stories about ghosts, but they're considered a version of Ionoth – memories of people.

Preliminary scripts for the first few episodes of the next season of *The Hidden War* have shown up. It's very interesting seeing what they're doing to reform Lastier to make the idea of him having a romance with me more believable. During the end of the last season they kept him pretty full of himself, and delightfully sarcastic, especially during the Arenrhon exploration, but emphasised the professionalism, and made sure that 'I' acted entertained by his cleverer remarks. And showed how completely his squad trusted him. They haven't put in any hint of obvious romance though, but just an underlying sense that there could potentially be something there.

The first episode will be an extra-long episode, starting with my log up to passing out in that bathroom, switching to the search for me, and then the rest of my log and then the discovery of my arrow and my rescue. Lastier stays supremely professional throughout, until news finally arrives of the arrow, and then they keep showing his reaction to things – the news that they're in range of me, that I'm critically injured, and then they get to me. And just for a moment his face shows how shaken he is, and he closes his eyes and struggles to put back a mask of cool evaluation. By the time people start watching my log and are being horrified about the Cruzatch he's enough the usual Lastier to snark about my fighting ability.

Amazingly (but perhaps fortunately) the kids hadn't discovered *The Hidden War* before Kaoren and I started discussing it over breakfast (although Sen's been watching that Setari Song Star show). Ys and Rye immediately looked for and found the first episode about me (neatly demonstrating how far they've advanced in their ability to use the interface, not to mention read/use the text-to-voice function). *The Hidden War* is classified the equivalent of PG for under-thirties, so we had to give permission for Sen to see it, and we watched it together instead of our usual after-dinner game. Ys wanted to know exactly what was true and what wasn't, and Rye was primarily caught up by the fact that Se-Ahn Surat looks nothing like me – and the discovery that both my eyes used to be the same colour. His reaction to Lastier was pretty much on par with Fourth Squad's.

It was a good opportunity to talk them through the problems caused by our notoriety, the impact that would have on them, and the fact that there was sure to be scripts in the future involving them. That was something we couldn't prevent entirely, but Kaoren told them that it was their decision as to whether anything 'true' about them was known, or if it was all left to scriptwriters to fabricate. I'd already made clear in my initial feedback that I wanted the kids kept out of the show as much as possible. Ys and Rye had already read quite a few news articles discussing the fact that Kaoren and I had expanded our family, but were of course less than impressed with the idea that there would be actors pretending to be them, and that a lot of people would believe that how they behaved on the show was what they were really like.

"Think over what you would prefer," Kaoren said. "The truth, an invented history, or leave them with nothing so that what they show is nothing of you."

Ys immediately vetoed making things up. Looking at the script outlines given to us, it wouldn't be until the next season that it becomes an issue, but as our shopping trip has already shown them, a great many people are going to be interested in them.

Knowing more now about Nuran culture, I'm glad we didn't just let them disappear into the eight thousand. Until all the Nuran children are adopted, this system of servants and Houses and Zarath would have put Ys and Rye in a bad place, no matter what opinion Tarens and Kolarens have of it, and it was important to get my three out of that to cut short any threat of them being separated. Sometimes I think I'm doing them more harm than good, and sometimes I'm just enjoying the hugs too much to care.

I keep trying to think of ways I can help my ghost-girl as well, but I have to face the near-certainty that it's way too late for me to do anything for her.

Tuesday, October 7

Reversed Polarity

I thought at first that last night's dream was exactly the same, but after surveying the city I realised that my ghost-girl just hadn't moved, was still sitting dazed and confused on the same roof a day later.

For today's session Tsur Selkie agreed to let me try and project just my ghost-girl and not her surroundings, if I thought I could do that. I wasn't entirely sure, and I feel increasingly embarrassed at the prospect of failing these experiments when I now have four squads sitting in attendance. Second and Eighth were the spares this time, since Third has been sent to Muina.

It was a struggle. It felt like trying to push the wrong ends of two magnets together – I could feel more or less how I needed to go, but then my mind would slip off focus. I was just about to concede defeat when that slippery sense of repulsion reversed, and I felt like I was being pulled into something, and clutched at my test chair in a panic, convinced I was going to end up back in that horrible room again. My vitals skyrocketed, and the near-space all around me started distorting, making everyone feel heavier. Tsur Selkie sent most of the squads backward, and sharply ordered me to stop the test.

I said, "It isn't me," sounding thoroughly freaked out, and shuddered as the drag got even worse and just for a moment I thought I saw my ghost-girl, but then there was an awful piercing pain in my head, and I passed out. That last was the interface deciding to start growing again. They still have no idea why the interface reacts this way with me occasionally, and they're talking about uninstalling it completely until further notice. But we're learning all my foibles and so were at least ready for the possibility, quickly shutting it down. My eye was damaged, but not very badly, and I'll be piratical for only a short while.

I woke in medical to the news that at the exact time as my attempted projection, all the platforms and malachite marbles on Muina had reacted. It had lasted for only for the few seconds before I'd collapsed, but the satellites and drones busy scanning Muina's surface had picked up a power reading in a region where no malachite marble had as yet been discovered. A new place to search.

Kaoren has this tiny frown-line between his eyes that was never there before.

I wasn't the one projecting. I stopped as soon as I felt that heaviness, and something else went on. We have the rough location of another malachite marble in return, but if I hadn't passed out I'm not sure what would have happened.

Thursday, October 9

Hooked

I didn't dream of my ghost-girl last night. She dreamed of me.

Or I dreamed of her dreaming of me. At any rate, I could tell it wasn't like my normal dreams. I dreamed that I was asleep on the scan bed, and Kaoren was asleep in the low lounge chair they'd fetched in for him. The lights were at half setting, but I could see straight away when my ghost-girl showed up – just there, looking at me.

Kaoren woke up immediately – he tells me it was because of my energy output, not because the girl registered as a threat – and after a long look at the girl (who was staring fixedly at me) he said: "Her name is Cassandra."

The girl only gave him the barest glance. "What happened to her face?"

She was speaking old Muinan, and there was a pause (while Kaoren accessed a translator for the words he didn't understand), then he slowly said in the best old Muinan he could manage: "She was injured by a communication device. She has been dreaming about you. Do you have the same ability to see and create projections?"

The girl gave him a suspicious look. "Who are you?"

"My name is Kaoren. Cassandra and I are...hand fasted. Will you tell me your name?"

That earned him a long second look, then: "Liranadestar. Where is this place?"

Kaoren's eyes were very narrow, and I could tell people were giving him a lot of conflicting instructions on what to say to her. "This is a world called Tare, a planet that some of the inhabitants of Muina fled to after the spaces were shattered."

From the little frown, I guessed the girl didn't quite understand at least part of what he said, but wasn't willing to admit it. So like Ys, who hates to show any form of ignorance.

"Can you take a message for me?" the girl (who can be called Lira because Liranadestar is a worse mouthful than Sen's name) asked. "To Peresadestar of Nuriath? Tell him that Naranezolen of Oriath took me away to a city I don't know. I haven't been able to reach out to him the way I usually do. I can't understand why."

"Do you remember going to a room with a dome made of black stone?" Kaoren asked very carefully.

"No," Lira said, but then paused and looked confused. "Will you carry my message?" she asked, with a ferocious frown.

Kaoren looked from her to me. I was starting to feel pretty bad, achingly exhausted, like I hadn't been to sleep for years. His mouth was a flat line as he looked back at her, and he said, "The people you're speaking of have been dead for centuries. Muina was abandoned centuries ago. Nuriath lies in ruins."

She gave him a disbelieving glare, but was shaken by the calm certainty in Kaoren's eyes and then wavered and vanished. I woke myself up, and held out a hand for him, and shuddered from the effort of just that.

"She was using me as anchor to look here," I said, as he helped me sit up a little. "But she's projecting herself. Can she be dead, and yet project herself?"

I didn't get an answer to this – still haven't – and a technician bustled in with a fortifier and made me drink it until I passed out for the better part of a day. At least I was already in medical. Kaoren stayed with me most of the time, with Maze, Zan, Zee and Mara occasionally spelling him. I felt pretty damn gluggy when I finally woke up, and took a long, cold shower to try and pep myself up a little. It hasn't really worked, but they don't want me to go back to sleep as yet, and are making me periodically walk around to keep my circulation up.

Everyone's a little freaked out about how much energy the projection was costing me. If I was right about it being her dream, not mine, then I mightn't even be able to wake myself up from it. Since I didn't try, there's a lot of unease about what will happen if she uses me as an anchor again. She's considerably more powerful than me – or, rather, they think she's actively linked to the platforms and malachite marbles on Muina, because they reacted again during this dream – which is another thing freaking everyone out. No-one's allowed to use platforms except for emergencies.

There's been a lot of Cruzatch sightings in Pandora near-space – and Taren and Kolaren near-space – and everyone's on high alert. KOTIS Command is debating taking me back to Muina to see if that reduces the energy cost of the dreams, but they're worried about exposing me to Cruzatch attack, not to mention the possibility of me getting trapped in that dark place again. But waiting till I'm stronger is no longer the safest option.

I'm giving people ulcers on their ulcers.

On the positive news front, they've found another of the Arenrhon-type places in the zone where the satellite picked up power readings. And they've located Oriath on the old maps recovered from Kalasa and are going to send an expedition there to scout around.

I am very bored with being in medical now, and am going to try my hand at bullying Kaoren into letting me go back to our apartment, at least while I'm awake.

Friday, October 10

To Atanra

On the way back to Muina to see if the energy cost of my dreams is less there. More ping-ponging between planets. I don't see what else KOTIS could do, but I am starting to feel like one of a mob of squawking chickens, running back and forth, back and forth, trying to find a safe place because the sky is falling everywhere.

My interface is still turned off, and it's very strange travelling without it. Makes me feel very isolated, for all I have four full squads with me.

We did have quite a debate about the kids, since we're not going to Pandora, but to a newly built facility called Atanra (the word means 'passage') which is very near Muina's rift into deep-space and is intended as a staging ground for planetary arrivals and departures. They hurried construction along at least in part so they could keep me close to the rift in case I get trapped again. No platform, no handy Ddura you can summon to play guard dog. Lots of shielding and defences, presumably. Because it's not considered a 'safe' zone, the kids will be going on to Pandora. And because the squads no longer have any members on sick leave, they've been assigned a babysitter.

I'm trying not to show how hugely entertained I am by the idea of Siame's first 'mission' being looking after three children who think they're well able to look after themselves. Not that, with all her Sights, Siame is probably in any doubt as to me finding the situation funny. She's being very self-assured – she really has a phenomenal poise, which only the drastic alteration to her close relationship with Kaoren has come close to upsetting. She decided to be coolly professional with me again, polite with a hint of Kaoren's dryness, not pretending to like me, but careful not to be hostile either. I can live with that.

It's been fun watching the squads react to her, particularly Fourth and Eighth, who have probably seen her before when they were Kalrani, but not had that much to do with her and thus see her entirely as "Tsee Ruuel's sister" and are rather wary. Most of the senior Setari are encouraging, but Lohn and Nils seem to regard her as Kaoren's 'mini-me' and are longing to tease her. They've taken her, Ys and Rye on a tour of the ship (it's the *Litara* this time – considerably larger than the *Diodel*).

I'm hoping they turn my interface back on soon, so that I'll be able to chat to the kids even though they're in a different settlement. Sen is particularly fond of sending a channel request to me at random moments, and it bothers her that it currently won't connect. She's not very happy at all right now. I've been taking the opportunity of the flight to be reassuringly well and alive, but the eye patch makes it a little unconvincing, and she's been latched on to me as much as possible. She's half-asleep in my lap 'helping' me write.

Theoretically we left Ghost behind, but I can feel her wandering about the ship. Since there's no Ddura at Atanra, I figure it should be okay. Nearly at the rift entrance, so it's time to go back to our pods.

Atanra is basically barracks, warehouses and a big landing spot for ships. One single building for all the living areas to make it easier to protect, furnished with very solid shielding. I spent my time being scanned while the Setari swept the area and checked the drone set in near-space for signs of Cruzatch activity. Ghost kept me invisible company, but is otherwise maintaining a low profile.

Thankfully the medics decided it was okay to turn my interface back on, and so I was able to read the kids their bedtime story and ask them what Pandora was looking like now (most of the flowers have moved on, lightning-quick, and all the trees are leaf-dusted). I'm feeling a little 'over-observed', since my room is a medical observation area. It's not too bad, I guess – it has two beds so that Kaoren can sleep in the same room as me – but I'm feeling like I should dig out one of my lab rat shirts.

Saturday, October 11

Ghosts

No dreams or projections of any sort last night. With four squads assigned to look after me, I'm going to spend my time feeling perpetually guilty about wasting their time. They've broken into a dayshift and a nightshift, and are busy clearing the area of nearby Ionoth and obligingly pretending they're not sitting around waiting for me to do something interesting. I'm not even scheduled for testing at the moment, until my eye is back to normal.

Atanra might be an interesting place to visit if I was allowed to go outside, but between health and safety issues I have a choice between the mess hall and my medical observation unit. I spent the day doing a lot of schoolwork, sleeping, and trying not to cringe during an examination of my eye. I was unconscious for a lot longer the last time my interface went haywire, so I missed the sensation of my eye not feeling 'right'.

I was in a bit of a mood most of the day. I always feel embarrassed when I'm feeling grumpy, given all the people who're stuck babying me, but I dealt with it by telling people I was feeling grumpy and was going to concentrate on schoolwork.

The highlight of my day was an actual conversation with Ys – who sent me a channel request after discovering an interface site devoted to "Caszandra's children", which had a lot of detail apparently culled from conversations with some of the Nuran survivors. About Ys and Rye they only seem to know that they were servants who had been assigned to look after Sen, but they had quite a bit of information about Sen's parents – Fiionarestel and Durenatar. The story (as retold) sounded a bit Romeo and Juliet – Fiionarestel was a highly respected scholar (and Sight Sight talent) and Durenatar some kind of architect. They'd been close childhood friends, but their families (or Heads of their Houses, rather) had a disagreement and they were forbidden from seeing each other. And had anyway, and had Sen, and were totally cut off from their families until they were found dead following what was widely believed to have been a murder-suicide.

Ys desperately doesn't want Sen to know any of this. She hated asking me, but her need to protect Sen trumps everything, and so she wanted me to find a way to suppress all information about Sen's parents.

Having finally reached this point, I asked very cautiously: "Does Sen not know anything about her parents?"

"She knows they were killed. She does not talk about them."

Ys sounded angry, which is her way of being very upset.

"You don't need me point out that Sen's Sight probably means she knows far more about this than you do," I said. "And you know perfectly well you can't control what other people say. If there anything to do, it's to see if there is truth to their deaths, rather than gossip. I can ask Inisar if he knows any details. Would you like me do that?"

She's decided she wants to think about it first, and went back to not wanting to talk to me. I'm tempted to ask Inisar anyway, especially given the conspiracies complicating Nuri over the past few years. But I think right now Sen's more likely to be upset by Ys' anxiety than what happened to her parents.

Sunday, October 12

Mind's Eye

I didn't dream of my ghost-girl last night. I dreamed about Nils. Well, to be exact I had a series of dreams about Helese Surion and Nils. The first dream was Nils and Helese on her fiftieth birthday (which is sixteen and two-thirds, when you shift to 'young adult' status according to Taren law and can take the exam to be granted adult rights). They'd gone out to dinner together, and then they made love (for the first time, I think). She and Nils looked fantastic together – Helese was tall and handsome rather than what I guess would be called beautiful on Earth, and she teased Nils about being prettier than she was, which at that age he was. He called her 'Lese' and so plainly lived and breathed for her that I could barely stand knowing that things wouldn't work out for them.

The dream shifted, and an older Helese was holding a party to celebrate her engagement to Maze. Nils was there, and was very gracious and happy for them, and flirted more than successfully with Mara, who took him back to her quarters. But after she'd fallen asleep he lay in her bed looking devastated.

And then another shift, to Nils sitting alone in what I guess was his apartment, conjuring an illusion of Helese and talking to it about Zee, about how she'd become so important to him even though he'd promised himself he'd never let himself really care about anyone again, and how fun it had been giving her the lowest possible opinion of him to keep her safely at a distance. But that he was feeling so tired of it all lately.

I was crying when I woke up, and was then in an extremely awkward position because my energy output had made it obvious I was having some kind of talent dream, and there I was with tears running down my face and not wanting to admit why.

Kaoren was sitting watching me, so I opened a channel. "Can I just say that my dream wasn't anything to do with Muina or Cruzatch or anything that needs to be talked about?"

"What was it about?"

"Senior Setari private lives."

My day would have been far less uncomfortable if he'd been willing to leave it at that, but Kaoren gave me a searching look and then asked, "If you were dreaming something like that, why didn't you wake yourself up?"

And the problem was that I hadn't been able to. Admittedly I hadn't tried immediately, fascinated when I realised that Nils had been dating Helese Surion, but I'd tried to wake up when she and Nils started making love, and hadn't been able to. It was just like when I was trapped in my ghost-girl's dream. And as soon as I told Kaoren that it hadn't been *my* dream exactly, he immediately wanted to know whose it was.

It didn't seem possible to avoid answering that, and after a quick interface conversation Kaoren confirmed that Nils had been sleeping – and dreaming – at the same time as me. But I was very firmly of the opinion that there was no way in hell I was going tell anyone what Nils had been dreaming, and escaped into the shower to buy myself some thinking time. Kaoren told me later that he could mainly sense overwhelming guilt from me, which wasn't easy for him, but he decided that the simplest thing to do would be for me to talk to Nils and confirm that we'd been dreaming the same thing, and that there was no need to record the actual content of the dream.

Talking to Nils was the absolute last thing I wanted to do – closely followed by talking to anyone in First Squad (who were fortunately still asleep) – but I knew that saying that would only compound an already mortifying situation, so I forced myself to go off to a neutrally boring little meeting room where Nils was waiting. He was looking down at his hands when I arrived, his expression remote and stern, and I instantly pictured him naked and miserable and wished I was anywhere else.

Nils glanced up and saw me cringing in the doorway, and the stern look went away as he smiled. "If you go about acting like I might eat you, I might be tempted to try."

"I'm sorry," I blurted out in response. "I didn't mean to do that to you."

For a second something harder came into his eyes, but he sighed and said: "I know. Sit down. Your very annoying boyfriend has given me a list of questions to answer."

I sat, and said, "I can guess. No I wasn't thinking about you or, uh, any other Setari before I went sleep. I was thinking about Sen's parents. It very much like the dreams I had when Lira dreaming of talking to Kaoren, though not nearly as tiring. Like I was there, but not. The dream went from birthday to engagement party to your apartment."

He lifted his eyebrows, amused, but I know now that Nils is not nearly so carefree as he makes out, and I cringed all the more inside. I've never done anything before which made me feel so completely in the wrong.

"Lohn and I are going to have to increase the scale of red we can try to make you turn," he said lightly. "Did you know that today is 'Lese's birthday? She would have been eighty."

I shook my head. "No-one talks about her."

"No. Helese, Cham, Senere, Mede, Suzlein. And two of the younger squads, all gone in a single blow. Alay was deeply involved with Suzlein. She plays around with some sour squitch of a technician now, I think to punish herself for being alive. Regan and Mede had been on and off for years, but they were on at that time and he – I barely recognise him. All of these people we'd known since our twenties, almost a third of all the people who we relied on to understand us, lost. We barely functioned in the aftermath. Kisikar retired. Do you know what the most frightening thing about you is?"

That I couldn't answer, but he wasn't expecting me to. "Not that you can cause someone to relive their past – for that was far more than a dream for me – but that you could far surpass me in conjuring up people to chat to. I've talked to 'Lese on every one of her birthdays since she was fifteen – I knew her before the Setari program began – and didn't let a little matter like her death end that. But it's just an image of her, and I'm not sure I'd make the image talk back even if I could achieve that. But you – you could create something which *was* 'Lese."

"At least until I passed out," I said.

"Mn, and I doubt 'Lese would appreciate being made an Ionoth, no matter how briefly. This isn't likely to be the last time you do something which hurts someone. That's why you're working to learn how to control it. The sheer scope of what you might do is undercut by your tendency to nearly die in the process, but if we ever get past current dramas you're going to have to expect people to realise you are frightening as well as amusing. And prepare for those who would use you, or remove you, because you are unutterably dangerous. I suppose it's fortunate you think someone like Ruuel a wonderful thing." He paused, considering me, then added with a sheerly wicked grin: "And I am going to *enjoy* telling people that you were having an erotic dream about me."

My horrified reaction to this made him laugh, and he stood up, opening the door. "The correct response to that should be 'And not for the first time!', but I'll forgive you the lapse. We've covered enough for me to write this report, anyway."

He left, but I sat there for a while, thinking about how different from the usual Nils he'd been, how he'd given me a lecture, and a warning, and calmed me down at the same time. And that he hadn't tried to pretend that I hadn't hurt him. Kaoren came to check on me, and since the meeting room is more private than my medical room, I climbed into his lap and kissed him a lot, then told him how awful I felt about invading Nils' privacy like that, and wanted to know if he had any suggestions for how to not ever do that again. I wish he'd said yes, that there was something instant and immediate and certain. He did say it shouldn't be overlooked that Nils is an extremely strong Illusion talent, which is a thing not completely dissimilar from my projection abilities, and suggested that I should think over any distinctive aspects of the dream so that I can try to escape it as it forms. I spent the rest of the day trying to find a big enough rock to crawl under.

But there's no place to hide in a facility designed to observe you, and I had little chance of escaping Maze, though he did give me until lunchtime, after First came back from a morning patrol. He took me up to eat lunch on the roof, which would otherwise be a treat given that I'm not allowed out of the compound.

He gave no sign of being upset, and when we were both sitting asked: "Did you know Nils was once a captain candidate?" He didn't wait for an answer, going on: "One of the best, but he withdrew his candidacy shortly before he and Helese stopped seeing each other. It bothered 'Lese a great deal, because she knew she was the reason, though she couldn't argue against his logic, since he said he wouldn't put a squad in danger because his focus wasn't on them. Nils doesn't argue, or discuss the things which matter to him: he decides his preferred course and carries it out. When he saw how powerfully drawn 'Lese was to me, he switched himself out of a position of responsibility and quietly ended their relationship. Almost everyone believes it was the mutual waning of interest he claimed, for he loathes exposing his true feelings, and hides them very well."

"Hope you're not trying to make me feel better," I said, feeling about an inch tall.

"I'm trying to identify what caused this," he said, grave and calm. "Today, there's only one thing Nils would have been focused on. The dream was about 'Lese, wasn't it?"

I nodded, mouse-like.

"That makes your dream far less likely to be only triggered by you, you see. The sheer strength of Nils' emotion may be the reason you dreamed as you did. In a way he may have shaped your power, just as it is believed the Ena is shaped by the minds, thoughts and feelings of the living."

"Do you believe that?" I asked. I've been far, far too interested in Zee's and Nils' relationship to regard a handily-delivered explanation as anything but the result of my own curiosity.

"I believe a dream about 'Lese on 'Lese's birthday is unlikely to be coincidence. This really matters to you, doesn't it?"

"It–" I was burningly embarrassed all over again. "Even if didn't mean it, it was violation. If someone did that to me, I don't know if could stand look at them ever again."

"Then learn how to prevent it," Maze said, straightforwardly. "Knowing that the dreamer is reliving their past will no doubt give you extra determination, even if the dream is not one you control." He gave me one of his glorious smiles.   "We're not going to hate you for this, Caszandra. Certainly not Nils, who is far too just. And we have a certain amount of experience accepting that Place and Sight Sight talents will know far more about our inner lives than we'd care to reveal. Like you, they are generally generous enough not to treat that knowledge as gossip."

But nor does anyone really like the fact, even without having it underlined by being forced to relive the best and worst days of your life. The idea that it was Nils driving the dream, not me, isn't any more comforting, since that means that my dreams, my projections, can be controlled from outside by people other than touchstones.

I've been stressed out all day, and don't want to sleep and I'm painfully aware that everyone, from Kaoren to the technicians, has been wracking their brains trying to find a way to calm me down. I didn't even want to write in my diary, but Kaoren asked me to because he thinks it will help.

I used to like sleeping.

Monday, October 13

Stasis

Kaoren did the otters visualisation with me before I went to sleep, and this was familiar and comfortable enough that I was able to recognise when I started projecting it, and to keep it as my own dream rather than manifest it. This small advance in control has made me feel vaguely hopeful overall, and at least I felt well-rested when I woke up, and not nearly so tense and sick.

But I still don't want to go anywhere near Nils or First Squad and so was less than keen to be sent for basic stepping exercises with Mara. Mara was a particular hurdle, since I had after all watched her have sex with Nils and didn't know how much that night had mattered to her, or the timing of her relationship with Lohn, or anything. But she didn't ask questions, only gave me a quizzical, evaluating look, then took me through the stepping exercises, and didn't act at all curious about what I may or may not have been dreaming. After that, Lohn showed up and wanted to know how the kids were going and how they were taking to Siame – which seems to be a hostile truce at the moment – and we ended up making a channel with them and playing games for much of the afternoon.

Siame approached the games in the same manner as Kaoren – incisive and methodically competent, not holding back, but not apparently concerned about victory. The atmosphere changed when Fourth came back from their patrol, and Kaoren joined in. Against him Siame was competitive.

Lohn was very amused by this, and afterwards when all four squads were together for dinner/breakfast, he told Kaoren that he felt he should be insulted by how Siame obviously rated him and Mara. Everyone was being chatty, doing their best to put me at my ease, and when Nils leaned down at dinner to murmur in my ear: "This is just to make you blush," of course I did, and managed to give him the proper annoyed grimace afterwards. But I don't know if I'll ever be able to not feel guilty every time I see him.

Tuesday, October 14

Forward

Big progress, not from me, but from the exploration team led by Third who have been exploring Oriath, the middle-sized city in the southern hemisphere mentioned by Lira. They've located an extra-large underground facility, with requisite malachite marble, a fair distance outside the city. Eeli is very proud of herself, and rightly so, since they're hoping this may be the headquarters of the House Zolen conspirators. Planning is already underway to create a research site there, and to my relief there's also discussion about moving me back to Pandora, since I've spent a few days on Muina now without having a major medical crisis. Particularly because they want to divert some of my excessive escort to the Oriath site. They've sent Eighth off to join Third already.

My attempt to dream of Lira last night didn't go anywhere, which at least means I had another good night's rest. The technicians are saying that I may be able to have my eye unbandaged tomorrow, and if I'm given an all-clear on health, they're considering a visualisation. The patrols haven't spotted any Cruzatch in this area, so KOTIS Command figures that they can have me test in the Ena here, and then if all goes well whisk me off to somewhere else.

Ghost has reappeared. I hadn't seen her since we flew here, and was privately rather worried. But she woke Nils up today sleeping on his chest. He seemed happy to see her, but I earned a minor lecture from Maze for failing to mention that she'd ridden along with us. Then she was fussed over a lot, and is happily seducing random technicians.

Partway through the day I had a nice long discussion with Isten Notra, who had read all my clumsy reports on my dreams, and spent a full kasse winkling every possible detail out of me, pushing me for all the impressions and opinions that I shy away from expressing.

We received further scripts for *The Hidden War* today as well, with the first few episodes rewritten in more detail – they'll be going into production on those soon I guess – and the next few episodes in first draft. I was highly amused to see that they had written in the whole stealing of my personal file, and me being made part of a Setari entertainment program. I can't say I enjoyed the script all about me being emotionally frayed, but the stuff about Lastier's squad being scandalised by their portrayal was very funny. Then there's the Velcro/Astroturf massive, which is another script I didn't enjoy, but was generally accurate.

Wednesday, October 15

Sudden Defence

I woke up in the middle of the night because Kaoren had been gone a while, and found him, Maze and Grif Regan down in the dining room, taking part in an interface meeting. There had been an attack on the Oriath expedition. Eeli's unconscious with a head injury, and Kade from Eighth is badly torn up. It was a huge surge of Cruzatch, and they only overcame it because the ships had weapons, and the Setari were able to retreat to them and blast everything in sight.

The attack suggests that Oriath is important to the Cruzatch, which I guess counts as useful information. KOTIS has withdrawn entirely from the site for now, intending to return in force.

This makes the question of what to do with me a tricky one, and Kaoren's just told me that they've decided on an Ena visualisation trip ASAP, and then to observe me sleeping afterwards, and they'll decide whether to send me back to Tare or on to Pandora depending on whether I have another 'episode'.

Tactical Survey

They had me visualise the site at Oriath, after showing me the mission log. Third and Eighth had been exploring a sprawling palace which was above the sealed installation, searching for entrances and any information. After I'd watched the log to just before the point where they were attacked, Kaoren stepped me through a description of the room they'd been in, but continually emphasising that there were no Cruzatch there, and I was able to project the room and the surrounding ones without effort. Fortunately without the Cruzatch, as ordered, although the theory was that I could just drop the projection if I produced them as well.

My minders (all three squads) fanned out and explored the nearby areas which Third and Eighth hadn't reached as yet, and then we headed back to real-space, leaving a drone behind to monitor for Cruzatch. If they showed up, it would suggest Cruzatch are able to detect my projections.

Back in real-space, they had me project the same area again, but this time *with* Cruzatch, emphasising what the area looked like right at that moment. So long as no-one moves the projected physical objects, or makes too much noise, projected Ionoth don't notice people in real-space and – depending on how strongly I'm projecting – are often only visible to me. In this case the Setari could sort of see the Cruzatch, and they could definitely see the crystallised webbing the Cruzatch were laying down, just as they had around the Kalasa platform. This is very good information to know, and I can now regard myself as a military spy satellite.

They debated having me try to project what the place had looked like back before the disaster, but this was deemed too risky, so I was sent to medical to be tired, and since I slept without even dreaming, let alone getting trapped anywhere, we're on the way to Pandora. Haven't told the kids yet, because I can't resist surprising them, whether they appreciate it or not.

Reunion

My morning visualisation and midday nap has messed me up rather thoroughly in terms of adapting to Pandora's earlier timeframe. I'd only been awake (again) for a couple of hours when we arrived at Pandora around its sunset. Everyone had been in a grim mood the entire day, and an undernote of anger was added in when we reached the Setari building and met up with Third and Eighth – those who weren't in medical, anyway. Only a few of them don't have some sort of injury – Cruzatch are quick close-combat fighters, and nanosuits only partially protect the Setari from their burning claws. They'd also proven adept at throwing chunks of rubble during combat, which is what had happened to Eeli. She's over at the main medical building.

Taarel's hair's really short. She was clawed across the back, and her long spirals of hair were severed and melted so she cut it all off. She looks amazingly different, but still very regal and commanding and very intent on the plans for the counter-strike, even though Third won't be going. I think she needs to concentrate on that to stop herself worrying about Eeli.

More squads are coming from Tare and Kolar, along with smaller combat-oriented ships. The exact timing for the attack hasn't been settled, and won't be until after another visualisation.

I only stayed down in the common room for a short while, then Kaoren and I went up to be with the kids (who were having their bath when we first arrived). Rye was first out, and stopped dead at the sight of the two of us talking quietly to Siame, and then went all formal, which was impossibly sweet and reminded me of those really old movies where the kids call their fathers 'Sir'. Kaoren put his hand on Rye's head by way of greeting and the poor kid just about died of joy. It was interesting watching Siame's shut-down expression – I think of the three she feels the most sympathy for Rye, but it really hurts her to see Kaoren being affectionate with other people.

Rye must have told Ys and Sen over the interface that we were here, because there was suddenly a shriek from the other bathroom, a rather magnificent splash, and then Sen pelted into the lounge, all wet hair and bubbles, to throw herself into my lap. Ys appeared a few moments later, clutching a mass of towels and brick-red with embarrassment. I dissolved into laughter and was half-choked by Sen's death grip as Ys dropped some of the towels over her. Kaoren kindly discovered a need to go into our bedroom for a minute, which allowed for some towel-readjustment.

It's impossible not to adore Sen, and I hugged her back, and told her how much I'd missed all three of them, and that it had felt much longer than a few days. Then I told her that she'd better get a little less soapy or she'd slide right out of bed while I was reading today's story. I squeezed Ys' shoulder gently and then gave Siame a kick on the ankle because she was staring at the part of Ys' back which was exposed, which fortunately Ys hadn't noticed, though Rye had. He'd gone white, but didn't say anything as Ys left the room and I went over and hugged him really hard, then asked him to tell me what they'd been doing at the talent school. Siame's far from stupid, so she took my heavy-footed hint, and showed no sign of curiosity (but no doubt had a discussion with Kaoren about it).

They've built another little bedsicle nook in the apartment for Siame (with her Sights, I suspect she'd very much preferred not to borrow our bed while we weren't here), and she retreated there during the kids' story and didn't re-emerge. Kaoren took a shower while I was stepping Sen through her Sights exercise, and when I went to find him he'd passed out on our bed, which put an end to my plans to really enjoy finally not being under observation in medical.

Friday, October 17

Laying their plans

Fifth, Sixth, Seventh, Ninth and Tenth, Tsur Selkie, and Squad Two arrived while I was having my eye patch removed yesterday morning. They mostly bunked on the *Litara*, but the Setari building periodically overflowed.

There were only two things on my personal list of things to do that day: visit Eeli and ravish Kaoren. Since Kaoren had planning meetings scheduled for much of the day, the first seemed easier to accomplish than the second, and I asked Mori and Glade to take me over.

Ista Tremmar was standing by Eeli's sense-bed when we arrived, and Mori asked her if there'd been any improvement.

"Not yet," Ista Tremmar said. "With head injuries of this nature, there's not a great deal we can do initially except relieve the pressure. When the swelling has gone down, I'll have a clearer prognosis."

Eeli was hooked to a machine to keep her breathing. That gave me a jolt, and I found myself only able to look at her in glances. Pale, still, somehow too small for Third's string bean of energy. I pulled up a chair and picked up her hand, but it was limp and clammy, like the kittens Mimmet had had too early. I put it down carefully.

"Eeli barely seems herself when she's not moving," Mori said, her voice thick.

"The perpetual motion machine," Glade said, small and shocked.

"I–" I took a breath so my voice was steady, then said: "I'm just going look for something."

I expanded my senses, pushing out. It's easy to do now, at least when there's lots of people around. Little points of life, with fainter hazes for plants, and the Setari bright blazes. I kept looking, pushing out, until I noticed a new bright blaze next to me. Kaoren.

Pulling back to myself, I took another steadying breath then opened my eyes, and wiped them.

"Sorry," I said. I tilted my head back so I could see Kaoren. His face was closed, grave. "You can tell, can't you? That she's not there."

He nodded.

I made myself pick up Eeli's hand again, so strange and wrong, and pressed the back of it to my cheek, just for a moment. Then I got up and hugged Mori, who was crying, touched Glade's arm and let Kaoren take me away.

We went to the top of the Setari building, and sat on a bench beneath fresh green leaves. I didn't try to speak for a long time, till the blow was something manageable.

"Does Taarel know?" I asked, eventually.

"Only that it's unlikely she'll recover," Kaoren said. "Sight is not an absolute in these cases."

"Eeli would hate so much missing out on seeing Taarel with hair cut short." My voice wobbled, and I stopped, then curled my fingers tighter through Kaoren's, leaning into his side. "Nils told me most frightening thing about me is I could bring people back."

Kaoren's horror was clearly transmitted everywhere we touched. He drew a breath.

"Don't worry," I said. "I know – I think she wouldn't want that. I know you wouldn't. I'm not sure if–" If Kaoren died, I have no idea how I'd react, but I like to think I would be strong enough not to make a copy of him. "I guess it's really not that different from making projections living people," I said. "Even projecting only the part of Eeli which isn't there. But it wouldn't last and it wouldn't be real. And that would make it worse than awful."

Kaoren stayed with me for quite a while, attending the strategy meeting virtually. I didn't feel babysat, just supported, and the way Kaoren had instantly been called out of his meeting to be with me feels like good sense when a few months ago I might have resented being treated as a so-fragile flower. The moment when it occurred to me that I could try to 'fix' Eeli gave me a better appreciation for why the Nuran Setari are dubious about me, and why there's an entire team of lawyers trying to draft an interplanetary agreement on what I'll be permitted to do.

I really don't want to know what the Cruzatch want me to do.

It was necessary to talk Kaoren out of keeping Fourth at Pandora, though. It's not that I don't want him here, and aren't just a little worried about sleeping without him – not to mention having to struggle with the spectre of him in Eeli's place – but I've seen how useful his Sights are in combat. Taking control of Oriath is important, and I want them to have every chance of coming through that battle without any more injuries.

Fortunately I managed to control myself overnight, replaying the otters visualisation, and only having one minor nightmare near dawn: nothing to give anyone reason to second-guess or change all the planning from yesterday. All the squads on Muina, including parts of Eighth, have gone, with considerable air support. The ships will be at the attack site soon, and they want me to visualise just before they arrive so they know how the Cruzatch react. Given the length of the visualisation, and the fact that I'll be in real-space, I'm almost certain to pass out after that, though I'm going to try and stay awake.

I'm really glad Siame's here. I'm sure she's worried about Kaoren as well – and she's not going to stop disliking me any time soon – but she's really helped me keep the atmosphere upbeat with the kids. They're tense, of course, but Siame's certainty that KOTIS is well prepared to take Oriath makes a big difference.

Saturday, October 18

Timing is everything

I'd tried valiantly to stay awake. My minders for the projection were Taarel and Sefen from Third, both of whom were just wounded enough to be disqualified for the attack, and spent their time tense and tightly controlled because they really wanted to be with the attack force, and are so angry and upset about Eeli. But Taarel stepped me effortlessly through the projection, and obligingly took me back to my apartment afterwards, where I promptly fell asleep on the couch, right in the middle of the battle.

But Siame was right to be confident, and the Setari rolled right over the dozens of Cruzatch waiting for them.

The battle was over almost as soon as it began, and Phase Two – establishing a defensible position – swung into operation. My sleep was occupied by an awareness of Siame giving Ys and Rye a basic combat exercise while Sen watched. Then Siame went out of the apartment – to get dinner apparently – and as soon as she was gone Lira was standing next to me. And my energy-use readings kicked up to 'dangerous', alerting medical.

Sen made the chirpy little noise she uses half as greeting and half as question – she's always willing to treat newcomers as potential friends. Ys and Rye's reaction was far less welcoming – Rye even took on a correct combat stance – but they're smart kids and we had told them about Lira, so after a pause Ys said: "You know that you make her sick when you use her to come here."

Lira looked immensely offended, and glanced down at me in an angry, dismissive way which I suspect was a disguise for guilt.

"Are you three her sisters and brother?" she asked then. "And that older one?"

"Siame is Kaoren's sister," Rye said. He's always very careful and correct about our relationship, and his voice wobbled a little when he added: "We are Cassandra and Kaoren's wards."

"Sweetheart!" Sen announced happily, snuggling herself between me and the back of the couch. "Ys, Rye, Sen," she added, pointing to each in turn, ending up with: "Lira."

Lira looked like she'd bitten a lemon, but turned back to Ys: "Is it true what he said? Has Nuriath fallen?"

"Hundreds of years ago," Ys said, bluntly. "Most people died straight away. Some survivors went through the Ena to different worlds and for a long time no-one lived on Muina at all, because something would kill them. Then Cassandra came and made it possible for people to live here, and they built this settlement, which is called Pandora. But whatever happened long ago is causing the walls between the Ena and real-space to tear apart, and there are Ionoth called Cruzatch who keep attacking, and they destroyed the world we come from. They keep trying to kidnap Her."

When Ys decides to talk, she's unsparing. I loved the obvious capitalisation on 'Her'.

"I heard Naranezolen say that they're running out of time. That it's not any more about self-reliance. They need another to work with me or it will be the Tzarazatch," Lira said, distress starting to leak through. "But I don't know for what – I'm not doing anything. Whenever they see me they chase me away. What–"

Ys, surprising me, stepped up and gripped Lira by the upper arms. "You need to stop now. Come back another time, or you'll make Her too sick. She'll help you if she can. She's soft like that. See if they say anything about a big fight today."

After a moment's offended glaring, Lira obediently disappeared. I woke myself, and struggled to sit up with Sen half-sitting on me, and weights of exhaustion attached to my whole body. The apartment door opened to show Siame, Taarel and one of the medics – Rye's response to Lira's appearance had been to immediately contact Siame. She'd brought Taarel and the medic, but they'd held off entering so as not to startle Lira.

"Lira's been observing us," I said, as Ista Mezan gave me a fortifier to drink. I looked at Ys and added: "She waited until Siame left so she could talk to you three."

"Perhaps she feels a link to someone her own age," Taarel said, steadying my hand, which had started shaking enough to slop fortifier down my front.

"Did the attack–?" I began, then choked as she tipped the fortifier down my throat.

"No injuries. They're going on with Phase Three."

Phase Three was finding all the tears into near-space in the area and putting boxes around them, since the theory was that the Cruzatch could only access real-space through the marbles or the tears, but couldn't pass through the unbroken parts of the wall between near-space and real-space. I didn't get any more explanation than that at the time, since I couldn't stay awake any longer. I guess it was Taarel who changed my clothes, and she was nice enough to put me in my own bed rather than parking me in medical. I was conked out for about fourteen hours – a stretch which made Sen coming and climbing on me rather perilous for my bladder.

Of course, now I'm awake, Kaoren's asleep, though he sent me an email telling me everything which had happened. It was a fast fight, but the Cruzatch kept coming back until the last of the nearby tears was boxed in. They're remaining on high alert.

I don't like Kaoren being away, but funnily enough I find Siame's presence almost as comforting as the kids do. She's just as habitually in-charge as Kaoren, and Kaoren's absence means she feels free to organise me. And watching Ys stubbornly ignore her and organise herself, Rye and Sen is highly amusing.

Wednesday, October 22

Zilla

The day after we took Oriath, I spent a morning medical chatting to Kaoren, asking him questions about the battle and describing the cloud of happiness Rye had been floating around on because Kaoren had told him 'well done' for contacting Siame so promptly. When I'm in-quarters the kids come and have lunch with me rather than sticking at the school, and we were sitting in a circle on the floor around our coffee table/dining table experimenting with the latest products of the culinary division, who spend their days in a state of bliss with a whole new world of food to play with.

I was feeling very queer and bothered and couldn't work out why, and found that Sen and Siame were both watching me attentively, and when I asked why Siame said she could see a shadow behind me, and Sen chirped up with "Lira come now?" Since I didn't feel the least bit like sleeping, I contacted Taarel and warned her that I was going to try expanding my senses, and she said that was okay, but told me to remember to use the scanner to record, and she stayed in-channel to watch. I managed to expand my senses fine, but that just made me feel even more queer and bothered, so I tried to create a projection of Lira, and that worked.

She was looking impatient and cross and said: "You are very dull and unnoticing," to me.

I smiled at her. "I know – I'm very bad at being alert. But is nice be able talk to you directly."

"I listened for them talking about an attack, like she said," Lira went on, glancing at Ys. "They were all very annoyed, but also pleased because they'd thought of a good thing to do. It's something about you. I've been trying and trying to tell you." She was highly aggrieved, anger hiding worry.

"Did they give any details?" Siame asked sharply.

"Only that they would stop something from being called. They were very pleased."

I reached out experimentally – it's so difficult for me to move while all expanded – and touched her hand, which felt solid and entirely normal. "Thank you, Lira," I said. "I wish I could find where you are."

I let the projection slip, and came back to myself as Siame was rapping out orders to the kids. The differences in dialect means I'm only translating Lira clearly in retrospect, but we'd all gotten the gist. Siame told us we were to go straight downstairs, to the level which is below ground and easiest to defend. There was an alert flashing over the interface – Taarel had put KOTIS staff on ready status and told the greensuits stationed at the amphitheatre to summon the Ddura immediately.

If I'd been a little less thick, if I'd realised sooner that Lira was trying to communicate, they'd still be alive. Two women and a man, Keeri Nell, Evva Nozen, and Barl Miks. The Cruzatch got them before they reached the platform. All I knew at the time was that as we came out onto the inner balcony, we abruptly shifted from a level two alert to a level five, which covers everyone in Pandora and means there's Ionoth on the loose and everyone's to take shelter.

Taarel came flying abruptly up to our floor, enhanced herself, and dropped us all down to the ground floor, where Bryze from Eighth was waiting. It was not as if Pandora was completely without Setari defenders – there was a Nuran, Mila, and various members of Third and Eighth – five of them not too injured to fight. And quite a lot of greensuits, and mounted weapons at certain key points. But as Tsur Selkie said later, the Ddura had made us complacent.

Bryze enhanced as well, but then kind of groaned, and we all froze looking out the big (fortunately closed) plate-'glass' doors over the lake, and the Cruzatch just outside. I gather that there were two groups, each numbering around thirty, one of which had hit the amphitheatre and the other had gone straight for the Setari building. That little fact is the cause of a great deal of consternation, because it means that the Cruzatch either can track me effortlessly, or had a very good idea of the layout of Pandora.

Taarel said: "Go!" to Siame, and sent us scurrying out of the common room. A haze came up to cover the outer doors – the Setari building has a good set of shields which can be brought up sectionally – but I could hear yelling and a crash off toward the direction we were heading. The Cruzatch had surrounded the entire building, and found a way in through the school, then torn through the physical barriers which had automatically sectioned off the Setari area, damaging some of the shield transmitters in the process.

Siame stopped short, then shooed us backward. The common room atrium is a very open area, and I glanced around frantically, spotted one couch which was set against the wall, and told Ys and Rye to take Sen and hide behind it. Trouban from Eighth dropped down from the upper levels, clutching a couple of the new breathing masks, and he, Bryze and Taarel headed toward the sounds of fighting at double-pace just as the Cruzatch came in

They moved like a swarm of spiders, racing over walls and ceiling, and while the tight entrance meant that Bryze was able to take out a whole bunch of them in a single shot, the way the common room opens up meant they could quickly spread out and get behind the three Setari.

I'm quite proud that I managed to dodge the net one of them threw at me. It's about the only time I've managed to properly dodge anything, and I did it with a stylish tumbling roll which looked like I'd rehearsed it. Unfortunately, all this earned me was a burnt arm, because another Cruzatch swooped down, grabbed me above the elbow, and tossed me on top of the fallen net. I have deeply-burned claw marks again and am extremely sorry I wasn't wearing my nanosuit – a sleeveless T, cargo pants and no shoes do not make an adequate combat outfit.

To my horror, Ys ran over and tried to bat the Cruzatch out of the air with a chair (which she could barely lift, let alone hit things with) and I grabbed her back against my chest and curled around her as it took a lazy swipe in retaliation – one thing which was clear was that they didn't want to damage me too much, so it was the best way to protect her, though this meant that when they inverted the net and hauled me into the air, Ys came too.

The Setari (and Siame) of course weren't just sitting back while this was going on, but there were so many Cruzatch and in an enclosed space with 'civilians' about, they couldn't be very wild using elementals, and were struggling not to be straightforwardly slaughtered. The Cruzatch seemed to intend a quick snatch and grab, which kept the casualty numbers down, but also made them very hard to counter. Bryze was very badly injured trying to stop them from hauling me off, but they say he'll recover.

By this time, Kaoren, Maze and Tsur Selkie were in channel with me, which was an exercise in frustration for them, and only served as a distraction for me. Kaoren told me to try breaking individual strands of the net, but it seemed to be made of some kind of rubber (vaguely resembling the stuff they'd used to build the traps around Kalasa's platforms) and would only stretch a little – not nearly enough to make a Cass-sized hole. It was also very hard to do anything while being banged around corners.

And then we were outside, soaring straight out over the lake toward what was later determined to be their entrance point, a tear on the far bank of the southern 'hook' of the lake. Siame was the only defender who'd managed to follow straight away – she doesn't have Combat Sight, but she's a stronger Light talent than Kaoren, more on Lohn's level, and since she hadn't enhanced was able to shoot Light bolts at the Cruzatch carrying me. It was dodging very well, but one of the bolts went through the top of the net, spilling Ys and me down into the lake.

I wasn't prepared for the drop, but managed to keep a hold of Ys and was lucky to take the impact on my shoulder. After a disoriented and panicky flounder we surfaced and Ys, coughing and gasping, nearly pushed me under again. At least the water made my burned arm stop hurting quite so horribly.

Siame was just above us, trying to fend off three Cruzatch at once. I turned in the water, and saw that we were quite close to Tupal Rock – the stony cluster which is the nearest island to Pandora. I told Ys to climb on my back, and managed a sluggish breast-stroke, and was trying to angle to the lower side when Siame and one of the Cruzatch fell out of the sky.

They landed very close, the Cruzatch producing a big hiss of steam. Taarel had shown up by then, racing two more Cruzatch, and took on the pair Siame hadn't killed. Siame barely seemed to be swimming, so I detached Ys and asked her if she thought she was able to swim to the rock and when she nodded I sprinted to Siame as she started to sink. Her Kalrani uniform doesn't provide half the protection of the nanoliquid suits, let alone built-in close combat weapons, and she'd been clawed across her abdomen, deep enough to do serious damage. She's still alive, but facing a long, painful recovery.

By the time I hauled her to Tupal Rock, Mila had joined Taarel, but they were both injured and struggling, and more Cruzatch were arriving from the group which had attacked the platform: a cloud of burning black moving in for the kill. Mila and Taarel were magnificent, fighting back-to-back, managing even as the numbers grew higher to keep all the Cruzatch's focus on them, picking off any who dropped toward me. But there were so many.

During the short swim to the rock, I kept thinking that Eeli wouldn't be able to bear it if Taarel died as well, and searching desperately for the best thing I could do to stop that from happening, telling myself that I'm powerful enough that they need to make laws about me, and could surely manage a few judicious lightning bolts.

I hauled Siame as high on the rock as I could manage, and told Ys to hold her there, then found a dip I could wedge myself into. "I'm going to try to help," I told Ys as I muted my interface distractions. "Be careful not to touch me."

There's quite a few scanners stationed along the Pandora shoreline, so when I woke I could watch what happened next on the news. I didn't have much of a view of it at the time – my perception is really vague when I'm expanded and I was concentrating very hard and only had my eyes open part of the time. They keep showing the whole sequence over and over again – Siame pursuing the Cruzatch with me and Ys in the net, and then us falling into the water and Siame's fight against them (Kaoren says she did extremely well) and then the expanded battle above us while I was trying to get Siame to the rock. And then Ys desperately trying to hold on to Siame and staunch her bleeding while I'm just sitting there very still with my eyes closed – like I'd gone into extreme denial.

Then the dragon shows up.

I'd abandoned the idea of lightning bolts almost immediately – there's no way I can aim while expanded. And I've known for ages that I can create Ionoth, after all. A dragon wasn't an obvious choice – most of them are evil in stories – but my mind had frozen when trying to think of really powerful flying things who could pwn a few dozen Cruzatch really quickly. I almost did Superman, but realised at the last moment that the sun mightn't be the right sort. And then I thought of Maze toasting dozens of Cruzatch, and thought of dragon breath.

Spirited Away was one of my favourite movies growing up, and there was a hint of river-spirit dragon in what I created: white with highlights of blue and gold, long in body, but with vast wings. And huge. It dove into view to snatch up two Cruzatch which were dropping toward me, and opening these truly incredible wings with a snap which echoed across the lake. It threw the two Cruzatch into the water as it started upward, and the gale was incredible, making me struggle to not lose focus.

I'm so glad that Taarel and Mila chose to pull free from the Cruzatch cloud at the dragon's appearance – I'm not sure I could have lived with it if they'd been crisped when the dragon tilted down again and *breathed*.

Dragonzilla. It was Light, not Fire. The kind of beam which you see in mecha anime which scorches a mile-long ridge into the landscape and cuts through mountains. It evaporated the swarm of Cruzatch just as they clustered in preparation for attacking and then scored down into lake, creating a great whomping cloud of steam.

And the energy cost for *that* hit me like a tank. I promptly passed out and toppled into the lake.

Poor Ys. She hates so much anyone seeing her when she's upset, and everyone on three planets has watched her frantic horror as she tries to keep hold of Siame while snatching at me as I drop. She couldn't keep me from going into the water, and wasn't strong enough to pull me out of it while keeping Siame in place, but she did manage to lift my head enough so that I was only a little bit drowned when Trouban from Eighth dropped down (half-fell, he was in bad shape) and joined us on the rock, while Taarel and Mila cleared up the few Cruzatch which had escaped the dragon.

I *so* should have yelled *Expecto Patronum.* Talk about missed opportunities.

I've been unconscious for the last couple of days, and I suspect I've damaged my projection talent again like I did with the Kalasa projection, but I got off a lot better than the Setari and Siame. Fourth, Sixth and the other parts of Eighth were sent back immediately, and things have been relatively quiet since – the expeditionary force digging in to work on the shielding around the new site, and the Cruzatch not as yet testing them again.

KOTIS has copped a lot of flak for leaving Pandora/me inadequately defended, which they've been taking a *mea culpa* attitude to, although the first battle at Oriath was so intense that going with fewer would have meant far more injuries, and they don't dare pull any more squads from Tare and Kolar. The injury list just keeps climbing, and they've made active as many of the Kalrani as they're willing to risk at this stage.

Kaoren was sitting beside me when I woke, looking so tired that I have extreme doubts he managed any real sleep the entire time I was unconscious. I suspect he and Sen were plagued by Sight dreams, since she didn't look much better by the time I got back to our apartment (after a meal, another long sleep and a medical exam). I'm writing this propped against Kaoren's arms on our couch, with Sen sprawled down one side of us. Both of them passed out almost as soon as we sat down. Ys and Rye looked pretty wrung out as well (if Sen's not sleeping, they're generally not sleeping either), but held out to have quite a long conversation with me about dragons and to grimace at me fiercely or blush and look at the floor depending on their inclination when I told them what I thought of their bravery.

Rye fell asleep sitting on the floor propped against the couch, after a long period of gazing up at Kaoren with unblinking devotion. Ys went and fetched him a pillow, and then my diary when I asked her for it, and actually tolerated me thanking her, and has stayed close playing with her modelling toy while I write – she's growing quite adept at using it, and seems to most enjoy making copies of Pandora's buildings. She's very exacting and precise.

I've been amusing myself using the scanner to record this scene for posterity, and also having interface conversations with a selection of almost everyone I know on the planet. The recurrent theme has been: "That bat-surri was incredible." It certainly made an impression on the collective imagination, and the interface sites are full of discussion about it, and me. The fact that I can outgun the Setari in a suicidal one-shot kind of way has certainly strengthened the "we need to make some laws about the touchstone" brigade. On a plus side there's a ton of positive comments about Siame (quickly identified as Kaoren's sister) and Ys.

I'm glad I was able find a way to fight back – and OMG I can make *dragons* – but wish I could have just paid enough attention to realise that Lira was trying to talk to me.

Thursday, October 23

Mine

Third and Eighth have been sent back to Tare, with only two of them lacking a significant injury. Eeli's still here, though, because the medics are worried about the impact of taking her through deep-space. Not one of Third could stand leaving her behind, and Taarel sent them off to the ship with her head high and her eyes hard.

Siame can't be moved either, but at least is periodically conscious. I went down to see her, but she likes me even less now – or is just too ill to disguise how little she wants to do with me. Other than not being able to project, I'm feeling fine today, with my burn thoroughly medicated.

The expeditionary force is having immense trouble working through the shielding at the Oriath site – it's on par with the shielding around Kalasa – but they've made a lot of progress setting up warning drones and creating a little fortress, dense with shields and bristling with weapons. Even without the Setari there, anyone inside the bunker could probably defend themselves against all but a massive attack. They're waiting for the next Cruzatch assault (should there be one) before sending any more squads back, so they can gauge how sufficient it is, but two more of the Nuran Setari have returned.

The shielding on the talent school hadn't been brought up during the Cruzatch attack because some of the kids were still outside and couldn't get inside quickly enough, and that's led to a revision of both the school and Pandora's Ionoth safety procedures. The proposed solution is emergency shelters outside some of these outlying buildings. Shielded shelters are a seriously sensitive subject for the Nurans, of course, but for certain critical buildings KOTIS Command has decided they can't risk leaving them open.

The question of whether there are spies for the Cruzatch here is also causing a headache. It's obvious to suspect the Nurans – and unfortunately this suspicion seems to be focused on the Nuran Setari – but it could be anyone on Muina, Tare or Kolar. Someone, after all, told the Nurans about me after I unlocked Muina. Thankfully practically no-one knows we've made contact with Lira – not that she's probably able to manifest at the moment with my talents taking a time-out. KOTIS Command hasn't decided whether to move me, pretend to have moved me, or even use me as bait.

At any rate, the kids are out of school for the moment because their presence reveals mine, and all of us are confined to the Setari building. They're quite happy about this. Sen because it means she spends more time with me, Rye because he gets to spend more time with Kaoren, and Ys because she doesn't have to spend any time with the children at the school.

The Setari building feels so deserted with only Fourth in residence. Mila, Orial and Korinal aren't tremendously social, and are often away mediating issues with the Nurans. Having the common room to themselves (windows set to be one-way) turned into a great game for Sen, who gleefully collected every cushion and made a massive mound of them, and kept climbing on top and rolling down the sides. Ys and Rye didn't try to stop her, just made sure there wasn't anything to hit. I sat on the table watching all three of them, not failing to notice how Ys and Rye would occasionally check the entrances of the room for annoyed adults. I'm pretty sure if someone had been mad they would have pretended it was all their idea and taken any blame.

I know they'll always be ready to do anything for Sen, but I am hopeful that one day the shadow of House Renar won't sit above them so strongly. They are improving. When it's just Kaoren and me with them, they're more inclined to show preferences in what to do each evening, and even Ys now asks questions if she can't work out an answer using the interface. Though that's becoming rarer – she's formidably intelligent.

It's so fun to watch Rye light up whenever Kaoren arrives, although today with a brief double-check to make sure that playing with cushions was allowed. It's also pretty damn cool watching Kaoren's response. I think the outright worship embarrasses him a little, but he really enjoys encouraging Rye, and says he has to keep resisting a temptation to show off for him.

It was a quiet day. Fourth had the morning free – or as free as they're allowed to be when they're the only squad on site – and Kaoren was in interface meetings, which is why I took the kids downstairs. In the afternoon we trained together. Since Halla is mildly injured, she was assigned to training with me, and Kaoren delighted Rye by having her include the kids in our training as well.

Isten Notra is coming to the Setari building tomorrow to discuss the conclusions she's come to from all the data my projections and dreams have given her. Of course, she could just tell us that over the interface, but since it appears that Lira can observe me, Isten Notra is hoping to tell *Lira* what she thinks happened.

Which is a cruel, hard thing, but I completely agree with Isten Notra that only the truth will do.

Friday, October 24

Planet Drac

Last night's attack on Oriath involved a full force of Cruzatch, plus a massive and attendants.

This time Taren and Kolaren technology ruled the day. Tare has tremendous problems fighting massives, because almost all their land surface is covered by buildings. Kolar has huge amounts of land surface, though all their cities are in two relatively small regions (parts of which are in permanent night, or permanent twilight, which leads to some *great* stories about things living in the dark), but while Kolar has difficulty dealing with small and medium Ionoth, with massives it usually just bombs the shit out of them.

KOTIS had expected exactly this tactic from the Cruzatch, and had been preparing launchers for missiles, which they promptly used to rain fiery destruction from the skies after checking that it wasn't the type which could reflect missiles. The Cruzatch plainly don't want to do any damage to this site, and hadn't brought the massive through right on top of it – hoping no doubt to lure the Setari away into battle. So a nice, comprehensive victory (which still involved a lot of mopping up work for the Setari at Oriath, but hasn't been nearly as fraught and injury-intensive).

This is by far the most protected of the malachite marble installations, and the shielding continues to delay further exploration. I'm still holding out hope for *Our Secret Plan and How to Foil It*, but I think it's no longer critical to find it, because we have Isten Notra.

The meeting was down in the common room, giving Isten Notra a chance to view the smoky spots and gouges on the walls which the pinksuits haven't quite found time to erase. The physical attendees were limited to Isten Notra, Tsur Selkie, me and Kaoren, with not even any of Isten Notra's minions along, but the audience over the interface surprised me. Not just Pandora's most senior bluesuits and the senior Setari representatives – Maze, Zee, Grif, Raiten, Inisar and Korinal – but about a dozen people whose names I had to look up: highest-echelon representatives from Tare and Kolar.

Isten Notra had brought one of the tablecloth screens with her, and started out by displaying a map of Muina with the platform towns highlighted.

"While much of what I'm about to discuss is not currently provable," she began, "we now have enough pieces that we are prepared to treat it as a working assumption. Given the increasing urgency of the situation, the recommendations I make today cannot wait for certainty, for the kind of expertise of those who built this system.

"The platform and Pillar system is a magnificent achievement, layering function upon function. The feed towns do not turn moonlight into aether, as you once suggested Caszandra. Instead they are drawing the substance of the Ena into real-space, and refining it – patterning it, if you will – so that it can be used as a power source: one so versatile it can even recognise and heal Muinans. The presence of the moon appears to be a control mechanism, to manage the volume produced, although there is some suggestion in the documentation recovered that the gravitational pull of the moon assists in safely thinning the wall between real-space and the Ena.

"The amount of aether needed to power the shielding dome at Kalasa, the teleportation platforms, and the Pillars is a fraction of the total aether produced by the feed towns, and the Pillars themselves appear to serve the dual function of stabilising the near region of deep-space and providing a storage channel for the excess aether. The whole system is integrated, and while it is likely those who built it intended to create further platforms, and to use the aether for other devices, maintaining a delicate balance would be paramount, for drawing and using the stuff of the Ena in real-space poses a monstrous risk, as we are all now well-aware."

Isten Notra glanced at the tablecloth screen and green dots appeared, showing the locations of the malachite marbles.

"Enter a parasite system," she said, sounding exactly like Agowla High's headmistress that time half of Year 11 held a panty-shot scavenger hunt. "When the platform and Pillar network was activated, the wall between real-space and the Ena began to tear like a cloth under strain, despite all the calculations of its creators. This secondary system is most likely the cause."

She changed the display again, this time to a schematic of the site at Oriath – the outline of the underground rooms revealed by the scanners – and highlighted one in particular, at the very centre of the facility.

"This room is the exact proportions of the aether-filled chamber Caszandra was trapped within, and projected for us." She zoomed in to the room, and though the scan was a little blurry, it was clear that the central pedestal was there. She replaced the image with a scan of the room I'd projected. "The diagrams covering the walls and ceiling appear to be symbolic references to the aether inflows – the platforms – and you will see from this projection that the aether is not simply contained in the room, but is slowly moving through it on spiralling paths from ceiling to floor. Scanner readings taken from the projection are not to be relied upon, but their measurement would suggest that the visible aether is merely leakage, and that a vast amount of aether is being channelled by this structure. It is probable that half, or even a majority of all the aether collected on Muina is being consumed by this room."

The image shifted to a close-up of the pedestal and the shrouded figure weighed down by tiny malachite marbles. I flinched a little inside, having no way of knowing whether Lira was watching, hating the thought of what was beneath that shroud.

"We believe these orbs represent the power stones placed across Muina," Isten Notra was saying. "You will note that if that correlation is true, we have three still to uncover. Those diagrams on the walls which do not relate to the platforms are considered likely to represent the large power stones. While the platforms are the power inlet, it appears that these power stones – large and small – are an outlet channel, drawing away and also consuming part of the aether output. Using the placement of the smaller stones in this projection, we have identified areas recommended for scouting."

Then she held up a small audio player and I winced, recognising the creepy whisper from my dream.

"We have spent considerable time attempting to enhance and separate the auditory component of Caszandra's projection. Multiple voices are speaking at once, and we are working with the theory that each voice is transmitted by one of the stones. We have separated the clearest."

She played one of the whispers, almost incomprehensible to me still since it was old Muinan and mostly names. Isten Notra had a translation which basically said "In [place], the immutable [person] has dominion over [this particular area]. The immutable [person] and [person] are as his left and right hands. No power is greater than the immutable [person] in [place], and nothing has strength to wound or weary or naysay his will. Beneath his power will dwell the immutable [person]..." And so on and on and on. I hadn't projected long enough for them to capture the full length of it, but it was all about the immutable this and that and how they lived at the pleasure of the person in charge of that area. Some of the whispers are male and some are female, and so far as they've been able to tell all the whispers are along the same lines, but with different areas and different people.

Isten Notra continued to speak aloud, even when directly addressing our interface audience: "It is believed that the shrouded figure in this room is the previously known touchstone, a child at the time of the disaster. Those of you who have observed the logs of Caszandra's testing sessions will be aware that a touchstone is able to create a projection of any object or place described to her, including fictional places." She let out a faint sigh. "The Ena is not a realm governed by simple physics. Our histories and our investigations suggest it is an expression of the minds of – not necessarily sentients – but of the living. It is the memory of hunters and hunted, of places etched strongly in thought and hopes and fears. In each of these power stone installations, barring the lack of sarcophagi at Kalasa, we have found a combination apparently of the willing and the unwilling, all of whom may have been consumed. We believe they were using both the touchstone, the aether, and the lives of those within the installations to attempt an act of creation."

"Something more than becoming Cruzatch?" asked one of the bluesuits. "Surely they could not have done all this for such an existence?"

"No. A grander ambition altogether. These are the projections of the location Caszandra has repeatedly visited in a dream state, where it appears some remnant of the previous touchstone's consciousness has been trapped. Our initial belief was that this was Muina's past, but I am now inclined to believe that what Caszandra has glimpsed is instead the end product of these machinations. A space perhaps in the Ena or possibly even separate to it – sealed and unreachable, maintained by the power system of the platforms. Created by their will, and by fixing their description of this place in the mind of a child whose connection with the Ena is profound. They tailored themselves a world."

"Then what are the Cruzatch?" I asked.

Isten Notra brought up the image of the weird balloon-tent room from my dream. "This has been interpreted by Sight Sight talents as a gate. It is obviously not a physical throughway. Still, to those who created a world which depends on this one for survival, there is an obvious need to access real-space. For decades we have been confused by a number of spaces where Cruzatch have appeared to belong to those spaces, generating regularly, but with the advice of our Nuran partners we have concluded that those spaces were a consequence of living creatures reacting to incursions of Cruzatch into their worlds – a secondary instance of them. The true Cruzatch are outside our experience of traditional Ionoth, and we believe they are either aether 'devices' controlled by those living on the parasite world, or even projections of their minds."

She displayed an image of the impossibly tall and golden people. "These are almost certainly the rulers of that world, and perhaps even the originals of the conspiracy on Muina, remade and sustained by the power stone system. To them, our activities must pose a direct and absolute threat. As we have grown more active in the Ena, so have they become more active in attempting to prevent our expansion.

"The fact that they are so eager to gain control of Caszandra suggests that just as we are experiencing increasing problems with the tearing of the spaces, the world they have created is not stable. Clearly they were unable, with a single touchstone, to create a world which existed independently of Muina. Now, the instability their system created in real-space is threatening their parasite world. It is probable that their activities on Nuri were an attempt to bolster their world's existence, spending lives to create stability. It is possible that Nuri is not the first world the Cruzatch have used so."

There was a little silence.

"And does this solve our problem?" asked Tsaile Staben, voice brisk and tight. "What impact if the power stone system is removed?"

"Unknowable." Isten Notra's mouth disappeared into wrinkles for a moment. "Suddenly removing the destabilising force is unlikely to be achieved without consequences. We will be forced to take an immense risk, and it would most certainly be disastrous to remove them sectionally. It is critical that we locate all of the power stones before tampering with them."

She turned to me. "Now – before we shift to the question of action. Caszandra, during your projection of this space, you objected with some considerable distress to the idea of moving the covering from the shrouded figure. Did you have any impression of consequences to that action?"

I hadn't been expecting to have to contribute, but at least have grown less easy to fluster, and so I thought before I answered.

"Something was going to change," I said. " I felt that looking would..."

I broke off, because my voice trembled, and Isten Notra smiled at me comprehendingly.

"The act of observation makes real? With the Ena, that is a factor which we will need to keep in mind when dealing with the question of what is beneath that shroud after thousands of years." She moved on to technical details about the stresses on the walls between real space and the Ena, and the increasing rate of growth of the tears, and what we could expect to happen if we didn't do something soon. And that we had to prepare the three planets for the high probability that interplanetary travel would be cut off at least temporarily if the platform/Pillar structure is damaged by the removal of the power stones.

The chickens have decided which way to run. It's just a matter of managing it before the sky falls. My job in all this is to recover, keep in hiding, and maybe do some visualisations. Most importantly, no dates with Cruzatch.

After the meeting ended, I took Isten Notra to visit our quarters and see the kids. She called Ys 'valiant', which made Ys go all pink instead of glaring like a basilisk. Ys has a lot of respect for Isten Notra.

Kaoren sat through a second meeting about the spread of resources for searching for the other malachite marbles. They've decided to import some of the older Kalrani for these theoretically 'easy' missions and will be splitting off the spares from Fourth to captain these junior squads as provisional Fifteenth and Sixteenth squads. Toren and Dae don't know that yet.

It's Siame's forty-fifth birthday soon (fifteen). I asked Kaoren what the Taren custom is for birthdays (they usually only celebrate every fifth, with fifty being the really major one). In Earth-years Kaoren will be twenty-one soon, and me nineteen, and we need to set birthdays for the kids. Rye will be first, since we think he's about to turn eleven, and then Sen and Ys a long while from now. Sen's the only one who any of the Nuran Setari could give even an approximate age for, and we probably won't ever have their real birthdays. The greysuits had entered a 'presumed birth date' when they'd given them their thorough medical, and we spent some time working them all out in the new Muinan calendar (or the old Lantaren one, since the technicians found what the Lantarens used to call months and days, and have adopted that). We're in "year one" of the New Muinan calendar – it dates from when I unlocked security access – and since the kids will be Muinan citizens we may as well stick with the Muinan calendar for these things. The year, like the day, is slightly longer than Earth's, but at least in Muinan-years Kaoren isn't sixty.

Kaoren grew rather distracted and then quietly annoyed in the middle of the afternoon, and when I asked him why he told me that since my dragon, he and Siame had been getting a lot of email from their parents, who are not unnaturally upset that Siame has been so severely injured. They still don't approve of the Setari program enough to want Siame to stay in it beyond the absolute minimum, and they want her to come back home to live with them until she's recovered. Which will take months – having your abdomen sliced into by red-hot claws is not something which can be fixed in a week.

Having to be rescued by me has not helped Siame's attitude toward being a Setari, for all that she'd been injured rescuing me first, and she's considering returning home. The thing which tied her most strongly to the Setari was Kaoren, and now that his attention has shifted to me, she feels crowded out, and less inclined to want to be part of KOTIS.

Kaoren is philosophical about this to a degree – he does mainly want Siame to be happy – but he thinks this was a bad time for his parents to start pressing her because she's still very ill. I gave him a long shoulder rub after this conversation and he fell asleep, leaving me to chew over everything Isten Notra had said.

The Photoshop Gods of the Parasite Planet. It sounds like a B movie. And that world is obviously a bad wrong thing which has to be stopped because it's tearing the universe apart. But I can't help thinking about a bunch of kids playing with a little cloth ball. They're just kids. They're plainly some kind of lower strata beneath the Photoshop crowd. If we destroy the power stones, then we're killing them.

And Lira.

Saturday, October 25

A Thousand Cats

I spent the morning in medical feebly trying to project. I can do a little – just enough to get a few good dragon pictures for the kids – but it gave me a headache and made me feel mopey about Lira. She's been trapped for so long, used and then ignored, and I know that almost certainly there's no living flesh under the shroud in that room. She was trapped there like I briefly was, but had no way out, and all that's alive of her now is a projection.

And I want to help her because I'm 'soft like that', but I don't think there is any way to help her. Part of fixing this problem means dismantling whatever is sustaining Lira's consciousness. She mightn't be properly alive, but we're going to finish her off, and I feel wretched about that, maybe even worse than I do about the kids on the parasite world, who presumably are just living their lives, maybe not even aware that their world is some kind of interplanetary vampire.

Sen could tell I was feeling down and, though it took a while for me to figure out what she was doing, kept fetching things to me in an attempt to distract me. Odd bits of equipment, cushions, clothing, and food from the kitchens. Once I realised what she was trying, I had her sit on the side of my med-chair and played interface games with her until they let me go.

My current role is to stay tucked away so the Cruzatch don't get me, and to work on my health in the hopes that I can be a spy satellite again. Kaoren had warned me that he's going to step up my physical training regime, so I wasn't looking forward to the afternoon, but was entertained at lunch because the ship carrying the Kalrani arrived and I got to watch Toren and Dae's faces when everyone was brought into a single channel and the provisional squads were announced. The Kalrani – ranging in age from fifteen to seventeen – were all being incredibly correct and yet so very excited. Even the girl I first encountered drooling over Kaoren outside the Sights training area was there, and studiously avoiding catching my eye.

Most everyone went out to the patch of ground the Setari use for training, and the squads did some practice training. I'm still not allowed outside, so Kaoren left me with Halla and Sonn, who proceeded to torture me all afternoon. They're not bad to me, but I prefer being tortured by Mara. I was particularly pathetic in my dodging and rolling because Something Had Occurred To Me which was well worth capital letters, and I didn't know what to do about it. Eventually Sonn and Halla just stopped and Sonn said: "What is it?"

I blushed, because she was being patient, and I didn't think I could answer her. "I think I need to ask Isten Notra something," I said.

"We'll take a rest then," Sonn said, then surprised me by giving me an almost warm look. "You're learning," she added.

I puzzled over what she meant as I went and grabbed a towel, and decided that it was a reference to my old issue of not speaking up. Then I sent a channel request to Isten Notra.

"What can I do for you, Caszandra?"

"Isten Notra, who is it who decides whether I'm on second level monitoring or not?"

"A large and squabblesome group of people," she said, then added firmly: "Who are not likely to consider altering that arrangement until this crisis is over."

"I guessed. But – do you have the power to suspend it, just for a few minutes? I want to ask you and Kaoren something, but it's...I think it would be a bad idea to log it."

Isten Notra took a moment before responding, then said she would make some arrangements, and be over to see me before dinner. After that I was better able to concentrate on not being beaten up by Sonn and Halla, and only told Kaoren that Isten Notra was coming to chat with me. He could tell, I think, that there was more to it, but didn't ask questions until we three were alone in one of the unused apartments.

Isten Notra settled herself on one of the couches, then nodded to me. "Very well, Caszandra – I've suspended your log. You've certainly made me curious."

I squeezed Kaoren's hand first, explaining: "I asked if I could ask you both something off-log." Then I looked at Isten Notra. "This parasite world – would you describe it as an idealised version of Muina, one where the rulers have been made more powerful, given abilities that the ordinary people do not have?"

"A fair enough description," Isten Notra said.

"But, you see, to me that's – that's a description of Muina."

I was watching Kaoren, saw his chin lift a fraction as he processed the idea, and his eyes narrowed.

I don't think it's often that Isten Notra is surprised, but she paused a long time before saying anything. "You're suggesting that Muina itself is a projection created by the people of your world?"

Her voice was calm, kind, but the way she said it made it sound like an awful insult. I flushed hard, but stumbled on. "Muina is so like Earth, just better put together. A little larger, with far fewer hot dry areas, a better mix of land and water – and all the water fresh, except for one shallow sea which conveniently happens to provide salt! The trees, the crops, the animals – so many are almost exactly the same, or variations of the kinds found on Earth. The one major difference is that the group of people in charge had psychic abilities which made them more powerful than those they ruled."

"Earth has no tears into the Ena," Kaoren said, his mouth a flat line, his eyes still narrowed. "Nothing you have described about it suggests that it's sustaining a parasite world."

"But the parasite world is a parasite because they didn't have enough power to make it permanent, to fix it in place. Something which endured, like my origami cranes. What if Muina was created by a more powerful system, one which wasn't latching on to something meant for other things. Or if they had two – a dozen – enough touchstones?"

My voice had gone a bit loud, so I stopped, and took a breath and told myself not to be upset.

"And so you take the question to Science and Sight," Isten Notra said, the smile returning to her eyes. "What does Sight say?"

Kaoren shook his head. "Sight Sight is rarely helpful with broad questions. I feel no immediate rejection, but nothing to suggest it's true, either."

"And I see no way to prove this," Isten Notra said. "If Muina was created, there does not appear to be any active link to the creator, and there is no sign of an external power source maintaining this world. Nor does it show any sign of being located within the Ena. Is there any known place on your world similar to the room with the shrouded child?"

I shook my head, and Isten Notra leaned forward to take my hand and briefly squeeze it. "Then I have no answer for you, child. What you suggest may be true, or may simply be fear and fancy. And I suspect I know why it weighs on you."

"We're going to kill everyone on that planet."

"Very likely. Or they will capture you and place you in a room and finish what they started, with who knows what effect on Muina. Or we will not find all the power stones in time, and everything around us will tear apart. When you are presented hateful choices, you can only measure the cost of not acting." Isten Notra stood up. "But you were wise to ask this off-log. Even though the restrictions against viewing such monitoring are not so easily ignored as you seem to think, I will set a process in place to ensure that logs of your daily life are deleted within the shortest possible timeframe. As for this discussion, I will note that you wished to speak openly about your concerns regarding the destruction of the parasite world, and also that you fear to be used in the way that the child, Liranadestar, was. Your log will restart in two joden."

Nodding to Kaoren she left, and I let out a breath. He sat down, then said: "An interesting irony if we, who have trained our entire lives to kill Ionoth, were a form of Ionoth ourselves."

"That's not what I meant!" I said, appalled. "It's totally–"

"Different? How far is the memory of a monster from the active projection of one?" His eyes were still narrowed, thoughtful, and he gave me one of his fractional smiles. "You ask difficult questions at times."

"Projections stop when I stop feeding energy into them. Ionoth are remembered by their spaces and come back," I said. "You – Eeli–"

"Will not. You've given yourself your answer." He held out his hand. "Even if Muina was made, it is a true world now, and does no damage by existing. That is certainly the answer I would choose to prefer."

And I will. I have to. Just as I have to accept that we are going to destroy what's sustaining Lira, because no other option seems workable.

Writing this down doesn't quite defeat the purpose of arranging to go off-log, but I guess I'm going to have to ensure my diaries are destroyed eventually, and not preserved as part of Muina's historic record.

Kaoren was more bothered by my questions than he wanted to let on, and this evening has continually tried to shift on top of me in his sleep. I've brought Sen into bed with us because she was struggling with her dreams too. I just want this waiting to be over, to have all the power stones found, and gone. And I'm trying to look at that positively, to think of it as saving what can be saved, and at least ending Lira's pain and confusion.

It's hard, though.

The expedition at Oriath is hoping to break through the shielding there tonight/tomorrow.

Sunday, October 26

Too Awful

Spoke to Lira last night. It wasn't a dream. I was asleep in bed with Kaoren and Sen when I felt Lira standing near us, and I woke myself up and she was there standing by the bed looking at us. I wasn't projecting, and didn't feel any power drain, so I was pretty surprised by this and only just stopped myself from elbowing Kaoren in the ribs, which wouldn't have been the nicest way to wake him up – I gripped his hand tightly instead as I said "Hello".

Lira looked at me, and at Kaoren as he lifted his head, then said: "Something's changed."

"It certainly has, if you can manage to be here all by yourself," I said, sitting up and reaching out to touch her arm. Warm and alive and at least temporarily real. "Thank you for warning us before."

"You were too slow," she told me. "The flying lizard was good, though."

"Were you able to see the meeting we had two days ago?" Kaoren asked (every bit a captain despite being dressed in the Singlet and boxer-briefs he wears to bed). "Where we discussed the site at Oriath and what we believe the people who kidnapped you did?"

"The old woman who kept talking," Lira said, in a flat tone which barely masked tight distress. "What room is it she was talking about?"

"It's underneath a palace to the south-west of Oriath," Kaoren said evenly. Then, after a brief pause added: "There is a shield about the complex, and today, just now, we succeeded in piercing it. Just before Cassandra woke."

Lira's no fool, and she knows that there's something dreadfully wrong with her, and she was being very brave trying to find out more. But she went so terribly white that I couldn't help myself, and scooped her into my lap and squeezed her hard. She reacted just like Ys, going rigid, but then when I – on the edge of hysteria myself – whispered "I'm sorry" into her ear over and over she suddenly gave a great shudder and clutched me and burst into tears – great, deep choking sobs full of confusion and fear and despair. We proceeded to cry all over each other, waking poor Sen up with a start (though she maintained her characteristic sweetness by patting both of us and making little comforting chirrupy noises and even pattering off and fetching water when we started to calm down).

Kaoren waited us out, no doubt having long discussions over the interface, though he did briefly squeeze my shoulder, despite what his Sights would make that feel like for him. Lira cried herself into limp exhaustion, and then faded away completely.

"Sorry," I said to Kaoren, taking the cup of water Sen was holding at a dangerous angle. "Not very useful to make her cry, but I couldn't help myself."

"It's what she's coming to you for," Kaoren said, briefly resting his hand on Sen's head so that she knew he approved of her being helpful. "Liranadestar must be aware that when she is conscious it's always in projection, that she is not returning to her physical self. And her captors interrupt the projection when they see it, which leaves her in a fragmentary and nightmarish state. It is comfort, more than answers, that she's seeking."

He didn't hide that this made him feel just about as bad as it did me. I leaned against him, then took Sen off and made us all hot drinks, and we carefully coaxed her back to sleep and sat up for a couple of hours watching the proceedings at Oriath over the interface. They had, as Kaoren said, only just made a breach in the shield when Lira had appeared, and had been performing scans when Kaoren contacted Maze. They actually waited out my weepy fit, which is going to look great on the mission report. "Pause while Devlin wept."

Then they sent First and Second in with Tsur Selkie, who had gone back to Oriath after the meeting because there's no other Place/Sight talents there at the moment.

The first floor wasn't too bad – was more of the same kind of living quarters and masses of dead people that we'd found at Arenrhon, but when they reached the ramp down they found that instead of a shield blocking their path there was...distinct weirdness. The ramp looks like it's underwater, and Tsur Selkie took a long look at it and then pulled the squads out and sent a drone in instead. The drone (a spider drone about the size and shape of a football but with lots of delicate pointy legs) made it about a third of the way down – measuring increasing pressure the entire way, and then collapsed and stopped transmitting. They sent two drones next time, and kept one at the top of the ramp recording what happened to the other one (which they sent down the ramp at a faster speed). It made it about halfway and then crumpled, metal bending and twisting.

This has rather put a damper on exploration, and they've set up drones to measure for any fluctuation in energy readings and eventually decided more Place Sight talents were now necessary, so they're swapping First and Ninth for Fourth, while sending Seventh back to Tare. I have to stay here still, which if it wasn't for Kaoren being gone would suit me fine, since I really don't want to go too close to that room. Mara, Zee, Alay and Ketzaren are going to take turns bunking on my couch.

No sign of Lira all day.

Monday, October 27

Ties

Another Cruzatch attack at Oriath last night. They tried to be all sneaky about it, but again preparation and technology defeated them. The greensuits have been taking great satisfaction in setting up very subtle scanners and traps throughout the aboveground palace, and it's become almost impossible for the Cruzatch to get in to where the research bunker is situated.

Kaoren and Halla completely failed to produce any useful information about the distortion at the ramp, and so they've switched to assisting the extremely careful search of the palace and upper floor for any intact information, or Sight impressions, while the technicians try and analyse the tendency of drones to go CRUNCH.

I hate sleeping without Kaoren. I had intended to have Sen in with me, but I ended up staying up very late talking to Mara and nodded off on the couch, so she put me to bed – where I promptly had vague and unsettling dreams about Lira. Not Sight dreams, I think, just ones expressing how sad I felt about her.

It's very nice having First back though. They've a few minor injuries – and two very glum juniors who missed out on getting their captaincies purely due to chance – but First is very much what I need when I don't have Kaoren around. They're just such an important part of my life, and having breakfast with them made me feel happy and worried at the same time. They look so worn.

I'm feeling horribly anxious about everyone right now.

Most of the day was filled with training – Mara obligingly including the kids in the torture session, and Lohn whisking them off for games and snacks when they'd run out of pep. She kept me going for much longer, until I could finally escape her and ease my aching bones into a bubble bath. Evil Mara.

I hadn't been in there very long when Ys surprised me by sending a channel request, and when I accepted it she said flatly: "Lira is in my room."

"She wanted to ask you something?" I asked.

"I showed her how to use my model," Ys said, even more flatly – it was hard to tell if she was annoyed, or daring me to object.

I thought about telling her to make a log (she has the ability now, having flown through infant's school already), but then said: "Let me know when you're ready for dinner."

I told Maze, of course, but he agreed that at the moment it was better not to distress Lira, and that if she'd heard anything important she would have come to talk to me. Sen and Rye soon joined Ys, and I settled on the couch listening to them playing *Pictionary*. If an afternoon with children who don't run away from her is all I can give Lira, I'm glad to at least give her that. I told Kaoren when he woke up that hearing Ys and Lira both laughing on the same day was almost too much for my feeble mind to process.

Lira left without coming out of Ys' room-nook – I'm willing to bet that breaking down and crying has made her all embarrassed and angry about it – she's so like Ys. Who came out and glowered at me, and then glowered even more when I hugged her and told her she was a very wonderful person.

We finished off Ys' book at story time, and I said it's my turn to pick the next one, which I have some plans for, but need to ask permission first.

Tuesday, October 28

Planning a Surprise

Ys' turn for nightmares last night. It's weird how, even though the kids' rooms aren't exactly close, I'm still better able to hear them tossing and turning than to notice people sneaking up on me. My kid-sense seems to be far stronger than my combat-sense. I took her a glass of water, and sat with her a little while. Of the three, she's most aware that Lira is probably not exactly alive, and we had a brief conversation (over the interface because she's aware Lira watches us) about whether we would be killing Lira by stopping whatever is going on, and whether it's better to release her from a half-life. Since I'm so confused about the question myself, it was hard to think of a way to be reassuring.

Ys has saved Lira's (rather good) attempt at creating a statue of a slinking cat, and kept looking at the model unhappily.

It was Zee's turn on the couch last night, and she was sitting up still when I went to fetch the glass of water, and waited for me to come back. My relationship with Zee has gone weird after my tangle with Nils' dreams. I'm pretty sure she really wants to know what I dreamed, but nothing could make her ask, and I'm busy pretending that there's no reason she'd be interested and having to stop myself from going: "OH BY THE WAY NILS LOVES YOU!!!1!!!" I'm definitely finding that it's not fun to know other people's secrets.

I was glad to talk to Zee though, about the kids and how they're coping with the dramas, and I particularly wanted to ask her about Siame. The medics are saying she'll be able to shift out of critical care soon, and I'm struggling with what to do about her current state of mind.

"I'm worried about her making decisions about her future based primarily on being upset because she couldn't fight three Cruzatch at once. Or because of me."

"Any Kalrani who can bring down even one Cruzatch should be congratulating herself," Zee said. "Nor does it sound like her relationship with her parents is as toxic as her brother's. No doubt, being Sight Sight talents, they'll prove to be perfectly tolerable people so long as you're doing what they think is right."

She was teasing me, and I laughed, and thanked her for letting me vent. Kaoren's family is one subject he and I don't seem able to discuss freely. I tried to talk to Zee about Eeli, but had to stop. It's too hard to talk about Eeli.

On the good news front, Dae's brand new Fifteenth Squad located one of the remaining malachite marble installations today. Two more to go, and then we...do something.

In the midst of Cruzatch raids and planet-wide marble hunts, KOTIS continues to push ahead with making Pandora a fully-functional colony as quickly as possible. Parts of the manufacturing 'outer suburb' is now operational, more and more apartment buildings have been completed, and including the Nurans we're coming up on the big twenty thousand residents mark, a number which amazes me.

Once the on-planet manufacturing process was functional, KOTIS Command was able to really move ahead, since they're now capable of producing the various components for fitting-out the apartments, from power units to waste systems to snotty goop that lives in your ducts and gives you nightmares. Mesiath was due to be made an active settlement this month, but because of the Cruzatch risk and the upcoming "doing something" they've postponed putting large numbers of people anywhere but Pandora, where the Ddura is now a near-constant background noise (for me).

All the incoming settlers are warned of the dangers, and are told firmly that they're taking a big risk coming here. It doesn't seem to have impacted application numbers greatly. Muina's so important to so many people, and also represents a big change in quality of life for many. And a big chance to become a land owner for others, judging from some of the discussions broadcast as part of the "forming Muina's laws" process. Everyone with any kind of interest is putting in their two cents about the next stage of the settlement. Once Pandora's not only self-sufficient, but able to provide for other colonies, people can start to expand out to the protected areas around other platform towns, and even further out, in individual houses rather than apartment block structures. An awful lot of people seem to have "lord of all they survey" ambitions, and I guess quite a few of them will get that to some extent or another. The designs for 'farming estates' are fascinating, and there's massive arguments about the process of giving grants for possession.

There were red pears on the table for lunch today and I just stared at them for a long time, and couldn't bring myself to eat one.

In the afternoon, I asked Maze if I could try to project something rather than do lots of exercise, and when they said okay (because they need to test how my ability to project has recovered) I said I'd need several scanners and all of First Squad's help, which made them very curious, but they obligingly didn't press me when I wouldn't say exactly what I wanted to create. I love that I can tell Maze "nothing anyone will object to" and he can give the go-ahead.

The thing I made was a bookshelf. The double-deep bookshelf where Mum keeps her favourites, and the classic children's books she used to read me as a kid. Everything from old-fashioned books like *Pride and Prejudice*, and the picture books which don't fit on the other bookcases. I had two main aims here – all the things I've been longing to read to the kids, and this really massive coffee-table book of Mum's which was basically "lush and glossy shots of really nice paintings throughout history".

While I did everything I could to maintain the projection, First Squad obliged me by rapidly flipping through for the scanners the particular books I pointed out. I especially wanted the art history book, and explained that I wanted to see if I can get it reproduced physically as a present for Siame's birthday (so a lot of care was needed in scanning it), and this naturally was a secret. Fortunately, I put so much focus on that one that even when I passed out it endured for about half an hour and they were able to get every page properly scanned.

Having it turned into a book (with suitable translation of the titles) isn't necessarily difficult, but having it done without everyone on three planets knowing about it and Siame reading it as an interface release before I'd even given it to her is the hard part. Maze is going to try and wangle something. I didn't even read the kids any of the stories First had scanned for me because I want to wait until after Siame's birthday, and instead picked a smallish Kolaren book to read to them.

It's the first time I've had a secret from Kaoren, for all it's a really mild one, but I felt very strange not telling him about it. I think I have enough of an understanding of his Sights to at least not be carrying a big "keeping a secret" flag when he talks to me, though that's probably working because he's not here right now. He's not even sure he'll be able to make it back for Siame's birthday.

And no Lira today, which worries me.

Wednesday, October 29

A Heavy Place

I dreamed of the Oriath expedition last night, of Kaoren and Halla and Tsur Selkie comparing their impressions of what was happening to little balls which a technician was tossing down the gravity ramp. They were bouncy rubbery balls which the technician sent ricocheting up and down at the beginning of the ramp, but which then on the next bounce up barely hopped an inch and then squashed flat to the stone, then crumbled.

I watched the next attempt, trying to work out a weirdness which I realised felt like Lira – it felt like Lira was there beside me, though I couldn't see her. And I realised I could, just barely, hear whispering.

That totally spooked me and I made myself wake up. Ketzaren was sitting on the side of my bed, waiting to see whether I was going to have a crisis, and let me squeeze her hand for a bit before having me explain what I'd been visualising. That, of course, created more than a bit of a problem, because they don't want to risk me getting mentally trapped again, and don't want me to be in Pandora if that's about to happen. Fortunately it was nearly morning and I'd had a reasonable rest, so I wasn't in immediate danger of passing out or anything, and after some back and forth discussion they decided that a few days back on Tare were in order, just to make sure, but that they could use the opportunity to poke me at the Oriath site first, to see if I could tell them anything useful.

This was a plan which didn't exactly please anyone, but beyond taking the "nuke the site from orbit" option, the technicians are starting to doubt they can get at the power stone for the Oriath site. Not anywhere near as quickly as we want. So after breakfast Mara stayed at Pandora with the kids, and the rest of First Squad took me to the nearest platform town to Oriath, where we were collected by a ship which took us the rest of the way. It was southern hemisphere, and quite cold, but not far enough south to be snowy. The 'palace' itself was covered in climbing vines which had dropped their leaves, so that it looked like it had been tied down with woody ropes.

They didn't want to risk me being there too long, so I arrived, glanced about, and then First and Fourth joined up to take me down along the main corridor only partially cleared of ancient corpses to look at the ramp.

Kaoren was being particularly upright and silent, with his eyes half-lidded. He loathes the 'poke Devlin at it' method. And it didn't help that this was one of those times where I wasn't feeling comfortable at all, having to force myself go through with it.

By the time we reached the ramp my heart-rate was spiking out of sheer scaredy-cat, and I leaned against Kaoren in a not very mission-like attitude as I streamed to them the whispering I could hear. And then over the interface I suggested that most everyone wander a little way away because I could still feel Lira there and I was hoping she would manifest herself.

Everyone except Kaoren, Maze and Tsur Selkie went off around a corner, and Maze and Tsur Selkie stood as far away from me as they were willing to go, and then I said out loud: "I'd really like to talk to you, Lira."

When she appeared, she was kind of tucked against my leg and behind me, as if hiding from having to look directly at the ramp.

"I'll try not to cry all over the place this time," I said, having to clutch Kaoren rather a bit to stop myself from being visibly upset. "We're trying to find a way to get further down."

"That's where you think this room is," Lira said, sounding very subdued. "Can you hear it talking?"

"Yes."

"What are you planning to do if you get down there?"

"Silence it," said Kaoren, his voice quiet and even and firm. "We don't understand what they did well enough to undo it gracefully. We can only try to pull it apart and hope we don't destroy everything else along with it. We don't know what will happen to you, Liranadestar."

I'm glad he was there. I don't think I could have said that to her. She looked up at him, this terribly grave, measuring stare. Then said: "It's the words which are making the things you put there fall apart," she said. "The words are eating them."

She vanished, disappearing from underneath my hand – and out of my senses. I felt too sick about it all to even talk, but I watched as they tossed a couple more balls down the ramp, and they now have a log of what I heard, showing that the quality and strength of the whispers changes when you toss something down there.

First stayed at the site, and Fourth was flown back to the platform town with me, and we hopped through Kalasa to Pandora, and we're all on our way to Tare now – including Siame and Eeli. Seeing Eeli in medical was a shock, but I think perhaps I'm glad I got the chance. Even though I still can't sense any hint of her inside the body they're keeping alive, I asked if I could spend some time with her, and told her all about Taarel's hair, and how I think Inisar likes Taarel, and how much everyone misses her.

After that, I managed to talk Kaoren into getting some sleep – he looks to me like he hasn't been sleeping since Fourth was sent back to Oriath, and when I need to go to sleep, I want him not to be exhausted. The kids and I sat next to him and played games most of the trip, with me being very reassuringly not ill and not vomiting and not in a coma. They've tanked now too, and most of the rest of Fourth, and I'm pretty tired, but I'm holding out till we're 'home'. Not much longer.

A couple of days on Tare has made my birthday plans for Siame fall apart rather, since I doubt she'll be returning to Muina with us, and barring dramas we're due to go back the day before her birthday. I'm trying to decide whether to buy something for her. It's made it easier to deal with Kaoren and Rye's presents, though. Kaoren's is something I've been experimenting with for a while – holding a nice stone I picked up and trying to fill it with feelings which he'll be able to sense with Place. The problem is I can't tell if it's worked. At least I can shop for Rye and maybe for Sen as well while I'm here.

Thursday, October 30

Spiritual

After all that fuss, I slept without any dreams at all, let alone being trapped anywhere. Kaoren says that just showed that the tactic of moving me before I was drawn in worked.

Nice quiet day, anyway. I had no medical appointments, no training, and since Fourth Squad has this time as leave, Kaoren and I could spend a lot of time together, and he could spend the morning with Siame. He's not happy because she's chosen to go home to their parents (she's only just reached the point of not being tubed up, and will be a month or so in straight recovery mode). He doesn't consider it a healthy environment for her, but he's not arguing and is taking her home tomorrow (a complicated trip because she can't really sit up for long periods). I am thoroughly relieved that there's no suggestion I go with them, even though it is a bit weird to not meet or even talk to the parents of the person you're engaged to. With the interface, Kaoren could arrange that easily, and the fact that he hasn't does make me wonder what they've been saying to him. I have seen pictures of them, and also his brother – they've inescapably been drawn in by the publicity surrounding my engagement to Kaoren and were also minorly well-known beforehand, at least in art circles, but haven't been interested in discussing Kaoren and me with the press at all, beyond Kaoren's mother giving the Setari program a bit of a serve.

I put in a lot of shopping – noting with some awe the way the amount in my account keeps going up, earning interest and adding in my wages. I also surveyed the current tone of the gossip about me and the kids, not to mention the universe falling apart, the inadequacy of KOTIS, and the Cruzatch spies in our midst.

In the afternoon we were able to take the kids swimming. Zan couldn't make it, but Ys and Rye are confident enough now that they don't need a person devoted entirely to them. Still swimming with frantic inefficiency, but no longer with overtones of panic. Ys swims with dogged determination – nothing like being dropped in a lake to demonstrate to her that this is a useful skill – but Rye's really loving it, and I cheerfully taught him some different dives (notably bomb dives). Sen is still slightly scared by the whole thing, but is happy enough so long as one of us is sticking within arm's-length.

And she always radiates a deep sense of contentment when we do family activities. I think the older two still don't fully realise that Sen sought me out not because she wanted parents, but because she wants Ys and Rye to have parents. I don't feel particularly used, though. Sen does genuinely like me – her Sights may have told her I was useful, but it's the way Kaoren and I behave which prompts all those joyous little hugs, and she will turn to me for comfort if she's upset.

Kaoren and I were sitting in my window-seat discussing the kids' development, but I got a little distracted by how beautiful he is and started kissing him, and enjoying very much Kaoren's usual reaction whenever I try to take charge. We've already learned not to go stripping off in unlocked rooms, and were just getting to the stage of deciding we needed to move when we realised we had an audience: Ys and Lira. I had to laugh at them.

"You look like twins," I said, which drew a fierce scowl from both of them.

"No we don't," Ys said. They don't, either, other than having typical Lantaren colouring. Lira is very good-looking, a bit similar in structure to Sen or Zee, with long, thick hair. Ys is skinny, almost boyish, and her hair is thin and fine and uncooperative. And Rye keeps reminding me of Nils, but without all the smouldering. [Thankfully!]

"You do when you're both pulling a face like this," I said, twisting my mouth with scornful disgust, and laughing at them again because they both reacted with the same angry annoyance. "Hello again, Lira," I said, before they thought to storm off. "Is it harder to project all the way to another planet?"

"Is that where this is?" Lira glanced past us to the towering thunderstorm approaching outside. "I suppose it might be. They're building another trap for you, so maybe it's good that you're not there."

"Did you hear what kind of trap?" Kaoren asked. He'd handled the interruption with almost his usual aplomb, but with just a little extra colour in his cheeks – and a cushion in his lap.

"They're making it hard for me to get near," Lira said, shrugging. "I only heard two of them arguing about how it was a bad idea because it risked speeding something up or making something break, but the other one said that it doesn't matter if it speeds up because if they have a second touchstone they'll be able to finish off properly and then they won't have to worry about it at all again."

"Any idea when their trap will be ready?" I asked, and she shook her head.

"They're frightened," she said, with some considerable satisfaction. "They need to get you soon. Can you show me what this world looks like?"

She sounded angry when she asked, which was a combination of very justifiable rage at the people who'd kidnapped her, and an attempt to disguise a resurgence of the sheer horror of her half-life, which she seems to be trying not to focus on in preference to revenging herself by foiling the plans of Photoshop Gods.

There was no way I was going to say no to showing Lira anything, and all five of us ended up taking her on tour, since Sen woke up when Ys went to tell Rye, and attached herself to Lira in a pleased and very protective way. And the kids were useful tour-guides, too, since they insisted on pointing out the things which most interested them as residents of a non-technological world. Moving walkways and elevators and the KOTIS ship dock, and the roof with its whitestone expanse and the enormous storm roiling in the distance. The one thing we didn't see was many people. Kaoren told me that the bluesuits pretended they were having a drill, put KOTIS on alert, and actually cleared corridors rather than have too many people see her, since Lira is very secret still, and stands out incredibly in her formal Lantaren outfit.

Sen was asleep on her feet by the time we reached the roof, and Kaoren carried her back down to our apartment and put her to bed, while I trailed along making sure Rye kept walking in his enthusiasm to describe what travelling in the ships was like (they're all immensely impressed by the ships). Lira faded away before we'd quite reached the apartment, and I spent quite a while talking to Ys and Rye over the interface, since Rye's caught up with Ys in understanding just how bad a situation Lira is in, and went all white-faced and horrified when I couldn't promise him that we'd save her. As soon as I left them they both hopped into Sen's bed, which is a sign of how deeply upset by this they are.

Kaoren's been in interface meetings ever since, but is very unkeen on letting me out of his sight. Another trap for me is not a good thing.

Friday, October 31

Little Gestures

Kaoren had Sight dreams about me all night. The same thing over and over – me falling and him trying to catch me but my hands slipping through his. Sight Sight isn't supposed to be prophetic, so it's likely a reaction to his awareness that there's an existing threat. He was a wreck by morning (and I wasn't that great, because he thrashed about and even kneed me in the stomach once), and when breakfast time rolled around, we came very close to having an argument because Kaoren wanted to arrange for someone else to take Siame home.

We were fortuitously interrupted by the delivery of a huge number of parcels – the results of my shopping spree – which certainly gave the kids some fun over breakfast. I'm trying to restrain the urge to buy them everything, but even things which are practical replacements in my eyes (like the endless amounts of bubble bath Sen gets through) also count as impossible largesse in their eyes.

To my delight, among the parcels was one which had been forwarded care of Maze, and I tore it open to find that Siame's book gift had been reproduced precisely as ordered, with my laboriously transcribed titles included. This was a serious distraction for Kaoren, who not only was very interested in the contents (and forced himself to not more than glance at it because it was Siame's gift), but also the fact that I'd managed to get it made without him knowing. I'd simply forgotten about it, which appears to be an excellent way to keep secrets from Sight Sight talents.

One of the things I'd ordered was some useful paper, a thick piece of which I folded and wrote on, and a big sheet I measured out against the (huge) book, then gave to the kids the assignment of drawing pictures to make a birthday card and wrapping paper. Kaoren I took off to the shower, to talk him into going with Siame. I don't want him not doing something which would normally be so important to him, just because he's afraid for me. I guess that might count as our first full and proper argument, because we definitely had the make-up sex.

He was pretty subdued afterwards, but quietly joined me in adding drawings to the wrapping and card – really exquisite pictures of some of the animals we'd seen on Muina, which he told me privately his parents would consider embarrassing just because they'd been done on something like wrapping paper. I think I'm going to struggle to like his parents, if I ever meet them.

But the present looked great, all wrapped up in embarrassing art: my little plan to convey to Siame that she's not lost a brother, but instead gained an extended family. But Siame's reaction, when we went down to see her off, was focused almost entirely on Kaoren's drawings. It was hard to tell if she was upset that I'd managed to break Kaoren's ban on drawing, or pleased that he'd drawn something for her. She was on her best behaviour otherwise, self-assured and very polite – despite being tremendously weak and shaky still. No wonder she's feeling down – being sick always makes you feel awful. Her birthday's the day after tomorrow, and I can only hope that the book wasn't just the thing to make her more annoyed with me.

Today was a rough day. Even though my move to Tare had been kept very quiet, and I was thoroughly guarded, being away from me for the seven hours it took to fly Siame to Unara, settle her in, and then fly back was not something Kaoren found easy to face – especially when it involved Siame being so ill, and having to talk to his parents. He ended up asking me to keep him permanently in-channel again, streaming what was around me to him, which I did (except for going to the bathroom) and of course nothing dramatic happened at all, but it helped.

Lira's warning has meant a higher level of alert on all three worlds. I was assigned to Twelfth for the day, and Zan simply incorporated me and the kids into their training regime, while ensuring I was thoroughly guarded at all times. She managed to make it seem almost natural that there were always at least two squad members within five feet of me. But the stress level among all the squads is high, and so many of the Setari look exhausted or are sporting injuries. We had the good news that all the malachite marble locations have been discovered, but the technicians at Oriath have made little progress with the ramp of crushing doom. They're experimenting with sonics as a way to 'keep the words out', but so far have only made it an extra foot or so down the ramp before the poor drone goes squish.

NOVEMBER

Saturday, November 1

Keyed Up

Another bad night for Kaoren. Beyond remaining notably unkidnapped, I don't know what I can do for him. It must be awful to have something like Sight Sight shouting at you that the person you love is in danger. Other than keeping tensely alert and taking all logical precautions, you can only wait and try and stop it when it happens. I'm less keyed up about it myself, but in a kind of determined way, because if I let myself think too much about it I'm going to have a few rip-roaring nightmares of my own.

Just picture me with my eyes shut, hands over my ears, going "La la la la la la".

Not exactly heroic, I know. But KOTIS has achieved what it needed from me, found what they think is a workable plan, and my role now is to just keep my head down until they open the way to the last of the marbles.

The rest of Fourth was back from leave today, and I could see that Kaoren's open exhaustion was a serious shock to them. Sen, oddly, isn't having nightmares, but I think her Sight has told her something because she's gone very quiet and wants to be carried about and held far more than usual. I'm not allowed anywhere without a guard, and a full squad within quick response time. Not even medical. Mori and Glade were with me today, and it was a relief to talk almost normally about the ads for the upcoming season of *The Hidden War*. They're hyping the hell out of the first episode as a major, history-making event, and showing the last few seconds of the last episode and then blackness and then a fragment of the actual audio from my log, ending in a huge splash and underwatery sounds.

I think if any of us have to wait any longer someone's head's going to explode from sheer stress.

Monday, November 3

Out from Underneath

It's over.

It's over and I'm not dead. Or trapped in a half-life or any of the things I halfway expected to happen to me. I've been quietly convinced for so long that I would end up dead that I can hardly believe it. Nor can anyone else, I think.

There's a good deal of cautious celebration going on.

Of course, I had to get through a lot of drama to reach this point. It started while I was still being a pin cushion in medical, when news came in from Muina that Second Squad had been lost.

Not lost as in dead: lost as in vanished. They'd been in-transit through Kalasa, hauling a fresh batch of sacrificial drones (now produced in Pandora). They stepped on the platform to the town nearest to Oriath – along with a greensuit and two greysuits who had been with them – and didn't arrive at the expected destination. As totally gone as I'd been when I vanished to Kalasa. All the scanners stationed by the platform could tell us was that there'd been a higher than usual power reading. The greysuits were guessing that the platform's destination had been diverted. That Second Squad had been caught by the trap meant for me.

There's a serious problem with using technology that your enemy understands far better than you.

They'd been missing about an hour by the time we heard the news, and we had to sit through way too much debate over whether to try and use me to visualise the missing. I desperately wanted to, not only because I've grown close to Second, but I just hated to think of Zee and Ketzaren, who would both be going out of their minds. But I was also scared spitless that I would visualise them and they'd be dead.

Before KOTIS was willing to risk a visualisation – particularly one which would require me going into the Ena – they sent every available squad out to scout multiple locations in near-space for any sign of Cruzatch, and then finally took me through a gate they don't normally use, with an escort of six squads.

The visualisation at least wasn't difficult to do and I felt a good deal of relief not to be seeing dead bodies. Nils was looking very captainly, quite unlike his usual self, talking to Jeh while unpacking one of the drones from a pallet of them. Jeh was trying to wake everyone else, all lying about on the floor of a rather familiar-looking doughnut-shaped room. The inside of one of the Pillars.

"The walls–" Halla began, and Kaoren said sharply: "Cut the projection!" and grabbed at me, but it was too late, and his hands went straight through me.

It's a little hard to describe what happened, even after watching several different logs of it. I guess it was the reverse of what I did when visualisating Inisar. I was sitting on the testing chair we'd brought with us, looking at all the symbols burnt into the whitestone walls of the Pillar, which had shifted from glowing mildly to vivid white, and from my point of view just sort of overwhelmed everything I could see and swept me away like a tidal force. I really thought I was in the undertow of a massive wave. The squads guarding me saw me just fade away, as if I was one of my own projections allowed to lapse. And to Nils and Jeh, off in the Pillar, the symbols began glowing and I suddenly blazed into existence, being pulled backward toward the central column of the Pillar.

Nils has Speed and excellent reflexes, and threw himself between me and the central column, which was a handy way to give us both a lot of bruises. I split his lip. The tidal wave kept trying to sweep me on, and he let out this low gasp of pain as he was crushed against the central column, but he managed to keep hold of me.

I felt like a super magnet was pulling me, and Nils was just a bit of squishiness temporarily between me and where I was going. The pressure made it very hard to breathe and Nils was even worse off, with me crushing into his chest, and his enhanced Telekinesis useless because it won't work on me. Even with Jeh's help they couldn't budge me at all, and my arms and legs kept getting sucked backwards around him and going straight through the substance of the central column into the aether stream. All three of us barely had the strength to haul them back, and it was obvious that if Nils didn't let me keep going both of us would suffocate.

"Get one – two – of the small drones," Nils gasped, then opened a channel for all three of us because he was barely able to talk. "Caszandra, open your suit and seal the drones inside it."

This wasn't difficult to do, though it did make me look ridiculously like I was pregnant with very argumentative twins, and spider drones aren't exactly something that are fun to put inside your clothes. Fortunately the legs folded away in non-dangerous ways or I probably would have ended up a drone-kebab.

Nils activated the drones, adding: "Sound your alert – it gives more people more ability to access your interface and suit controls," and gave me a little squeeze after I did, then with Jeh's help struggled out from between me and the symbol-covered central column. I promptly smacked into it and vanished, falling into a river of light.

I've watched the mission log from back on Tare, where I and my projection had both vanished at the same time. Kaoren stays frozen before my empty chair for all of two seconds, eyes wide and horrified, and then goes totally captain, ordering everyone back inside at double-pace and asking Halla for her Sight impressions during the brief trip back inside. His voice was maybe a little more curt than usual, and his eyes nearly totally closed, but otherwise he didn't show any sign of his feelings. He says he couldn't let himself pause until he'd made sure everything he could think of doing was being done.

Once back in real-space he was very absolute in his discussions with the bluesuits – though at that time he thought that I was trapped at the Pillar with Second, and didn't know I'd spent barely any time there at all. But knowing Second was at a Pillar, and with drones, meant they had a shot at finding them, since all the Pillar locations found so far open out into deep-space. Kaoren had a scanning ship which was stationed at the rift island sent into deep-space immediately to try and contact the drones, and then arranged for a second ship to take a mix of scanning technicians and some of the best Kalrani path-finders on a trip through to Muina. And the kids, because Lira has shown a marked tendency to speak to them, and the search would be coordinated from Muina.

I can only be relieved that he did that – and that the weather was good so that they could fly quickly and weren't still in deep-space when it happened. Fourth and Eleventh travelled to the rift island via the Ena – a route which has been included in the regular rotations ever since I got myself trapped the first time – and they joined up with the scanning ship as it came back from its initial survey.

There had already been a project underway to try and locate the Pillars from deep-space. They hadn't succeeded as yet, but then they hadn't had drones and a squad sitting handily at any Pillar locations. Deep-space isn't a great environment for drones – the physics there aren't exactly helpful – but drones and ship instruments have a far greater range than the Setari. The scanning ship hadn't detected anything when it went in to hover around the rift entrance, but after returning to collect Fourth and Eleventh, they headed on the usual course to Muina, scanning madly all the way, and finally detected a signal just before the Muina rift. Whereupon Nils told them that I was no longer with them.

Since they were inside the Pillar and relatively protected from Ionoth, Second Squad (bruises and aether-drunkenness aside) weren't in immediate danger, so the ship continued on to Muina to let them know I'd been taken, only to find out that this was old news.

From the squads on Muina's point of view, they'd been continuing their search for Second Squad when I suddenly popped into interface range, deeply unconscious with my alert blaring away. Nils had dropped both our logs to the drones before letting me go, so they knew what had happened to me before I'd passed out. And they knew exactly where I was, too – right near the bottom of the Oriath installation.

As soon as the Oriath team detected me, they'd accessed the drones, and withdrawn my nanosuit so that they could make a visual scan. The visual had shown that I was lying alone on a (symbol-etched) platform being busily unconscious. The technician driving the drones detected movement nearby and very sensibly didn't leave them sitting on top of me, but scuttled them down one side of the platform and tucked them as far out of sight as she could manage. She even powered them down to a ready state, and I gather that she's likely to get some kind of commendation for this, since the Cruzatch invariably destroy any drones they spot, and it was a group of Cruzatch which came and took me away – up to a room directly below the room holding Lira.

After a suitable pause, KOTIS repowered the drones and did some cautious exploration of the lower reaches of the Oriath installation. The Cruzatch had taken me up, and one drone tried to follow and was promptly crushed on a ramp. The other searched down and found a particularly grand and magnificent series of sarcophagus rooms, ending in another malachite marble. Once it reached here, the drone was tucked into a corner and KOTIS Command had a fun argument over whether to have Palanty from Fifth teleport down straight away, or to wait. They didn't want to precipitate a countermeasure by the Cruzatch, and if they lost the drone's visual feed, it would be much more difficult and dangerous for Palanty to teleport down.

And they didn't particularly want to blow the place up while I was still in it. Unless they had to.

The eventual decision was to hold off doing anything until they'd broken through to the malachite marble in the last of the other installations. Isten Notra had stressed that leaving one marble functional might create catastrophic stress on the spaces, so KOTIS has been shielding each marble against Cruzatch retaliation and planting bombs ready and waiting.

And they were still waiting when Fourth brought news of Second's location. Fourth stayed on Muina, headed for Oriath, while Eleventh went back to trace a path to the Pillar where Second were stuck. KOTIS was already well into full battle mode, most of the Setari squads massing at

Oriath, and two groups of technicians frantically trying to overcome the ramp of doom and work through the last of the shielding at a final installation up near the northern icecap.

All that time they were trying to wake me up, but I was suffering from an extreme overload of aether and was totally non-responsive. Other than them finally breaking into the other installation and planting the second-last of the bombs, there really wasn't any progress until I *did* wake up – by which time Fourth was about two-thirds of the way to Oriath and Second been recovered and had just emerged from the rift.

Waking up was the worst thing.

I was lying down and I couldn't move and I couldn't see. There were voices. The whispers.

The whispers were still whispers, but somehow they were so loud, so dominant, that the large mass of people trying to talk to me over the interface were just noise. But then that noise dropped away and became Kaoren, just Kaoren, talking to me steadily, and very sensibly sending the words to me in text as well.

Reading his words helped me hear him, repeating my name. And then, in some of the bare few words of English I'd managed to teach him: "Please. Need. Hear."

That did start to shift me out of my groggy state, and I tried to turn my head and failed, discovering that the stuff covering me would only expand and contract a few millimetres, like strong elastic.

The whispers started to build up, trying to drown out Kaoren, and that made me angry, giving me impetus to respond.

"There's ten Cruzatch near me, and more somewhere down. I'm tied up and can't move my arms or legs. I think they've used the same stuff that net was made of," I said, struggling with the annoying rubberiness of it. "There's something over me making it too dark to see. I can hear the stones whispering. They're a little further away, but otherwise it's very like my dream."

Although I held it together starting out, I sound openly terrified by the time I reached the end. And the log has helpfully captured my gasping breaths when Tsur Selkie told me they needed me to wait, to lie there and tell them if the Cruzatch went away.

I opened a private channel to Kaoren and asked him to keep talking, and especially to keep sending it in text to reinforce the words, to tell me what had been happening. I needed that to keep back the whispers, which kept sucking at my attention, this steady stream of old Muinan, building a hierarchy of gods.

It might have seemed like forever, but apparently it wasn't more than five minutes after I woke up enough to respond that until the Cruzatch in the room gathered together, then moved away.

"They are going down," I said. "None left near me."

"Tell us immediately when you can no longer detect them," Kaoren said, his voice shifting to measured captain-mode. "As soon as that happens, the drone will be activated so a team can teleport into the room of the power stone. We can't teleport to where you are, both because we cannot see the room, and because you're in the heavy zone. Once you're free, you need to move either down toward the power stone or up to the surface – whichever way is easiest. Once the teleportation group are in, I'm going to take you through a visualisation to help free you."

"I can only feel a couple now," I said. "I – no, they're gone as well."

"Good. We'll start the visualisation now."

Kaoren began to describe a drone, a very solid, squat drone furnished with a vast array of cutting tools. It was his usual clear, concise description, and by that time I'd shrugged off more of the aether effect, but–

"The whispering's getting louder." My voice was high.

"Then concentrate, Cassandra." Kaoren's words were clipped, stern, the tone he only uses with me in emergencies.

He continued with the visualisation, and I think I did succeed in making the drone, or at least there was suddenly a loud crunching sound right next to me, as if a solid, squat drone with a vast array of cutting tools was being compacted for recycling.

Then Zee's voice, loud and abrupt. "Use her suit. Caszandra, we're going to cut you out."

Nanosuits can be cloth, they can change colours, and they can make an edge sharper than steel. Lots of them, all over. Caszandra Scissorsuit.

It worked too. While Palanty and Kajal teleported down to the malachite marble room with the last of the bombs and a round dozen drones to send skittering off exploring, my uniform grew dozens of blades, effortlessly slicing through the stuff holding me down. My hands came loose first as a technician cleverly manipulated the suit to slice as well as pierce.

But the whispers had me.

As I stopped hearing anything else, my vitals began climbing through the roof, and waves of distortion started rippling out: slow billows of heat which increased with every repetition. Not confined to the room either – they felt them at Pandora. For all I know, they felt them on Tare.

Tsur Selkie ordered Palanty and Kajal out immediately, and recommended that the bombs be triggered as soon as they were clear. All they could do was hope that the malachite marble would be destroyed without much damage to my floor. Palanty and Kajal teleported, but then the next wave of heat and distortion rolled out and that one–

Quite a few people have tried to describe to me what happened next. Maze says he felt 'thin', Zee that she was made of glass. Everyone on Muina had some variation of this: flattened, washed away, erased, frozen, unable to move, to think, to do. To trigger explosions. Kaoren says he felt painted. And all of them could see another place, a Muina where enormous statues stood above the cities to proclaim the reign of golden gods.

I didn't feel thin, or made of glass. I felt like I was being cooked alive while my brain was pierced by a half dozen needles. My scissorsuit hadn't cleared away the covering over my face, but even through it I could see there was a bright, burning light directly above me.

There was just enough of me left outside the brain piercing to be aware that they were going to blow the malachite marbles. I didn't realise the entire world had fallen into a pit of distortion with no way to dig itself out, and so I was pretty much lying there waiting to die. Which was pathetic of me, but it had just felt so inevitable for so long. I was the Supa Speshul Magick Gurl who had appeared from nowhere and made it possible to win, but who had to die at the end so that the people she cared about could live on.

Which would SUCK.

Especially when I was the one doing the dying, and particularly when it involved being slowly roasted. If I was going to be blown up, I decided, I at least wanted to get away from the mega-sunlamp first.

I wanted to not break my promise to Kaoren. I wanted to not have been wrong to let three children care.

My body didn't feel quite my own, but I managed to lift a hand and flail clumsily at my face, swiping away the rubbery shroud. But the whispers were getting louder, louder, and I'm not sure if I would have managed any more if not for Lira.

I don't know how long she'd been there, trying to push me off the altar. She was quite a sight to see, looking like a proper ghost instead of a little girl, with great streamers of light warping off her, being pulled toward this glowing starburst above where I was lying. Every time she reached out, her arms would thin out to light and be caught by the starburst, making it impossible for her to reach me.

But she kept trying, and mouthed words I could barely hear: "You have to *move*!"

The sight of her galvanised all the parts of me which weren't caught by whispers. Not to any rational, measured plan of action. No, my response could best be summed up as BAD LIGHT EATING LIRA! The amount of thought space I had left was definitely at Lolcat level. Which is probably why I decided that the important thing was to save the little girl who'd been dead for centuries.

But it got me to move, to roll off the altar, trying to push her backward, looking for the quickest route away from the light. There was no door. That betrayal of expectation actually cleared my head a little, enough to realise that the burning sensation in my chest was at least in part because the air was really, really hot. Still focused on saving Lira, I grabbed her to me, and staggered drunkenly toward the corner of the room, trying to shield her from the light.

As soon as I moved from the altar, the ground began to shake, and heading to the corner increased the amount of earth-shaking to a spectacular degree. And it felt like the needles in my brain were being dragged out, with every treacle-pull step.

Then the floor heaved up, but at least it tossed us toward the corner, whereupon I shoved Lira underneath me and tried to cover her as much as possible, desperately trying to project a shield or wall to keep away the light.

The sky fell.

The earth-shaking was worldwide. The damage at Pandora wasn't too bad – there's a crack in one of the science buildings and one of the towers in the old town fell down. More spectacular was the split which appeared in the moon. Instead of a bullet-hole, it now looks like a comma. That happened just before all the painted glass people found themselves real again, and immediately blew the charges.

The destruction of the malachite marbles caused a great surge of power to be released through the platforms. They aren't working any more, though Isten Notra thinks that's because their aether supply was exhausted. Moonfall happened at the platform villages where the moon was visible yesterday, anyway. And the Ena is currently a no-go area, all heaving and disturbed, so we're cut off from Tare and Kolar. They think it will settle down, but not necessarily to the way it was before, and it's very likely the Pillars are no longer operating.

But all that was later. They blew the charges just after I started causing earthquakes, and a world was thrown from its feet. When the dust settled I was alive but unconscious, my vitals not critical, but not likely to improve with a palace and four levels of subterranean installation collapsed spectacularly on top of me. It took nearly two kasse for them to get me out.

I woke in my home-away-from-home less than a day after my visualisation of Second Squad. Kaoren was asleep in the chair beside me, but came awake with a start which meant he'd had an alarm set to trigger if my state shifted to consciousness. I tried to say hello, but after all that burning hot air, my throat is pretty painful, so I said "I can't believe I'm not dead," over the interface.

He made a face at me, and then just leaned forward and rested his forehead against my shoulder. I put my hand on the back of his head and we stayed like that without speaking, appreciating that we could, that we got to be alive together, and go on.

My cheek and forehead felt more than odd, so eventually I tried to touch them, but Kaoren caught my hand, then showed me what I currently looked like, with my left eye swollen shut and the skin around it red and angry beneath a coating of salve, the eyebrow gone along with most of my hair, which had been melted and frizzled and then chopped unevenly off by the medics. I also have a broken arm and cracked ribs, but altogether this has been one of my less serious forays into injury-land. I'm planning on it being my last.

"The kids okay?" I asked, and he nodded, and told me he'd fetch them and squeezed my hand painfully hard, then left me to the embarrassing things medics do to me.

Sen arrived first, running ahead enthusiastically, but stopping just short of leaping on me and instead climbing very cautiously into the bed with me. She didn't say anything at all, just welded herself to my side and stuck there no matter what anyone said to her. It wasn't too bad – she'd chosen the side without the broken arm – and I patted her on the head, feeling quite overwhelmed. Rye had followed along hastily behind, but stopped short and just stared at me.

I gestured for him to come closer, and tugged at one of his thick, wavy locks, then brought all three of them into the channel with Kaoren and me and said: "We have to get Kaoren give both of us a haircut, I think."

Ys came in then, and completely floored me. Because Lira was with her. Lira. Dressed in Ys' clothes, with some bruises of her own, glowering at me in an unusually subdued way.

"But how?" I asked, holding out a hand for her in complete disbelief. I hadn't been wanting to think about what the destruction of the installation had meant for Lira, and certainly hadn't expected to find her with Ys.

"We're not certain," Kaoren said, helping me sit up so I could hug Lira. "She was beneath you when we reached you."

"How wonderful," I managed to say aloud, my throat sounding like it had been sandpapered. "I'm so glad."

"There's no reason she can't use Siame's room," Ys said – a pronouncement rather than a question, and I had to laugh, which hurt a lot. Ys is so protective of her family. I'm so glad she's decided to expand it to Lira.

"I think we can manage a room of her very own," I said, with some effort, and when Kaoren had given me a drink to make it easier, added to him: "If Cruzatch are gone, was hoping they let us build house on that island where we go swimming."

"I was thinking the same thing," Kaoren said, looking pleased. "When you're a little better we can all work on the design together."

I fell asleep before I really got to see more than their initial reaction to that. Rye was the only one looking openly delighted, but I think they were all pleased, and Kaoren told them that they had to make sure they had a good idea of what they needed for their rooms. I've had a chance to talk to them all individually since, and every single one of them has obviously put considerable thought into the kind of room they would like, for all that it's quite hard to drag the details out of some of them.

So Kaoren and I have four children now, though Isten Notra has told me quite bluntly that there's a strong possibility that Lira will one day simply fade away, just as my origami cranes apparently have begun to. Isten Notra isn't sure if she will age, or remain as she is now, and if she counts as an Ionoth or not. She's something very new and unexpected, and there's a huge amount of scientific and public interest in her, which we're going to have to shield her from. Kaoren vetoed an awful lot of the tests the greysuits wanted to run on her, and fortunately Isten Notra is backing him up. Lira, in turn, is claiming to no longer be able to visualise or project, which we're not altogether sure is true. She certainly enhances the Setari when they touch her (and without the distortion I cause). They're holding off implanting the interface for the moment, given its tendency to try and kill me, but I'm going to argue against keeping her permanently unconnected since I can see she already has realised the lack. She and Ys are thick as thieves, which I find a very handy thing.

After a long second sleep I've been awake for most of today (well, with occasional naps). Sen has stayed stubbornly by my side, sneaking back if anyone tries to remove her, and seems to have appointed herself as my social secretary, happily bullying everyone who comes and visits me. The only times she's left of her own accord is when I've spoken to Ys and to Lira, and the rest of the time she gives my visitors their marching orders when she thinks they've stayed too long. Unfortunately I can't convince anyone that I'm well enough to not need to be in medical, despite not being that injured and in no apparent further danger.

It really is over.

It's been very interesting seeing First and Second Squad particularly. There's just something different about their eyes. Relief, of course, that we escaped any more deaths (on Muina, anyway), but also this introspective quality. They're all thinking rather seriously about a different sort of future. The tears between real-space and the Ena haven't miraculously vanished, and Isten Notra says we won't know if destroying the malachite marbles has had a positive effect until the initial disruption has died down, but she does think that removing the pressure of the parasite world can only be a good thing.

What exactly happened to the Cruzatch and the parasite world is anyone's guess. It might all still be there, but it's far more likely to have been destroyed or to now be fading away. Just desserts for the Photoshop Gods, but I don't think I'll ever forget those children. Calling their world a parasite makes it easier, but it doesn't make their lives any less gone. I can only choose to count what's been saved, rather than who was lost.

I'm still having trouble believing I'm not dead.

Tuesday, November 4

Out of Touch

Slept a lot today, in between various medical things being done to me. Then Alay and Ketzaren came and kidnapped me in the afternoon and gave me a proper haircut. It's now shorter than Kaoren's but at least even. Still, I was able to emerge from medical to have dinner and watch the sunset and enjoy sitting around in the common room and on the patio with the mass of Setari now filling the building, watching their faces, listening to the changed note in their voices.

The squads – everyone on the planet – are currently gathered in Pandora, not even a hardy few trying to sift through the rubble at Oriath. For safety reasons, KOTIS is keeping everyone in one place until the rift stops letting out strange power surges, and so we've all these squads with only a little guarding duty between them. They've mostly been given a break to recover from the past hectic weeks and their various injuries, and are otherwise helping with colony work. They're not even allowed in near-space.

This means accommodating First, Second, Fourth, Fifth (who are being low-key, at least), Sixth, Ninth, Tenth, Eleventh, Fifteenth, Sixteenth, Squad One and Squad Two. Plus the Nuran Setari. Everyone's doubled up, and they've started a second (or third, given the school) building on the south side. It will be more exposed, since there's less hill there.

There are far more squads on Muina than on Tare and I know Maze is concerned about what this will mean to the squads defending Tare. Especially since so many of those on Tare are there because of injuries. Though it seems from the cautious drone surveys they've done of near-space here that the unstable environment might discourage most Ionoth anyway.

The prospect of the separation from Tare and Kolar being a long, extended one is naturally upsetting for many Pandorans, since it represents a complete loss of contact with friends and family. It's mainly Zan I'll miss, and Ghost, who we think maybe is on Tare. I can only be thankful that Kaoren insisted on moving the kids here, since Zan would have been practically the only person on Tare they've spent any time with at all.

The dinner discussion remained firmly on rebuilding Muina, and the progress of the colonies, at least partly because it was Lira's first large group outing and I'm willing to bet that everyone's under strict orders not to upset her. I spoke to Isten Notra today about the way everyone is itching to pick Lira's brain about all things Lantaren, and fortunately they're willing to hold off until Isten Notra gives them the go-ahead, and she doesn't plan to do that for weeks or months, and even then only sparingly. She says they can just live with whatever Lira chooses to volunteer until then.

And I am very extremely happy to no longer be so important – not even the only touchstone! I'm still not allowed out without a guard, at least until they're absolutely certain the Cruzatch won't reappear, and there'll be laws about my visualisation and projection abilities regardless, but it's the beginning of a new phase, and I can look forward to just focusing on looking after the kids and being with Kaoren and escaping the cycle of injuries which seems to be the inevitable consequence of playing hero.

And maybe occasionally making dragons. Because!

Kaoren's asleep in the chair next to my bed again. I haven't had enough chance to be alone with him. He needs to be able to hold me, I think, and know properly that I'm still with him.

Wednesday, November 5

Looking Ahead

Considerably better today, and cleared to not have to live in medical, so I immediately went for a walk down to the lake's edge all by myself and sat on a rock feeling very daring. I'm a sad case. It was quite five minutes before anyone noticed (for all I was in full view of the common room) and I sat there sunning myself and looking forward to the days when no-one is assigned to guard me.

Par and Glade were my current watchdogs, and Glade came out very aggrieved and said: "You have no idea the tortures we'll be subjected to. If you're going to sneak off, make sure it's when someone from First is assigned to you."

I grinned at him (as much as my very sore face would allow anyway). "I won't tell Kaoren if you don't."

"He'll know. He always does." Glade gave me an equivocal look. "I think for the moment it's just easier on all of us to know exactly where you are, and to be sure you've someone with you."

He meant that Kaoren has been stressed beyond the point of endurance, and I wrinkled my nose, but nodded. "I know. But I give fair warning that I'm going to be a lot less biddable and obedient about staying where I'm put in future. Just walking out here is the first time I've gone anywhere by myself in months. Once we're sure that the Cruzatch aren't able to get here anymore, I hope to go back to not having people assigned to guard me at all."

"I'm glad it's not me you have to win that argument with." He glanced toward Pandora's heart, probably thinking about Tsur Selkie, who had summoned all the captains for a meeting with Muina's leaders to talk about colony-building. "Not that the rules haven't changed in a big way. But Cruzatch aren't the only thing we're protecting you from, and given all that you've done and *could* do, I don't see any end to your guard roster."

"Maybe they'll guard me secretly, like the Nurans do those at Nurenor," I said, and saw from Glade's lack of reaction that he thought it very likely, if I kicked up too much of a fuss about people following me around.

That kind of put a damper on my day, but I'm still too pleased and amazed to be alive to get too upset about it. Instead I went up to the seats on the very top of the Setari building – the tree is very leafy and shady up there now and it was a warm day – only to find Nils asleep in the grass, surrounded by little daisies. There's a bruise on one side of his mouth from impacting with the back of my head and his split lip has only started healing, but somehow this made him look smexier than usual.

I'm pretty sure he woke up straight away, but pretended not to, and I decided to act like I thought he was still asleep. Nils' quick thinking with the drones basically saved the planet, but I'm still uncomfortable with him – mainly because I'm bursting to tell him that he's being very unkind to Zee, or tell Zee just how hurt Nils is – and I don't think either of them would forgive me for raising the subject.

After finding a position on the bench that didn't pinch my ribs, I opened a channel to Mara (who had the kids for the morning and was teaching them more basic combat moves) and asked if I could borrow Ys for a while. Ys duly came up, her expression particularly fierce. It made my heart turn over, because I knew it meant she was feeling uncertain. I'd never 'summoned' any of them before. Glade and Par had retired a little down slope, and Nils continued pretending to be asleep as I pointed to the seat opposite.

"You're supposed to be in medical," Ys said. She much prefers attack to defence.

"I escaped while they were looking the other way," I said cheerfully. "I have a particular job for you. I found this program which we can use to help try and work out what our house will be like. It's a bit fiddly and annoying, and I keep getting a headache trying to use it. See if you have better luck, and if you think you can work it properly, we'll have a family meeting and start figuring out what we'd like to have where. Let me know if it's too hard for you, and I'll ask Kaoren instead."

Nils lifted his head and gave me an amused look, but Ys was properly insulted by the suggestion that anything might fall in the too hard basket for her, and promptly lost herself in my thinly disguised present for her.

"You're building a house?" Nils asked, propping himself on one hand.

"We want to try get permission to build on one of the islands. Barracks living some good points, but this give us more privacy, and I can have garden to neglect, and we won't have to be escorted about as much for fear of passers-by." I shrugged. "It's just more what I'm used to."

"And given your capacity to acquire children, the barracks won't be large enough," he added over the interface. "Are you planning on many more?"

"Not for a while. Four's more than I was thinking of, already. We won't worry about that until after we're married anyway."

My face had gone hot, and Nils laughed at me. "So easy," he said aloud, making Ys give him a deeply suspicious look. Fortunately Lohn showed up, and told us about a ceremony of thanksgiving that the provisional council had decided they wanted, to celebrate the colony's survival, and to honour the Setari for their work in fighting the Cruzatch.

That news was a sign that the captains had been released from the meeting, and Kaoren and Grif dropped down a couple of minutes later. Kaoren just rested against me silently, without saying anything at all. He's finding it incredibly difficult to be away from me at the moment, so I'm glad I've been cleared to sleep in our quarters. Mara arrived with the rest of the kids, so I had Sen for my other side, and smiled to see that Sen and Lira are both wearing their hair in two beribboned braids and are looking disconcertingly like sisters. Ys seems to have donated all her girlier clothes to Lira.

Lira is very upright and distant with most everyone, and is being very formally polite to me, as if she's a guest with relative strangers, but she immediately sat down beside Ys and the pair of them kept whispering comments to each other.

When Maze arrived he gave me one of his super smiles while he brought all the Setari – Taren, Kolaren and Nuran – into a single channel. He spoke aloud, though, specifically so Lira could hear what was going on, I think.

"The drone which managed to return from the rift shows that while the power flares are dying back, the landscape there is continuing to shift," he said. "It is likely that the Pillars have either been destroyed, or have shut down. This does not mean it's impossible to reach Tare and Kolar, but that an extremely time-consuming process will need to be undertaken to map the currents of deep-space. The route is not necessarily closed, or even altered, but it will be a matter of delicate timing to navigate. Once we establish the timing, there is likely to only be a narrow window for travel, so multiple daily journeys will be a thing of the past unless we can re-establish the Pillars. That's a matter for the long-term future."

He shifted, looking thoughtful. "In any case, it's highly unlikely we will re-establish contact in the next year – Taren year – so these will be the arrangements until such time as that occurs. Most significantly, for day-to-day assignments the squads will be broken apart. Although we will nominally keep our squad designations, current squad make-up is designed for Ena work, and that will be the minority of our duties.

"They believe the platform system is recovering, so bringing Mesiath up to a self-supporting level is to be our first task. The bulk of our work will be assisting in settlement – land clearance, seeding and feeding whitestone, survey and collection work, but also work on the recovery of information at Kalasa and the Oriath site. Expect to be working in groups of two to four. There will be opportunities to apply for extended leave, should you wish it. The provisional council has also established a land grant for all serving Setari, in recognition of the role we have played in making settlement possible. The grant is very generous, and I'll post details of the process as soon as it's finalised."

After shooting me an amused glance in exchange for my pleased smile, he went on more seriously: "Construction work is not what we spent so many years training for, and I know that many of you will prefer using your talents more fully. We have a little leeway with the assignments, and we will require more traditional rotation work at Kalasa and the Oriath site, and once it's deemed safe, with escorting the survey ship attempting to remap the path to Tare and Kolar. Feel free to message me with any preferences, or other concerns. This is a new phase for the Setari program, but it is something we have achieved, and should be proud of. There is a ceremony of thanksgiving scheduled in two days, and then our new assignments will begin."

We ending up having a big picnic lunch on the top of the building – all the squads, even most of Fifth and the Nurans – and everyone talked about parts of Muina they'd seen and liked, and the prospect of owning land or building houses there. The estimate of it being months before there's any real likelihood for re-establishing contact with the other worlds was actually reasonably comforting to most people, because they'd been worried about it being permanent.

Sen had a wonderful time, as usual, and Rye is blossoming more in social events. Ys and Lira stuck together as if glued, and were very polite to everyone who said anything to them, but I also had a stern message from Ys that I had to arrange for Lira to have the interface installed Straight Away because it wasn't fair on her.

It was a really nice time until someone noticed that the "Setari party" was being featured on the news and that we were being live-streamed via long-range lenses (and quite a few members of the talent school had taken up nearby vantage points and were watching in fascination). Nils said that islands sounded like a good idea to him too, and we all went inside.

It was the first time any images of me post-squishing had leaked, and there was plenty of discussion about how terrible I looked. It was also the first time Lira had been publicly seen, and I have my doubts about how she'll take all this discussion about how beautiful and mysterious she is. Fortunately, what little information KOTIS has released about her has made absolutely clear that she spied on the Cruzatch for us, and saved my life, and deserves a lot of credit for any of us still being here.

Obedient to Ys' edict, I checked with Isten Notra, then took Lira down to medical and described to her how completely horrible she was going to feel over the next few days while the technicians gave her a medical exam and then a shot to the temple. It's unlikely they'll ever expand the interface for her as they did with me, though they do have a theory about why mine keeps going strange – the language injection they gave me, to jump-start me in learning Taren, is basically a pared-back impression of someone else's mind, and they think that's what's creating the conflict. Since Lira doesn't need the language injection, they're more confident about giving her the interface.

Ista Tremmar wanted to keep Lira in medical for observation, which she was extremely unkeen about, and eventually I talked them into putting a medical sense-chair up in our apartment so they'd know if she was having a crisis overnight. I want to keep her close because, even though there's times when she seems like she is taking naturally to her strange rebirth, I often catch her with a lost and lonely expression. She's not only survived a great deal of trauma, but I think she's well aware of the 'fading away' possibility.

I'm never going to forget the sound of her crying, and the way her whole body shuddered while I held her. I'd like to think that I've done more than give her a new form of half-life, that she'll be able to live normally, but since I have no way of knowing, all I can do is offer her as much welcome as she'll accept.

My throat was pretty worn by the time it was dinnertime, and both Lira and I were feeling very off, so we had a quiet meal, and Kaoren read the evening's bedtime story. We dimmed the lights in our lounge and put Lira's medical bed there, instead of in the kids' lounge, where it had been originally. I fell asleep before everyone but Sen, and woke a few hours later with an extreme need to take my pain meds.

Kaoren still can barely talk to me about how he felt while I was trapped. He's been holding me and watching me write for this entire entry, and I think he's going to be like that for quite some time. He's worried now about having a nightmare and hurting me thrashing about, but I told him to just sleep on my unbroken side and we should be fine.

Thursday, November 6

Arcadian

Lira had very little sleep last night, and looked fantastically depressed all day. She spent more of her time in Siame's room with the lights off. Sen, when she wasn't making a huge mess in the lounge, was tremendously sweet, running down to the kitchens every couple of hours and getting ice which she would wrap in a towel and then sneak into Lira's room and silently give it to her and take away the old towel.

I still made her clean up the mess.

Kaoren and I stayed in all day, rarely out of sight of each other, and along with spending time with the kids, managed to talk about not being dead, and what we would be doing next, and whether to change the timing of our wedding, and how to not have to keep relying on other people to take care of our children for us (this mainly involves me not being injured all the time so he and I can better balance the time we spend with them). They'll be going back to talent school quite soon, but we want Lira especially to have more time to adjust and no longer feel so uncertain about me.

We're not going to bring our wedding forward, even though the provisional laws they've written up for Muina don't have anything close to the time delay requirement of Tare. We'd been considering it because it would make formally adopting the kids easier, but Kaoren very much wants Siame to be there, and I still have hopes of contacting my family. We won't think about having more kids until after the wedding, which I think should give the ones we currently have enough time to feel that they really belong.

In a few days it's the day we decided would be Rye's birthday. He hasn't mentioned it at all, and from the occasional fulminating glare Ys has been directing my way, I imagine she thinks we've forgotten. The presents I bought were unfortunately left behind, but I figured out a replacement and Kaoren and I have been colluding with Lohn and Mara in getting it ready, and also arranging a surprise party. Rye's not openly looking concerned, though, and was in Seventh Heaven this afternoon because Kaoren took him out on the balcony and cut his hair off. It does make them look faintly alike, and it just made Rye so happy.

I'm not a Setari, so we weren't sure if the Setari land grant counted for me, but when Kaoren queried the contact person they kind of laughed at him, asked if I had a piece of land in mind, and said 'hold on a moment', and all of a sudden I owned an island. The whole island, since my land grant appears to be 'anything I take my fancy to'. I asked if I could change its name, and now my island is called "Arcadia", which pleases me to no end. It was that or call it Sydney.

Kaoren will keep his land grant and decide on where to use it much later. Possibly at Mesiath, because we both like it there, or possibly someplace we haven't even seen yet. A summer house, or something for the kids. I wasn't expecting to get the entire island, and could probably keep getting myself given bits of Muina, but the idea embarrasses me – especially because the grant of Arcadia hit the news about five minutes after it was made official. That at least pleased Rye – he's the most excited by the prospect of living on the island and he came running out to ask if it was true. And Lohn and Mara dropped by, and said that they were going to apply for land on one of the cluster of islands just south of Arcadia, and that a lot of other Setari were thinking of following suit. The largest island is currently called Siriath, and is about three times the size of Arcadia and very close – you could shout at each other over the gap.

Makes me want to try and get a canoe made.

Friday, November 7

Public Speaking

Today was the ceremony of thanksgiving.

I was too tired for it (contributing no end to the talk about how horrible I look) because I'd woken up a few hours after midnight to sit with Lira, who was having a terrible time. I took her down to medical, but they're still very unwilling to give any form of pain relief during interface installation, and because she's taken a strong dislike to medical (no surprise there) I took her back up to our rooms and sat out on the balcony with her.

Lira didn't particularly want to talk to me, just wanted not to be alone until she was finally exhausted enough to fall asleep. Thankfully the interface installation has completed, which not only means that she no longer has the headache from hell, but she has some incredibly distracting new toys to play with. Ys, Sen and Rye have all been very quick to show her the things they find most special about the interface, and she and Ys spent most of the ceremony talking silently to each other.

If I hadn't been semi-conscious, I suppose I would have found the thanksgiving ceremony quite touching. Even the huge Moon Piazza isn't nearly big enough to fit Pandora's entire population any more, but the main ceremony was there, and there were multiple other gatherings across the city, along with a broadcast. The provisional council is a mix of three Tarens, three Kolarens and three Nurans nominated to draft and recommend laws (although they have to be ratified by KOTIS for some time to come). They did most of the speaking, but kept it relatively short, and then someone sang and I was just wondering if I could get away with falling asleep leaning against Kaoren when they announced me as the next speaker. Kaoren promises me he would have warned me if he'd known, but it was my own fault for not reading my email. Or their fault for having ceremonies in the mid-morning.

So I went up looking like a car-wreck survivor, with extra circles under my eyes from lack of sleep, and my voice all croaky. I've never stood up before that many people, and only got through it by focusing on the black-clad rows at the front.

"It's nearly a full Muinan year since I first saw Pandora's old town," I said. "It was the first sign of civilisation I'd found. I was so glad. And it was so empty." I paused, looking past the Setari to the endless swell of people, most sitting on cushions or the stone paving. "Even after I was found by the Tarens, I still felt alone, because everyone I cared about was on another world, and I couldn't speak the language, and everything was strange. Some very kind people put a lot of effort into making me feel less alone, but I missed my family and I just wanted to go home. I'm not sure I would have believed a day like today could come so quickly. That Muina would not be an empty world, and that I could stand here and look out and in every direction see people who mattered to me, who have become part of a very extended family, and that they would have made this place home. I am so lucky to know you all, and I am very glad to be here."

That's totally not the speech I would have made if I'd put any thought into it, and I was bright red at the end of it, and got off stage as quickly as I could manage before I burst into tears. I could tell from the way Kaoren's eyes were nearly shut that he'd thought me tremendously funny, but he tucked me under his arm and Sen came and sat in my lap and I hid behind her. My punishment for looking so sick and exhausted during the ceremony was to be sent off to medical afterwards, where I promptly fell asleep.

Kaoren woke me in time for bedtime stories, and having finished the Kolaren story I began the rather challenging task of translating *The Lion, the Witch and the Wardrobe*. My Taren is still a little shaky on complex dialogue (and some of the scans were blurry), but it went reasonably well with only a few extended tangents for explanations of exotic concepts like lions. Fortunately the version we'd scanned was illustrated.

I ended up with five engrossed listeners, since Kaoren is very interested in Earth's stories as well. I want to read them every story I loved growing up. I think that more than anything else will finish making this home.

Kaoren's asleep now, busy looking gorgeous. The squads are all back on duty tomorrow, and the platforms have been very obliging about starting to work again. Kaoren will be working at Kalasa. They want me to do some visualisations of Tare and Kolar as well, but the "she's too injured" people are currently winning the argument.

Saturday, November 8

Education

Kaoren was at Kalasa most of the day, while almost every strong Telekinetic and Levitation talent was off in Mesiath clearing trees and seeding and feeding whitestone. Mori and Alay were my guards – I failed to win the "I don't need babysitters" argument, but so long as I stay inside the building I don't have to have them sitting right on me. Alay says I can consider them the day's trainers, though with an arm in a sling and ribs protesting whenever I bend even slightly, it's more training for the kids at the moment.

Rye's fine with anyone giving him combat training, but both Ys and Lira are very doubtful about the whole thing. I told them that knowing how to beat up anyone who might attack them is a good thing, and Alay laughed at me and said I should take my own advice.

Alay's laughing a lot more these days.

We've set a tentative date of five days from now for the kids to start attending the talent school again, since that should give Lira some time to adjust to the interface, and to just be more comfortable with being here. I can tell that Ys hates the idea, but is being very good about not arguing or showing how she feels. If anything, she seems even less eager to go than before.

Discussing the school has started me thinking about Rest Of My Life issues. I'm sure to have a fairly full schedule being Mum and whatever touchstone duties I can't get out of, but I am thinking through a few possibilities for other things to do.

We're waiting up now, until all the kids are thoroughly asleep, and we can put Rye's birthday present in his room.

Sunday, November 9

With Candles

Rye's reaction this morning was so much fun. He woke before we did, and came running into our room, excited beyond words and then was too overcome to wake us up and stood there gasping, which *did* wake us up. And then he couldn't speak, and when Kaoren sat up and put a hand on his head and said: "Welcome to your honour day" (the Taren equivalent of 'Happy Birthday'), he flung his arms around him, and then got incredibly shy and tried to pretend he hadn't. Kaoren hugged him carefully, and helped me up so I could too.

Rye's present was a terrarium – one we'd had great difficulty fitting into his room and inspired by Taarel's particularly magnificent one. We'd spent the last few days arranging for the plastiglass tank and the lights, and consulting with the botanic experts about plant selection. Once it had been assembled and planted up, Lohn and Mara had kept it in their room, and brought it in to us when the kids were asleep. They got a big kick out of the whole thing, and it was definitely a present which Rye appreciated. He was particularly amazed by one of the plants, a small-leafed ground cover with some little daisy flowers sticking up on slender stems. This was something called "gilly", which is a Nuran herb, and which the technicians very kindly resurrected from the flower Sen had given me, way back when I first met her.

They're actually quite pleased with it, and I gather it was a useful cooking ingredient on Nuri. Rye has one of the first clones they managed to construct, and most of the rest of his plants are Muinan herbs. Looking after them all will be exactly the kind of thing he most likes.

Even Ys approved, and showed it by leaning briefly against me as I watched Rye showing Kaoren each and every plant, and going over the information the botanists had provided. For Ys, that's extremely demonstrative, and I squeezed her shoulder in return, but didn't annoy her by actually saying anything.

Nor was this the only birthday treat we had in store. Since Maze was in charge of the duty roster, he had no trouble arranging for a couple of hours in the middle of the day so we could have a picnic lunch at Arcadia. Well, actually, given how complex the duty roster is, I think it was a lot of trouble, and it was extremely nice of him. But he looked so relaxed and happy that I think he was glad to do it. First, Second and Fourth were invited, and we brought huge picnic baskets of food (including a cake with candles, which is an Earth tradition I insisted on, although I had to get the candles specially made). They'd brought breathers this time, and Kaoren compounded Rye's ecstasy by giving him a personal underwater lesson. I wasn't in the condition to do more than sit in shallow water, but that suited Sen just fine, and I don't think Ys is quite ready to go swimming underwater either, although she'd probably have nerved herself up to do it if pushed. Lira has never even been allowed to go near something as dangerous as a large body of water, and was very stiff and doubtful as Mara and Zee took her through her first swimming lesson, but Ys was quick to take her in hand, and I think helping Lira increased her own confidence.

After lots of swimming, we ate ourselves sick, and I taught everyone a translated version of "Happy birthday to you" and we all sang it to Rye, who went crimson and blew out his candles very enthusiastically. Then we went for exploratory walks, and checked out where the house would go according to our tentative plans, and looked at the forest behind it (discovering enough little animals to make Rye even more enthusiastic about living here). More than a few of the Setari went and had a look at the neighbouring islands, and the one south of Arcadia could pretty much be renamed "First Squad Island", judging from some of the discussions I overheard.

I don't think I've ever seen anyone as unremittingly joyful as Rye was today. He radiated full-wattage joy until finally running out of steam around bath-time, and then he went all tired and sweetly shy again. It was a marvellously happy day for everyone, and I was particularly pleased with how much Maze enjoyed it. Houses and plants and children and animals he doesn't have to kill.

Best of all, no pictures of us showed up on the news. The islands are far enough away from shore that if the Setari go ahead with their plans to snap up all the available land there, it will be an enjoyably private place. And with the generosity of the lands grants, they have enough to split the grant to a house there, and also land somewhere else. It'll be quite a neighbourhood.

Monday, November 10

No Secrets

Kaoren and I have succeeded in arguing against Lira being on second level monitoring on the grounds that it will distress her. I have vague hopes of arguing my way off it as well. But she needed to know that everything I see and hear is recorded, and that if she tells me something important enough I'd have to tell at least Kaoren, who would then have to decide whether we can choose not to pass it on. That the things which were reported to KOTIS were theoretically private, but that stuff like my file being stolen could very well happen.

As you can imagine, Lira wasn't terribly pleased, but was nicely sympathetic about me being stuck on second level monitoring. And, even more fortunately, Ys and Rye already knew about the monitoring from watching _The Hidden War_, since I belatedly realised that I'd never discussed this with them. I'm not altogether sure Ys would have forgiven me for telling Lira things she doesn't know, and of course it hadn't been necessary because KOTIS doesn't feel the need to have reports on what any of the kids but Lira might say.

Tuesday, November 11

Settlers

Having my arm in a sling is driving me crazy. It's awkward and clumsy and makes getting dressed and undressed a complete pain, and I'm very tired of doing everything one-handed. Today I've been wearing my uniform just because Kaoren was gone early and I couldn't stand trying to put on anything more than my harness. I've got it in Summer mode, and it made me realise that I've been making an unconscious decision not to wear my uniform generally. Although it was very useful when I was kidnapped, overall I've just been happier to dress in my own clothes.

I've been doing schoolwork with Lira. She can read and write, but in Old Muinan, and she was very frustrated with the sudden leap backward. She doesn't have Ys' absolute love of knowing things, and was finding Ys' explanations frustrating. Ys is relatively patient, but she's so smart that remembering new words is incredibly easy for her, and in some ways it's simpler for her, Rye and Sen because they haven't learned slightly different characters, and slightly different spellings, and slightly different rules.

Lira's no more of a fan of getting things wrong than Ys is, and more likely to get frustrated and give up, so I spent the morning doing basic kindergarten lessons with her, and laughing over the things I got wrong, and talking about what it was like when I first got here, having to repeat infant-grade school a couple of months after doing my high school final exams. And I managed to settle a convenient arrangement where Lira would do her lessons with Sen, to try and encourage Sen to pay a little attention in school. And Sen, of course, wants to be helpful to Lira.

We're all getting quite good at understanding each other speaking, in Taren, old Muinan or Nuran, though often the subtleties of what we're trying to say is lost. And I was disconcerted to discover that I seem to have introduced a few English words into the general language here – 'okay', and 'cool' particularly – and I've been trying to work out *how* since *The Hidden War* didn't have details of my actual speech, and there's very little publicly available of me speaking. I think it's gone out from the Setari and the support staff who work in the Setari building – maybe describing how I speak to people?

Wednesday, November 12

Future

Today was the weekend, and when we asked the kids what they wanted to do, I wasn't altogether surprised to find that Arcadia was top of their list. Ever since our picnic on the roof was live-streamed, they've become extremely reluctant to go outside in exposed places (except possibly Sen, who thinks people being fascinated by her is a right state of affairs, and would probably most like to go visit the café again).

Nils and Jeh were my guards for the day, and Lohn and Mara came along too, but they all stayed off out on the shore while we had another swimming lesson. Lira was more confident this time around, and even Sen started paddling about as they played a game of water chasies. I sat paddling my legs in the water and leaning against Kaoren and feeling a weird sense of achievement every time one of them laughed.

After a group lunch, we all went on a walk to the island's centre (Nils carrying Sen) and found a grassy meadow not quite in the middle which had things like partridges which shot off into the air and gave me a near heart attack. But it also had butterflies, and Sen revived and ran about trying to catch them. Nils was in a very laid-back mood and teased me mildly, but mostly just watched the kids with a smile while Mara told me about some of the work the senior Setari have been doing with the kids at the talent school. Assisting with talent training is something they're used to, but the focus is rather different with the Nuran kids – not so intense and purposeful and disciplined.

"Even though the Kalrani were away from their families, they still had a home and returned to it during holidays," Mara said. "And always there was the focus of our purpose. The school here couldn't be more different. Harder, in a way, for us to deal with."

"It doesn't help that they think we're shopping," Nils said. "Or want us to be. It adds a raw edge, although also some high entertainment. Most of the Kalrani try to impress, but they don't try to sabotage each other in the hopes of winning some secret competition to be adopted."

"There's only a couple like that," Mara said, with a wry glance at Nils. [I'm getting better at not picturing them having sex, but I'm always going to be aware that there's history there.] "The Nuran household structure, full of feuds and rivalries and alliances, hasn't quite let go of them. Those who have other household members here or in the town seem more secure and comfortable, grouping together. In some ways it helps, but it's causing a lot of issues because some also tend to act as if they've inherited control over anyone who was once of their house. That group that took off to Nurenor, for instance, were almost all from three of the larger houses, and some of those of lower status were simply unable to bring themselves to disobey orders from seniors of the house. And belonging to a major household meant immediate prestige, even if you weren't at the head of it, and so there's children who no longer have any semblance of a house and miss it terribly, and even when they have others of their house with them, find that their house has no power here, and they're in a culture which heavily emphasises individual merit. All this on top of losing their parents."

"And the news service is constantly providing touching adoption stories," Nils said, dryly. "Where lucky brat number 4000 catches a family's eye and is no longer just one of many powerless orphans herded about with the mass. An immediate gain of security, prestige. The oldest ones are finding it hardest – less likely to be adopted, struggling with schooling requirements they would never have dreamed of, and facing the prospect of filtering to the bottom because no-one is going to reach out and pick them and they'll be transitioning to being responsible for themselves soonest. And then we go and dangle ourselves in front of them – beyond you showing up and saying 'I need a few more', we're probably as close to instant prestige as they can see right now."

"I don't think I could do that," I said. "Pick, I mean. Sen adopted me, not the other way around, and I got too emotionally involved with all three of them to not keep caring. Lira was the same way – she just happened. But you're thinking about it, aren't you?"

I was asking Mara, who nodded. "Jeh, Ketz and Grif, too. Of course, right now we're all in barracks, and don't have the same push to retire, but if we can get these houses built, then between us and the school we should be able to manage it. And you're right – the idea of picking is strangely daunting. Not so much for making a choice which will work for us, but because then there are all these children we didn't pick. And for every atrocious creature shamelessly trying to win favour, there are a half-dozen who I would be glad to know better. And even the atrocious creatures are breaking themselves apart inside. It's one of the big downsides to having Muina cut off from a fresh influx of settlers – KOTIS intended to have each and every minor settled with families as soon as possible, because they need that level of care. You only have to look at these four to see how much a sense of belonging does to offset the weight of trauma."

The idea of 'Jeh, Ketz and Grif' kept me occupied for a while, and I still don't quite know if they're intending to set up one house together, but I can see how much Mara's looking forward to the idea of having a home and building a family. She says she and Lohn are thinking of simply having two weddings (commitment ceremonies) to handle having lots of important people on two different planets.

I also couldn't help but notice that Nils was very quiet the rest of the day. He and Maze, who would both be great fathers, and are both caught up in their feelings for someone who's dead. Maze, though, seems to be at peace with where he is, while Nils is just cutting himself apart inside. I'm willing to bet Zee and Raiten are bothering him, too – they're working together on squad coordination to give Maze more time off, and always seem to be off somewhere chatting.

Ys also went quiet in the afternoon. It's because of going to talent school tomorrow, and she makes me want to tag along and stand over her protectively. Really, given how brave Ys was trying to help Siame and me in the lake, you'd think there'd be some kids there who would see her as more than a servant. But at least I think she's readier to believe that Kaoren and I value all four of them, and that I have succeeded in creating the sense of belonging Mara was talking about.

Friday, November 14

Friends, Family, Home

Ys came back from school today looking immensely relieved. Mara was able to clue me in on why, since she'd been at the talent school that morning. Ys hasn't suddenly become popular or anything, although one or two of the kids seem to have made slight overtures (which unfortunately Ys is completely disinterested in). But Lira is the focus of an immense amount of fascination. An actual Lantaren, beautiful, a second touchstone, hailed as my saviour and a brave spy who'd worked against the Cruzatch and – perhaps most importantly – with lots of syllables in her name.

I should have seen it immediately. Lira's the first friend Ys has ever had – a rather different relationship to Sen and Rye both, who she treats in a more parental way. Lira and Ys bonded thoroughly sharing moments of scorn for me, and just get along very well. Going back to the talent school meant there would be dozens of rivals for Lira's friendship, and the fact that Ys and Rye were 'just servants' would almost certainly be underlined, and Ys wasn't quite certain how Lira would react to that. Mara couldn't give me all the details, but it was plain that Lira wasn't terribly keen on the mass overtures, and when Mara had headed out for her shift Lira was welded to Ys' side and was glaring furiously at one particular clutch of kids.

Lira gave me an earful herself when Ys and Sen were safely in the bath (Ys still gives Sen a bath, and I suspect hasn't realised that Lira's probably perfectly aware of the scars on her back, after days of watching us invisibly).

Lira had said a few very rude things to Ys' greatest detractors and been lectured (no doubt very gently) by their age-group's supervisor about good manners, and wanted to make quite clear to me that she had no intention of being nice to anyone who thought Ys and Rye didn't belong with us. I just said: "Good for you," and told her to let me know if anybody bothered them too much.

I had a lot of fun reading the latest chapter of *The Lion, The Witch and The Wardrobe* to them this evening. They're very caught up in Edmund, about whether he should be rescued or deserves his fate. Sen adores Lucy, of course, and she's far more sympathetic toward Edmund than Ys, Lira and Rye are. Ys is monstrously impatient to know what happens next. I suspect she usually reads ahead for these night-time stories, and because it's in English she can't. Being all impatient does mean that she doesn't let Sen linger in the bath a moment longer than she considers necessary. So funny.

I adore them. Kaoren and I are both finding abrupt parenthood surprisingly to our taste, and the awful tension and after-effects of the Oriath collapse is fading. We're growing increasingly confident that we're safe now, that the Cruzatch aren't coming back, and the pressure tearing the spaces apart is gone. My only real downside at the moment is my complete lack of sex life. My face has only just stopped hurting enough that Kaoren's willing to kiss me, and neither of us find it much fun when I get into an uncomfortable position at night and wake up really needing some pain medication. It's getting better though – wonders of Taren technology and so forth.

Just asked Kaoren what he most wanted to do as a Setari over the next few years – whether he wanted to continue with Ena work, or was more interested in exploring Muina.

He had to pause to think about it, but then said very firmly: "Both. There is an intensity to Ena work which I – which all of Fourth, I think – are not quite ready to give up. The standard we need, the care and the challenge, that is very much a part of what we have been, and it is something which is still needed, even with the Ddura's aid. But the explorers of Muina, those who rediscover and see with new eyes this world which is our past, that is what the Setari are becoming. Some, like First, have already made that shift, but we all will. We are all changed. We cannot go back to what we were before."

He held up his hand, palm-down, and recognising the moment I reached up to meet him, palm-to-palm.

"We would not want to."

Saturday, November 15

Citizen of Muina

A little boy drowned today, which has sent me into a minor spin of parental stress over all the things my four could do to themselves on an island. The interface does make it safer, since they can call for help, and an alarm is set off if they're unconscious. The kid who drowned was one of the interface hold-outs, and I can't help but think about whether he'd be alive if he'd had it.

KOTIS is also struggling with moonfall. For a long while people stayed respectfully away from the old town during moonfall, but gradually 'free breathable alcohol' has meant more and more people of all ages deciding they want to stroll through the old town when the moon's out. The new law-makers have to decide whether it should be allowed, and how to cope with all the accidents and problems which might be caused by people who are aether-drunk.

That's something they're going to be dealing with at every platform town as Muina grows in population. Great pictures this morning of mounds of people sleeping in the amphitheatre. All very well in Summer, but probably not so good a thing in Winter.

I figure the old Muinans living here must have just gotten drunk once a week, since the aether flowed down off the roofs of their houses. Even little kids. The pro-aether people are arguing that it would function as a kind of health care, and you don't get to overdose levels if you don't go and sit on the roof or dance about in the amphitheatre. At least it doesn't seem to make most people violent, like real alcohol, but obviously there'll be incidents like Kajal deciding to force Kaoren to fight him. I suspect aether-effects are one of the reasons the old Muinans specially built the platform towns, rather than incorpor–

...

Wow. Had to stop writing because Zee just dropped out of the sky on me. I'd been writing sitting under the tree on top of the Setari building, with Par and Sonn spending their guarding time in a training session down the lake-side slope, when all of a sudden I looked up and Zee was there.

There in a Goddess of Thunder and Lightning kind of way, standing over me in all of her toned six-foot-whateverness, glaring.

I don't think I squeaked. Probably. But I certainly felt mouse-like, staring up at her, and couldn't find anything more useful to do than gape at her.

"I've had it with being told that those dreams were so traumatic and secret that you can't discuss them in any way," she said, her voice tight and angry. "What were they?"

I opened my mouth, searching for some way to explain that I simply couldn't, but she made a chopping motion with her hand. "Just tell me."

I've never seen Zee act remotely like that before, so full of repressed anger and frustration. I had no idea what to say, of course, because I really *wanted* to tell Zee, but was sure Nils would hate me for it. But Zee was looking like she'd hate me for not telling her.

"Did you know that night was Helese Surion's birthday?" I asked cautiously. Zee made a dismissive gesture and I hurried on awkwardly: "I had no idea that Nils and Helese had been together. The first dream was a real shock to me, that this person who everyone only ever mentions in connection with Maze was someone who was everything to Nils. No-one acts as if she was important to him, even though he was just – so completely hers."

Zee had had no idea. She stopped looking quite so angry and just stared at me.

"Maze had to explain it for me – that when Nils saw how strongly Helese felt about Maze, he made out that they'd just drifted apart, for all that it came close to destroying him to see she felt that way. He's too good an actor – no-one seems to think Helese had any real history before Maze because Nils goes about trying to make sure no-one ever takes him seriously, because he has this promise with himself to never really care about anyone again. But with you, he can't stop, so he–"

I broke off, a little afraid of the expression on Zee's face. Absolutely furious. Then she just left without another word, and I looked down the hill at Par and Sonn staring up at me, and wondered what to do.

After a lot of agonising I sent a channel request to Maze and told him very guiltily that I thought Zee was going to go kill Nils and that it was my fault. I can just picture Maze's expression.

But he calmly contacted Nils and told him to head in Zee's direction (because he's not keen on having senior Setari arguments played out in front of an audience). He didn't go after Zee himself, but instead came to see me and assured me that no matter how angry Zee might be about anything, she wasn't likely to try and kill Nils. I think he also came to check to see if Zee had yelled me into a wibbling heap. Maze was very good at making it all into much less of a drama, and came down and distracted Par and Sonn during lunch so that they at least wouldn't ask why I was all wide-eyed and blotchy.

The details of what Nils and Zee said to each other I don't know. I haven't seen either since because Maze told them both to take a week's leave, and they did exactly that – by setting their status to 'do not disturb' and going off on a camping trip together. Nils did open a channel to me briefly, but only said: "Just because Zee bullied you into that doesn't mean you're not getting spanked," and laughed and broke the connection. He sounded awesomely happy. Kaoren's right about the senior squads being most changed: they're all starting to move on with their lives.

I'm having to use all of my dubious moral fibre to not make a projection so I can see what Zee said to Nils.

Sunday, November 16

This day today

So it's been one year today. I spent the afternoon writing a letter to Mum, in preparation for the realignment of the natural gate to Earth. The technicians think it's going to open in the next couple of months, and I'm putting together a well-protected package to send, complete with nanotech-forged Australian stamps.

Along with the letter, I've had a number of photos printed up to include. They were a bit tricky, since I didn't want to have anything undeniably alien in them, and I particularly didn't want any pictures of me with fading yellow and green bruises down one side of my face, or a sling. Fortunately that's all on the same side. One recent image showing me in profile, tickling Sen's feet on the couch (Sen is fantastically ticklish and goes into spasms of delight), and I included a few older ones where my hair was still long (particularly one from when Kaoren, Sen and Rye fell asleep on the couch with me, and I'm looking down at Ys). The rest don't have me at all. A shot of Ys and Lira practicing their synchronised scowling. First Squad. Our waterfall.

And I'm going to send Mum these diaries.

I've been keeping them up out of habit, rather than out of that need to talk that it helped with early on, and nothing could explain more clearly to Mum just why I'm staying. We'll be together every time she reads them, and she too can come to love First Squad, and Kaoren, and four children who were alone and frightened, and are so happy to belong.

I'll still have my log record of the diaries, so I can read them to Kaoren, and look back over how much everything has changed. At all the people I've been since I walked home from school. Survivor. Stray. Lab Rat. Caddy. Assignment. Love. Weapon. Spy. Celebrity. Maker of dragons. Machine component. Saver of worlds. Mum.

And, soon, uni student.

I'm hoping to beat Ys there, though she's sure to go excel in sciences, while I'm thinking of a vague selection in the Arts: Literature. Mythology. Archaeology. Learning this world's stories so that it continues to become mine, and then maybe bringing some of my world's stories to Muina.

And one day I am going to figure out a way for the rest of my family to become Muinans as well. Till then, I hope words will cross galaxies for me.

Letter

Dear Mum (and Dad and Jules and Aunties and Nick and Alyssa and everyone)

I am here, not there, and that's now a choice that I've made. I'm no longer trying to get home, because this has become home. I hate that it's an either/or choice, and that there's no way to visit. I miss so many things, but I'm happy here now, and unless I was sure I could get back here, I can't risk even trying for a quick visit. I'm hoping for a yearly letter, at least.

I'm glad you had the chance to see Kaoren when you last saw me. He and I have been engaged nearly four months now. I think you might like him. The wedding's scheduled for six weeks after my twentieth birthday. The long wait was initially because of legal requirements and is pretty meaningless, since we live together already, and are working on plans for getting a house built. And we have four children!

They're orphans, and kind of adopted us, and we're going through the process of formally adopting them in return. Ys is the oldest (we think). She, Lira and Rye are all around eleven. Sen is four. They're really great kids, and far less bratty than I ever was. I'm not really 'Mum' to them, but I feel very parental, and I think we've built up some trust. Fretting over them makes me want to hit myself for all the times I was a complete bitch to you.

It's been a very dramatic year for me, on top of ending up here in the first place. I guess you could say I've been gainfully employed, and Kaoren and I are well settled for money, so I'm not having to stress about day-to-day stuff. It was very hard to adjust at first, particularly because I had to learn a new language, and I was just so outside everything. But some very nice people took me under their wing and it was a bit like gaining six older brothers and sisters, and I've developed an extended family of people who look out for me.

I'm hoping that one day it'll be easier to get between here and there and it would be great if you could come here. I've enclosed a bunch of photos of me and the kids and some of the people who are important to me and the place where our house will be. I had to get my hair cut really short and hate it and hope it grows back quickly.

I love you. I should have said it a thousand times. Miss you always.

Always.

Cass.

The End

TOUCHSTONE GLOSSARY

Agowla	The (fictional) high school Cass attended in Sydney.
AI	Artificial Intelligence.
Arenrhon	Settlement at site of underground installation of the Lantarens.
Aspro	Aspirin. Headache relief.
Atanra	A facility constructed near to the Muinan rift into deep-space. The word means 'passage'.
Authoritah	This is an indication that Cassandra has watched *South Park*, and not a typo.
Aversan	The old Muinan name for the platform town discovered in her month on Muina (initially called Goralath by the Tarens).
Beanie	A close-fitting knitted hat.
Breaking, The	A Taren term for the disaster which shattered the spaces.
Buckley's chance	Buckley was a convict in Australia who escaped and survived by living with Australian Aborigines. The phrase means "nearly impossible".
Café Crescent	Pandora's first café.
Carche Landing	The main airport in Unara.
Casszilla	Rawr!
Caves of Nonora	A Taren children's story, where Til, Magara and Nosk discover an entrance to the kingdom of the Tarull, deep below Unara.
Channa	A rocky planet inhabited by ex-Muinans living a nomadic tribal life. Tare has established a mine on Channa in an area of land isolated from the inhabitants.
Chapstick	Lip moisturiser.
Chune	One of the ships KOTIS uses to travel between Tare, Kolar and Muina.
Copped a Serve	Received a barrage of anger.
Council of Tare	The Lahanti (mayors) of the cities of Tare.
Cruzatch	A dangerous humanoid Ionoth, shadow burning white.
Dazenti	Swarming phasic Ionoth: capable of passing through walls.
Ddura	An enormous energy being created by the Lantarens.
Deep-space	The large portion of the Ena which exists between the 'memory spaces'. It is white in appearance, and filled with gates which open directly to real-space worlds.
Deep-space Ionoth	Ionoth which are formed and dwell not in the relatively small Spaces, but instead in Deep-space.
Delar	A Taren measurement unit – roughly 75 centimetres.
Despawn	Disappear, vanish. Taken from computer games where a monster is said to 'spawn' when it appears in the game world, and 'despawn' when it disappears (usually after being killed).
Diodel	One of the ships KOTIS uses to travel between Tare, Kolar and Muina.
Do Not Go Gentle	"Do Not Go Gentle Into That Good Night", a poem by Dylan Thomas.
Dohl Array	A series of underwater farms on Tare.
Drone	An advanced robot, usually used for scanning and monitoring.
Drop Bears	Important Tourist Advisory: Please wear protective head gear when walking beneath gum trees in Australia.
Ena	A dimension connected to the thoughts, memories, dreams and imagination of living beings.
Ena manipulation	A psychic talent which can change the substance of the Ena, particularly in stabilising gates between spaces. It can also be used in a limited way to change 'reality'.
Expecto Patronum	Looks like Cass has read *Harry Potter*.

Escort quest	A mission in an online game involving protection of a non-player character while they travel.
Faer	The Senior Captain in the Taren entertainment *The Hidden War*. Played by Eyle Sured.
Fahr	Kolaren treacle tea.
Falazen	A platform town ruled by border collies.
Fan service	Revealing or provocative shots of characters in anime/manga.
Fanfic	Fiction based on the stories of others and/or fiction involving a person of whom the writer is a fan.
Firiana	A platform town east of Pandora, situated among the islands of the surri.
First level monitoring	Interface monitoring which triggers an alert if certain conditions are reached (eg. loss of consciousness, heart attack). All residents of Tare are on first level monitoring.
Francesca	Francesca is a flowering shrub also known as "Yesterday, Today, Tomorrow" because its flowers fade from purple to violet to near-white as they age.
Gate	A tear or rift between spaces/worlds.
Gate Sight	A psychic talent which can judge the status of gates between spaces.
Gate-lock	An enclosure built around a gate from near-space to real-space to prevent Ionoth from passing through.
Gelzz	A now nearly-extinct cave-dwelling Taren insect noted for its tendency to admit a lingering rotten odour as a defence mechanism.
Goralath	The name originally given to the ruins where Pandora is later established.
Gorra	The first island settled on Tare.
Hasata	A city on Tare.
House Dayen	One of the leading Lantaren groups on pre-destruction Muina, and architects of the Pillars project.
House Renar	A Nuran House which was given the care of Sentarestel after her parents' deaths.
House Zolen	A Lantaren group on pre-destruction Muina believed responsible for the Arenrhon installation.
HSC	Higher School Certificate. Received when graduating from high school in Australia.
Ian Thorpe	A famous Australian swimmer.
In-skin	An immersive interface experience where most of the senses – sight, hearing, touch, smell, taste – are stimulated.
Interface	An in-body nanite installation used by Tarens as personal computers/the Taren internet.
Ionoth	Creatures which form in the Ena, usually remnants of the dreams and nightmares of inhabited planets.
Ista	An honorific for medical doctors.
Isten	Professor.
Joden	The Taren equivalent of a minute, though the unit is longer than an Earth minute. One hundred joden equal a kasse.
Kadara	Naturally-forming massive Ionoth.
Kalane	A medium-sized island city near the Dohl Array.
Kalasa	The training city of the Lantarens.
Kalrani	Trainees not yet qualified as Setari.
Kasse	The Taren equivalent of an hour, spanning approximately two and a half Earth hours.
Kaszandra	The KOTIS research facility on Kalasa's island.
Keszen Point	An outlying island of Konna used for warehousing.
Kolar	A hot, arid world settled by Muinan refugees, and advanced technologically by the Tarens.
Konna	Both the city and the island where the main KOTIS base is located on Tare.
KOTIS	An acronym for the "Agency for Ionoth Research and Protection".
Kuna	Supplementary memory provided by the interface.
Lahanti	Leaders of the cities of Tare – an equivalent to a 'mayor' of a city-state.
Lantar/Lantarens	The ruling class of Muina before the disaster. Powerful psychics.

Lastier	A fictional equivalent of Kaoren Ruuel from the Taren entertainment *The Hidden War*. Played by Teral Saith.
Litara	One of the ships KOTIS uses to travel between Tare, Kolar and Muina.
Lolcat	I can haz cheeseburger?
Lord Vetinari	A most Machiavellian ruler, found in the Discworld books of Terry Pratchett.
Luim	One of the ships KOTIS uses to travel between Tare, Kolar and Muina.
Machiavelli	To Cass, Machiavelli is "Lord Vetinari, except real". Niccolo Machiavelli was an Italian Renaissance writer whose book *The Prince* sets out a model of political stability achieved through not necessarily moral means.
March of Dawn	A traditional Muinan ceremony held in Spring. Flowers are carried to symbolise the birth of a new year.
Massives	Ionoth of unusually large dimensions.
Mea Culpa	'Through my fault' - acknowledging an error/taking the blame.
Mesara	One of the ships KOTIS has assigned to Muina.
Mesiath	A southern hemisphere city in a tall tree forest.
Moon Piazza	An enormous crescent shaped open area at the eastern base of the amphitheatre hill at Pandora. [Desza Tohl in Taren.]
Muina	A world abandoned after a disaster brought about by the Lantaren psychics.
Nanites	A machine or robot on a microscopic scale.
Nanna Nap	A short nap in the daytime, for the less active grandmothers.
Near-space	The envelope of Ena immediately surrounding a world, full of reflections of the world as it currently is – and it's most recent nightmares.
Night on Bald Mountain	A composition by Modest Mussorgsky. Cass has encountered it in Disney's *Fantasia*.
Nikko Pen	Permanent marker.
Noob	A new gamer who does not fully understand how to play/someone new.
Nori	The main character of the Taren entertainment *The Hidden War*. Played by Lanset Kameer.
Not happy, Jan	A popular phrase taken from an Australian television commercial for Yellow Pages.
NPCs	Non-player characters – a gaming term for characters in a game which you are not expected to fight.
Nuri	A pastoral moon inhabited by ex-Muinans.
Nurioth	One of the largest ruined cities on Muina.
OMGWTF	Oh my god, what the fuck?!
Oriath	A Muinan city, ruled by House Zolen.
Ormon of Nent	The hereditary ruler of Kolar's northern kingdom.
Pandora	First Taren settlement on Muina.
PAoN	Profound Awareness of Nils
Path Sight	A talent for location.
Pelamath	An equatorial platform town located on top of a plateau.
Pippin	A small animal of excessive cuteness.
Pissed off	Made angry. ['Pissed' can mean 'angry' or 'drunk' in Australia.]
Public Space	Virtual décor visible to all interface users/anything accessible to all interface users.
PVP	Combat in online games where players fight other players rather than computer-controlled opponents.
Pwn	Defeat comprehensively – a gamer term.
Rotation	Setari missions in the Ena designed to cover Ionoth respawn near Taren cities.
Rotational space	A space in the Ena which moves so that its gates regularly align and move out of alignment.
Rukmor	Appointed heads of various sciences and arts on Tare. Forms part of the world government.
Rule 34	Rule 34 of the Internet: If it exists, there will be porn of it.
Schoolies	Australian high school graduates celebrating the end of school during "Schoolies Week". Primarily located around the Gold Coast in Queensland.
Searns	A Setari squad member on the Taren entertainment *The Hidden War*. Roak Larion.

Second level monitoring	A safety/security interface setting causing all sights and sounds experienced by the monitored person to be retained in a secure log which can be accessed under exceptional circumstances.
Setari	Psychic combat 'Specialists' trained since childhood to combat Ionoth.
Sf&f	Science fiction and fantasy.
Shared Space	The interface equivalent of a conference call.
Shattering, The	A Nuran term for the disaster which shattered the spaces.
Shim	A 'Squad Emerald' Setari in the Taren entertainment *The Hidden War*.
Smex	Sex with added m.
Smutfic	Erotic fanfiction.
Solaria	An icy world settled by ex-Muinans. Currently not located by Tare.
Southern Ancipars	The three elected rulers of Kolar's southern country.
Soylent Green	Is people!
Spaces	A concept used in multiple contexts on Tare, covering 'world', 'dimension', 'area', 'region of the interface', and many others, but most particularly 'a bubble containing a fragment of a world remembered and reproduced by the Ena'.
Stickie	A parasitic Ionoth capable of living within a host human. Difficult to detect.
Stilt	A spindly-legged deep-space Ionoth.
Stray	A person who walked through a wormhole through the Ena to another planet.
Super Sight Six	An old Taren TV series about psychic detectives.
Surri	A native Muinan animal with an appearance of slender, dog-like seals.
Suyul	A pink flower (also pink/white-skinned).
Swoops	A variety of deep-space Ionoth resembling a pterodactyl.
Tai	Old Muinan for Lake
Tai Medlair	The Old Muinan name for the lake where Pandora is located.
Tairo	A kick-ass ball sport.
Talent	A psychic ability.
Tanty	Tantrum.
Tanz	Taren air transport.
Tarani	A many-legged deep-space Ionoth reminiscent of a caterpillar.
Tare	A harsh, storm-wracked world settled by Muinan refugees. The highly technologically advanced inhabitants live crammed into massive whitestone cities.
Taren year	One third of an Earth year.
The Hidden War	A Taren entertainment based on the Setari.
Therouk Island	A food processing island, with a small residential portion.
Third level monitoring	Active observation of everything a subject sees and hears.
Thousand Cats, A	See Neil Gaiman's "Dream of a Thousand Cats" in the *Sandman* series.
Thredbo	An Australian ski resort.
Timesa	A food processing island, with a moderate residential portion.
tl;dr	Too long; didn't read.
Tola	A classification of Ionoth which have little physical substance.
Toolies	Adults preying on teenagers during Schoolies Week/pretending to be a Schoolie.
Touchstone	The subject of the story.
True-space	The world, not the Ena.
Tsa	An honorific which is the equivalent for Mr/Mrs/Ms/Miss.
Tsaile	Commander.
Tsee	Setari Squad Captain.
Tsur	Director.
Tupal Rock	A small cluster of rocks which form the nearest island to Pandora.
Twig/twigged	Realise.
Tyu	A zither-like musical instrument.
Unara	The largest city on Tare, located on the island of Wehana.
Unco	Uncoordinated.

Unstable rotation	A rotation where the spaces are more likely to change and bring unexpected situations.
Wangst	Self-indulgent angst.
Wehana	The largest island on Tare, almost entirely covered by the city of Unara.
Wharra	One of the ships KOTIS uses to travel between Tare, Kolar and Muina.
Whitestone	A building substance formed with nanites.
Wuss	Wimp, coward.
Wut	What, with added incredulity.
Year 10 Formal	An end-of-year dress up dance held by schools in Australia.
Zarath	The nobility of Nuri
Zelkasse	A quarter of a kasse.

CHARACTER LIST

Squads

First Squad	Second Squad	Third Squad	Fourth Squad
Maze Surion (m)	Grif Regan (m)	Meer Taarel (f)	Kaoren Ruuel (m)
Zee Annan (f)	Jeh Omai (f)	Della Meht (f)	Fiar Sonn (f)
Lohn Kettara (m)	Nils Sayate (m)	Eeli Bata (f)	Par Auron (m)
Mara Senez (f)	Keer Charal (m)	Tol Sefen (m)	Glade Ferus (m)
Alay Gainer (f)	Enma Dolan (f)	Geo Chise (m)	Charan Halla (f)
Ketzaren Spel (f)	Bree Tcho (f)	Rite Orla (f)	Mori Eyse (f)
Kian Farn (m)	*Trill Nala (f)*	*Shin Morel (m)*	*Rada Dae (m)*
Az Norivan (f)	*Somal Joen (m)*	*Elory Tedar (f)*	*Sael Toren (m)*
Fifth Squad	**Sixth Squad**	**Seventh Squad**	**Eighth Squad**
Hast Kajal (m)	Elen Kormin (f)	Atara Forel (f)	Ro Kanato (m)
Dorey Nise (m)	Est Jorion (f)	Pol Tsennen (m)	Pala Hasen (f)
Faver Elwes (f)	Juna Quane (m)	Tez Mema (m)	Seeli Henaz (f)
Kire Palanty (m)	Del Roth (m)	Bodey Residen (m)	Zhou Kade (m)
Tralest Seet (m)	Meleed Aluk (f)	Aheri Dahlen (f)	Kye Trouban (m)
Seyen Rax (m)	Kester Am-roten (m)	Saitel Raph (m)	Zama Bryze (m)
Forrez Wen (f)	*Ture Melodez (f)*	*Kahl Anya (f)*	*Terel Revv (m)*
Tyne Upzor (m)	*Sade Seeny (f)*	*Hea Keth (m)*	*Wyrum Zak (m)*
Ninth Squad	**Tenth Squad**	**Eleventh Squad**	**Twelfth Squad**
Desa Kaeline (f)	Els Haral (m)	Seq Endaran (f)	Zan Namara (f)
Zael Toure (f)	Loris Darm (f)	Kire Couran (f)	Roake Lenton (m)
Rebar Dolas (m)	Sell Tens (f)	Yaleran Genera (m)	Dess Charn (f)
Oran Thomasal (m)	Joren Mane (f)	Palest Wen (m)	Sora Nels (m)
Moraty Less (m)	Fahr Sherun (m)	Zare Seeth (m)	Tenna Drysen (m)
Dyru Keszaden (f)	Netra Kantan (m)	Den Dava (m)	Tahl Kiste (m)
Tath Ba-Raften (m)	*Treeku Wize (m)*	*Marine Kasaty (m)*	*Sare Elehy-Ahl (f)*
Olena Kyru (f)	*Kivel Nu (m)*	*Velven Arava (m)*	*Dunare Rial (f)*
Thirteenth Squad	**Fourteenth Squad**		
Teer Alare (m)	Kin Lara (m)		
Tekly Roth (f)	Pen Alaz (f)		
Elsen Dry (f)	Greve Sanya (f)		
Next Urally (m)	Taree Jax (f)		
Rail Sorela (m)	Parally Goff (m)		
Paza Lagden (m)	Rish Udara (f)		
Kolar's Squad One	**Squad Two**	**Squad Three**	**Nuran Setari**
Raiten Shaf (m)	Taska Ayle (f)	Arat Turian (f)	Inisar (m)
Arad Nalaz (m)	Integel Fel-Argen (m)	Doar Noran (m)	Korinal (f)
Meral Katzyen (f)	Roka Deslenkar (f)	Tana Brez (f)	Serray (m)
Laram Diav (f)	Mete Arby (f)	Kasan Olan (f)	Orial (f)
Dell Taranza (f)	Saleek Argule (m)	Dree Mittaha (f)	Mila (f)
Korali Aerieword (m)	Hearan Brookend (f)	Ness Tuse (f)	Trelasetar (m)
			Jaselasker (m)
			Selreven (f)
			Otarien (m)

Other

Alyssa Caldwell (f)	Cassandra's best friend.
Arden Ruuel (m)	Kaoren Ruuel's older brother. An artist and former Kalrani.
Barl Miks (m)	KOTIS security detail at Pandora.
Cassandra Devlin (f)	An Aussie teenager not enjoying her big adventure.
Cham Anore (m)	Taren Setari and member of the original First Squad, killed by massive.
Clere Ganaran (m)	KOTIS liaison.
Dase Canlan (m)	A junior KOTIS archaeologist.

Deen Tarmian (f)	KOTIS liaison.
Denasan (m)	A Solarian stray advising at Pandora.
Durenatar (m)	Sentarestel's father.
Elemnar (f)	A Nuran Setari. Sight Sight talent.
Elless Royara (f)	KOTIS technician.
Elizabeth (Bet) Wilson (f)	Cassandra's aunt.
Evva Nozen (f)	KOTIS security detail at Pandora.
Far Dara (m)	A warehouse keeper.
Fiionarestel (f)	A murdered Nuran Sight Sight talent. Her daughter is Sentarestel.
Hedar Dayn (m)	Kalrani Ena manipulation talent.
Hadla Esem (m)	KOTIS security detail.
Helen Middledell (f)	aka Her Mightiness or HM. A well-off and popular girl who goes to Agowla School.
Helese Surion (f)	Original First Squad captain, killed by a massive.
Intena Jun (f)	Former KOTIS publicity officer.
Iskel Teretha (m)	Administrative person in charge of the KOTIS research facility Kaszandra on Kalasa's island.
Islen Lap Dolan (m)	Senior KOTIS botanist.
Islen Lothen Ormeral (m)	KOTIS archaeologist.
Islen Merle Nakano (f)	Senior KOTIS animal expert.
Islen Rel Duffen (f)	Senior KOTIS archaeologist.
Islen Rale Tezart (m)	Senior KOTIS 'psychic technology' expert.
Ista Tel Chemie (f)	KOTIS medic assigned to Setari.
Ista Del Temen (f)	KOTIS medic assigned to Pandora.
Ista Kestal Leema (f)	KOTIS medic assigned to Pandora.
Ista Noin Tremmar (f)	KOTIS medic assigned to Setari.
Isten Sel Notra (f)	Pre-eminent scientist researching the Ena.
Jelan Scal (m)	'Psychic technology' scientist.
Jenna Wilson (f)	A friend of Cassandra's in Sydney.
Jorly Kennez (f)	The first Setari to die on duty.
Julian (Jules) Devlin (m)	Cassandra's younger brother.
Karasayen (f)	A Nuran orphan of remorseless perspicacity.
Katha Rade (f)	A junior KOTIS archaeologist.
Keeri Nell (f)	KOTIS security detail at Pandora.
Kess Anasi (m)	Kalrani Ena manipulation talent.
Ketta Lents (f)	Wife of Orren Lents – stockbroker.
Kimirenar (m)	Head of the Nuran House Renar.
Kinear Rote (m)	Kalrani Ena manipulation talent, one of twins.
Kisikar Sorn (m)	Taren Setari and member of the original First Squad, retired.
Laura Devlin (f)	Cassandra's mother.
Leam Marda (m)	Unara Transport Department official.
Liane Lents (f)	Daughter of Orren and Ketta Lents.
Lianzrenar (m)	Nuran orphan of House Renar.
Liranadestar (f)	An earlier touchstone.
Mede Orra (f)	Taren Setari and member of the original First Squad, killed by massive.
Michael Devlin (m)	Cassandra's father.
Naranezolen (m)	Head of House Zolen.
Nenna Lents (f)	Daughter of Orren and Ketta Lents.
Nick Dale (m)	Sue Dale's stepson.
Noriko Yamada (f)	A friend of Cassandra's from Agowla.
Nona Maersk (f)	Aide to the Lahanti of Unara.
Palan Leoda (f)	Wednesday Addams, junior reporter.
Paran Ruuel (m)	Kaoren Ruuel's father. A mathematician.
Peresadestar (m)	Head of House Destar, ruling family of Nuriath.
Perrin Drake (m)	KOTIS security detail – weapons trainer.
Purda (f)	A Solarian stray advising at Pandora.
Roke Hetz (m)	KOTIS security detail.
Rye (m)	A Nuran orphan, formerly belonging to House Renar.
Se-Ahn Surat (f)	An actress who plays Caszandra Devlin on *The Hidden War*.
Sebreth Tanay (f)	Lahanti (mayor) of Unara.
Senere Amallay (m)	Taren Setari and member of the original Second Squad, killed by massive.
Sentarestel (f)	A Nuran orphan, given to the care of House Renar, and the daily care of Ys and Rye.
Shon Notra (m)	Grandson of Istsen Notra.
Siame Ruuel (f)	Kaoren Ruuel's younger sister. A Kalrani.
Sue Dale (f)	Cassandra's Aunt.
Suzlein Dor (m)	Taren Setari and member of the original First Squad, killed by massive.
Teor Ruuel (f)	Kaoren Ruuel's mother. A sculptor.
Torenaltelasker (m)	One of the potential heirs of House Telasker, the ruling house of Nuri.

Truss Estey (f)	Administrator in charge of the Pandoran talent school.
Tsa Orren Lents (m)	An anthropologist working part-time with KOTIS.
Tsaile Nura Staben (f)	Overarching Commander of Muina settlement forces.
Tsana Dura (f)	A teaching program.
Tsana Ridel (m)	A teaching program.
Tsel Onara (f)	Captain of the *Diodel*.
Tsen Neen Helada (f)	KOTIS officer in charge of the Arenrhon site.
Tsen Rote Sloe (m)	KOTIS officer in charge of Kalasa site.
Tsur Gidds Selkie (m)	Senior coordinator and trainer of Setari. Sight Sight talent.
Voiz Euka (m)	A KOTIS technician who created an Earth clock and calendar.
Ys (f)	A Nuran orphan, formerly belonging to House Renar.
Zelekodar (f)	A Nuran orphan.